"For once we are in co[...]
sounded pleased, but he di[...] look it. He let his gaze
wander over her again, though standing this close, it was
impossible for him to see farther than her breasts where
they were crushed against his body. "Not more than a
month ago, I would have sworn I'd never give a woman
like you a second look. But I'd risk every penny I have that
I could still seduce you. Right here and now. In spite of
everything that's happened, I swear I could, and have you
begging for more."

Torie was as startled by the suggestion as she was by the
realization that he was absolutely right. To cover both her
shock and her amazement, she made a small noise of
disgust. "I don't think you'd enjoy it," she said.

Obviously as staggered by the whole thing as she was
and not as loath to admit it, Gabriel shook his head in
wonder. "Damn me," he said, "but I think I would."

Torie knew it was impossible for her heart to stop
beating, yet she could have sworn that it did. She stood as
if spellbound, watching the blue-black lightning that glimmered in Gabriel's eyes, transfixed by the mellow sound
of his voice and the full, deep beat of his heart against
hers.

She didn't move, not even when he lifted her hand and
pressed a kiss to her fingers.

"I could take you here and now," he said, his voice low
and ragged, his words creating a swirl of hot, dangerous
desire deep in Torie. Twining his fingers through hers,
Gabriel pinned her arm against the wall and slid his lips
from her hand to the underside of her wrist. From there,
he glided his lips to the sensitive, soft place inside her
elbow . . .

EARTHLY DELIGHTS

❋

CONSTANCE LAUX

ZEBRA BOOKS
KENSINGTON PUBLISHING CORP.

ZEBRA BOOKS are published by

Kensington Publishing Corp.
850 Third Avenue
New York, NY 10022

First Printing: March, 1995

Printed in the United States of America

For my good friend Peggy Svoboda who is always willing to brainstorm and always ready to read. Thanks, Peggy!

Prologue

Sussex, England
October 1821

"I've seen them, Torie! I've seen them again!"

At the sound of the front door banging shut, Victoria Broadridge looked up from her journal. A crisp autumn breeze flooded in from the entryway, guttering the candles that stood on either side of her desk. The wind carried her brother's cries into the library.

"I've seen them again, Torie!"

Roger Broadridge burst into the room, his words still ringing in the sharp air. His eyes wide, he paused a moment inside the doorway and swept the room with a look that sent the short hairs on the back of Torie's neck standing on end.

It was a look she knew all too well, one she had prayed she would never have to face again.

"Of course you've seen them." Even to her own ears, Torie's comfort sounded forced. Her soothing words were in painful counterpoint to each frantic beat of her heart.

Carefully, she put down her pen and pulled her spectacles from the bridge of her nose. She set them down, precisely, slowly, hoping the familiar repetition of everyday habits would help calm Roger and quiet his fears. She stood, her hands against the desktop, and somehow managed to make herself smile at the same time she made her voice sound far calmer than she felt.

"You see them each time you walk home after dark. It's only natural that tonight—"

"Stop it! Stop patronizing me!" His chest rising and falling to the staccato tempo of his breathing, Roger paced to the fireplace and back again. Though his cheeks flamed with crimson color, it did not look to be caused by the stinging winds out on the downs. The rest of his face was as gray as the ashes in the grate.

Torie fought against the disapproval that shone like fire in her brother's eyes. She took a step toward him, her hands out.

"Don't." He slapped her hands away. "Don't look at me that way. Don't think you can treat me like a child. I know what you're thinking. I know what you and Spencer Westin say behind my back. You say I'm mad. You all think I'm mad." Roger swept both his hands through his thick thatch of golden hair.

"I'm not," he said, his words far more assured than the look in his eyes. "I know what I see. Every time I'm alone on the downs at night. I know what they are. Lights. They are lights. And they follow me. Trying to lead me out over the chalk cliffs. Out to where I might tumble into the sea."

Relieved, Torie let go the breath she was holding. This was not a new delusion. It was the same hallucination Roger had struggled against all this past summer. She would simply cajole him out of this peculiar mood as she had before, she decided. She would humor him.

Torie broadened her smile and lowered her voice, cooing to him as one would to a distraught child. "There is frequently marshfire on the downs. We've both seen it. Will-o'-the-wisps. Out along the horizon. But we are scientists, Roger, we know what causes the lights. Remember? The spontaneous combustion of the gases that—"

"Spontaneous combustion!" Roger threw his head back and laughed, not with amusement but with another, more disturbing emotion, one that was rough and unsettling and made Torie's stomach lurch. His laughter died as quickly as it started and he gave Torie a piercing look. His pupils were dilated so that his eyes seemed black, like the bits of obsidian displayed in cases around the room. There was no depth in his gaze. Roger's eyes glittered, flat and sharp and as dangerous as broken glass.

"This is no bit of phosphorescence caused by rotting vegetable matter." His words hissed across the short distance between them. "I've told you before. They are lights. Lights that follow me."

Roger spun away. He stalked to the fireplace and, one hand against the mantelshelf, dropped his head onto his arm. His voice rose, high and thin, his words punctuated by the sobs that shook his slender shoulders and caused his other arm to twitch fitfully against his side. "It never happens right away," he said. "Never near Westin's house. But after I'm down the lane a bit, after I'm around the bend near Newberry's farm, it starts. I see them from the corner of my eye. Small, dancing lights. Like the marshfire you think they are. Like the marshfire, yet not."

Roger looked up. There was a sheen of perspiration on his forehead and another that glittered along his top lip. His fingers twisted against the cravat at his throat, working it over and over until it was stained with the sweat of his hands. Finally, the knot came loose, and Roger yanked the neckcloth away and flung it across the room. His fingers trembling, he ripped at the pearl studs along the front of his shirt, gasping for air.

He darted a gaze around the room as if he could see beyond the walls of the cottage. "They are all around me then. All the lights! Blue at first. Then yellow." He swallowed hard. "And then the white lights come. The white lights." With the heels of his hands, Roger pressed his eyes shut against the memory.

"They follow me. They follow me here."

This disclosure sapped the last of Roger's strength. He sagged against the chimneypiece and looked at Torie through eyes that were red and bright with unshed tears.

"All will be well. You'll see." Where Torie found the courage to say the words, she did not know. She squeezed her eyes shut, struggling to tell herself it was true, and repeated the words to herself, a litany against the worries that swirled through her mind like fog, thick and impenetrable.

"All will be well, Roger." Torie repeated the phrase, as much to convince herself of its truth as to reassure Roger. She stepped forward and offered her brother her hand.

This time he took it and held on tight while tears spilled from his eyes and cascaded down his cheeks. "They are not lights that blink far out over the horizon," Roger said, his gaze locked with Torie's, his voice a whisper. "They are close, so close I could reach out and touch them. If I dared."

"I know." It was a useless bit of mindless consolation, yet it was all Torie could think to say. She chanced another step closer and when Roger did not shy away, she laid her hand on his arm. He collapsed against her and Torie wound her arms around her brother and cradled his head against her shoulder, all the while murmuring words of comfort in his ear.

His sobs quieted then and Torie whispered a prayer of thanks. It was over. At least for this night.

It was over and she could lead Roger to his bed and go to her own.

She could go to her bed and worry what she would do the next time he came home with stories of the lights.

"It's time for bed." She straightened and urged Roger

to stand on his own. One hand still gripping hers, he allowed her assistance and moved to leave the room.

They had gone as far as the passageway outside the library when Roger jerked to attention. He stared at the front door, all the wildness back in his expression. Torie felt his hand begin to tremble, and then his arm, slow at first, then quicker and quicker still, until his entire body shook. With a mumbled curse, he cast Torie's hand away and rounded on her, his gaze darting from the door to Torie and back again to the door.

"They stop out on the downs most nights." His voice was low, as if he were afraid someone might overhear. "I have willed them to stop far from the house. I have prayed long and hard that they would never cross our threshold. That you would never . . . never know the horror, the madness of the lights. But tonight . . ."

Roger stared at the door and his mouth opened and closed in a silent scream.

"Tonight they are here! They are here for me, Victoria!" Tears streamed down Roger's face and a thin trickle of blood dribbled from one corner of his mouth. He grabbed Torie's shoulders between fingers that were hard with desperate strength and held on until her bones ground against each other.

"No!" Instinctively, Torie fought against him, not to ease the pain he was causing, but to drive the panic from his mind. She did not try to move from Roger's grasp, but took his cheeks between her hands and forced his face to hers. She held him there and refused to let him look back to the door.

"You're with me, Roger. You're home. With Torie. Nothing's going to hurt you here." Torie raised her voice, fighting to break the claw of fear that held him in its grip. "I won't allow anything to happen to you, Roger. I won't let the lights come in. I—"

Her words were interrupted by a terrible sound. It

started low in Roger's throat, like the whimper of a wounded animal, and rose until it was a shriek. "Tonight they are here, Victoria." His hands still locked on her shoulders, Roger turned so that he was facing the door.

A single spasm coursed through him, quivering over his shoulders and tightening his grip. His muscles tensed and his body went rigid.

"Tonight," he cried, "they have come to claim me."

His gaze snapped back to Torie's and held there. Still staring at his sister, Roger collapsed to the floor.

Chapter 1

Oxford, England
April 1822

"Two hundred bloody pounds!" Gabriel Raddigan strode into the foyer of his lodgings, banging the door shut behind him with so much force the oak panels rattled.

He slammed his walking stick into the umbrella stand just inside the door. "Two hundred pounds! It's a bleeding fortune!" He grumbled while he stripped off his top hat and his greatcoat and tossed them to his waiting manservant. "Can you imagine that, Hoyle?"

The solemn expression on Hoyle's face did not change. He caught his master's hat and coat in midair, set the hat on the nearest table, and proceeded to smooth the wrinkles from the coat and drape it over his arm. "No, sir," he said, his voice as stolid as his face.

"Well, neither can I. It's unconscionable! The blighter!" Gabriel stomped the length of the entryway, his boots keeping time to the exasperated rhythm of the blood that hammered through his veins. "That bastard, Kresgee, wants his two hundred pounds by the weekend." Underscoring the statement with a series of slaps against his thigh, he turned and covered the space to the door in five long strides. "That bloody fool doesn't trust me.

That's what it is, Hoyle. He doesn't know a goddamned gentleman when he sees one. And what in the bloody hell—"

Hoyle cleared his throat. "Sir?"

The question was hardly enough to attract Gabriel's attention; the audacity of Hoyle's interruption was. Surprise mingled with Gabriel's anger and caught there in his throat, checking his stinging rebuke. His mouth open, he stared at his servant.

Hoyle directed a meaningful look at the library door. "Sir, there is a woman here to see you."

"Is there?" Gabriel pulled up short and gave the closed library door a questioning look. He'd drunk two glasses of brandy with Kresgee—or was it three?—but that shouldn't have been enough to make him forget an appointment. Especially one with a woman. His eyes narrowed and his lips thinned with vexation. He ran one hand through his dark hair and gave Hoyle a questioning look. "Damned if I can remember. Did I send for a girl?"

Hoyle met his master's eyes, but only for a moment. The next second, he fixed his gaze firmly ahead of him. "It is not a girl, sir," he said. "It is a lady."

"Damn!" Gabriel spun away and headed for the staircase, dashing up the steps, two at a time. "Then I know I didn't send for her." He tossed a final comment down to Hoyle. "Bring up a bottle of brandy, will you? And the largest tumbler you can find."

"And the young lady, sir?"

Gabriel dismissed the question and the mysterious young lady with a brisk wave of one hand. "Tell the baggage to go away. I have too much on my mind to waste my time with any woman. Particularly if she's a lady."

"Even if she's Roger Broadridge's sister?"

"Most especially if she's Roger Broadridge's sister."

Gabriel did not realize he'd spoken aloud until he

heard his words fall dead against the frosty silence that greeted them. It was an instinctive response, quick and piercing, the one conceivable answer to a question only half-heard. He pulled himself to a stop and wondered if his ears and Kresgee's cheap brandy were beginning to play tricks on his mind. It was not Hoyle who had asked the question. He would swear it. It was a woman.

Gabriel glanced downstairs. The library door stood open.

"Damn!" He underscored the oath with a sharp whack against the bannister and added the finishing touches with an especially foul word.

In the seven years since they'd shared digs at Magdalen College, he'd tried his best to forget that Roger Broadridge ever existed. It seemed as if that was not about to happen.

He couldn't take a drink at any of the pubs frequented by the Oxford students without hearing Broadridge's name. He couldn't stop at his club without listening to someone extol Broadridge's reputation. He couldn't pick up a scientific journal without seeing Broadridge's name in print.

Roger Broadridge was as much a damned nuisance in his absence as he had been when he was a student here at Oxford. He was a pretentious ass of a fellow with a sour, pinched face and the disposition to match, a scholar of little promise, who had somehow managed to parlay his less than stellar academic credentials into a career of some distinction in the fields of anatomy and paleontology.

The idea filled the back of Gabriel's throat with a taste far worse than that of Kresgee's brandy. He pushed the thought to the furthermost corner of his mind where it belonged and with his fingers drummed an irritated rat-a-tat on the bannister.

The last thing he needed today was a social call from

Roger Broadridge's sister. He knew as much without another moment's thought. The last thing he needed today,
or any day, was a reminder of his past.

His mind made up, Gabriel raised his voice so that it
echoed against the wood-paneled walls. "Hoyle, tell the
young lady I am not receiving visitors today." His words
were as distinct as the pounding beat of his pulse in his
temples. "I will be up in my room. My private room," he
added for good measure, glaring down to where the
woman stood. "And I do not wish to be disturbed."

"Yes, sir." It must have been a trick of the light. He
could have sworn Hoyle cast a look at him, his lips puckered with disapproval. The next second the expression
was gone. Hoyle pulled back his shoulders and took a step
toward Miss Broadridge. With a sweeping gesture, he
directed her toward the door. "If you please, miss."

Even from this perspective, Gabriel could tell the
woman was not pleased. She looked from Hoyle to the
door. She did not keep her gaze there long, but stepped
forward and turned her face up to look at Gabriel where
he stood upon the stairway. "I did not travel here all the
way from Sussex to be dismissed as if I were nothing more
than a common strumpet."

"God's eyes!" Gabriel swore beneath his breath, a note
of incredulity stoking the flames of his anger. The spectacle was beginning to play like a scene from one of Mr.
Sheridan's comedies.

And he had never liked Sheridan.

Gabriel stalked down the steps and across the foyer
until he stood toe to toe with the woman. He frowned
down into eyes that were as impossibly green as he remembered her brother's to be. "Is that so? Then I am
sorry to disappoint you, Miss Broadridge, for that is exactly what's happening. You are being dismissed. Like a
common strumpet. And like the last common strumpet I

had occasion to dismiss from my home, I hope you will have the good sense not to return."

She gathered herself. It was the only word he could think to describe her actions. Drawing her arms closer to her body, raising her chin, and snatching her lower lip between her teeth, she gathered herself, and looked directly at Gabriel without backing down.

"I have never been accused of being sensible, Mr. Raddigan," she said, her voice as resolute as the determined tilt of her head. "Nor am I easily bullied. I did not think you would be especially pleased to see me, for I have heard you keep much to yourself these days and avoid your former colleagues, but I did expect at least some modicum of courtesy. Obviously, I presumed too much. It is not so much to ask, I think, especially when you consider that I have something of particular importance to discuss with you."

"Do you?" The woman's attitude was so confident, her words so absurdly assured, Gabriel could not help but smile. It was not a friendly expression, not like the smiles he reserved for his drinking companions, or his bookmaker, or the serving girls at the local pubs who were as willing to take care of a man's physical needs as they were of his thirst. This smile was meant to intimidate, and Gabriel put the full force of his personality behind it. He raised his brows and crossed his arms over his broad chest, stepping back to get a better look.

The infuriating Miss Broadridge was younger than himself by a year or two, he guessed, about the same age as her insufferable brother. She had the same slightly squared chin he remembered Roger having, the same straw-colored hair, the same thin, firm lips. Her nose was slender and slightly pointed, though not unattractively so, her cheekbones were high beneath eyes that, this close, were flecked with gold and blue.

It was not so much Miss Broadridge's physical resemblance to her brother that made Gabriel wince as it was the expression she wore. Her face was somber, as somber as her black gown. Her eyes were fixed on Gabriel's with that same tiresome expression Roger used to wear, sober as hell.

A brief twinge of pity flooded through him, and Gabriel shook his head.

She was Roger Broadridge's sister, right enough, and poor thing, she looked exactly like her brother.

"Miss Broadridge." Gabriel let out her name along with a sigh of impatience. "I hardly think we have anything to discuss."

"But Roger—"

"Roger." Gabriel turned up the edges of his smile. "And how is Roger?"

The question was innocent enough and not prompted by anything stronger than the simple rules of propriety, yet it caused a momentary wavering in Miss Broadridge's very formidable self-control. She sucked in a small, sharp breath and lowered her gaze. "Roger," she said, "is dead."

She did not give Gabriel time to respond. As quickly as her hesitation came, it passed, and she raised her eyes to his again. "That is what I've come to see you about."

Like the sun just beginning to burn off a morning's worth of heavy fog, the purpose behind Miss Broadridge's visit unfolded before Gabriel's eyes. But the cold light of reality was nothing like the warm rays of the sun. The realization solidified in the pit of Gabriel's stomach like a block of ice, driving out his anger and replacing it with panic.

His hands out in front of him as if to ward off the implications of her statement, Gabriel backed away. "Really, Miss Broadridge! You have come to the wrong place if you are seeking assistance. I am a bachelor, with no female relations who might be able to take you in. And as you yourself so aptly pointed out, I am averse to involving myself with others, no matter how difficult the situation. If there is no place for you to go—"

"Mr. Raddigan!"

Gabriel's desperate excuses were cut short by the brisk sound of Miss Broadridge's voice.

"I am not here seeking charity," she said, her eyes sparking green fire, like absinthe held up before a candle. "Nor am I hoping for a reference. I am here to make you a business proposition. Nothing more."

Gabriel breathed a sigh of relief, a feeling that was as short-lived as his sigh. He had reached the limits of his patience. It was time to put an end to the game.

"And I," he said, pronouncing each word carefully so she would not fail to understand, "am not the least bit interested." Spinning on his heels, Gabriel marched to the far end of the foyer. Because Hoyle had never been dismissed, he was stationed there still, watching the proceedings with open interest. Gabriel thrust out his chin and pinned his servant with a look. "Hoyle," he said, "show Miss Broadridge to the door. And this time, make sure she leaves through it."

Without another word, and without another look at Miss Broadridge, Gabriel whirled back to the stairs and started up.

"Perhaps you'd be a little more interested, Mr. Raddigan, if I told you I can help you raise the two hundred pounds you need."

Miss Broadridge's words reverberated through the air like the click of Gabriel's boot heels on the stairs. He stopped, and glared over the bannister at her.

"And how do you know about that?" he asked.

She shrugged off the intensity of his expression with a gentle lift of her shoulders. "You were hardly reticent about expressing your distress when you came in," she reminded him. "The acoustics in here are really quite splendid. I heard every word you said. Even the vulgar ones. I could help you out of your unfortunate predicament with the notorious Mr. Kresgee."

"And how precisely do you intend to do that?" Gabriel asked, all the anger and exasperation back in his voice. "Are you a sorceress, perhaps, in addition to being the irritating Mr. Broadridge's sister? Or are you just a repentant saint, willing to do punishment for your sins by selling yourself to Kresgee in exchange for the release of my debt?"

Even Gabriel recognized the question for being as cruel as it was, yet Miss Broadridge did not seem to care. She returned his look, the steely spark of determination more dazzling than ever in her eyes.

It was a damned unnerving trait in a woman, this unyielding willfulness, and Gabriel looked Miss Broadridge up and down.

What he saw did not ease his mind.

He would find no chink in this woman's defenses, not this easily. Gabriel mumbled a foul word and dismissed both Miss Broadridge and the unsettling effects of her maddening composure with a snort. "I withdraw that last statement," he said. "I know Kresgee too well. He wouldn't have you."

"But *you* would have two hundred pounds." She shot the reply back at him without a moment's hesitation. There was no vexation, no fluctuation in her voice. She spoke the statement like she had all the others, simply and calmly, as if she knew without a doubt what Gabriel's answer would be.

It was impossible to admit he wasn't interested. Gabriel cursed himself for the thought at the same time he knew it to be true. He was a desperate man. A man desperately in need of two hundred pounds. And here was a woman who claimed she could get it for him.

He threw his hands in the air and gave Hoyle a look

heavy with significance, one he hoped effectively communicated what he needed.

Deliverance.

The word burned through Gabriel's mind as if, the more intensely he contemplated it, the sooner Hoyle could read his thoughts. And the sooner Hoyle read his mind, the sooner he could help extricate his master from the dilemma in which he found himself. "What am I to do, Hoyle?"

Hoyle cleared his throat and stepped forward. With no more than a glance, he told his master he understood the situation fully, understood it, and had it well in hand. "If you please, sir. I should invite the young lady to sit down."

"Would you?" It was no wonder he paid Hoyle so handsomely. The man was a godsend! Gabriel smiled and hoped he was a good enough actor to make the expression seem more like one of disbelief than relief. He raised his brows and looked at Hoyle as if the man's impertinence would be all but unforgivable if he himself had not asked for the advice. "And then what would you do, Hoyle?"

"I, sir?" Hoyle paused as if considering the unlikely prospect of being asked his opinion. He delayed long enough to give the moment its full dramatic effect, then pulled his shoulders back and continued. "It is quite cold outside, sir. I should offer Miss Broadridge some tea. And I should have a glass of brandy myself. It helps clear the mind, I think you'll agree, and puts one in a state more conducive to discussion. And then, once I was comfortable and more inclined to listen to what the young lady had to say, I should find out why she is willing to give me two hundred pounds, sir, and what I had to do to earn it."

"Splendid! Absolutely splendid!" Propelling any note of interest from his voice and replacing it with a wry edge of amusement, Gabriel applauded. "You are to be commended, Hoyle, and I would be tempted to follow your advice if I did not suspect that beneath your very sound reasoning there lurks a soft spot in head and heart, one of immense proportions."

He peered down at Miss Broadridge. "He is not doing this for me," he confided to her with a glance that indicated Hoyle. "The devil take him! Beneath that hard and polished exterior lurks the heart of a true romantic. He is championing your cause, Miss Broadridge. Poor Hoyle cannot resist the request of any young woman. It is a fault I would never tolerate in myself." He shrugged off the thought good-naturedly. "But reliable servants are hard to find, so what am I to do but listen to the man?"

Gabriel gave up the fight with as much good grace as he could muster. He bounded down the stairs and motioned Miss Broadridge into the library.

For a moment, he thought she was as weary of the game as he, and that, finally facing victory, she might toss it aside for the satisfaction of besting him. She stared at him across the small space that separated them, not as much triumph in her eyes as there was skepticism. Her determination apparently overcame whatever suspicion lurked behind those bright green eyes, for settling her lips in a thin, scornful line, she nodded her acquiescence and moved into the library ahead of him.

There were two chairs set before the fire, and Miss Broadridge settled herself in the one Gabriel knew to be the most comfortable. She straightened the skirt of her gown, tugged her sleeves demurely down around her wrists, and gave Gabriel a level look.

"I am Victoria Broadridge," she said, her voice as unemotional as the look in her eyes. "Roger's twin. We have had occasion to meet. I believe you were present at least twice when I visited Roger here in Oxford, the year you and he shared digs at Magdalen."

Oh, bother!

Torie swallowed the malediction along with the last of her words. She had not meant to bring up the scandalous shadows of Gabriel Raddigan's past so early in this interview. She fought back her chagrin and dared a look at him from beneath her lashes.

If the mention of his ill-fated academic career bothered Gabriel in any way, he did not show it. When they entered the room, he had perched himself on the arm of an overstuffed chair across from hers, and he sat there now, balanced precariously between his eagerness to know what it was she had to offer and his reluctance to show any interest.

Torie remembered Gabriel Raddigan from the days he and Roger were acquainted. Gabriel had been a young man of splendid promise then. His academic achievements were legend. His intellect was astounding. From what she remembered, he had an equally admirable physique.

Torie pushed the thought away. Gabriel's body had been dissipated as surely as his intellect. He had grown fleshy. She could tell as much, even though he tried to hide the fact beneath a layer of finely tailored clothes. There was a bit too much fabric in his patterned waistcoat. It was designed, she presumed, to hide a stomach that was not as fat as it was fubsy, soft, and out of condition.

There was a bit too much extravagance in the knot of Gabriel's cravat, a bit too much practiced nonchalance in his looks, in his manners, and in his voice.

His face might be handsome if it were not for the lines that underscored the ennui in his eyes and marked the corners of his mouth with the telltale souvenirs of what Torie could only guess was too much gambling, too much liquor, and far too many women. The excesses had left his skin pale and heightened the contrast with hair that was black as a raven's wing and eyes as pitchy dark as a midnight sky.

Still, there was a certain suggestion of mettle in his jaw,

and a kind of engaging boyishness in his smile. She would give him that much. It was a pity that smile never made it all the way into his eyes.

Torie nearly felt sorry for the man until she reminded herself of everything she'd heard about Gabriel in the four days she'd been here in Oxford. He was overindulgent, intemperate, and idle, she reminded herself. He was dissipated and rash, a rake of the worst sort.

Holding a tight rein on a sympathy she feared would be sorely misplaced, Torie felt a certain smug satisfaction overtake her pity. She hid the secret smile that threatened to reveal her thoughts.

Gabriel Raddigan was the embodiment of everything she despised in a man.

That was what made him so perfect for her plans.

Settling herself, Torie raised her eyes to meet Gabriel's. "You are exactly the kind of man I'm looking for, Mr. Raddigan," she said with all sincerity.

"Am I?" This seemed to amuse him. Gabriel tipped his head back and smiled, the grin broad and wide and guileless. As quickly as the emotion brightened his face, he extinguished it. He leaned forward, his face only inches from Torie's, his breath heavy and sweet with the smell of brandy. "And what kind of man is that?" he asked.

Torie was not sure if she should recoil from the look in his eyes or challenge it. She decided instead to get on with her business as quickly as possible. Certainly the singular proposition she was about to offer him would drive away Gabriel's irritation and suspicion. How could it not?

Allowing only the smallest smile of enthusiasm to tease at the corners of her mouth, Torie raised her chin. "The kind of man," she said, "who would be honored to continue Roger's work."

"Roger's work?" Gabriel bolted upright, his lips twitching in what Torie supposed was meant to be a smiling, gracious acknowledgement. It was, instead, more of a dubious smirk, one that quickly changed into a full-sized grimace. "Why the hell would I give two bloody damns about Roger's work?"

"Really, Mr. Raddigan!" Torie sloughed off the profanities with a shake of her shoulders. "There is no need to be quite so hasty. Perhaps you do not realize the significance of my offer. If you kept up with the literature—"

"Oh, I keep up with the literature well enough." Gabriel rose from his chair and went to stand near the windows. With one hand, he toyed with the draperies, his fingers working over the edges, impatient and severe. "Does that surprise you, Miss Broadridge?" He tossed the question over his shoulder at her, his voice suddenly filled, not with the impatience and irritation she had heard in it before, but with disdain. "Does it astound you that a man of my tarnished reputation dares to look upon the journals filled with the wisdom of the great thinkers of our time? That is what Roger was supposed to be, wasn't he? One of the great minds of the century?"

"His findings were unquestionably sound." Torie fought to control the note of tension in her voice which she feared might give her away. "His research was flawless. His methods unparalleled. He surely—"

"He surely is as damned bothersome in death as he ever was in life!" Gabriel dropped the curtain and spun to face her. "Let me remind you, Miss Broadridge, that your brother was a mediocre student at best, barely competent, much less brilliant. He got through University by the seat of his well-tailored pants. It is impossible for any right-thinking person to figure how he managed to make such a name for himself on so little talent, and even more preposterous to think that I might be willing, in no matter how small a way, to continue his dubious legacy."

His words rushed through the room at Torie like stones thrown by an angry mob, each one stinging where it

landed. She bolted from her chair, an instinctive response
to the attack, and fought to repress the anger that seethed
in her. Gabriel had come closer to the truth than she
dared admit, even to herself, and his words burned
through Torie, as hot and dangerous as the fire blazing in
the grate.

"Had my brother lived, he would have been preparing
yet another monograph for the scientific journals." This
at least, was true, and Torie wrapped the realization
around herself like a shield against the censure that
showed in Gabriel's eyes. She held it tight, her words
giving her courage, her courage fanning the flames of her
conviction.

"What he was about to report, Mr. Raddigan, would
have revolutionized the world of natural science."

"Revolutionized?" Gabriel threw back his head and
laughed, his teeth glinting even and white in the firelight.
He took three steps toward her and eyed her like one
might eye a peculiar specimen in a menagerie. "Miss
Broadridge, in the short time we have spent together, I
have discerned that you are willful and headstrong and
entirely too outspoken." He held up one hand to stop her
when she opened her mouth to dispute him.

"These are not criticisms," Gabriel said, his voice far
more pleasant than the spark of exasperation that was
quickly growing into a blaze in his eyes. "Far from it. I
have met few women with such spirit. I have also met few
women who irritate me more." He whirled away from
her, swung back again, and his voice rang through the
room. "You are a damned nuisance, Miss Broadridge,"
he said, emphasizing the point with a jab of one finger.
"As much of a nuisance as your brother ever was. And
now, now you are determined to prove to me that you are
also mad. It's too much. Far too bloody much for me to
endure."

He marched to the door, flung it open and waved her toward it. "Get out," he said. "Now."

"Very well." When Hoyle had shown her into the room earlier, Torie had deposited a hard-sided valise on the cherrywood desk that stood near the door. She picked it up, and holding it before her, she went to stand opposite Gabriel. "Perhaps I am mad, Mr. Raddigan. But be so kind as to grant a madwoman one last request, will you? I will ask only one more minute of your time." She looked down at the case in her hands. "I will show you what I came to show you. After that, if you are not interested, I will leave, Mr. Raddigan. Leave for good. I swear it."

Gabriel did not readily agree, but he did not object, either. Torie took his silence as a good sign. She set the valise on the nearest table, snapped it open and reached inside.

The fossil felt cool in her hot palm. She closed her fingers around it and weighed it in her hand, finding renewed courage in the familiar feel of it.

Torie drew in a deep breath and turning back to Gabriel, she held out her hand. She opened her fingers and showed him the tooth.

Chapter 2

"Of all the damned nonsense!" Gabriel looked down at the object that lay in the palm of Victoria's hand and his mood veered sharply from outright annoyance to unmitigated anger. Not even trying to check the short bark of scornful laughter that escaped him, he ran one hand over the back of his neck.

"It's a goddamned, bloody elephant's tooth," he said, his voice tearing through the blanket of Victoria's expectant silence. "You're all in a dither over an elephant's tooth?"

In spite of his stinging reproach, Victoria's hand remained rock-steady and there was no wavering in the firm line of her shoulders. "Perhaps you spoke too quickly, Mr. Raddigan," she said, her voice as brusque as her suggestion. "Perhaps you spoke too impulsively. Perhaps you did not look closely enough." She thrust her hand—and the tooth—out to him. "If you did, I do not think you'd be so quick to dismiss me."

Gabriel mumbled a curse. On the best of days, he had but a small store of patience. On a day like today, the well had long since run dry. He sighed, eager to have this absurdity over and done. Bending from the waist, he peered at the tooth. "I will admit, it's old. It's fossilized." He straightened and looked at her. "I suppose to the inexperienced scholar, that would be enough to give the specimen some importance. But honestly, Miss Broadridge, other than that," he shrugged away the significance of the tooth, "it has little interest. And even less value. Not the stuff of which revolutions are made."

"An elephant's tooth." Victoria wrapped her fingers tight over her palm and held her fist to her heart. "Is that what you think?" She looked at Gabriel, a kind of mysterious, satisfied smile playing its way around her mouth. "Why?"

"Why is it an elephant's tooth?" Gabriel ran his tongue over his lips and tried to swallow, though the dryness in his throat made it devilishly hard. At the same time he wondered where the hell Hoyle was with his brandy, he offered Miss Broadridge a tight smile. "It is an elephant's tooth because it is an elephant's tooth," he said, and cringed at his own lackluster reasoning.

A wide smile cracked the solemnity of Victoria's expression and she turned from Gabriel and strolled across the room. She stopped near one of the lamps and, holding the tooth between thumb and forefinger, examined it in the light. "You have been removed from the groves of Academe for far too long, Mr. Raddigan. Your reasoning is weak. Your argument, inconclusive." She snapped her gaze to Gabriel's, and her words rang through the room with all the conviction of a thrown gauntlet. "Try again. Tell me why it is an elephant's tooth."

It had been years since Gabriel had felt the surge of emotion that came from such a flagrant challenge, and he reacted instinctively to it, reacted like he used to back in the days when the fires of learning still raced through his gut and ignited his mind and his imagination. He nodded brusquely, accepting the invitation to combat.

Without a word, Gabriel crossed the room to stand directly in front of Victoria. He planted his feet, and held out his hand.

Obviously the woman recognized a declaration of war when she saw one and surprisingly, she had the sense to keep quiet and get on with it. Her silence as deafening as his, she handed him the fossil and stepped back to watch.

Gabriel weighed the tooth in the palm of his hand, and a strange, barely remembered excitement awakened inside him, as if he'd been out of school six days, not six years. Just looking at the thing, just holding it, brought back not so much memories as it did sensations. Like primal passions, the emotions stirred: the thrill of discovery, the excitement of newfound knowledge, the astonishing feeling of advancing hypotheses that were as astounding as they were original.

Where it came from, he wasn't sure, and with Miss Broadridge peering at him like a testy don he wasn't about to question it. The feeling rose up somehow from beneath the sea of brandy where Gabriel had tried to drown it these past years. Like a man breaking the surface of the water after being too long submerged, he gulped in a breath and plunged headlong into his explanation.

"Obviously worn down from years of chewing food." Gabriel held the tooth up to the light. "See here. The surface is smooth. My initial assessment was right. The tooth is from a herbivorous animal." He looked up at Victoria. "That is, in case you are not familiar with the nomenclature, an animal that survives solely on a diet of vegetation."

The remark was as acerbic as the look he tossed her and Gabriel regretted neither. It was worth it, simply to see Victoria's reaction. There was a quick spark of anger that flared just beneath the surface of her maddening calm, an almost imperceptible quiver at the corners of her mouth that revealed her annoyance.

Satisfied that he had goaded her into at least this bit of emotion, Gabriel returned his concentration to the tooth.

He held it closer to the light and bent to examine it more carefully.

"Perhaps not an elephant," he said, almost to himself, narrowing his eyes and wishing he had not sold his reading glass to pay Hoyle's last month's wages. "But certainly a large pachyderm of some sort." He looked to Victoria, waiting to see a note of approval on her face. There was none. She crossed her arms over her chest, tilted her head, and waited for more.

There was no more. Gabriel was certain of it. He shoved the tooth back at her. "Upper incisor of a rhinoceros," he said, confidence ringing in his voice.

"Is it?" Victoria accepted the tooth. "Then what would you say, Mr. Raddigan, if I told you Roger found this tooth near Lewes, on a roadbed that was being repaired? What would you say if I told you he traced the stone they were using for the repairs to a quarry in Cuckfield in the Tilgate Forest?"

"You mean it came from here in England?" The question popped out of Gabriel's mouth before he could stop it. He cursed himself for his impetuosity. Such thunderstruck astonishment might be appropriate to an inexperienced student who had never before faced such persistent, though weak, arguments. It had no place with a man of true intellect, such as himself.

Miss Broadridge's feeble rationale may have been enough to put off a less experienced man, and that might have been just what she was counting on. Gabriel smiled. Though the woman purported to know a great deal about him, she obviously had not counted on his prodigious memory.

"There are stories," he said. "Stories of the Romans bringing fantastic animals to Britain when they ruled this island. Perhaps your brother never told you?" He dangled the suggestion in front of her like a fisherman proffering an especially juicy worm. Would she rise to the bait, he wondered?

It did not take more than another moment to find out.

Victoria's chin furrowed. "Then why has no other evidence been found?" she demanded. "Why are there no written records of those animals? Why are there no skeletons?"

Gabriel shook his head. Had the girl been anyone else's sister, he might have felt sorry for her. It seemed even his tolerant explanations were not enough to convince the young lady. She'd been manipulated into believing the importance of this insignificant discovery by someone— probably her miserable brother—and there was little he could do to soften the blow of reality. But if she would not credit this simple, and quite rational, explanation, he would simply have to dazzle her with erudition.

Gabriel hitched his fingers together behind his back, stuck out his chin, and began. "These are not new theories," he said in his most didactic voice. "And they are not my own. Roger Plot, in his *Natural History of Oxfordshire* describes a thigh bone dug up in Cornwell, not far from here. He determined it was from an elephant brought over with the Romans. His book was written in 1676."

"And in 1677, the real skeleton of a real elephant was brought to Oxford," Victoria shot back at him. "There wasn't one bone in it that was anything like Plot's bone."

"And Plot then reversed his findings and concluded that the bone came from a human giant. Does that make more sense to you than the elephant theory?"

"Of course not. But—"

"But that is an end to it, Miss Broadridge." Gabriel brushed his hands together, ridding himself of her argument. "There is no other accounting for the bones, just as there is no other justification for your tooth. It is from a large animal that exists on a diet of plants. A pachyderm, surely, what else could it be?"

It was meant as a rhetorical question, nothing more, yet Victoria seemed to take the query to heart. She gave Gabriel a steady look while she pulled in a long breath and let it out slowly, as if measuring the proper moment for her answer.

"Mr. Raddigan," she said, "when you were a boy, did you ever read about dragons?"

Gabriel opened his mouth to throw a rejoinder back at her, but there was such a gleam of fervor in Victoria's eyes, such a touch of intensity in the rigid way she held her jaw, he found there was nothing to say. He snapped his mouth shut at the same time another, more disturbing idea snaked into his mind.

Perhaps his earlier assessment of Miss Victoria Broadridge was closer to the mark than even he had supposed.

Perhaps she really was as mad as a March hare.

Gabriel eyed Victoria warily. She even looked a bit like a rabbit, her eyes soft and glowing, her lips and the small muscles around her mouth twitching with excitement.

Finding the analogy altogether too capricious for a situation that was at once both pitiful and frightening, Gabriel pushed it out of his mind. He backed away.

"You have no reaction to my question? No rebuttal?" If Victoria saw the apprehension that clouded Gabriel's vision, she did not acknowledge it. She held tighter to the tooth. "I confess, I am disappointed in you, Mr. Raddigan. I was told you were a scholar of great promise at one time. The years in which you've dulled your senses with wine and women have obviously dulled your mind as well, and robbed you of whatever singular intellect you may have once possessed. No scholar of any merit would dismiss a theory so out of hand."

"A theory about dragons?" Gabriel found his voice. His question came rushing out along with a ragged breath. "I do not dismiss your theory, Miss Broadridge. To dismiss a theory is to imply that you give it some credence, enough at least to consider and discard it. I refuse to give your statement even that much validity."

Gabriel's argument had not the least effect on Victoria. She spun around and crossed the room, and when she reached the far wall, she turned again to him, her face aglow. "Think of the evidence!" she said her voice rising with excitement. "In China, huge teeth were dug up as early as the sixteenth century B.C. and the Chinese are finding them still, today. They call them dragons' teeth and they grind them down and drink a tea made with the powder. They claim it gives them great power."

"But—"

"And they say they have exhumed dragon bones. It's in their written literature dating back as early as the third century."

"But—"

"And the native Indians who live in the lands of the Americas tell tales of giant bones as well. They say they are the skeletons of monstrous serpents. Why, even William Clark who went out to map the American lands beyond the Missouri River with Meriwether Lewis, even he wrote of such bones. And that was not twenty years ago."

"But Miss Broadridge, really!" Gabriel interrupted as quickly as he could, hoping for a chance of inserting even one rational thought into her argument. "Dragons? It is laughable. Dragons are the stuff of children's stories. Fables and fairy tales. You don't really think what you've got there is a dragon's tooth, do you?"

"A dragon's tooth?" Victoria looked at the tooth in her hand. Her golden brows dipped in a vee and she looked at Gabriel as if he'd grown two heads. "Don't be ridiculous, Mr. Raddigan. Who said anything about believing in dragons? I merely endeavor to put the problem in historical perspective for you. I am not suggesting this tooth belonged to a dragon."

"Good." Gabriel let out a ragged breath. "Very good."

"No. What I am suggesting is that the bones and teeth our ancestors attributed to dragons are very similar to this tooth."

Finding no fault in this bit of her logic, Gabriel nodded. "I will grant you that," he said.

"And because those peoples could not account for such an anomaly in any other way, they made up stories to explain the teeth and bones they found. Stories that included gigantic winged reptiles."

"Again, you are right. There is every indication that is exactly what happened, but—"

"But what I am saying, Mr. Raddigan, is that perhaps we should have paid more attention to those fairy tales all along. What I'm saying is that perhaps they are based on facts. Not written evidence of any kind, but some innate and incomprehensible ability that helps us make sense of something we dig out of the ground, something for which we have no explanation. What I'm saying is that perhaps what our primitive ancestors called dragons were really some sort of large, herbivorous animals. Those," she said with a sidelong look and stinging note of sarcasm in her voice, "are animals that exist on a diet of vegetation."

Victoria did not wait for his reaction. With quick, impatient steps, she crossed the room and came to stand in front of Gabriel. She opened her hand to again reveal the tooth. "What would you say if I told you the rock strata where this fossil was found was Cretaceous?"

"That rock would be at least sixty-five million years old." Gabriel rejected the notion with a snort. "Impossible!"

"Impossible! Impossible!" Victoria's hands curled into fists and she whacked them against her sides and squared her shoulders like a pugilist preparing for another round of a match. "Nothing is impossible in the eyes of a true scientist, Mr. Raddigan. Don't you see? Everything is possible. Everything. All we have to do is open our eyes and our minds and find the possibilities where others think only impossibilities exist."

"God-amighty!" Gabriel ran one hand through his hair. Perhaps she was not mad, at least not as mad as he thought her to be, but Victoria Broadridge was certainly stubborn.

While he considered the prospect, Gabriel took a moment to study Victoria. In the heat of their debate, a wisp of her hair had come loose from the tight knot at the back of her head. The straw-colored curl hung close to her slender neck and fell soft and easy over shoulders that glowed, flushed and pink above the dark fabric of her gown.

A corresponding blush stained her cheeks, and Gabriel noted with an acerbic smile that the excitement of conflict obviously elevated the young lady's color as well as her temper. Still, no matter what the cause, the rosiness added a certain softness to her expression, one that was not there earlier. It accented the fresh green of her eyes and nearly made her face look pretty, as pretty as any stubborn young lady might look.

Stubborn?

Gabriel reconsidered.

Perhaps he was wrong.

Perhaps Victoria was not being as obstinate as she was just being female. Perhaps a woman, being a simpler creature, merely needed things spelled out to her more clearly.

Gabriel felt the stiffness in his neck and shoulders relax. This was certainly an arena where he felt comfortable, far more comfortable than he felt trying to debate anything even vaguely intellectual with a woman, and he found himself smiling in spite of the irritable look Victoria was giving him.

His luck with the cards and the ponies may have

slipped away, his credit may have gone to hell, his reputation was surely in shreds, but this was one facet of his life he had firmly under control. If Gabriel Raddigan had nothing else, he still had an easy charm and the remarkable gift for talking a woman—any woman—into exactly what he wanted.

Gabriel smiled the smile that had melted female hearts from one corner of Oxfordshire to the next and lowered his voice as if he were explaining some everyday thing to a simpleton. "Miss Broadridge," he murmured, "let me elucidate. There have been many fossils found in Cretaceous rock strata. You might have heard your brother say as much. But what he may not have explained—or perhaps he did explain and you simply did not understand— was that the fossils found there are generally of fishes and shells. There has never been any evidence of the remains of mammalia in strata that old. Never. And since your fossil is obviously, as I pointed out earlier, that of a mammal, that means it is undoubtedly from a diluvial deposit, a much newer rock layer forced into the Cretaceous strata by a flood or glacier. I stand by my original conclusion. Your dragon," he emphasized the word, "is nothing more than a misplaced pachyderm."

Victoria did not respond and Gabriel relaxed even more. He had her. Had her for certain now. The irrefutable logic of his argument and the simple words in which he'd couched it, had robbed her of all her bluster. Finally seeing an end to her vexatious badgering, he forged ahead. "Think about what you have," he suggested, his voice smoothed of all its aggravation. "Go over it in your head. Say it aloud if you must. You will come to your own decision, and I think you will see that there is but one conclusion. Your findings will, no doubt, correspond with my own."

Victoria gave him a tight smile and Gabriel found himself smiling back. The girl could actually be civilized when she had a mind to. The thought cheered him and he settled himself against the nearest table. His long legs out in front of him, his hands braced against the tabletop, he waited for her to reason her way through to the one and only possible conclusion, the one he had already proposed.

"Very well." She agreed graciously enough and Gabriel was ready to relax even more. He caught himself just in time, in time to hear the subtle note of exactness in each word she spoke, in time to note the rigid, formal way she held herself, her shoulders back, her head high and steady. There was something about her attitude that did not speak acquiescence as much as it did defiance, and Gabriel sat up and listened.

"What we have," Victoria said quite precisely, "is a tooth. The surface of the crown is worn, smooth and oblique, and that would indicate an animal which chews its food. We are agreed on that much, I think." She did not give Gabriel a chance to answer, but continued.

"We also agree that no mammalian fossils have ever been found in Cretaceous strata, nor are they likely to be. There is no evidence of mammals existing as long ago as sixty-five million years. That, it appears, we also agree on. While you are convinced the tooth comes from a pachyderm, I am saying you have not considered all the possibilities. For instance, in your somewhat tenuous argument, you neglected to mention that the tooth could belong to a fish. Such fossils have been found in Cretaceous strata. You may have heard as much mentioned by Cuvier, or Buckland, or one of the other eminent scholars in the field. Or perhaps you did hear and you just did not understand." Victoria fixed him with a look, long enough to be sure the stinging reprimand was not lost on him.

"The fish that springs to mind, of course, is *Anarhicus lupus,*" she continued after she was sure her arrow had found its mark. "The wolf fish. But if you recall anything of animal anatomy, you will realize the wolf fish had teeth that were prismatic in form. Quite different from this one.

"By the same bit of logic and the application of applied anatomy, I stand by my earlier argument that the teeth and bones that have been found in this country and in others, though similar to the large pachyderms we know to exist today, are not quite identical. Not enough to be from the same animals.

"I rule out fish, Mr. Raddigan," Victoria said with another one of those penetrating looks that seemed to dare him to follow to whatever curious place her logic might lead. "I rule out mammals. Obviously, the tooth did not come from a bird. I assume that in addition to anatomy you also took philosophy classes when you were a student? Then you will recall the simple process of elimination. And by the process of elimination, that leaves only one other class of animals."

"Reptiles?" The word was tight in Gabriel's throat. It was preposterous, of course, yet something about the idea sent a tingle up his spine. He fought back with the first argument that came to mind. "But reptiles don't chew their food. They gulp it and—"

"The reptiles we know of today don't chew their food." Victoria let the simple statement seep into the farthest corners of his argument. She leaned closer so that the light gleamed in her eyes like the outward sign of an inner fire. "But don't forget the dragons! What I have here, Mr. Raddigan, is the tooth of a herbivorous reptile, the likes of which no longer lives anywhere on the face of this earth."

Now that Victoria had finally come to the denouement of her little drama, Gabriel felt nothing more than relief. He laughed. "Stuff and nonsense!"

Victoria ignored his response. Gathering her dignity, she pulled herself up to her full height. "You need further proof? Then you should know Roger traveled to London before his death. To the Hunterian Museum of the Royal College of Surgeons. There are thousands of specimens there, current and prehistoric, and he looked through every one of them, every bit of tooth and bone in the place. He found one animal, and only one animal, with teeth that are almost exactly like this one. The iguana, a reptile which lives today in Central and South America."

The very idea was mesmerizing, if not for its plausibility then at least for its singular inventiveness.

Gabriel shook the thought out of his mind. "But look at that tooth. It's the size of a hen's egg." He turned away and went to stand near the fire, chafing his hands together, not to warm himself, but to give him some way to release his pent-up energy. "I know a bit about the animal in question. An iguana grows to five feet at the most and its teeth are nowhere near as large as that. If what you're saying is true—"

"If what I'm saying is true, the animal this tooth belonged to was very much like an iguana." Victoria followed him across the room. She came to stand next to him and tilted her head to catch his gaze, her voice no louder than the crackling fire. "Except that it was thirty feet long."

Gabriel's head came up. "Like a dragon!" He whispered the words, the full meaning of Roger Broadridge's findings just beginning to make their way through the swirl of confusion that filled his head. Yet there was another niggling piece to the puzzle, a problem Gabriel had forgotten in the heat of debate. It presented itself now, as clear as the flames that danced in the grate. He gave Victoria a curious look. "And you've come to me with this dragon's tooth. Why?"

This was apparently the question she'd been waiting for. Victoria's expression brightened with the excitement of her words. "I believe . . . Roger believed," she corrected herself, "if there are teeth to be found, there are also bones. Mr. Raddigan, I want you to find them for me."

It was just as well Hoyle chose that moment to bring their refreshments into the room, for Gabriel was certain he would not have been able to respond to the astonishing proposition. His mind awhirl with both the prospects and the irony of the situation, he watched Hoyle set a teapot and cup on the table nearest Victoria. It was a rather awkward performance, one that would have been far more seemly had Hoyle had a tray.

The trays had gone with the last batch of silver Gabriel sold. The thought prickled over him like chicken-flesh and he wished Hoyle would hurry back with his brandy so that he might damp it down.

Hoyle did not disappoint him. He returned with a bottle and tumbler and set them near his master. His task complete, he backed out of the room and snapped the door closed behind him.

Damn, but he needed a drink!

Without waiting for his guest to pour her tea and without offering to do it himself, Gabriel popped the cork from the brandy bottle, filled his glass, and tossed it down. The little time he had spent with Miss Broadridge had left him as thirsty as he was confused. He refilled the glass instantly and stood contemplating the amber liquid.

"One summer. That's all I ask of you, Mr. Raddigan." Torie's voice snapped Gabriel out of his thoughts. He looked up at her, an emotion she dared hope was interest gleaming in his dark eyes. "One summer of your time," she said, trying to convince him before the gleam had a chance to fade in the harsh light of reality. "One summer in Cuckfield to try and find the bones."

Gabriel swirled the liquor in his glass, his gaze returning there and settling. She knew what he would ask next, it was inevitable, and Torie braced herself for the question.

"What's your part in all this?" Gabriel's voice sounded far more inquisitive than it did concerned, and relieved, Torie dropped into her chair and poured her tea.

"I was Roger's assistant," she said, her well-rehearsed response sounding as natural as she'd hoped. "I transcribed his notes, made sure his journal was kept up to date. I would be more than willing to provide you with the same services. Once the bones are located and excavated, you, of course, would publish the findings and present them to the British Association for the Advancement of Science."

Gabriel considered the prospect in silence and Torie drew in a deep breath of calming air. She stirred her tea, daring to hope the most critical phase of the interview was over, praying all her worry had been for nought and he would not raise the question she most feared.

"Why?"

As if he were reading her thoughts, Gabriel's single word ripped the stillness and solidified somewhere between Torie's stomach and her throat. Still stirring her tea, she waited for more.

Gabriel took one step toward her, his eyes dark with sudden realization. "Why would you come to me?"

"You are eminently qualified." Meticulously, Torie tapped the rim of her cup with her spoon and set it on the saucer. "You were known as a student of some promise when—"

"When I was at University." Gabriel finished the sentence for her, his voice suddenly as cold as the chill that made its way up Torie's back and into her shoulders. "You seem to know a great deal about me, Miss Broadridge. Do you know why I left University?"

She did not look at him. "Yes."

"Yet you are still willing to entrust your brother's work to me. Why?"

"Why?" The question was too much for her. Torie

bolted from her chair and went to stand close to the half-empty bookshelves that lined the far wall of the room. "Because I need someone to finish the important work Roger began," she said. "I need a man of imagination and intellect, and yes, one who is just foolhardy enough to dare the things I ask. I need a man who is not afraid to advance exceptional hypotheses, ones that may not be accepted readily."

"And you think I am that man?" There was no joy in Gabriel's voice, none of the satisfaction she expected would naturally follow such blatant flattery. He asked this question like he had asked the questions about the tooth, his voice as keen as the edge of a well-honed knife.

It was not easy to face such brutal honesty and still lie, yet Torie knew she had no choice. She clutched the tooth in her hand tighter for courage and turned to Gabriel. "I do think you are that man," she said, her voice sounding infinitely calmer than her insides felt.

"And you know I have no credentials? No credibility?"

At least this time, she did not have to invent an answer. "What does it matter?" Torie asked. "We are about to turn the world of natural science upside down, Mr. Raddigan. To find the possibilities where others think only impossibilities exist. I do not think credentials or credibility would do either of us any good."

Gabriel took another long drink, all the while looking at her from over the rim of his tumbler. For one foolish moment, Torie dared to believe she had talked him into the scheme. His dark eyes were alight with interest. His voice and face were as innocent as a that of a child unborn. "And you did say you'd pay for my services?" he asked. "Three hundred pounds?"

"Three hundred—!" A blast of outrage sharpened Torie's voice and stiffened her spine. She should have known better than to expect rationality from a man as depraved as Gabriel Raddigan.

The realization did nothing to make her feel any better. "The offer was two hundred," she reminded Gabriel. As much as she would have liked to, she refused to back down from the unnerving traces of audacity that glimmered in Gabriel's eyes. She set her jaw and fixed him with a look. "I am certain you heard me quite clearly when I proposed it," she said, her words clipped by her clenched teeth. "Two hundred pounds in exchange for one summer of your time."

"One summer of my time is infinitely valuable." Gabriel rolled his head and stretched his broad shoulders. If he had done nothing else in the years he had been banished from polite society, he had at least perfected the fine art of total and complete boredom. He had also learned more than a little something about the shrewd craft of bargaining. The way he saw it, there were two ways the negotiations could go.

He could get Miss Broadridge to up the ante, or he could get her to go away.

Right now, the second possibility looked to be the most promising. And the most pleasant.

Gabriel glanced at Victoria, gauging her response. "There is much for me to do here in town," he said. "Entertainments. Diversions. You wish to take me away from it all. To set me out in the middle of some godforsaken place where my only entertainment will, no doubt, consist of visiting with the vicar's wife. If I'm lucky, she'll be young and pretty." He underscored the possibilities of the situation with a shrewd smile. Of course Miss Broadridge did not respond. He should have known she wouldn't.

He turned up his smile a notch and tried his best to goad her further. "If I'm particularly lucky," he said with a quirk of his brows, "her husband will be old and shriveled and she'll be chomping at the bit for a little excitement." The thought was not nearly as appealing as

Gabriel tried to make it sound. In spite of himself, he shook his shoulders with distaste.

He recovered as quickly as he could and tipped his head back, pretending to be deep in thought. "Let's see, what else will there be to do in Cuckfield?" He chewed over the unpleasant prospects for a while, long enough to be sure Miss Broadridge was irritated beyond measure. He did not look at her again, not until he heard her let go a sigh of impatience.

"I could watch the moss grow on the window ledges," Gabriel suggested with a bright smile. "I could count the clouds that float above my head. I could pick flowers, or learn to imitate the calls of birds." He may have had to force the smile, but he needed to do nothing to his voice. It was filled with all the loathing he felt for Miss Broadridge's preposterous plan. "You see," he added, "I must ask for ample compensation. The tedium would be severe."

He had accomplished his objective. Miss Broadridge was not only annoyed, she was utterly vexed. Her steps quick, her movements crisp, she replaced the tooth in its valise and snapped the bag shut. She pulled on her gloves, tugging each finger in turn. "It would not seem to be so different from what you do now," she said, her voice as pinched with anger as her mouth. "Two hundred pounds is more than adequate compensation. And it is all I am going to offer." Lifting the valise, she went to the door. She paused when she got there, her hand on the brass knob.

"Perhaps you will reconsider when the weekend arrives and Mr. Kresgee demands his money."

Gabriel gave her a devastating smile. "Perhaps," he said, "I will reconsider when hell freezes over and the devil dances in ladies' drawers."

Just as he hoped, the brazen vulgarity was too much for Miss Broadridge. Choking on an expression of outrage, she yanked open the door and disappeared into the hall-way.

Gabriel didn't move. Not until he heard the front door bang shut. Only then did he allow himself the luxury of dropping into the comfortable chair in front of the fire-place.

He supposed he should be congratulating himself for dispatching the vexatious Miss Broadridge so quickly and neatly. Yet something in the back of his mind would not let Gabriel savor the moment.

"Damn the woman!" He mumbled the words while he poured himself another drink. "Damn her brother! Damn her nonsense about giant reptiles! Damn her two hundred pounds!"

Gabriel gave the fireplace fender a vigorous kick.

Damn the two hundred pounds, indeed.

Staring into the amber liquid that swirled in his cup, Gabriel turned the problem over in his head.

The idea of having his debt to Kresgee paid appealed to him. He would admit that much, at least to himself.

But there were other unpaid accounts as well, accounts that Miss Broadridge had no way of knowing anything about. And some of them were even more pressing than his debt to Kresgee.

His tailor, damn the man, had been after him for weeks to pay for his newest clothing. His greengrocer, curse him, was eager to settle their bill. Then there was his book-maker, devil take the man! Not even two hundred pounds would be enough to satisfy him. And what was it he'd said the last time they'd talked?

From what Gabriel recalled, there was some mention of broken limbs, and the distinct and unsettling reference to damaging another portion of Gabriel's anatomy that made him wince.

Gabriel shook the thought from his mind.

And as for playing mop-up boy to Roger Broadridge . . .

Gabriel downed his drink and frowned into his empty glass. Mumbling a curse, he reached for the brandy bottle. It was empty, too, and he tossed it away and watched it spin on the bare floor where only three months ago, expensive Savonnerie carpets would have stopped its tipsy whirl.

Even furthering the reputation of a man as repulsive as Roger was not as daunting as the thought of spending the entire summer with his irascible sister.

It was a damned bothersome problem. And there was only one way to deal with it.

Gabriel kicked off his boots and raised his voice so that it echoed through the flat.

"Hoyle!" he called. "Bring me another bottle of brandy!"

Chapter 3

"Damn!"

Gabriel tossed his cards on the table and rubbed his eyes with the heels of his hands.

It was late, and he was tired. Too tired to play well. What had started as an evening of small but significant victories had quickly deteriorated into an out-and-out disaster.

He heard Kresgee chuckle and watched as he reached for the wager in the center of the table and scooped it into his already huge pile of winnings.

"Another hand?" Kresgee's red-rimmed eyes lit. He ruffled the cards in Gabriel's direction.

Gabriel shrugged and sat back in his chair. He waved toward the barmaid to bring another round of drinks. "Another hand, another drink. Why not? I've nothing better to do on a night as dismal as this. Nowhere better to go."

"Are you sure?" James Elliot was sitting on Gabriel's left. He was the younger son of an MP from Kent and as a student at Queens, he should have been back in his digs hours ago. He didn't seem the least bit concerned about either the time or the place, a house of such ill repute it was strictly off-limits to Oxford undergraduates.

Elliot swilled down half his glass of ale before the barmaid ever had a chance to set it down and leaned over the table. Reginald Barnstrom was sitting on Gabriel's right, and Elliot gave him a knowing wink. "Raddigan says he has no better place to be." He chuckled and turned to Gabriel, a lecherous smile sparkling in his dark eyes. "Are you sure about that, Gabe?"

Gabriel snorted his annoyance. Even at the best of times, Elliot was a bothersome young rakehell. The only reason he and Kresgee ever agreed to play cards with him was that he was easy to beat and not ungenerous when it came to supplying his companions with as much liquor as they could hold. Elliot was annoying when he was sober; he was even more obnoxious once he was in his cups. This was one of those times, and the night—and Gabriel's luck—were too far gone for him to take Elliot's cryptic remarks with anything even close to equanimity.

By now, Kresgee, Barnstrom, and the others at the table were all watching Gabriel, waiting for his answer. "I would remember if I had some place to be," Gabriel told them, not even trying to disguise the annoyance in his voice. He signaled Kresgee to begin the deal for the next hand. At the same time he whisked one card after another off the table when they came his way, he tossed Elliot a curious look. "What makes you think I've an assignation?"

"Oh, just a notion!" Elliot snickered. "Though she doesn't seem your kind at all. A real bluestocking if ever I saw one. Pale and proper. You know the type. As prickly outside the bedroom as they are cold between the sheets. Not your kind, I'd hazard. Not your kind at all."

"Who doesn't seem—?" Exasperated, Gabriel threw down his cards. He turned in his chair. "What are you talking about?" he demanded, staring down the younger, smaller man until Elliot squirmed and ran one finger around the inside of his collar.

Elliot laughed self-consciously and poked his chin to-

ward one of the tables that was set along the wall to
Gabriel's back. "There," he said. "She's been watching
you like a hawk for the last quarter hour. Naturally, I
assumed it was someone of your acquaintance. And just
as naturally, I assumed if there was a woman waiting for
you . . . well . . ." A flood of crimson rushed up Elliot's
neck and into his cheeks. "You know what I mean."

"I know what you mean, right enough. The real question is, who do you mean?" Gabriel swiveled in his chair.
The room was dark and thick with the smoke of shag
tobacco. He squinted through the acrid cloud.

And didn't like in the least what he saw.

Gabriel hurtled out of his chair and strode over to
where Victoria Broadridge was seated, an untouched
glass of ale in front of her, her hands clutched primly on
her lap.

"You!" He poked one finger in her direction. "What
the hell are you doing here?"

"I am watching you play cards." Victoria flicked a
thread from the sleeve of her dark pelisse and gazed up at
him, her expression as nonchalant as if she'd run into
Gabriel somewhere no more remarkable than a church
fete. "It's no wonder you lose so very much money," she
said matter-of-factly. "You aren't very good."

"Not very—!" The words strangled in Gabriel's throat.
He had no intention of debating the merits of his card-
playing skills with the woman. "That still doesn't answer
my question," he said, glaring down at her. If he expected
her to squirm and acquiesce like Elliot, he was sorely
disappointed. She looked up at him, her green eyes unwa-
vering, her shoulders as straight and rock-steady as a
dragoon's. "That doesn't tell me what you're doing here.
How you got here. Who let you into this back room to
begin with? It's supposed to be private. And how the
bloody hell have you been here a quarter of an hour when
I haven't noticed you?"

"You did not notice I was here because you were engrossed in your cards when I came in," Victoria answered him coolly. "Playing the queen in that hand was really quite a tactical error. You might have played the ten, of course . . ." Her voice trailed away along with her interest in the topic. "No matter." She dismissed the subject as inconsequential.

"I was allowed access to the back room because other people are not as boorish as you." At the memory, the smallest of smiles cracked her earnest expression. "The proprietor did not wish to grant me access to this room. He said public trade is out front. It took quite a bit to convince him. But it seems that after all, he is a good man, a conscientious provider for his wife and seven children. Once he heard how you took advantage of my poor younger sister, once he knew how you left her and the baby with not a penny to call their own, he was more than willing to allow me back here to speak with you."

"You what!" Gabriel's mouth opened and closed. His hands balled into fists. Too appalled to keep still, he spun away from Victoria.

The sight that met his eyes did little to soothe him. Kresgee, Elliot, Barnstrom, and the others were watching the little drama eagerly. They might not be able to hear everything he and Victoria were saying, but it was certain they could hear enough to know the girl was up to something. And they couldn't wait to find out what it was.

Kresgee jabbed Barnstrom in the ribs. Behind his hand, Elliot said something in a stage whisper that made the others roar with laughter. Gabriel heard a clink and saw a coin land in the center of the table, and he knew what was happening.

They were betting on the outcome of the curious rendezvous, and Gabriel could well imagine why. He heard Kresgee mumble something about having done with it here and now, about taking the girl home to bed before she changed her mind. Barnstrom winked and made an unmistakable gesture.

Gabriel wasn't sure if he should be offended by their insinuations or amused. He threw his hands up in resignation and turned back to Victoria.

"I am willing to wager a rump of beef and a dozen claret that you don't have a younger sister," he said, his voice sharp with frustration.

"I never gamble." Victoria stood and smoothed her skirts. "But no, I do not have a younger sister. I'm glad of it. I would not have liked risking her reputation in a lie."

"And what about my reputation?"

Victoria cocked her head. "Mr. Raddigan, from what I've heard, you don't have a reputation. Certainly not one that would be damaged by the story of an indiscreet love and a bastard child."

"God's eyes!" Gabriel shook his head. He was hearing it, hearing it all. But he still wasn't believing any of it.

Drawing in a deep breath, he fought to calm himself. There was no use causing any more of a scene than they already had, he reminded himself, just as there was no use losing his temper with the woman. Not here and now. And there was no use even trying to reason with her. Obviously there was something in the Broadridge hereditary makeup that caused any sort of rational discussion to be completely incomprehensible to anyone of that name.

But in spite of his good intentions, Gabriel could not control himself. "How did you find me?" The question exploded from him before he could stop it. "How did you know I was here?"

This too seemed to present not the least problem for Victoria. She gazed at Gabriel with utter sincerity. "I called at your home this morning," she told him, a crease furrowing her brow. "Hoyle would not allow me in. I don't know why. He seems a decent enough man. Sadly, the only logical conclusion seemed to me that you had instructed him not to permit me access to your person. What choice did I have?" She made a gesture with her hands that was at once full of both resignation and defiance. "I waited for you to come outdoors and then I followed you." For the briefest of moments, her eyes clouded with confusion.

"You rise very late," she said. It was clearly a curious habit, one she did not understand in the least. She discarded it with a shake of her shoulders that reminded Gabriel of a terrier just out of water. She was just as persistent as a terrier, too, he noted with a sour smile. Once her teeth were into something, she wasn't about to let go. "I've been following you all day," Victoria continued, as if to confirm his theory. "The coffee house. Your tailor's. The pawnbroker's."

She paused only long enough to make it quite clear she knew exactly why he'd visited the moneylender's shop in Holywell Street. The realization did little to help Gabriel's mood. It did wonders for Victoria's. Her point made without another word, she breezed on. "You were quite absorbed in what you were doing. I did not have an opportunity to speak with you. Until now."

Gabriel slashed one hand through the air, cutting off her words before she could continue. "We have nothing to say to each other."

"Don't we? My offer still stands, Mr. Raddigan." On the empty seat next to where Victoria had been sitting was a cloth reticule. She opened it and drew out a handful of bank notes. "Look," she said with the most triumphant of smiles. "I've brought the two hundred pounds with me."

"Miss Broadridge!" Praying no one was watching, Gabriel glanced over his shoulder. As seemed the nature of things these days, his prayer was not answered.

Every eye in the place was on them and sometime while he and Victoria were speaking, all other conversation in the crowded room had stopped. Cards and drinks were nothing when compared to entertainment as interesting as they were providing.

Mumbling a curse, Gabriel grabbed Victoria's hand and shoved it and the bank notes back into the depths of her reticule. He didn't let go, not even when she squirmed and tried to draw her hand away. He held on tight and pinned her with a look. "Are you mad?" he asked, his words filling the small space that separated them. "You can't come into a place like this and start waving around such a large amount of money. What possessed you, woman?" For a minute, Victoria didn't know what to say. Her cheeks flushing with color, she stared up at him, her lips parted in an expression that was certainly not a smile, but wasn't quite an outraged expression of protest, either.

Gabriel congratulated himself. It was a small thing, but tonight, even as insignificant an event as keeping Miss Victoria Broadridge quiet for a minute seemed like a victory of the most immense proportions.

In spite of the anger that raced through Gabriel like a horse at the gallop, in spite of the aggravation he felt when he stopped long enough to realize that he and Victoria were the center of sport for his drinking companions, in spite of the way the woman boiled his blood and the irritation that flared in him every time he thought of her . . . in spite of it all, he smiled.

Whatever words she was about to speak, they stuck in Torie's throat. She looked up into Gabriel's dark eyes and a feeling assailed her, not unlike the time she twisted her ankle in the wet sand while walking along the seashore with Roger. A wave had come up suddenly. It swept over her and before she knew what was happening, she was sucking in seawater and gasping for breath.

That was exactly how she felt now, though she couldn't for all the world understand why. She was unable to catch her breath and her heart was pounding. It must be the wretched smoke in this abominable place, she told herself. Or the lateness of the hour. It certainly could not be because Gabriel was holding on to her hand. Or because he was standing not six inches from her, so close, she could feel the heat of his body and smell the mixture of smoke and brandy that clung to his clothes and skin.

It could not have anything to do with the fact that for just a moment, there had been a flash of real amusement in Gabriel's eyes, she told herself. Or the unsettling realization that the laughter there had already stilled into something deeper and more disturbing, something that made Torie's insides feel warm, like the wax trickling from the candles on the nearby tables.

"The money was not meant to make you feel uncomfortable." Torie managed to croak out the words even though her mouth was dry and her voice sounded odd, as if her tongue were stuck to the roof of her mouth. "It is nothing more than a temptation. A temptation for you."

Her words broke whatever spell held them.

Gabriel let go of her hand and backed away. If Torie didn't know any better, she might have suspected that he was as much at a loss for words as she was. Of course he was neither flustered nor unsettled, she reminded herself in no uncertain terms. Even after only one meeting with Gabriel, she knew him well enough to know he was not easily upended. He may very well be a profligate, but he was not a man who lost his composure easily, nor was he one who would let a woman know when he did.

He was, quite simply, angry. Angry enough so that a vein bulged at the side of his neck. Angry enough that he held his well-shaped chin rigid and when he spoke to her, each word was clipped.

"Miss Broadridge, I thought I made myself clear to you the other day. I am not interested in your offer. I am not interested in your money. Don't!" He held up one hand to stop her when she opened her mouth to speak and hurried on, his words harsh.

"Don't bother to ask why. My reasons are varied and there are hundreds of them. Let us keep this as simple as we can. Let us just say I am not interested in passing my summer in Sussex. I am not interested in helping with your brother's work. For God's sake, woman, we are in Oxford, the center of learning for all the world. If it's a scientist you need, go up to the High in the middle of the afternoon and toss a stick. You're bound to hit five or six men of science and if you count undergraduates, another ten or fifteen besides. Go to Christ Church and talk to Morrison. Go over to New College and see Granger. Hell, go have a talk with Cronkite at Magdalen. I knew him when I was an undergraduate. I'll take you there myself and introduce you if they'll deign to let me through the front gate. Go tell them about your dragon. Your remarkable rhetoric and your boundless charm surely will be enough to convince one of them."

If harsh words were the only thing Gabriel Raddigan understood then he would have them, measure for measure with his own. Torie made no attempt to school her voice. "I don't want Morrison," she said, her words ringing through the silence that filled the room. "I don't want Granger. And I certainly don't want Cronkite. I want you, Mr. Raddigan." She stopped just short of stomping her foot to emphasize the point. "No one else will do."

Behind Gabriel, one of the men he'd been playing cards with choked on his drink. Another one collapsed on the table in fits of laughter. Torie couldn't imagine why. Right now, she didn't care. Ignoring everyone but Gabriel, she lifted the valise from the bench by her side.

"I've brought the tooth," she said. "Just in case you've forgotten how important it is. Perhaps if you have another look—"

"That's enough!"

Torie swallowed the rest of her words. She could not recall ever seeing a person turn the same remarkable shade of scarlet as Gabriel was right now, and some instinct warned her it was best to keep silent, at least for the moment. Eying him as if he were a wild beast, she took a step back and watched as Gabriel spun away from her and stomped back to the card table. He dropped into his chair.

"Deal the cards!" he growled.

Torie was not about to give up so easily. Gathering her composure as well as her courage, she marched over to where he was sitting. "Mr. Raddigan, I—"

"Deal the cards." Gabriel paid not the least bit of attention to her. He motioned to the man who was holding the cards though how the man could have seen the gesture was beyond Torie. He was staring at her, the cards loose in his hands, his mouth open.

Leaning forward, Torie placed one hand on Gabriel's shoulder. "Perhaps if you'd just listen," she suggested.

With a quick, impatient movement, Gabriel pulled away. The man holding the cards shook himself and began the deal.

Gabriel kept his gaze fastened straight ahead of him. He might have been carved from stone, except that his chest rose and fell with each irregular breath he took. He grabbed his cards almost before they'd had a chance to skitter across the table and propped them in one hand.

Torie settled her shoulders and raised her chin. She might be headstrong, but she was certainly not foolish. She knew when to quit, even if it was only for tonight. "Very well," she said. "If that's the way you want it, Mr. Raddigan. I am certainly not the kind of woman who will stand here in a public place and argue with you."

In spite of the fact that he was pretending not to listen, Gabriel snorted.

Torie disregarded the impertinence just as she ignored

the looks both she and Gabriel were getting from the other card players. She held her head high and steady and clutched her hands at her waist. "I am staying at the Golden Cross on Cornmarket Street," she said. "I will be there through the weekend. If you change your mind—"

"I won't." Gabriel slapped three cards down on the table.

He didn't look at her, and Torie didn't wait to see if his resolve would crumble. Keeping her head high, she collected her reticule and valise and walked out.

The street outside the pub was deserted.

Torie set down her valise and reticule long enough to turn up her collar. Sometime while she was inside, it had started to rain. She sighed, considering the wet walk back to the inn.

Just as quickly, she scolded herself for being foolish. Standing here worrying about the rain wouldn't get her to bed any sooner. Lifting the valise into one hand, the reticule into the other, she started toward the Golden Cross.

It wasn't a long walk and any other night, Torie imagined she might actually enjoy it. Whether it was soggy with rain or ablaze with summer sunshine, there was no city in the world that could match Oxford for beauty, no place on earth where the atmosphere was so rich in learning that it felt as if the very stones at her feet were alive with it. Torie took a deep gulp of air, imagining that she could breathe in the incredible knowledge that seemed to seep from every crack and crevice in the ancient cream-colored walls that surrounded each of the city's colleges.

Any other night, she knew what feelings would assail her next. She would not be beguiled by the city and all its singular charms for long. Soon, she would remember that as a woman, she was prohibited from attending school here, barred from the halls of learning where her male counterparts, whether academically gifted or not, were welcomed with open arms.

But even that thought did not bother her tonight as it had every other time she had visited Oxford. Tonight, her thoughts were as far from education as the earth was from the moon.

Tonight, all she could think about was Gabriel Raddigan.

"Scoundrel!" Torie kicked at a pebble that lay in her path. "Villain!" How any man could be so difficult was beyond her. In her naivete, she had imagined all scholars to be like her brother, Roger: learned, polite . . .

"Civilized!" Torie grumbled the word. "You'd think an educated man would at least be civilized."

"Good evenin', miss."

Torie's sullen thoughts were interrupted by a man who was standing in the center of the path. He smiled and tipped his hat.

"Not a good night to be out, what, miss?" The man's words hovered on the damp air along with the sour smells of cheap liquor and unwashed clothing that hung around him like a putrid vapor.

"No. It certainly is not." Torie stepped to her right to get around the man.

He stepped to his left.

Torie pulled to a stop. The man was not tall but he was powerfully built. Even in the dark with raindrops dribbling into her eyes, she could see that his feet were planted far apart. His right hand was curled into a fist. In his left hand, he held something long and flat. It looked like a cudgel, except that it was covered with leather and one end was bulging and heavy, as if the leather covered a knob of metal.

Too late, Torie remembered Gabriel's warning about showing her two hundred pounds inside the pub.

Swallowing hard, she spun on her heels.

The man was too quick for her. She hadn't gone five yards when he caught up to her. He darted directly in front of her.

"There you go, miss." The man hissed the words close to Torie's face, his breath as stale as yesterday's breakfast. "I'll just relieve you of your things here." As slick as a snake, he whisked the reticule out of Torie's hand and reached for the valise.

Torie did the only thing she could think to do. She screamed as loud as she could and swung the hard-sided valise.

Her weapon hit its mark. The ruffian shrieked in pain as the valise slammed into his mid-section.

It was the last thing Torie remembered.

As if it came out of nowhere, a sharp blow struck the right side of her head and she fell to her knees. The last thing she saw before unconsciousness claimed her were the paving stones that were suddenly right up against her cheek. They were slick with rainwater and wet with blood.

Torie closed her eyes and her stomach lurched into her throat. She knew the blood was her own.

Chapter 4

Gabriel turned in his chair. He crossed his legs, then uncrossed them. His fingers beating an impatient tattoo against the table, he waited for Elliot to deal the next hand.

If Elliot was trying to devil him, it was certainly working. His expression intense, his eyes focused on his hands, the young whelp shuffled the cards, reshuffled them, and shuffled them again. Just when it looked like he might actually get around to dealing them out, Elliot's facade crumbled. He burst into laughter.

"I don't want Morrison," Elliot said, his voice raised three octaves in a shoddy imitation of a woman's. "I don't want Granger. And I certainly don't want Cronkite."

Barnstrom joined in the fun. He fluttered his eyelashes and waved one limp-wristed hand in Gabriel's direction. "I want you, Mr. Raddigan. No one else will do."

Everyone at the table laughed.

Everyone but Gabriel.

Crossing his arms over his chest, he leaned back in his chair. "That wasn't what she meant," he said, with a look at his companions that would have sent them running for cover had any of them been sober enough to discern it. "The girl's devilish queer. She's bird-witted. Green as duckweed. I can assure you she had no idea what she was saying. She doesn't want me." He poked his thumb at his chest. "She wants . . . Oh, hell!" It was impossible to explain, even to himself, and Gabriel gave up trying. Mumbling one curse at his companions, another intended for Victoria, he glanced at the door where only a few minutes ago she had disappeared in a flurry of black bombazine and high indignation.

She was green as duckweed, right enough.

The thought niggled at the back of Gabriel's mind and try as he might, he could not expel it.

Only a woman as foolish as she was green would have brandished two hundred pounds in a gaming hell such as this. And only a fool would attempt to make the trip back to the inn by herself after doing so.

"Hellcat!" Gabriel tossed another glance at the door and his upper lip curled in disgust. He rapped his knuckles against the pitted surface of the tabletop, each whack in perfect rhythm to his angry words. "Annoying, vexatious, irritating hellcat! You're going to walk out of here and right into some good-for-naught wretch with an eye for your purse. Maddening woman!"

If he had been less angry and had more presence of mind, Gabriel was certain he would have been able to talk himself out of his foolish concern for the troublesome Miss Broadridge. She was, after all, an adult, and as such, was fully capable of taking care of herself. If he had any doubts of that, he need only remember how thoroughly aggravating the young lady could be. Besides, if she ever was confronted by a ruffian, she would not have to worry about surrendering her purse. She would probably offer the man a position continuing her brother's work and give him the money blithely.

The thought appealed to Gabriel's sense of humor, but even that did little to improve his disposition.

He reminded himself that he was a clever man. He should have been able to devise any number of things that could be done to get rid of Miss Victoria Broadridge. If the hour was earlier and the brandy less abundant, he supposed he might actually have been able to think of some of them.

"Hell and damnation!" Without another look at his companions, Gabriel scraped his chair back from the table.

There was only one thing to do, that was for certain, and he cursed himself at the same time he made up his mind to do it.

He had no choice but to go after the woman.

". . . hadn't heard the commotion . . . never would have found you . . ."

As if she was slowly being hauled from the depths of a dark and murky lake, Torie rose from the black clutches of unconsciousness. She heard a voice not far from her ear, or at least she thought she did. It was loud one second, completely gone the next, and she drew in a sharp breath and tried to focus on it, using it as the beacon that would guide her back to wakefulness.

". . . should never have . . . told you . . . of course, you wouldn't listen . . . some kind of bloody character flaw . . . completely irrational . . . headstrong . . . willful . . . if only you'd listened to me."

Torie didn't have to open her eyes. She knew whose voice it was.

"Mr. Raddigan." She had not meant to make the words sound so much of a sigh, yet she could not seem to help herself. Her confrontation with the thief had obviously left her weaker than she realized. There was nothing she would have liked better than to hop to her feet and prove to Gabriel Raddigan that she was as fit as a fiddle. But in spite of her intentions, she did not move. There was something uncommonly reassuring about the feel of Gabriel's arms around her, just like there was something singularly comforting about the way he cradled her head in his lap.

She couldn't move if she wanted to, and right now, she wasn't sure she wanted to.

Opening her eyes, Torie found herself staring directly into Gabriel's. He was bent over her, his nose nearly touching hers, his eyes screwed up as if he were examining her carefully, searching for signs of life. She wasn't sure if he looked relieved or disappointed to see that she was not dead.

"What . . ." Torie passed a hand over her eyes and peered into the darkness around them. They were completely alone. There was no sign of the thief. "What happened?"

"What happened?" Gabriel shook his head. Whatever had happened, he looked none the worse for wear. Even with rain streaming over his dark hair, he looked just as self-assured and maddeningly cocky as he had at the pub. He was holding a silk handkerchief that was stained with something dark and while Torie propped herself on her elbows, he dabbed it under her nose. "You went and got yourself coshed, that's what happened. If you had listened to me——"

Torie bolted upright. "The tooth!"

Both his hands to her shoulders, Gabriel pressed her back on his lap and glared at her, a not-too-subtle indication that he expected her to stay there. He reached around to his back and dragged the valise over to where she could see it.

"Your dragon tooth is fine," he said. "Though you'll need a new bag." He looked to where one corner of the valise was bashed in, and chuckled. "After the way you hit him, that beggar will have a pain in his gut for days. That's the only way I found you, you know. I heard the poor devil bellowing like a stuck pig."

It must have been an optical illusion caused by the peculiar mix of dark night and even darker shadows that played across Gabriel's face, Torie decided. For just a second, she could have sworn his eyes lit with something very close to admiration. Then just as quickly, that emotion was gone. In its place was another that was even more incredible. If Torie didn't know better, she might have said the look was one of genuine concern.

She wondered if her own surprise was written across her face, if her eyes were wide with amazement or her mouth open in astonishment. Whatever the reason, Gabriel mastered his traitorous emotions in the blink of an eye. His expression chilled. His eyes grew as hard as the precious tooth in the battered valise.

"I have no doubt you thought you were saving yourself, Miss Broadridge, but don't you realize how foolish that was? Resisting a desperate man . . . fighting back . . . That is all well and good in those silly romantic adventure stories you women so enjoy, but this is real life. You are no more than a slip of a thing, despite the fact that you have the temperament of a dragon. You could have been hurt. You could have—"

"But I wasn't." Torie struggled to sit up. When Gabriel tried to assist her, she pushed his hands away. "I was not hurt," she told him in no uncertain terms. "And you said yourself, you would not have found me if it were not for the blow I dealt the man. It seems what you deem foolish was, in fact, quite wise. I saved the tooth, didn't I?"

Gabriel sat back on his heels. "And the money?" he asked.

"The money!" For the first time, Torie remembered the two hundred pounds. She drew in a painful breath and darted a look around.

The place was empty. Her reticule was nowhere to be seen. The money was gone.

It was not all her money in the world, Torie reminded

herself. On the deaths of their parents, she and Roger had been left with a sizable fortune, a fortune that came into her sole possession when Roger died last autumn. Torie tried in vain to console herself with that thought at the same time she attempted to ignore the ministrations of Gabriel's hands. Her nose was bleeding again. She could feel the blood, hot and wet against her top lip. By now, Gabriel's handkerchief was soaked with rain water. He touched it to her face anyway, gently wiping away the blood.

Torie supposed at any other time she might have welcomed the aid. Any other time. From any other person.

Now, Gabriel's care and her bleeding nose only served to remind her that she had proved him right. She was foolish to bring the money to the pub, just as he said she was. She was foolish to flaunt it. She was foolish to think she could leave by herself and travel the deserted streets carrying what, to most people, was a king's ransom.

Gabriel had been right. And that hurt more than the blow she'd received to the side of her head, more than her bloody nose. It hurt nearly as much as the fact that she knew without a doubt that it was something he would never let her forget.

Torie's shoulders drooped. No matter how hard she tried, she could not keep the gloomy note of despair from her voice. "The money," she groaned. "It's gone."

"Hell." Gabriel grumbled the word at the same time he set Torie upright. Reaching inside his greatcoat, he drew out her reticule and shoved it at her. "It's a shame I'm as good-natured as I am," he said, his tone of voice no more good-natured than the look on his face. "You deserve to suffer more for your lunacy. Here." Torie was too stunned to take the reticule straight off, and he pushed it toward her again. "I'm sure the money's all there. Not that I've had time to count it, what with picking you up off the pavement and tending you like a nurserymaid. Take it." He dropped the reticule into her hands.

Torie didn't say a thing. It was not the welcomed sight of her reticule that snatched her words and blocked her throat. It was not relief for her found money that welled up in her along with the tears that suddenly filled her eyes. It was the condition of Gabriel's hands.

"Mr. Raddigan!" Before she could stop herself and before Gabriel had even the slightest chance of pulling away, she grabbed his hands and turned them over in her own. His knuckles were scraped and bleeding and even in this meager light, she could tell they would be black and blue before long. He winced when she touched a finger to the wounds, but Torie didn't let that stop her. While he was still too stunned to argue, she pulled the handkerchief from his grasp.

"You're hurt!" she said, all the while trying to hold on to his hands. They were slick with rainwater and he struggled hard to pull them away, but Torie would not be put off. She was nothing if not determined, she reminded herself. And she was determined to help Gabriel Raddigan, whether he wanted it or not.

Setting her lips in a hard line, she gave him a look that told him she would tolerate no opposition. Satisfied that he'd seen and understood, she proceeded to wipe away the blood that coated his knuckles. "Resisting a desperate man . . . fighting back . . ." Torie clicked her tongue as she continued to rinse away the dirt and blood. "That is all well and good in those silly romantic adventure stories you men so enjoy, but this is real life, Mr. Raddigan. You could have been more seriously hurt. Imagine! A man in your . . ." She eyed him dubiously, allowing her gaze to rest for a moment on the small paunch that showed beneath his finely tailored shirt. ". . . in your questionable state of trim. That ruffian looked to be built of bricks. You might have been . . . you might have been . . ."

In spite of her attempt to give Gabriel back as good as he'd given her earlier, another thought made its way into Torie's head and her words caught in her throat. Her breath suddenly gone, her heart pounding as hard and fast as it had when she fought off the attack of the thief, she looked up into Gabriel's eyes. "You might have been killed, and you fought him nevertheless. You fought him to save me."

She didn't know what sort of reply she expected from Gabriel. She supposed he could laugh off the entire thing. She supposed he might tell her he only came after her because the night was dull and he had nothing better to do. She supposed he very well could hop to his feet and berate her for inconveniencing him so. Instead, he lifted one hand and gently touched it to the sore spot on the side of Torie's head.

"You look a bit like you've been to an Irish wedding yourself." Gabriel's voice was as soft as the sound of the rain against the pavement. He gave her a small smile. "It's not your nose that's the problem, you know," he said, brushing the tip of her nose with one finger. "You must have hit that when you struck the ground. It's this clout to the side of your head that will hurt like the devil tomorrow." Lightly, he ran his fingers over the wound. "I wouldn't be surprised to hear if by morning, you had a black eye to go with it. And your clothes . . ." He looked down at her and shook his head. Torie looked, too.

Her pelisse was soaked with rainwater and covered with mud. Her shoes were filthy. Where her coat fell back, she could tell that even her gown was dirty. There were wet smudges along the hem and a patch of brown mud coated much of the front of her skirt.

"Come on!" Gabriel hauled himself to his feet and offered Torie a hand to help her up. With his other hand, he lifted the valise. "You certainly cannot go back to the Golden Cross looking as if you spent the evening paddling the Isis from shore to shore without a punt. We'll take you back to my flat and clean you up a bit."

Reluctantly, Torie allowed him to cup her elbow and pilot her down the street.

It was not that she objected to his aid. She knew it was true, she would cause an awful scene if she went back to the inn looking like something the cat dragged in from the gutter. Her bonnet had disappeared, and she knew the pins were gone from her hair. It hung around her shoulders in long, wet strands that clung to her face, a face she knew was caked with dirt and crusted with dried blood.

Torie shuddered. It was one thing accepting the aid of a stranger in her moment of need. It was another altogether to expect him to keep her company when she looked no more presentable than a common mudlark.

The disheartening thought clattered through her head as they made their way through the quiet streets.

But, she asked herself, if she looked as terrible as she feared, why did Gabriel smile, all the way home?

Gabriel's good humor lasted only as long as the walk home. No sooner had they turned into Paradise Square then the smile vanished from his face.

"What the—?" Gabriel pulled to a stop on the pavement opposite his lodgings and stared across the street, the muscles in the hand that held Torie's arm suddenly as rigid as his expression. He darted a look around and, satisfied no one was about, he signaled Torie to stay where she was and ventured to the other side of the street, his gaze riveted to the front door and the small square of colored silk that trailed from the knob.

"I do think you are overreacting just a bit, Mr. Raddigan." Her hands clutching her reticule at her waist, Torie fell in step behind him. When Gabriel realized she was following him, he mumbled some unintelligible word.

From the look he gave her over his shoulder, she thought it just as well she did not know what that word was.

"You look at it as if it's some token from the devil himself," Torie said, following his gaze back to the bit of fabric. "It is just a square of silk. Someone has tangled it around the knob. Surely there is nothing there to trouble you."

"Just a square of silk." Gabriel grumbled the words beneath his breath. Again, he darted a look up and down the street.

Though they were quite alone, he still didn't seem satisfied. Snatching Torie's arm, he pulled her into the narrow walkway between his block and the one next to it. A flight of shallow stone steps led up to Gabriel's house. Standing where she was, Torie could look up and see the iron railing that flanked the stairs and from there, the front door.

Gabriel craned his neck, trying for a better look. There was nothing to see besides the closed door and the scrap of silk and he mumbled a particularly vulgar word. "It's not just a square of silk," he said, his dark brows low over his eyes. "It is a signaling system and this late at night it can only mean trouble."

The idea was so absurd, Torie was tempted to laugh. The notion did not last long. She needed to do no more than look at Gabriel's face to know it was no laughing matter.

In the shadow of the stairs, it was dark, but not dark enough to disguise the thin set of Gabriel's lips or the rigid fix of his shoulders. His eyes were shot through with copper-colored flecks that sparked and flashed, as wild and dangerous as lightning. His movements as restless as a hunting animal's, he stalked over to the row of tall, close-set windows that flanked one side of the house.

"Hoyle ties a green silk to the door if there is a trades-man waiting to discuss my account," he said, attempting

to see into the first window. The draperies were shut tight
and he went on to the next window at the same time he
gave Torie a sidelong look. "We use yellow for a woman
I want to see, red for one I don't." This window proved
no more serviceable than the first, and Gabriel slapped his
palms against the side of the building in frustration.
"Damn you, Hoyle," he muttered. "Why do you have to
be so diligent about following my instructions to keep the
draperies pulled?"

"And white?" Torie asked, glancing up to where the
fabric hung, wet and limp, against the oak door. "What
does a white silk mean?"

Gabriel marched back to the stairway and pulled to a
stop in front of Torie. "White," he said, "is more serious
trouble. I have a feeling I know who is here. And that
means this may not be pleasant. That's why we've got to
do something with you." He cast a glance around. There
was no place to hide, not even here beside the front stairs,
for if anyone looked over the railing, they could surely see
the walkway and anyone trying to conceal themselves in
it.

Without so much as a word of warning, Gabriel
grabbed Torie's shoulders, spun her around, and gave her
a firm push toward the street. "Get back to the Golden
Cross," he said.

Torie shook off his hold. Far too interested to leave
now, she turned on her heels, crossed her arms over her
chest, and glared at Gabriel.

His patience snapped. "Go on!" he snarled. "Go! Get
out of here. If it's that thief you're worried about, don't.
He won't be back for your purse. I have no doubt word
has already gone 'round the lower orders in town. All
about the fierce woman whose bite is every bit as vicious
as her bark. You have less to fear out there," he said, with
a tip of his head toward the town, "than you do here." He
looked at the house.

As if to support his words, they heard a heavy thump from within the house, followed by a crash. Gabriel headed for the stairs, stopping only long enough to shove the valise into Torie's hands. "Anyone comes within thirty feet of you, use this."

Instead of taking the valise, Torie grabbed Gabriel's sleeve. She planted her feet and held on tight. "And where do you think you're off to?" she asked, meeting his look with one she hoped was as tenacious as his own. "You can't go marching in there if there's trouble. Not all by yourself."

Gabriel's body tensed the moment she touched him. The look in his eyes veered between utter disbelief and absolute outrage. He took a step nearer and glared at her. "What's that?"

His voice was infinitely calm, but the look that flared in Gabriel's eyes warned Torie to tread carefully. She ignored it.

"I said, you cannot go in there by yourself," she said, meeting his look head-on. "I won't allow it. Whatever is happening, it is apparent that it is something you can't handle on your own. You might get hurt and—"

Another loud crash came from the house and Gabriel ripped his arm from her grasp. "And what about Hoyle?" he asked, his words splitting the air between them. "Shall I leave him in there? Shall I—"

Before he ever had a chance to finish, the front door flew open.

With one arm, Gabriel pressed Torie further into the shadows next to the stairway, but even she knew that would do little good. If the man whose beefy form filled the doorway chose to look over the railing, he would surely see the two of them standing there.

"And ya can tell Raddigan that there's no more than a warnin'!" The man's rough voice preceded him out onto the front step.

He was the largest, most hideous-looking man Torie had ever seen, roughly dressed and ugly as bull beef. Even from this angle, she could see the jagged scar that slashed across his right cheek and his fists, as big as country hams where they curled around the silver head of a walking stick that look wicked and heavy.

A second later, another man followed the first out the door. Torie stared up at him from the shadows and her stomach lurched like it had the one and only time she'd been on a boat. Her heart pounded so loud, she was certain it was echoing all through town, as loud as the bell that tolled through Oxford each evening from Tom Tower.

For this man, though his form was slighter and his clothes impeccable, had eyes with all the warmth of a rat's.

Glancing up and down the street, the second man pulled on his expensive kid gloves. He tossed a look at Hoyle who appeared just inside the doorway, pale and shaken, but with his shoulders set and his head held high. "Mr. Raddigan is quite a forgetful fellow," the man said, his accent as flawless as his attire. "Perhaps our visit will jog his memory about paying his gambling debts." The first man moved aside and let the second precede him down the stairs. "Tell him we will find him. I'm not sure where and I'm not sure when, but when we do, there will be more broken than worthless crockery and shabby furniture."

"Shabby, indeed." Gabriel's angry growl rumbled in the narrow confines of the walkway. His fists up, he stepped toward the stairway.

Torie's heart leapt into her throat. Though she had known Gabriel Raddigan less than two days, she knew she could not let him walk out into the open and face these two ruthless men alone.

She was not sure why it mattered so very much, she only knew it did.

Perhaps, Torie told herself, it was because she could not watch any creature suffer without suffering some herself. Perhaps it was because, no matter how dishonest and depraved he was, Gabriel had rescued her tooth and saved her two hundred pounds, and she could not forget that. Perhaps, Torie admitted with more cynicism than she usually allowed herself, it was because she knew that with two broken arms and two broken legs, he would be of little use to her this summer.

Whatever the reason, Torie knew she had to do something. And she had to do it quickly. She had to keep the men on the stairs from seeing and recognizing Gabriel. She had to keep Gabriel from letting them know he was here.

The solution hit Torie with all the force of a physical blow. She did not stop to consider it, for if she did, she was certain she would talk herself out of the plan.

Taking a deep breath and swallowing hard, she seized Gabriel by the arm and pushed him back against the barrier formed by the risers of the stone stairway.

She didn't look at him. She couldn't, not without swooning from embarrassment. Ignoring the odd, rushing noise in her ears, and the peculiar feeling of her blood pumping like quicksilver through her veins, and the certain, irrefutable, incontrovertible fact that Gabriel, who had always thought her mad, was certain to believe it now, Torie kissed him.

Chapter 5

It was an awkward kiss at best.

Trying as hard as she could to keep the men on the stairs from seeing Gabriel's face, Torie tipped her head to the right. Though she had little experience in the art of kissing and even less in hiding from cutthroats, she suspected that leaning her head to the left would have been far more natural and much more comfortable. She supposed, too, that she would never convince the men that she and Gabriel were lovers caught unawares in a compromising position. Not unless she moved nearer, and touched his shoulders with more than the very tips of her gloved fingers, and forced her lips to do something other than just brush his in a kiss that had all the warmth of the chilly rain that fell over them.

She knew it all, but still, she could not make herself do any of it.

For the first few seconds of the preposterous performance, Gabriel was too surprised to do anything more than stand there, as still as if he'd been carved from stone. His amazement did not last long. As if he could read Torie's thoughts and knew exactly what she was trying to do, his lips softened and his rigid posture relaxed. Though Torie suspected it was neither the time nor the place, she was certain she felt a rumble of laughter vibrate through Gabriel's body.

"You can tell your master we're not finished."

Torie heard the voice of the well-dressed man with the cruel eyes. He was coming down the stairs; Torie could tell as much. In another moment, he would surely see them.

"Perhaps we will be back," the man said, punctuating his warning with the kind of laugh that made Torie think of the way the wind howled over the downs in winter. "Perhaps tomorrow. Perhaps another day. Make no mistake, we will find Raddigan. And when we do . . ." The man's voice trailed away into icy silence.

Gabriel was just as aware of their danger as Torie was. Beneath her fingers, she felt his body tense. He pulled away and looked down at her, but while she thought she might see anger or even fear written on his face, instead she saw a look that took her breath away. It was as if there were fires burning inside him, candle flames of light that warmed his expression and sparkled in his eyes until they were the color of sherry.

Gabriel's lips parted in a smile. "If this is going to work," he whispered, "we're going to have to be much more convincing."

Still smiling, he scooped Torie into his arms and spun her around. Before she could even think how to respond, his mouth came down on hers in a kiss that was as much like the one Torie had given him as night was from day.

Gabriel didn't simply touch his lips to hers, he covered her mouth with his and pressed her back against the cold, damp stone, the length of his body full against hers.

If her life depended on it, Torie could not have said what was more frightening, the prospect of being discovered by the two ruffians, or the extraordinary sensation that erupted inside her. It was as if a flame had kindled in the pit of her stomach, one that raced through her bloodstream and flowed through her, burning each and every place Gabriel's body touched hers.

Her spine tingled where the fingers of his left hand splayed against it. Her neck burned where his right hand smoothed back her hair and stroked it. Her breasts ached where his chest pushed against them. Gabriel's greatcoat was open and the thought that his frill-fronted shirt and her three-year-old pelisse, muslin dress, chemise, petticoat, and corset were the only things keeping their hearts from beating one against the other, was enough to make Torie feel tiddly as a drunkard.

For a moment, she wondered if perhaps the blow she received to her head earlier in the evening had done more damage than she realized. Her brain was spinning with the unrestrained intensity of a child's top, and a giddy sensation suddenly and inexplicably filled her from head to toe. She relaxed against the wall, her muscles slackening at the same time something deep inside her tightened like a closely wound clockspring.

Gabriel tasted like brandy and rainwater, and she moved her mouth against his, drinking in the flavor. He smelled like the night, and she drew in as much of a breath as she could, filling herself with the scent.

One small part of her remained detached enough to know that the two ruffians were still on the stairway. She could hear them talking. Their voices droned on and on in her ears, a backdrop to the rushing noises that filled her head and the drumming of her heart. Another small part reminded her that Gabriel's sudden enthusiasm, no matter how intriguing, had more to do with self-preservation than it did with passion. With her back to the wall and Gabriel in front of her, the men would see her face if they looked into the walkway; they would see only Gabriel's back.

Another thought made its way into Torie's head and she scolded herself for being so suspicious of Gabriel's motives. Standing this way, Gabriel was shielding his identity, but he was also shielding her body with his.

Through half-closed eyes, Torie watched over Gabriel's shoulder. The two men came down the stairs and turned onto the pavement. They stopped just at the entrance to the walkway and Torie's heart stopped with them.

"What's that? Who's there?" The first man, the large, ugly one with the savage-looking stick, took a step nearer.

Torie knew Gabriel heard the men, too. Beneath her hands, she felt his muscles tense. His lips changed instantly from soft and inviting, to firm. He risked lifting his mouth from hers and slid it along the curve of her neck and up to her ear.

"Run when I tell you," he whispered.

Torie was not a woman who frightened easily. She reminded herself of the fact over and over again. Though she had fretted and worried, she had never been frightened when Roger's spells of madness came over him. Though she was alarmed and upset, she had not been frightened when she was accosted by the thief earlier in the evening. But she had heard the cruel threats the man with the stick made against Gabriel. She'd seen the wintry chill in the second man's eyes. Now she was frightened, and the panic made her reckless.

She grabbed Gabriel's face between both her hands and forced his mouth back to hers. "Oh, Alfred!" She giggled and snuggled closer. She spoke loud enough for the two men at the end of the walkway to hear and added a pleasured groan for good measure.

Even Torie was surprised at how skilled an actress she was. If she hadn't known better, she might have actually convinced herself that she was enjoying the charade. There was just enough desire coloring the edges of her words to make them sound believable, just enough longing in the ragged breaths that trembled through her to make them seem sincere.

Torie set the thought firmly aside. It was not as easy to dismiss the effects of Gabriel's mouth on hers. He must have realized that running would do little more than get them both hurt. He followed Torie's lead. He deepened the kiss, and Torie tipped her head back. He parted her lips with his tongue, and Torie moaned.

It was like being carried away on a cloud, she decided. A cloud of light and pure sensation. A cloud that took her up and into the atmosphere, one that carried her closer and closer to the sun. She would surely be incinerated once she got there, she knew. And right now, she didn't care.

"Come on."

Torie's thoughts were interrupted by the sound of the well-dressed man's voice. The reminder was enough to make her cloud come plummeting to the ground. Her lips still on Gabriel's, her fingers tangling in his hair, she dared to open her eyes a bit. She peered over Gabriel's shoulder in time to see the smaller man slap his hulking confederate on the arm.

"There's nothing here to interest us," he said, clicking his tongue in disgust. "Just those two, and they're no more than common rabble, coupling like cats!" He shuddered.

The giant peered into the shadows. "You don't suppose Raddigan . . . ?"

"Don't be ridiculous." As if he'd just bit into a lemon, the other man's lips puckered. "For all his sins, even Raddigan's not enough of a rogue to take a woman out in the street."

The first man still did not look satisfied, and he didn't move an inch. Torie could feel his eyes on her, his gaze raking over what he could see of her, appraising her like a bolt of two-penny muslin in a shop window.

Neither his leering nor the way his massive bulk

blocked all exit from the walkway mattered right now, Torie told herself. All that mattered was getting Gabriel out of here alive.

Torie pulled away from Gabriel. She tossed her head back and moaned at the same time she whispered a prayer of thanksgiving for the darkness. If there was any more light, her flaming cheeks would surely give away their ruse. Swallowing her chagrin along with what little was left of her pride, she nudged one knee between Gabriel's legs and wrapped her other leg around his hip.

"Oh, Alfie!" she groaned, affecting a lower-class accent she hoped did not sound as spurious to the ruffians as it did to her own ears. "I know I ain't never goin' to be able to wait until we get 'ome."

For all its absurdity, the maneuver had a remarkable effect, both on the ruffians and on Gabriel. Torie would swear there was some subtle change in him, though she could not say for certain what it might be. Perhaps he was dazzled by her daring, or, as was much more likely, perhaps he was appalled by her lack of moral rectitude. Whatever it was, she felt Gabriel's chest rise and fall against hers and heard him suck in a sharp, ragged breath.

Torie hardly noticed, she was too busy concentrating on the two ruffians. The smaller of the fellows turned away in disgust. The larger ran a tongue over his lips and his mouth dropped open, like a hungry dog who is no more than a spectator at an especially sumptuous banquet.

"I suppose you're right," the bigger man said with a heavy sigh. "From what I've heard of 'im, Raddigan's got better taste than that, and brains enough to know when to get out of the rain." He cast a look at the lowering clouds as if wondering why he didn't, and ran one beefy finger across his forehead, flicking away the drops of water that sat like oily beads upon his balding head. "I know where there's a damned good lot of pieces like that," he said. With one last look in Torie's direction, he turned and followed the other man down the street. "They're just waitin' for them what's got the right amount of money. Why don't we take ourselves over there and . . ."

His voice trailed off into the night.

For a long time, neither Torie nor Gabriel dared to move. They stood there with their arms around each other, their legs entwined, their breaths mingling to create a fog that floated around them on the cool night air.

They might have stood that way for an eternity if they had not heard a sound above their heads.

"They are gone, sir."

As surely as if a current of electricity had suddenly and unexpectedly been thrust between them, Torie and Gabriel flew apart. They found Hoyle standing on the stairs, staring down at them, an enigmatic look on his face, a fireplace poker raised like a club in his hands.

He lowered the poker and bent over the railing. "They are gone, sir," he said again, as if he wasn't sure Gabriel heard him the first time.

"Right." Gabriel ran one hand through his hair. He wasn't sure why. There was no way he was going to look one whit better from this small bit of grooming, just as there was no way he was going to still his heart or calm his breathing by pretending he had something to do with his hands. "Right."

Now that the danger had passed, there seemed little left to say.

Gabriel looked over to where Victoria stood, as still and frosty as one of the ice sculptures he had once seen in a fashionable London restaurant. But unlike a statue, her face was suffused with color and her breaths came in small, quick gasps that pressed her breasts against the dark fabric of her coat. She didn't say a word and she didn't look at him. Though Gabriel couldn't remember doing it, her pelisse was unbuttoned, and she bowed her head and made much more of a task of buttoning it again than was necessary.

Gabriel was glad to see that her hands were trembling, if only just a bit. It meant he was not the only one who was unnerved by their encounter, though in his present state of mind, he did not want to even begin to wonder why.

"Perhaps it would be safer and drier for you and the young lady if you were to come inside, sir." Hoyle looked from one to the other of them, his typically sober expression tipped with what in better light might very well have been a smile. As usual, he made his advice seem not at all like a suggestion, but simply a mere statement of fact. Gabriel knew exactly what he was doing. Hoyle was rescuing him, as Hoyle always did.

Nodding his thanks, Gabriel offered Victoria his arm and led her into the house. She was stiff as a board at his side, all her famous starch back in spades. Her lips were pinched tight, her chin was high, her shoulders were back. She looked more like a dutiful soldier marching off to certain death than a woman who'd just shown him a tantalizing hint of the fires that burned beneath her surface of vinegar and ice.

That was a thought for another time, too, and Gabriel firmly set it aside as he watched Hoyle move respectfully out of the way to allow them to enter the house.

What they found inside was no worse than Gabriel feared. The furniture was smashed. The porcelain was demolished. Only the least valuable paintings had not been sold off long before now, and these were destroyed, their canvases dangling from their frames in pitiful shreds.

In the center of the foyer, Gabriel swung around, taking in the destruction with a surprisingly dispassionate eye.

He did not think it was shock that deadened his emotions and robbed him of his voice. He did not believe it was anger. He wondered, for only the moment he permitted it, how much his detached reaction had to do with his incredible encounter with Victoria, how much of the anger he should have felt right now had been used up in passion, how much of his outrage had been dissipated by the taste of Victoria's lips and the feel of her hips moving against his.

The memory was as sharp as a razor's edge. It twisted through Gabriel, forcing him to glance from the devastation of his home to where Victoria still stood near the door.

Her face was as pale as candle wax. Her eyes were wide with horror at all she saw. But she did not look afraid, and she certainly did not look as disconcerted by their encounter as Gabriel himself feared he did. If it were not for her lips, he might have imagined the entire thing.

But her lips . . .

Gabriel let his gaze rest there.

Her lips were swollen and red, still moist from his kisses.

"Hell and damnation!"

Gabriel allowed himself a hearty curse and left it to Victoria and Hoyle to decide who, or what, he was cursing.

Spinning on his heels, he marched into the library and waited for Victoria and Hoyle to join him. Luckily, there was at least one bottle of brandy that was unscathed, and he poured out three glasses. One he handed to Hoyle. The second he gave to Victoria. The third, and the bottle, he kept for himself.

After the first glass, he felt better. After the second, some of the strange numbness that had assailed him from the first moment Victoria's lips met his, faded away. He downed the rest of his glass and, noticing Hoyle had finished his, poured his manservant another drink.

"And you?" Though she hadn't so much as touched her drink, he tipped the bottle in Victoria's direction.

"No. Thank you." Victoria glanced around the room. The destruction was extensive here, too, but to her credit, she neither whimpered nor cried as so many other women of Gabriel's acquaintance might have done.

Not Victoria. She merely studied it all, as if it were some illustration from a particularly interesting text, her eyes measuring and evaluating, her expression unreadable.

The sound of Hoyle sighing snapped Gabriel out of his thoughts. Though usually reticent and reserved, as any good servant should be, Hoyle was known to respond quickly and easily to even a touch of liquor. Gabriel had seen what one glass of port could do to both the man's inhibitions as well as his tongue. And Hoyle was already well into his second glass. His ears were red. His eyes were bright. He shook his head with what Gabriel would have liked to think was a look of admiration. He feared it was, instead, an expression of wry amusement.

"I will give you a great deal of credit, sir. Miss." Hoyle bowed in Victoria's direction. "That was a resourceful way to get rid of those two ruffians. Very realistic. If one did not know better, one might have imagined that you were actually . . . that is, that you were really . . ." Hoyle may have been on his way to intoxication, but he was not insensible to the presence of a lady. He searched for the right words.

Before he could find them, Victoria broke in.

"One does what one has to do." With a businesslike clink, she set her untouched drink on what was left of the nearest table. "Mr. Raddigan was in danger," she said precisely, dispelling whatever bizarre fantasies Hoyle may have been entertaining with a look that would have dropped a lesser man at twice the distance. "We had no choice but to pretend a dalliance. You cannot think—"

"No. No, miss." To Hoyle's credit, he didn't retreat. His voice as ingenuous as his face, he looked from Victoria to Gabriel. "I am merely complimenting you both on the resourcefulness of the whole thing. If it were not for your clever initiative, miss, and Mr. Raddigan's eager participation—"

"Right you are!" Anxious to keep Hoyle from the tongue-lashing he knew was waiting at the other end of Victoria's sour look, Gabriel thumped his glass on the table and made a great show of crossing the room to check on what was left of his library.

Most of the history books were untouched and he thanked whatever mercurial fates had granted him at least that much mercy. The religious tracts that had been given to him years ago by his father were damaged beyond repair, he noted with a caustic smile. It seemed the ruffians had done him one kindness, after all.

One by one, Gabriel retrieved those books which were salvageable from the floor and set them again on the shelves where they belonged. It was mindless work, and he supposed he should have left it until morning, but there was something comforting in the repetition, something therapeutic about the monotony of the thing, so that when he was done, he felt more like himself again. Brushing his hands together, he leaned against the bookshelf and directed a questioning look at Hoyle. "Upstairs?" he asked.

Hoyle took his meaning in an instant. "Thank the Lord, no, sir," he said. "They did not go as far as upstairs. The kitchen is also untouched, as are my quarters. I think you should know, though, that they did promise to return, and they did say if they do not find you here, they will find you in some other place. The racetrack, they said, or your club."

"Right!" Gabriel slapped one open hand against his

thigh and hauled himself back to where Hoyle stood. "You have a sister, don't you, Hoyle?" he asked.

Hoyle seemed to have to consider the question. He nodded uncertainly, and Gabriel wondered if it was because the question was highly personal and thus inappropriate, or if it was because Hoyle did not himself stop to consider his sister very often.

"Y . . . yes, sir, I do," Hoyle finally said. "Younger than me by fifteen years. Lives in London with her husband. He's a banking clerk and quite respectable. Six children they have, sir. Little Elizabeth, and then there's Thomas, and Margaret, and Percy and Bartholomew and—"

"Good." Gabriel waved away the rest of Hoyle's explanation. Though she was trying her best to look as if she knew exactly what was going on, Victoria looked as confused as Hoyle. Her reticule was dangling over her arm and Gabriel reached over and snatched it away. He pulled open the drawstring that held the bag closed and rifled through the banknotes inside.

"Fifty pounds," he said, holding the money out to Hoyle. "That should take care of your salary for the next good while."

Hoyle looked at him in wonder.

"Take it!" Gabriel shoved the money into his hand. "And go," he said, turning Hoyle by the shoulder and pointing him to the door. "Go visit your sister. Bounce your nieces and nephews on your knee."

Hoyle's face went ashen. He looked from the money in his hand to Gabriel. "May I ask, sir, am I being sacked?"

"Sacked?" Gabriel laughed and clapped Hoyle on the back. "No, you are not being dismissed, Hoyle. You are being put on leave. Until further notice. They're bound to come back, you know. Those two bullies. I have no doubt I know who sent them. It must have been Simon Stone, my bookmaker."

In spite of his attempt to remain as nonchalant as

possible, Gabriel felt his lips compress. "Stone is not a pleasant man to have as an enemy," he admitted. "I have no doubt he will not be happy until he gets satisfaction, and the only thing that will satisfy him is either the money I owe him, or my broken bones. They will be back, Hoyle. And when they do, I don't want you to get hurt. Go. Now. Tonight." Gabriel gave Hoyle as much of a friendly smile as was allowed between a gentleman and his manservant. "Please."

Hoyle looked as if he wanted to argue, but he didn't. Still staring at the money, he backed out of the room and clicked the door closed behind him.

"Well, that takes care of that, doesn't it?"

As if the snap of the door latch was enough to prompt Victoria to action, she crossed the room to stand in front of Gabriel, her movements as crisp as her words. "I will hire a coach as early in the morning as I can," she said. "With any luck, we can be to Cuckfield by—"

"Stop!" Gabriel held up his hands to drive back the barrage of words. "What are you talking about?"

"You can't stay here. You said it yourself. If there is danger for Hoyle, there is certainly more danger to you. Those two ruffians will be back. Certainly, the solution to the problem is clear."

"Is it?" Gabriel was tempted to laugh. He might have if it wasn't so damned clear that the woman was, for the first and only time since he'd met her, absolutely right.

"I helped save your life, Mr. Raddigan," Victoria continued, reinforcing her argument. "The least you can do is—"

"The least I can do?" Suddenly, Gabriel knew why he hadn't been angry at the way Stone's bullies destroyed his home. He was saving all his anger, saving it for now. He pulled himself up to his full, considerable height and glared down at Victoria, who had the temerity to look not the least bit unnerved. "Are you telling me I am obliged

to come and work for you because I owe it to you?"
Gabriel asked, his voice sharp. "That's ludicrous! No one
forced you into that absurd farce out there. No one made
you—"

"What was that you said outside, Mr. Raddigan?" Victoria's voice was as guileless as the look on her face. His
argument thus gently but effectively cut in two, she sauntered over to the windows and nudged the draperies aside,
acting for all the world like she wasn't listening to a thing
he was saying. "One color silk for women you want to see,
another color for those you want to avoid. Had I been one
of the latter, you would not be standing here now." She
turned to him, her head cocked, her eyes wide.

In another woman, he might have taken the look for
that of a coquette. Gabriel knew better. Coming from
Victoria, the look might be innocent as a lamb's, but there
was surely a lion lurking somewhere beneath.

"Would any of those women have been willing to do
what I did?" she asked.

Gabriel snorted. He answered too quickly and much
too honestly. "They'd do that and more."

"Yes. I can well imagine." Victoria saw his mistake as
surely as he did. She clutched her hands at her waist, her
lips tight. "That is not what I meant," she said, pointedly
avoiding naming exactly what she was referring to,
though they both knew precisely what it was.

"You mean would any of them have helped save my
neck?" Like it or not, it was an intriguing thought. Before
Gabriel had a chance to tell her as much, Victoria
marched back across the room, retrieved her reticule, and
went to the door.

"My offer still stands," she said, barely able to contain
a self-satisfied smile. "A summer in Sussex. Dull, boring,
hideously provincial Sussex. After what I've seen tonight,
I would venture to guess that watching the moss grow on

the window ledges is infinitely preferable to the alternative. Are we agreed, Mr. Raddigan?"

"I never said—"

"It seems to me," Victoria said, looking down at her reticule, "that you owe me fifty pounds." She opened the door. "I will send the coach to collect you at eight."

Gabriel waited until he heard the front door shut to crash his fist into the back of the overstuffed chair in front of the fireplace. He raked one hand through his hair.

"Damned woman!" He headed out of the library and into the foyer, his boots crunching against the splinters of mahogany and rosewood that coated the place like carpeting.

He took the stairs two at a time.

Hoyle had assured him that nothing on the first floor had been touched, and that was just fine with Gabriel.

There was a bottle of very fine, very expensive brandy in the wardrobe alongside his bed.

Tonight, he thought he might need it.

"And damn it," he grumbled with one last look over his shoulder at the front door, "if I don't finish it, I'll take whatever's left and drink it on the way to damned Cuckfield."

Chapter 6

Perhaps it was the late hour.

Perhaps Torie was tired from the journey.

Perhaps spending the better part of the day in a closed coach with Gabriel Raddigan, his bottle of brandy, and his repertoire of tavern songs sung poorly but with great enthusiasm, was simply too much for any one person to bear and still remain in possession of either her temper or her composure.

Whatever the reason, the sight of Spencer Westin sprawled comfortably in one of her library chairs was not the first thing Torie had expected to see when she arrived home. It did little to improve a patience already stretched far too thin.

"Mr. Westin."

At the sound of Torie's voice, Spencer hopped out of the chair. Completely ignoring the slightly sour look on her face, he hurried to the door, his hands held out to her, his eyes darkening with worry when they alighted on her bruised face and blackened eye.

"Miss Broadridge!" He coughed away his embarrassment, obviously deciding not to ask what had happened for fear he might not like the answer. "How delightful to see you again!" One hand solicitously on Torie's elbow, he bent and touched a kiss to her cheek.

"You have been too long gone," Spencer said, smiling broadly and conveying her into the room as if it were his home, not hers. "It has been sadly uneventful here without you."

"I had not thought to find you here on my return." Torie fought to keep her annoyance from spilling into her voice. Spencer Westin was a friend, a good friend, and it was not right to make him suffer for either her exhaustion or her displeasure.

She glanced around the room, hoping the familiar and cherished surroundings would help relieve her weariness and soothe her ill temper.

After three weeks of being away, the orderly rows of fossils and rock samples displayed in cases along the walls looked especially welcoming. Torie let her gaze settle there. She breathed in deep, and the wonderful scent of leather-bound books, musty papers, and good, country earth, filled her nostrils and brightened her disposition.

She offered Spencer a smile, one she feared could never quite equal his in enthusiasm. "How did you know I would be arriving this evening?" she asked.

"Luck, I suppose." Spencer's smile widened. His long, thin face and square teeth always reminded Torie of a donkey, and today was no exception. He stuck his hands into his pockets and peeked out at her from beneath a shock of brown hair prematurely peppered with gray, exactly the color of a donkey's fur.

"I've been coming by periodically, just to make sure nothing was disturbed. When I heard the carriage which brought you from Cuckfield . . ." Spencer scuffed his boots against the bare wood floor. "Your journey was successful, I trust?"

"Quite." Crossing to the desk, Torie set down the hard-sided valise that contained the tooth. Her journal was lying there and she fingered it idly at the same time she scolded herself. She was not usually such a careless housekeeper and she could not imagine how she had left the book out instead of placing it in the desk drawer where it belonged.

"You went to the Hunterian Museum in London?"

Spencer's question chased her thoughts away. Torie's head snapped up and she looked at him. "How did you know?"

Spencer shrugged. "A guess. Really only a guess. Roger talked about doing it last autumn, but . . . well . . ." As they usually did when he discussed Roger, Spencer's eyes misted. He dashed away the emotion with the back of one hand. "Roger never had the chance, of course. When you were gone so long . . . Well, I am as much a scientist as Roger, after all," he said. His chest puffed with pride at the same time his cheeks reddened. "The evidence was there before me. I simply came to the most logical conclusion. I assumed you had taken the tooth and—"

"The tooth? You know about that, too?" Torie was not sure if the emotion that roiled up inside her was annoyance or simply surprise. The discovery of the reptile tooth was supposed to have been a secret, she and Roger had decided as much the day it was found. They had pledged to keep the knowledge to themselves, at least until other evidence could be uncovered that would substantiate the animal's identity. "How did you—?"

Spencer dismissed both Torie's apprehension and her suspicions with a wide smile. Stepping closer, he scooped her right hand into both of his. His eyes warm and gentle, he captured her gaze and his smile melted into a look of tender affection.

"As well as being colleagues, Roger and I were the best of friends," Spencer said, his voice dipping at the same time his gaze dropped.

Torie followed the glance down to his hands, as workworn and calloused as her own, his skin browned from days spent in the sun. He moved his fingers over hers, the touch neither intimate nor bold, but warmhearted and tender.

It was not so much his touch that robbed Torie of her voice as it was the understanding of what Spencer intended to convey by it. Spencer Westin, who had always been a friend, was declaring himself something more, and Torie blinked at him in bewilderment, her astonishment complete.

Spencer raised his eyes to hers. "Roger and I dined together the evening he found the tooth," he said. "He was so terribly excited, of course he told me all about it. Probably before he ever told you." He pressed her hand between his, unspoken sympathy written in every one of the fine lines that spread from the corners of his eyes like webwork.

"I know how much Roger's work meant to you. But Roger and I, we were associates, after all, and friends. It is a different thing to discuss a matter of importance with another man of science than it is to discuss your work with your sister, no matter how interested or involved she is. I'm sorry." Spencer leaned closer, his eyes swimming with sincerity, his mouth only inches from Torie's. "It must be terribly hard to know Roger shared the intimate details of his discovery with someone outside the family."

"Where do you want these bloody trunks?"

With a thud that shook the walls of the cottage, Gabriel Raddigan burst into the room and dropped the trunk he was carrying to the floor. His gaze slid from Torie, to Spencer, down to where their hands were intertwined, and when he looked up again, his dark eyes lit with what, for a moment, Torie thought was admiration. It was not. She realized as much before the gleam even dimmed. It was mocking amusement, and Gabriel underscored it with a lopsided smile.

"Delightful of you to have arranged a welcoming committee!" His smile still firmly in place, Gabriel turned his attention to Spencer. "Raddigan," he said by way of introduction.

"Mr. Raddigan." Spencer let out a breath that was almost a sigh. He tipped his head to acknowledge the introduction at the same time he released Torie's hand and turned to Gabriel. "I am Spencer Westin," he said. "A friend of Roger's and I hope," he added with a quick glance at Torie, "a friend of his dear sister." Spencer's eyes narrowed and he tilted his head back, sizing up Gabriel with one keen look. "Raddigan. The name is familiar, yet I do not believe we've had the pleasure of meeting." He stuck out his hand. "Are you a relative, Mr. Raddigan? A friend?"

Gabriel sauntered across the room and accepted Spencer's hand. Standing this close, Spencer could not help but detect the conspicuous odor of the brandy Gabriel had consumed in the coach. He brought his knuckles to his nose, decorously sniffing back the distinct smell at the same time he gave Gabriel a closer look.

Torie followed Spencer's gaze. An entire day in a cramped, uncomfortable coach had left Gabriel as disheveled as Torie knew she must be. His hair stuck up at odd angles at the top of his head and fell over his forehead and into his eyes. His chin was dark with the shadow of an evening beard, the stubble accenting the hard lines of his face, making it look more than ever as if it had been carved from stone.

Gabriel returned Spencer's look measure for measure, the tiniest of smiles stealing over his mouth.

Torie found she was obliged to turn away. After all that had happened between them last night, she could not look at Gabriel's lips without thinking of the extraordinary effect his kiss had on her, both physically and mentally. It was an awkward realization, damned awkward, as she knew Gabriel would say. It made her uncomfortable though she couldn't quite explain why. It made her angry, though for the life of her, she couldn't say who she was angry at. She would have liked to think it was Gabriel, but she very much feared it was herself.

"Mr. Raddigan is neither friend nor relative," Torie said, her irritation crackling through her words. "He is here in a professional capacity. He will be continuing the work Roger began before he died."

"Continuing . . . ?" For a moment, it seemed as if Spencer might challenge the statement. He looked at Torie in wonder, and his mouth opened and closed like that of a fish newly hooked and brought onto land. He controlled the reaction, his courtesy overcoming whatever emotion caused the tremor in his aplomb.

"Welcome to Sussex, Mr. Raddigan," Spencer said with a polite nod. "Although my own interests lie in the consideration of geology rather than paleontology as Roger's did, he and I discussed his work many times. If I may be so bold as to admit it, my understanding of the subject is exceptional. If there is anything I can do to assist you in any way, please feel free to call on me."

Gabriel accepted the generous offer with a bow. "I suspect," he said, with the slightest lift of his eyebrows, "there is more you will be doing for Miss Broadridge than you will ever do for me."

With that, he turned on his heels. He paused at the door. "We have not met before," he said to Spencer. "But you may, indeed, have heard the name. It is Gabriel." He disappeared into the outside passage, his last words rumbling back at them like the echo of distant thunder. "Gabriel Raddigan."

"Gabriel Raddigan?" Spencer turned to Torie, his face suddenly as red as the sun setting outside the window. "Do you know who that is?"

"Of course I know who he is." Torie brought her chin up, daring Spencer to question her further. "He is a

scholar of some note, I believe, and he will be living here
this summer."

Spencer's eyes popped open wide. "Good heavens,
woman! Don't you know? The man was sent down from
University!" Spencer waved one arm vaguely in the direction in which Gabriel had disappeared. "Did you know
that much about him before you went out and invited him
into your home?"

"Yes." Annoyed at Spencer for questioning her, annoyed at herself for being bothered by his questions, Torie
spun away from him and went to stand near the fireplace.
Fitfully, she straightened and restraightened the orna-
ments on the mantelpiece. "I know what happened at
Oxford."

Spencer came up behind her, his boots rapping against
the floor with all the displeasure he fought to keep from
his voice. "Do you? Do you really? You may think you
know the story, but you cannot know the entire truth. If
you did, you never would have made such a foolish decision."

When Torie did not respond, he leaned over her shoulder, trying to capture her gaze. "Raddigan is something
of a legend in academic circles," Spencer said, his voice
heavy with derision. "At one time, he was expected to be
the most brilliant practitioner in the history of modern
natural science. Perhaps the next Baron Cuvier, some
said. Perhaps even greater. He threw it all away." Spencer's voice dropped, his words harsh in Torie's ear.
"Threw it all away the day he traded a handful of pound
notes for the questions on an examination."

"I know all that." Torie edged away, putting distance
between herself and the brutal truth of Spencer's words.
"I knew it all the day I offered him the position."

"Then why on earth . . . ?" Spencer threw his hands in
the air. "I admit, the workings of a woman's mind do
confound me at times." He drew in a loud breath. "My

dear Miss Broadridge . . . Victoria." His hands on her shoulders, he turned Torie to face him.

"I wish with all my heart that Roger were still here to tell you these things. But he is not, and the world is a sadder place because of it. In his absence, I hope you will allow me to address you as I know your brother would have. I am sorry if my words sound harsh and insensitive, but I confess, I am sorely troubled by what's happening here. Perhaps you have tried to take too much on yourself. Perhaps it is simply too much to expect any woman to make the right decisions without the benefit of the kind of worldly knowledge only a man can have." Spencer cocked his forefinger beneath Torie's chin and lifted her face to his. His expression was gentle, indulgent.

"You should have asked my advice before you did this imprudent thing. Perhaps you do not understand the gravity of the things to which I refer. The man isn't accepted into polite society." He cast a look at the door. "Not even the most liberal of intellectuals will go near him. Gabriel Raddigan is an outcast, a cad who's spent the last years consoling himself for his perfidy in every bottle of spirits he can find. You smelled him when he came into the room. Is that the kind of man you want continuing Roger's work?"

Torie clutched her hands at her waist. "I know very well what I am about," she said. "What I decide to do with Roger's work is my business and mine alone."

Spencer dropped his hands to his side, a spark of displeasure flaring in his brown eyes. "You are absolutely right, of course," he said, his words as tight as the look on his face. "What you decide to do with Roger's work is none of my affair. But you, dear Victoria, you are." He took her hands, and held on tight, as if the very feel of her skin next to his was all that was holding his temper in check.

Spencer's voice trembled with emotion. "The man is a

wanton! He is known throughout the academic community as a rogue and a villain. You cannot think that you
can spend the entire summer with such a man living
under your roof. I would not be able to sleep at night for
worrying about you."

"Is that what troubles you?" In spite of Spencer's fervor, Torie laughed. She squeezed his hand in assurance,
but she did not meet his eyes. How could she, when she
was about to tell him a colossal lie?

"Mr. Raddigan is surely the most aggravating man I
have met in many a long year," she admitted, that much
of her confession absolutely honest. "But he has been
nothing but a gentleman toward me."

That was true, too, Torie told herself. After all, Gabriel
was not the one who initiated the embrace in the walkway. Gabriel was not the one who began the kiss. He was
not the one who wrapped his legs about her and moaned
with something very like pleasure when their tongues met.

Heat spread through Torie's face at the memory. To
hide her mortification, she turned from Spencer. "From
what I have been told, Mr. Raddigan's preference is for
licentious and beautiful women," she said, not sure if she
was trying to convince Spencer or herself. "And since I
am neither, I am quite sure he will not give me a second
look. I am safe, Spencer. There is no cause to worry for
my virtue."

"It isn't funny." Spencer's lips puckered with displeasure. He sucked on his teeth and the sour look intensified.
Finally, as if he'd made up his mind about something
monumental, he drew in a great breath.

"Victoria, you give me no choice. Something must be
done to correct this ghastly mistake of yours. Mr. Raddigan simply must be made to leave. I will pay whatever
money it is you have promised him."

The offer may have been well intentioned, but it was as
offensive as it was generous. Torie's temper flared. "I

have reached my majority," she said. "I do not need a keeper."

"Don't." Ignoring her outburst, Spencer placed a gentle hand on her arm. "Do not let us argue today when we have been apart these last, long weeks. Perhaps I am not making my intentions clear. Perhaps that is why you misinterpret them as being so presumptuous. What I mean to say, Victoria, is that I know you can be something of a spitfire when you have a mind to. You will be pleased to know it is a fault I am willing to overlook, just as I am willing to disregard the matter of your age. You are five and twenty, after all. Your best years are behind you. If your mercurial temperament does not frighten off potential suitors, your age certainly will. I am willing to accept you as you are."

There was nothing to be said in reply to a declaration this astonishing, and Torie did not even try. She stared at Spencer, her mouth open. She exhaled, drew in another breath, and let it out again. Still, there were no words that would give voice to her surprise.

Spencer did not seem to notice. His smile firmly in place, he beamed down at her. "You do not disappoint me, Victoria," he said. "I knew you would not protest like a callow girl or bemoan the fact that there is no mention in my little speech of anything about love." Spencer laughed.

"Love. It is a foolish woman's notion, I fear, one derived from reading too many stories filled with tripe and onions. You know as much, Victoria, you are as rational a woman as ever there was. That is what makes you so far superior. You know the truth as well as I do."

The full intent of Spencer's speech made Torie's words whoosh out of her as if she'd been struck in the stomach. "Whatever are you talking about?" she asked, though she was sorely afraid she would not be pleased with the answer Spencer was bound to give. "I am afraid the long hours on the road have muddled my mind. If I did not know you better, I would think you—"

"But that is exactly what I am saying!" Spencer pulled his shoulders back and set his jaw, looking for all the world like a man standing before a firing squad. "Victoria," he said, "I would like you to be my wife."

"Mr. Raddigan?"

Torie stepped back and glared at the door of Gabriel's room as if staring at it long enough and with enough intensity would cause him to answer her knock.

The plan was uncertain at best and, just as she suspected, it did not work.

There was no answer this time, just as there had been no answer one hour ago when she'd come by and knocked.

Frustrated, Torie shook her head. Gabriel had not joined her for dinner, though she'd called him twice. He had not appeared in the library where she sat reading after the meal. He had not ventured out of his room at all since their arrival this evening, and she found the fact more than a bit perturbing. That may have been what she had in mind for the rest of his summer, but for now, the least he could do was accknowledge her presence.

"Mr. Raddigan!" She tried one last time, her voice betraying the annoyance that welled in her. Still there was no answer and she decided there was only one thing to do.

Situating the bottle of brandy she was carrying behind her back, Torie settled her shoulders and raised her chin. She opened Gabriel's door.

She was familiar with the room; it had been Roger's for the months they'd lived together here, and she was grateful now for the familiarity. The curtains were drawn on each of the room's two windows and there were no candles lit. The room was nearly as black as the night outside.

Torie peered into the gloom. There was a small fire in the grate, one that had obviously not been tended in the last hour or so. Its forlorn flames licked the sides of a spent log, their meager light just enough to show her the outlines of Roger's favorite chair, the one he had always kept at his writing desk across the room.

The chair had been pulled up in front of the fire, and Gabriel was propped in it, his head against the overstuffed back, his eyes closed.

Torie took a tentative step over the threshold, her gaze drawn to Gabriel whether she would have it or not. For, as many times as she had seen Roger in the chair, she had never seen him as she saw Gabriel now. And if she had, she knew somehow that the effect would never have been the same.

Gabriel must have been exhausted from their long journey. His boots were off, kicked into the corner, his stockinged feet were stretched toward the fire. He had obviously begun to undress before he fell asleep. His shirt was off, revealing far more of his anatomy than Torie had seen of any man's. She took another step forward, fascinated, and assured herself in no uncertain terms that her interest had everything to do with healthy curiosity and nothing to do with the singular tingling that had begun in the pit of her stomach.

There was a fine thatch of black hair on Gabriel's chest. Torie leaned nearer, examining it closely. It was soft and silky-looking, skimming over muscles that might have been impressive once, and Torie followed the path it laid from his chest, to his stomach, down to where it disappeared into the waistband of Gabriel's trousers.

A sudden burst of heat rushed into her face, and Torie fanned it away with one hand, her heart thumping against her ribs.

"You'd better get used to it. You'll be seeing more than

just his chest once you marry the incomparable Mr. Westin."

Gabriel popped open one eye and watched with perverse delight as the color drained from Victoria's cheeks. She stepped back, startled, and blinked at him, her usual bluster gone in the face of her mortification.

It didn't take long for her to recover. No sooner had the echo of Gabriel's words faded in the room, than Victoria's surprise melted. As surely as embarrassment had paralyzed her, a flare of anger revived her. "You were eavesdropping." Victoria frowned, the light of the fire picking up emerald sparks in her eyes and throwing them back at him. "You heard everything Spencer said. That is rude, Mr. Raddigan, rude and—"

"The acoustics in here are really quite splendid." Gabriel interrupted her with the same comment she had made to him on their initial meeting in Oxford. He smiled when her expression showed that none of the sarcasm was lost on her. "I couldn't help but hear," he told her, taking full advantage of the breach in her composure to irritate her even further. "Unfortunately, your voices dropped too low after a while. I heard Mr. Westin's passionate proposal, but I did not hear your tender consent."

Victoria looked away. "That's because there wasn't one," she said.

Gabriel's brows rose, his lips tilted into a smile of begrudging admiration. The woman had far more sense than he'd given her credit for, though he wasn't about to let her know it. He draped one arm across the back of his chair.

"I find it difficult to understand how any woman could resist Mr. Westin's enticing proposition," he said. "Especially when it was phrased in such sentimental terms. What was it Westin said?" He cleared his throat and tried to speak in the same high-pitched, nasal voice Spencer used.

" 'You are five and twenty, dear Victoria, no other man would have a woman so old and wrinkled.' " Gabriel chuckled. "You are a much stronger woman than I thought if you can resist such courtship."

Victoria's lips pinched with annoyance. "Spencer Westin is not as much a buffoon as you would make him out to be," she said. "He was a good friend of Roger's and he has been my friend as well. His offer was not motivated by sentiment as much as it was by concern. He is clearly disturbed by the prospect of us spending the summer together under one roof." She gave Gabriel a stinging look. "I told him there is not the least cause for worry."

"Not on my part." Gabriel held his hands up in mock surrender. Just to refresh his memory as to what the woman was really like, he slid his gaze from the top of Victoria's head to the tips of her shoes. With her back as straight as a broomstick and her face as sour as bad ale, she was the most forbidding-looking woman he'd ever known. And, he reminded himself, she had the personality to match, as prickly as a hedgehog. Still, he would admit one thing: there was something about the firelight that brought out the best in her.

The last log in the hearth split and shattered, sending up sparks of light, fitful flares of yellow and orange that accented the golden highlights of Victoria's hair and softened the firm ridges of her countenance. Part of her hair was unbound, as if she had unloosed it absentmindedly, pulling some of the pins away and leaving others in place. The shorter hairs over her ears floated like a downy cloud around her face, casting it in lacy shadows that blunted the sharpness of her expression.

The effect was ethereal and Gabriel sat back, as surprised as he was pleased. Victoria had changed from her traveling dress into a gown of lighter-colored stuff, the kind of delicate and airy thing a woman would wear around the house but never in public. Though it was not

frivolous by any means, the dress was far less severe than
the mourning gown she'd worn to call on him in Oxford,
its simple lines skimming a waist that was far smaller than
he had noticed, and hips that were slim and long and
well-proportioned.

Gabriel shook his head, amazed. In this light, he could
almost see why Spencer Westin had proposed to Victoria.

The thought should have sobered him like a splash of
icy water. It had just the opposite effect. Suddenly uncomfortable, Gabriel shifted in his seat.

It must be all this damned fresh country air, he told
himself. Or the fact that he was already bored and tedium
always opened his mind to fantasy.

Why else did he keep thinking about the taste of Victoria's lips? Why else did he keep feeling the shock of
electricity that hit him when he pressed his body close to
hers?

Before Victoria could suspect what was going through
his mind, Gabriel looked away. He gathered what was left
of his wits and looked back at her, his face—he hoped—
perfectly composed. "There was something you wanted
to talk to me about?" He stared across the little room at
Victoria, hoping the reality of her presence would scatter
the overworkings of his imagination.

"Yes." Whatever she had been thinking, Victoria
snapped out of her own thoughts as clearly as Gabriel
came back from his. "I wanted to let you know that we do
not need to work tomorrow," she said, her voice recover-
ing all its chilly preciseness. "It is Sunday, after all. I will
be going into Cuckfield for services. If you'd care to join
me . . . ?"

"Yes, of course."

"And this coming week . . ." Victoria hurried on. "This
week, I have a great deal to do to prepare for our summer.
I have been away too long and there are supplies to
purchase, correspondence that must be answered. I need

to stop in at Newberry Farm and see if they can spare someone to do our cooking."

"And what am I supposed to do while you're busy with all that?" Gabriel sounded like nothing if not a young boy who had seen an especially delectable sweet snatched from him. He winced at the petulance of his own words.

Victoria did not seem to notice the tone of Gabriel's voice as much as she did the question. Her eyes widened, as if she were surprised. "You could keep busy reading, I suppose," she said, looking at him uncertainly. "There are any number of interesting books in the library . . ."

"And we begin excavating when?" Gabriel asked.

Something about his simple inquiry caused a noticeable crack in Victoria's stiff demeanor. She turned from Gabriel and went to the door. "There is no hurry," she said, glancing at him over her shoulder. "We have all summer."

"But I thought—"

She did not give Gabriel time to voice his concerns. In three quick steps she came back across the room. "This is for you," she said.

Gabriel looked from Victoria to the bottle of brandy she held out to him.

"We've always kept spirits in the house." Victoria hurtled into her explanation. "For visitors. Roger was not one to enjoy them and neither am I. This bottle is some years old. It's unopened, but I'm told it will go bad if it is not used soon. You might as well take it."

She thrust the bottle into Gabriel's hands and without another word, turned and hurried from the room.

His astonishment complete, Gabriel sat back in his chair. For a woman who showed a decided lack of social grace and a definite mistrust for the finer things in life, Victoria could be remarkably agreeable when she had a mind to.

Imagine, an untouched bottle of brandy, an entire

week of relaxation, and the undeniably pleasant thought
that he was far from the dangers that awaited him in
Oxford.

It was enough to cheer any man's spirits.

Smiling, Gabriel turned the brandy bottle over in his
hands and examined it. For a bottle that had been on the
shelf for years, it was remarkably clean. He paused to
consider the puzzle, but only for a moment.

The next second, he popped the cork and raised the
bottle in salute to himself. "And to you, Victoria Broadridge," he said, with a smile and a wink at the door. "As
unlikely a means to a man's salvation as any woman I've
ever met."

He gave voice to the thought even before he had a
chance to consider it. Sitting there listening to himself, he
realized it was true. Gabriel sat motionless, his gaze fixed
on the closed door, an improbable thought making its way
into his head.

Perhaps this chance to continue Roger Broadridge's
work was his means to salvation.

The theory was so absurd, Gabriel knew he should
have been laughing. But he wasn't. His smile vanished as
a sudden rush of emotion filled him, one he had not felt
in so long, it took him some moments to work out what
it was.

Hope.

The single word burned inside Gabriel's mind as if it
had been branded behind his eyes.

Hope.

The hope of one last chance to prove to the world that
there was more to Gabriel Raddigan than the man he
himself had spent the last six years creating. More than a
buck of the first head. More than a drunken sot. More
than the man who had blackened his family's name, and
gambled away his family's fortune, and done every reck-

less thing he could to help him forget his past and blunt the pain of his present.

Perhaps it would take a woman whose kiss was as remarkable as her scientific theories to do all that, Gabriel thought. Perhaps it would take a woman who believed in dragons to help put his own demons to rest.

Gabriel rammed the cork back into the brandy bottle and set it down on the floor.

Suddenly, he wasn't very thirsty.

Chapter 7

"Red seven on the black eight. Black four on the red five. Red queen on the . . . oh, hell!"

Gabriel hurled his deck of cards at the far wall of the library. "Bloody hell!" He swept his forearm over the table, demolishing the neat rows of cards he'd been so careful to arrange and rearrange. Pushing away from the table, he paced to the far end of the room just as the clock on the mantelpiece struck the hour.

"Four o'clock," Gabriel grumbled, slapping his hand against his thigh, "and no sign of the woman. What in the bloody hell—"

"Mr. Raddigan?" Victoria poked her head in the library door. "I thought I heard a noise and—"

She took one look around the room and her golden eyebrows rose. There was a seven of clubs perched precariously in the bunch of flowers she'd picked only yesterday; a three of hearts stuck between two books on the shelf. There were cards on the chair in front of the fireplace, cards on the floor. There were cards on the plate that held the remains of the chicken, bread, and cheese that had been Gabriel's lunch, cards strewn over the top of the desk.

Victoria stepped into the room, and Gabriel could tell from the way her mouth tightened that it took all her effort not to click her tongue and shake her head as one might at a naughty child. "The game is called Patience," she said, with a patronizing look that sent Gabriel's blood past the boiling point. "Surely if the cards were not going your way, there were better ways to deal with your frustration."

"The cards were going my way very nicely, thank you." Gabriel went to the table and scooped up the few cards that were left on top of it. He knelt to retrieve the ones that had landed on the floor nearby. "It is not the cards that trouble me," he said, looking at Victoria from between the table legs. "It is this interminable boredom. I simply cannot continue to—"

"Really, Mr. Raddigan!" As if his vehement protest were no more important than the buzzing of an annoying insect, Victoria shook it off. From his position on his hands and knees under the table, Gabriel saw her set down the lumpy bundle she was carrying. He watched her cross the room, only the tips of her boots and the hem of her gown visible now that she was closer.

"What you perceive as tedium is what others would surely consider a holiday," she said. The annoying exuberance of her voice was dulled to a nearly tolerable level by the thickness of the table between them. "Besides, there must be a better way of dealing with your boredom than chucking cards all about the room." Gabriel heard her sigh and watched as she bent to pluck the cards that lay around her feet like the petals of a spent rose.

It was warm today and Victoria was wearing neither a pelisse nor mantle. She was dressed in an out-of-fashion gown, as he'd learned was her habit when she was not making social or business calls. It was black, as was appropriate for a woman who had lost her only brother less than one year earlier. The dress had short, puffed sleeves and a bodice gathered up high under her breasts and cut low over her shoulders.

Gabriel watched her collect the fallen cards one by one, and, as if he were a conspirator who knew some secret he was not about to share, a smile tipped his mouth.

When they were together, he reminded himself, Victoria was careful to keep her words crisp and her movements brisk. In the past two weeks, he had learned that these things were inherent in her character, as much a part of her nature as the way her nose wrinkled with disgust each time he filled a brandy glass, or the way her fingers moved idly through her hair as she sat in the evening reading a book or writing in her journal.

But there was another side to Victoria, one that she revealed only in those moments she thought Gabriel was not watching.

When Spencer Westin came by a week ago to show her a particularly unusual rock sample, Gabriel saw the way Victoria's eyes sparkled with excitement. When Westin stopped in again three night ago and broached the subject of some scientific theory or another, Gabriel heard the way Victoria lost herself in the passionate defense of her own opinions, ones that were completely outside the realm of what was either accepted or acceptable.

At times like those, Gabriel was reminded that there was another woman hiding beneath the priggish exterior Victoria Broadridge showed to the world.

That was the woman who could fight off a thief using only her native courage and a cumbersome valise, the one who would help a man defend his home and himself even though he was practically a stranger, and a belligerent one at that. That was the woman who had kissed him in the walkway outside his Paradise Square home. The woman he saw now.

Watching each of Victoria's smooth, feminine movements, Gabriel's body instinctively reminded him that there were better ways to alleviate boredom than with a deck of cards. Suddenly, his thoughts were as far from Patience as they could possibly be.

Unable to reach all the cards, Victoria knelt and stretched out her hand. The action itself was innocuous enough. Its results were anything but.

Stooped over the way she was, Victoria revealed far more than Gabriel had seen of any woman of late. Certainly it was more than he'd ever seen of any woman he did not call by first name. And if memory did not fail him—and it seldom did—he'd go so far as to say it was more than he'd seen of any woman who he did not, by the end of the evening, compensate for services rendered.

She could not have imagined what she was doing. She would be mortified beyond belief to know it. Gabriel wrestled with his conscience, torn between saving Victoria from further embarrassment and savoring the splendid view.

There was little doubt which would win.

Still on his hands and knees, Gabriel let his gaze wander over the tantalizing glimpse of flesh and shadow that showed just below the neckline of Victoria's dress. She was surprisingly bronzed, a color like the mix of good, strong coffee and quantities of the palest cream. Her skin was dappled with freckles, flecks of brown bits like sugar that sweetened her shoulders and dusted her breasts.

There was a tantalizing shadow between her breasts and like it or not, Gabriel could not keep himself from wondering if it was as soft and warm there as it appeared to be. If his tongue tasted that secret place, would she toss back her head and moan with ecstacy as she had when they kissed? The question popped into his head before he could stop it. It was just as well he did not have long to consider the answer.

Victoria reached for another card, one that was farther from her, and all thought scattered from Gabriel's mind like the playing cards strewn about them. The movement pressed one breast tight against Victoria's gown and moved the other just far enough from the fabric that Gabriel could see all the way to where her skin darkened.

"God's eyes!" Gabriel swore beneath his breath. He was not sure if it was a curse of frustration or annoyance. Perhaps it was simply an expression of complete and utter admiration. Whatever it was, there was only one thing to do about it.

He needed a drink.

Gabriel admonished himself the moment the thought made its way into his head.

After promising himself two weeks ago that he would use this summer to turn his life around, he had indulged in little more than a glass or two of brandy each night after dinner. Now here it was, the middle of the afternoon, and he suddenly found himself as dry as a desert. His tongue felt too big for his mouth. His mouth felt parched and arid, scorched by a heat too fiery to bear.

Blessedly oblivious to all that was going on inside Gabriel's head, Victoria picked up the last of the cards and rose to her feet. Gabriel could not help himself, his gaze followed her every movement and his body just naturally trailed along. He sat up beneath the table.

For his efforts, he was rewarded with a sharp knock on the back of the head.

Gabriel did not even try and restrain himself. He swore mightily and hauled himself out from under the table. If nothing else, the pain in his head made him forget the ache that had begun in another, even more sensitive part of his body. His momentary lapse of good taste and common sense thus painfully terminated, he sat back, rubbing one hand to the knot that had already formed on the back of his head. His foul mood returned in full force.

"Where have you been all day?"

He might as well have asked the question of the walls around them. Ignoring Gabriel's query as well as his injury, Victoria tapped the handful of cards she was holding into a neat pile and set them in the center of the table. She did not answer him.

Gabriel pulled himself to his feet. "I asked where you've been."

"Yes. I heard you." Torie looked across the room at Gabriel. After his brief foray beneath the table, his clothes were disordered and his hair was mussed. It was difficult to deal seriously with a man in such a sorry state, yet something about the way Gabriel's eyes flashed at her told her it was the only way he would be dealt with. It was a storm she'd felt brewing these past few days, though when and how it originated she could not say. All she knew was that she was no better prepared to deal with it now than she had been then.

A tactical retreat was in order.

Grabbing the bundle from where she'd left it, Torie stepped to the door. "Where I've been and what I've been doing is hardly any of your concern," she said. She tried to make her voice sufficiently cold so that Gabriel would, perhaps, become angry enough to forget the question she was so obviously avoiding.

She did not have to try hard. Suddenly, the possibility of him knowing the truth seemed all too real. The thought made Torie's words stick in her throat just enough that when they finally made their way out, they sounded clipped and terse. "You are here in my employ and as such, may I remind you that—"

"If I'm here in your employ, then employ me." Gabriel dashed across the room and shot out one hand to seize her arm and hold her in place. He fixed her with a look that made it impossible to turn away. "I've been penned up here for the better part of two weeks," he said. "While you are off all day, Lord knows where, I am left here waiting for some instruction. Instead, you come home with a tidy sum of weak excuses and the feeble promise that, tomorrow, we will begin our work. If I'm to be of any use to you this summer, I need direction. Each evening, you avoid conversation and dodge my questions. Each morning, you are nowhere to be found. You want me to excavate, but you haven't told me where. You want me to continue Roger's work but you never bothered to tell me his papers were stored away in the bottom desk drawer."

"You found Roger's papers?" Torie's show of icy indifference melted in the heat of the anger that burst in her like water through a tumbledown dam. Afraid that if she didn't move away, Gabriel would surely feel the tremor of fury that rippled through her, she jerked her arm from his grasp.

She tossed her bundle down on the floor and faced him, her hands on her hips. "You have no right to pry," she said, her voice rising louder than she would have liked. "There are private things . . . private papers . . . you had no right to go looking through—"

His frustration complete, Gabriel tossed his hands in the air. "What the hell else do you expect me to do? Sit on my behind with my feet up, sipping brandy and dreaming about all the pleasures of town that I've given up for this wonderfully monastic existence?" He glared at her, waiting for her answer.

Something told Torie he would not be satisfied until he got it.

She turned from him and crossed to the fireplace. Thanks to Mrs. Denny from Newberry Farm who came in to do for them each day, the mantelpiece was spotless. Regardless, Torie brushed her index finger along the length of it, stalling for time.

Had it been anyone else waiting for her answer, Torie knew she would have had no worry. She could have lied to another man. But if she had learned nothing else about Gabriel Raddigan in the last two weeks, she had learned he was a man who would accept nothing less than the absolute truth.

And that was something she could not give him.

A feeling very much like panic rose in Torie, strangling her breathing and making her heart beat so loud and fast she was sure Gabriel could hear it. She controlled it with a deep breath, and squaring her shoulders she turned to face him. She wasn't sure what she was going to say, not yet, she only knew she had to say something.

She was saved by the sight of a letter propped against the vase of flowers. Torie took a step forward, pointing to it. "What's that?"

Gabriel's expression soured, but Torie wasn't sure if it was because of something about the letter itself or because by finding it, she had also found a way to change the subject.

"It's a dinner invitation," he said, crossing his arms over his chest and leaning back against the table. "From Spencer Westin. Six o'clock tonight."

"A dinner invitation?" Whatever misapprehension Torie felt only moments before dissolved in a healthy measure of outrage. She grabbed the letter and held it up so that Gabriel could not fail to see her name written on the front of it in Spencer's distinctive, spiky hand. "It's addressed to me," she said. "And you opened it. What if it was something personal?"

Gabriel shrugged, the movement so casual and yet so insolent it made Torie want to scream. "Another proposal?" His mouth tipped with a cynical smile that ate through Torie's argument like vitriol. "What else is there to do in a place as dull as this?"

"So you read other people's correspondence?"

Again, a shrug and, again, it took all Torie's strength to hold her temper in check.

Gabriel knew it. She could tell from the gleam in his eyes. Stretching, he strolled over to stand in front of her.

"Dinner will be served at six and from what I understand, it is a walk of some distance." He slid his gaze from her face to her dress.

Not for the first time, Torie wished she could read the expression in Gabriel's dark eyes. She supposed his look was meant to remind her, in no uncertain terms, that she was not dressed appropriately for dinner and that she had better change right now if they were to get to Spencer's on time.

But that was not how the look seemed to her.

It seemed to Torie that Gabriel's expression softened even as his gaze slipped from her eyes, to her shoulders, to her waist. It seemed to her that there was just the smallest catch in his breathing, just the slightest slackening in the firm line of his jaw. It seemed to her that his thoughts were very clearly no longer on where she had been all day or on what she had been doing, just as it seemed that he was not as interested in what she would be wearing tonight as he was in what she had on right now, and how it fit over every curve of her body.

It seemed to Torie a very precarious thing to even begin thinking about.

She dashed the thoughts from her head and moved away from Gabriel as quickly as she could.

"Your own attire is hardly acceptable for dinner," she said, giving him the kind of critical look he had given her.

She was not at all sure what he had seen when he looked at her a moment ago. She didn't even care to think about it. But what she saw when she looked at him shook loose the last bits of Torie's self-possession.

Sometime in the last two weeks when she hadn't been paying attention, Gabriel's slight paunch had disappeared. He was leaner now, and the play of his linen shirt against the muscles that rippled beneath it was enough to make Torie's pulse quicken.

Sometime in the last two weeks while she had been

busy and left Gabriel to his own devices, a trace of color had made its way into his face. His cheeks were burnished by the wind of the downs. His eyes flashed at her from a face newly creased with a network of fine lines caused by the warm, spring sun.

Sometime while she hadn't been looking, the jaded, dissolute, and desperate man she had been so careful to select had transformed himself into something else altogether, a man whose every motion spoke his impatience, one who was eager, and even excited, to begin the work she had hired him to perform.

It was unsettling at best, and not something Torie cared to think about. Not here, with Gabriel watching her every move. She pushed the misgivings from her mind and looked pointedly toward the door, indicating to Gabriel that, whether he liked it or not, their discussion was at an end. "You'd better put a cold cloth on your head," she told him. "And do get into some appropriate evening clothes. Even though we are here in the country, Spencer insists on a formal dinner."

She thought, perhaps, that Gabriel wanted to reply.

He didn't. With a nod that was not quite polite, but not quite rude either, Gabriel left the room.

Torie was not one to curse. She never had been, and now that Gabriel was in the house, she supposed she would never have to even consider the habit. He cursed enough for the both of them, and the entire population of Cuckfield, and most of Sussex as well.

Yet right now, she could not help herself.

"Damn!" Torie was not game enough to let the oath explode from her. She mumbled it below her breath and kicked the leg of the nearest chair to emphasize her point.

She thought she had everything under control.

Marching across the library, Torie retrieved the last of the cards lodged between the books. She slapped them down atop the rest of the deck, her gaze automatically going to the door, her thoughts full of self-reproach.

She thought she'd done her prep work well and chosen wisely. Now she found to her dismay that Gabriel Raddigan was not the man she wanted him to be.

She feared he was the kind of man who asked too many questions and when he was put off, did not wait long to find the answers for himself.

She feared he was the kind of man who was not as content as she hoped he would be to sit idly and drunkenly by while she went about her business.

She feared—she very much feared—that she had made a very big mistake.

Spencer Westin emerged from his cottage like a moth from a cocoon that was far too small to accommodate its wingspan. His shoulders hunched, he stooped to get through the low doorway. Outside, he shook himself to his full height, straightened his long, lean frame and held out his hands to Torie.

"Victoria! So good of you to come," he said, his smile wide and earnest. "You look splendid!" He let his gaze drift over her, obviously pleased with the gown she had chosen. It was Bishop's blue, trimmed with black in honor of Roger, with close-cut sleeves and a high neck. Because the dress was new, the style more fashionable than the dresses Torie wore around the house, the bodice was not cut high and snug around her breasts. The waist was dropped low, nearly to where a woman's waist was meant to be. The dress was comfortable enough to accommodate Torie on the thirty-minute walk to Spencer's cottage and, she suspected from the look on Spencer's face, formal enough to satisfy his need for convention.

"You must be thirsty after your long walk," Spencer

said, winding Torie's arm through his. "Come inside
and—"

Spencer's enthusiastic expression wilted like a rose on
a hot summer day. Torie looked over her shoulder to
where his gaze was fixed.

Gabriel Raddigan came puffing up the last small hill-
ock that hid the path from Spencer's view. His cheeks
flushed, his forehead rimmed with perspiration, he glared
at Torie. She would have liked to think the pained expression on his face was caused by the fact that he was staring
directly into the sun, but she knew better than that.

In one look, he told her he did not appreciate the brisk
pace she had set across the downs, a pace that had left him
far behind, scrambling to catch her up.

Torie paid his expression no mind, just as she'd paid
him no mind when she knew he'd fallen far behind her on
their trek to Spencer's. After all his questions this afternoon, the last thing she wanted from Gabriel was more
conversation. Fortunately, his casual pace had provided
her the perfect excuse to release her from the obligation.
Not far from home, Gabriel made the mistake of stopping
to admire the view from High Brill, the tallest of the area's
hills. Torie saw her opportunity and took it. She forged
ahead, and left Gabriel to follow in her wake.

"I didn't know . . ." Spencer looked from Gabriel, to
Torie, and back again to Gabriel, his expression as pitiful
as any Torie had ever seen. He looked like nothing if not
a child who had a particularly lovely sweet snatched
away, though Torie could not imagine why. To Spencer's
credit, he concealed his bewilderment behind a wide
smile, one that looked to be painted on by an artist who
had made it a little too stiff, a little too forced.

But no matter how spacious Spencer's smile, he could
not disguise the puzzlement in his voice, just as he could
not hide the sharp, quick look of resentment that darkened his eyes when Gabriel came near.

"Good evening, Mr. Raddigan," Spencer said, inclining his head to acknowledge Gabriel's presence. "How kind of you to walk Miss Broadridge all the way here." The required pleasantries neatly disposed of, Spencer turned to lead Torie into the house.

In spite of the fact that Torie would have liked nothing better than to leave Gabriel there until he rooted to the earth, she could not believe Spencer's ill manners. It was so unlike him, it stopped her on the spot. It did not, however, hamper her ability to speak her mind. "Surely you are not going to leave Mr. Raddigan standing out here while we are inside?" she asked, gazing up at Spencer, baffled. "With only so much as a feeble thank you?"

"No. Surely. No. You're right, of course, it was rude of me." Spencer's face reddened. Clearing his throat, he looked back at Gabriel. "You needn't worry," he said. "I will not let Miss Broadridge attempt the walk home alone after dark. I will accompany her myself and—"

"Spencer!" Torie extricated herself from his hold and turned to him in wonder. "Mr. Raddigan is as much your dinner guest as I am and certainly—"

"Dinner guest?" To his credit, Spencer recovered in less than a heartbeat. He gave a hearty, if not quite convincing, laugh. "Dinner guest. Of course! Of course!" Spencer rubbed his hands together. "I will just go inside and make sure Cook has everything under control," he said. Before either of them could move further, he ducked into the cottage. "If you'll wait one minute please—"

Spencer's voice trailed off as he disappeared into the house.

Torie shook her head in wonder. "What was that all about, do you suppose?"

Gabriel pursed his lips. He was trying very hard to keep from laughing, but it wasn't working. The muscles around his mouth twitched. His shoulders shook. "I suppose," he said, "it's all about me not being invited to dinner."

"What?" Torie rounded on him. "What do you mean? You read the invitation. You told me—"

"I told you there was an invitation to dinner. From Spencer Westin." Gabriel grinned down at her, his smile widening as her chagrin grew. "I never said I'd been included. You're the one who told me to get dressed for dinner."

Torie felt the color drain from her face. "Oh, dear." She pressed one hand to her lips as if the feeble gesture could contain her mortification. "Then you're not supposed to—"

"Of course I am!" Before she could utter another word of protest, Gabriel snatched Torie's arm and led her into the house. "Shall we go in to dinner?"

"Bah!" Westin pushed away from the table. Though their dinner was simple, it had been delicious, the food both well prepared and abundant. Yet Westin did not look pleased.

His long, thin face was mottled with red splotches. His fingers plucked fitfully at his serviette. He was too much of a gentleman to shout, but Gabriel could tell beyond the shadow of a doubt, that was exactly what he was tempted to do.

At his right hand, Victoria sat still and stiff as if she had been carved from one of the chalk hills that made up the downs. Her chin was high, her shoulders were steady. Though she did not show her perturbation as easily as Westin did, Gabriel knew exactly what she was thinking. She was giving Westin that same, direct, unnerving look she had used on Gabriel the first day she'd come to see him in Oxford. The day she told him about the dragon. And that surely meant Westin was in for trouble.

Stretching out his long legs, Gabriel sat back in his chair. He wasn't sure why he was looking forward to seeing Westin and Victoria go at it tooth and nail, he only knew he was.

Perhaps it was because Victoria had led him such a merry chase over the downs this evening.

Gabriel rubbed a sore muscle in his thigh. He was not usually a vindictive man, just as he was not usually the kind who forced himself on others, whether he had been invited or not. But something in Victoria's behavior this afternoon, something in the way she evaded his questions and avoided his eyes, had pushed him over the edge.

She had only herself to blame, he told himself, the rationalization a balm for his conscience. If she had done a little more listening and a lot less talking, he might have told her the dinner invitation was intended only for her. But he didn't. And he was glad of it.

If he had, he would have missed this most interesting of disputes, and that would have been a shame.

Perhaps he was enjoying this squabble between Victoria and Westin so because in his heart, he felt they deserved each other. The idea appealed to Gabriel's imagination as well as to his sense of humor.

Not that Westin and Victoria were at all alike.

Where Victoria was tight-lipped, pontifical, argumentative, and brusque, Westin was polite, soft-spoken, courteous, and, when it came to Victoria, attentive to the point of smothering the poor girl. Where Victoria was too rigid in her opinions, too set in her habits, and far too stubborn for her own good, Westin went out of his way to please.

It was a match made in hell, where, Gabriel was convinced, all really interesting matches originated. Watching Westin and Victoria square off had all the fascination of watching a cock fight. And like most of the cock fights Gabriel had ever attended, it promised to be grisly, ugly, and thoroughly entertaining.

His knuckles white where they pressed against the damask table linen, Westin made the first move. He leaned forward and caught Victoria's gaze, the momentary wavering in his aplomb under control, his look as benign as hers was fierce.

"You missed my point, I think, Victoria," he said, in tones so indulgent, they put Gabriel in mind of the way a father might speak to a difficult child. "The Plutonists are wrong, surely. I know my beliefs are held to be somewhat old-fashioned now, but think of the evidence. It is bad enough the Plutonists believe that rock is actually formed by the cooling of hot lava from volcanoes. But this nonsense of uniformitarianism!" Westin tossed back his head and laughed, the sound of it like a braying donkey.

"It's ridiculous. Roger knew it. He never subscribed to that sort of nonsense. It's a wonder you do, and I would question your logic if you were not a woman. Being of a gentler disposition and a simpler mind, you obviously do not understand the theories behind—"

"Theories?" Victoria's control cracked. Even from where he sat on the other side of the table, Gabriel could feel the heat of the gaze she fixed on Westin. "Uniformitarianism is certainly more than a theory. How can you say otherwise? The belief that the earth is gradually changing, the realization that it continues to change, these are at the basis of Hutton's philosophy and thus the beliefs of all the Plutonists. They are sound ideas. And sensible. I—"

"Victoria, Victoria, Victoria." As if seeking patience from the vast heavens that lay beyond the roof of his small, neat cottage, Westin raised his gaze to the ceiling and shook his head. "The teachings of Werner are certainly far more convincing than those of Hutton," he said. He looked from Victoria to Gabriel, his words honed until they were as sharp as those of a dispirited university fellow tutoring a roomful of simpleminded charges. "The entire earth was once covered with ocean," he said, his hands at chest level making a waving pattern.

"The chemicals in the water slowly settled," he continued, bringing his hands down to rest them on the table, "and formed layers. Those are the rocks we have today. And that is the basis of Werner's theory. It is convincing. I know. I heard Werner himself lecture in Germany, you know, at the Freiberg School of Mines."

Westin dropped this bit of information as if it were very special, a windfall apple from the tree of knowledge that stood square in the center of Eden. He sat up a bit straighter, his cheeks pink with excitement.

"That is what the Neptunists who follow Werner's teachings believe. And how you can even think to dispute it, Victoria, is far beyond me. It is a proven fact. All rock is formed from that first, global ocean. No further changes in the earth have occurred since. No further changes will ever occur. The earth was formed six thousand years ago and only rare catastrophes can change its features. That is the common thinking among the scientific community and it is logical, rational, and accurate." He turned to Gabriel, effectively dismissing Victoria and all her arguments. "Am I not right, Mr. Raddigan?"

Gabriel thought the problem through. On the one hand, though he did not believe in the Neptunists' preposterous theories for even a moment, it did occur to him to agree with Westin. His concurrence was sure to annoy Victoria beyond belief and that in itself might make the long walk over here worthwhile.

But then again . . .

A flash of memory cut its way through Gabriel's thoughts like a hot knife through butter.

Rigorous days of schooling, still more arduous nights of study.

He would not have backed down from a controversy in those heady days at University, by the Lord Harry, not even for the sake of deviling a woman.

Before Gabriel had the chance to speak, Westin

reached out one hand and patted Victoria's arm. "Women have no business dabbling in science. And those who think they do should attempt to read the literature. I guarantee you, my dear Victoria, even the most simply written is beyond your understanding. Far beyond what any woman could possibly comprehend."

It wasn't Westin's words so much that made up Gabriel's mind as it was the look he was giving Victoria. He was smiling at her, the kindest, most patronizing smile Gabriel had ever seen.

Gabriel smiled, too, and turned the full of his attention on Westin. "It seems to me I have seen a copy of Playfair's *Illustrations of Huttonian Theory* on the shelf in Miss Broadridge's library," he said, carefully pronouncing each word to see what Westin would do.

Westin did not react, but Victoria did. He saw a slight stiffening in her spine, a tiny tightening in the muscle that ran along the base of her jaw. She was ready to match wits with both of them if need be. Her expression told him as much. She was ready for a fight.

"I believe I have also seen a copy of Hutton's *Theory of the Earth* there, too, if I am not mistaken," Gabriel continued. "I certainly do not pretend to know Miss Broadridge as intimately as you do, Westin, but I would surmise from the evidence that she has read the literature."

Gabriel's unexpected support was enough to stun Victoria into silence. Her head tilted, her eyes bright with the light of the candles that winked on the table between them, she looked at him in wonder.

Devil take it, that a woman as troublesome as Victoria should have so clear and direct a gaze, and eyes so green as to remind him of a summer's day.

The thought broke over Gabriel like a cold wave. It did not leave him refreshed, as he knew a splash of seawater would. He was uncomfortable with it, as uncomfortable as he was with the sudden prickle of awareness that streamed through him like the molten lava Hutton and Werner were so intent on arguing about.

Gabriel shifted in his seat, hoping to banish the feeling. It didn't help when Victoria flashed a smile of thanks at him, an expression so bright and unexpected, Gabriel could not help but smile back. "I wouldn't doubt, too, that Miss Broadridge has studied the work of Desmarest," Gabriel added for good measure, unaccountably buoyed by Victoria's approval. He pulled his gaze from her long enough to glance at Westin. "You surely know about Desmarest, don't you, Westin? He's that chap who proved that the rocks of the Auvergne region of south-central France are, indeed, volcanic. If memory serves me correctly, two of Werner's most famous students went over to the Plutonists after that. Von Buch and von Humboldt. Perhaps you forgot. Or perhaps Werner failed to mention it when you heard him lecture in Germany."

Where Westin had thought to find solid support, he now saw the ground yawning before him, an endless, dark chasm filled with pitfalls and treacherous allies. Caught between Victoria's uncompromising arguments and Gabriel's startling support of them, he did the only thing he could do. He ended the discussion.

"We'll have brandy now," he said, leaping to his feet and pulling back Victoria's chair in a gesture that, while gracious, made it clear the debate was over. "You do not mind waiting in the parlor, do you, my dear?"

"Surely that's not necessary!" Even Gabriel was surprised at his impulsive protest. He wasn't sure why he objected so strongly to Victoria's dismissal, he only knew he did. He schooled the emotion in his voice before he dared to speak again. "There are only just the three of us, Westin, you don't expect Miss Broadridge to—"

"I shall be quite all right." With a rustle of her blue gown, Victoria stood and moved to the door. "You gentlemen," she gave the word a curious lift, "can drink your brandy in peace without the cumbersome presence of a woman to hold you back from the discussion of important things. In any event, they are matters that, as a mere woman, I surely would not understand."

Westin could not possibly have seen Victoria's face, not from where he was standing. But Gabriel did not fail to notice that she was smiling a smile that spoke her feelings far more clearly than her words. Expertly, she erased the look before she turned to Westin again.

"It is a pleasant night. And warm," she added. "I will wait in the garden." She cast a glance toward Gabriel. "Spencer has a wonderful garden. Brimming with flowers and herbs."

Westin's brows dropped low over his eyes and a shadow like that of worry darkened his features. He caught at Victoria's sleeve. "It will be dark soon, do you think it's wise?"

"Spencer!" Victoria left the room shaking her head, but whether it was with wonder or disgust at what he'd said, Gabriel could not tell.

Westin watched her go and clicked the door closed behind her. He went over to the mahogany sideboard and splashed brandy in each of two glasses. He crossed the room and handed one glass to Gabriel, his gaze darting again and again to the door. "I don't like it, I can tell you that much." Westin sipped his brandy precisely, the way a woman drinks her liquor.

Gabriel tossed down his drink and held out his glass for a refill. If Westin was at all surprised by his boldness, he didn't show it, or perhaps he was simply too preoccupied to care. Westin's face was shadowed with anxiety. His mind seemed not a million miles away, but gone only so far as the garden that lay around at the back of the house.

Without a word, Westin set his glass on the table. He went to the sideboard and brought the brandy decanter over, setting it down and letting Gabriel pour for himself.

His first drink gone, the second just about finished, Gabriel felt better able to deal with whatever strange issue occupied Westin so.

"What is it you don't like?" Gabriel asked, catching Westin's eye. He held his glass up, tipping it toward the door. "Miss Broadridge? Something about Miss Broadridge?"

"Something about her wandering around outdoors after nightfall," Westin answered, almost to himself. Finally, as if he'd just woken from a sleep filled with frightening nightmares, he shook his shoulders and looked at Gabriel.

"I'm sorry." Westin dropped into his chair and reaching for the decanter, he refilled his own glass though not half of the brandy in it was gone. "You don't know, do you? You don't know about Roger."

Gabriel shrugged. "I know he's dead."

"Dead, yes. But do you know how?"

It was something Gabriel had never taken the time to consider. Roger Broadridge was dead. That was all that seemed to matter. The manner of the man's death? That looked to be as relevant as Werner's foolish theory of a global ocean.

What mattered so little to Gabriel obviously meant a great deal to Westin. He lowered his voice to a reverential hush and fixed his eyes on some far off thing Gabriel could not see. "Roger was my friend," he said. "My very good friend." He swallowed hard, as if trying to keep the rest of the explanation from coming out, and Gabriel could not help but imagine some invisible hand around Westin's throat, extracting the rest of the story from him against his will.

"It is not something I like to discuss, Mr. Raddigan," he said, as if to give substance to Gabriel's fancy. "But I feel I owe it to you. I think you should know. After all, you are living there, you have some right to know what you are up against."

"Up against?" It seemed a peculiar choice of words. His curiosity piqued, Gabriel leaned forward, waiting for more.

Westin threw back his head and swallowed the rest of his brandy in one gulp. Gabriel felt sure, had he been alone, he would have coughed and choked on the potent liquid. To the man's credit, he held his reaction in check, though he could not contain the flush that rose like fire in his cheeks or the film of tears that shone in his eyes.

"Roger died in a fit of madness," Westin said. "It was a horrible, agonizing death. His reason was gone. His mind was no more rational than an animal's. Madness, Mr. Raddigan. Ugly, terrible, terrifying madness."

Westin sat in silence, waiting for Gabriel's reaction.

There was little Gabriel could say. He supposed, somewhere deep in his heart, that he should feel pity for Roger, pity and perhaps sympathy. He supposed his reaction should be one of dismay, or shock, or even disgust. Instead, he felt nothing. Absolutely nothing.

It was a shame. But there it was, the truth, unadorned and uncomplicated, as ugly as Roger's demented last days.

Thoughts as uncomfortable as those deserved to be drowned, and Gabriel obliged them. He poured another drink and sat back to enjoy it.

It was not, apparently, the response Westin anticipated. He snapped his gaze to Gabriel's, his eyes bright with unshed tears, his voice breaking with emotion. "Don't you understand what I'm trying to tell you? They are twins, after all, Roger and Victoria. And they say madness runs in families."

Chapter 8

Gabriel pushed his glass away, his appetite for warmth and spirits suddenly gone. "Are you saying—?"

"That Victoria is mad?" Westin shook his head and passed one trembling hand over his eyes. "No. Thank God, no. Not now. Not yet." He glanced over his shoulder at the door. "I pray it will never come to that. But for her to be out alone at night . . ."

There seemed no logic to Westin's ramblings. At least none Gabriel could find. Suddenly uncomfortable, both with what Westin was telling him and with the feeling that filled his insides in reaction to it, he scraped his chair back from the table and rose to his feet. He paced to the sideboard, hoping the action would help dispel his uneasiness. Gabriel balled one hand into a fist and slapped it against the open palm of his other hand.

"Damn it, man, what does being out at night have to do with it?" Gabriel asked, though he wasn't sure he wanted to hear the answer.

Westin did not move. He didn't look at Gabriel. His hands clutched on the table in front of him, his shoulders hunched, he began his explanation the way a storyteller might begin his tale, his voice low and mysterious, and though Gabriel would never admit it, not even to himself, Westin's words sent a shiver up his spine.

"They say the downs are haunted, Mr. Raddigan," Westin said, sounding old and suddenly very tired. "That's what the locals say. They say the hills are filled with the spirits of the ancients who made the chalk caves their homes and forged their iron instruments from the ore they found in the area. They say . . ." Westin drew in a long breath and let it out again, guttering the candles set before him on the table.

"They say that those who are unlucky see the spirits at times out on the downs at night. Flickering lights that can bewitch a man and send him to his death. Lights that can lead him over the cliffs to the sea or into the impassable woods. Lights that can make him plummet down the slow, inescapable path to madness. That is the same as death, I suppose, only worse. I have heard the stories countless times. I never paid them much mind. But Roger did. Roger listened."

Westin rose from his chair and went to the window. He pulled aside the draperies. From where Gabriel stood, there was little to see: His own reflection looking small and out of proportion because he was so far from the glass. Westin's image, larger, closer, and more in focus, his features impossible to see in the blend of shadow and darkness, the place where his eyes should be, black like the empty sockets of a skull. The vast sweep of the downs, dark and unending.

"I've lived and worked here these four years," Westin said, looking outside. "In all that time, I have never seen anything beyond these windows that gave me cause for alarm. Not in daylight. Not in darkness."

Gabriel could not help himself. As much as he would have liked to dismiss the whole thing as nonsense, the story held some macabre fascination. "But Roger?" he asked.

With a heavy sigh, Westin turned from the window. He leaned back against the oak frame, his hands in his pockets, and when he spoke, his voice was heavy with the memory. "It started a year ago. Roger didn't tell me, and he certainly didn't tell Victoria. Not at first. He didn't want us to worry. He hid it well enough, but then Roger always was the kind of man who could keep a secret."

Even though they were speaking of the dead and Gabriel knew he should in all rights show some respect, he could not help himself. His own memories of Roger Broadridge and the kinds of secrets he was, indeed, capable of keeping, intruded on Westin's story. He snorted with derision.

Westin did not seem to notice. He went on with his tale, weaving a tapestry word by word, a picture of the last terror-filled months of Roger's life. "I remember the day I finally confronted him. I'd noticed the change in him weeks before. He was nervy, tense. He paced to the windows when he was here after dark, looking out over the downs as if he expected Old Nick himself to be standing there waiting to claim his soul. He glanced over his shoulder constantly and started at the slightest noise. It took some doing, but I finally badgered him into telling me what was wrong. When he did, I was almost sorry I'd asked. You see, Mr. Raddigan, Roger had seen the lights."

Gabriel let out a short bark of laughter. "You don't believe that, do you?" he asked. "That nonsense about lights and ghosts? You're a man of science, Westin, at least you make a fine show of it. You don't think—"

"What I think hardly matters." Westin shrugged. "What I know is that Roger believed what he saw. He said the lights were small at first. Innocent. Almost pretty, sparkling there upon the horizon. But each time he saw them, they grew in his sight and in his mind. Toward the end, he saw them every night, stalking behind him across the downs like hunting animals, closing in on him until that last night, when they were there with him in his home, swallowing him up like a big cat swallows its prey."

"You were there?"

Westin waved away Gabriel's question. "No, not I. Victoria was, of course. She told me about it later. About the terror etched on Roger's face and the horror in his eyes. There were violent convulsions, apparently, and some paralysis." Westin sighed. "He died there in the hallway, outside the library doors. Died in Victoria's arms."

It was not a pretty picture, and imagining it made the implications of Westin's words all the more real. Gabriel pulled himself up. He felt cold, suddenly, though he could not say why. The night was mild, the windows remained shut. "And you think . . . You think Miss Broadridge is next?"

"I pray not. I may be too overprotective, but I hate to tempt fate. I'm not comfortable with her being out alone at night." Westin laughed self-consciously. "Before you think me as mad as Roger, let me assure you, I do not believe there are spirits prowling the downs. But a woman's mind is easily influenced, her imagination is prone to play tricks on her. And as I said, madness does run in families."

The cold that Gabriel felt in his shoulders settled in his stomach. How many times since the day he'd met Victoria had he called her a madwoman? How many times had he told her her schemes were crazy? Her theories insane? It seemed a travesty now, and he felt like an invader who had trespassed over the boundaries of what was right and decent.

At the same time these disturbing thoughts rattled through Gabriel's mind, another picture formed there. One that showed Victoria with her chin held rigid and her shoulders squared. Victoria spouting off facts about Hutton and Werner and Cretaceous strata like they were no more troublesome than the names and ages of beloved nieces and nephews. Victoria who, even though she probably did not understand Roger's findings fully, was bright enough to recognize them as both forward-looking and important, and brave enough to try to make the world take notice.

Victoria was a lot of things. She was a stubborn, willful nuisance who didn't know when to keep to her own business. She was a headstrong hellcat who had taken that most unsettling of female proclivities—the ability for finding a man's weakness and using it to her full advantage—and developed it into one of the higher art forms. She was forceful and tenacious, confident and bold. The Rock of Gibraltar swathed in black muslin.

The notion appealed to what was left of Gabriel's sense of humor and he smiled in spite of himself, leaving it to Westin to wonder if the Broadridges were the only mad people in the neighborhood.

A second later, Gabriel's smile faded. Victoria was Gibraltar in muslin, right enough, but with a hint beneath of something more, the something she had shown him in the smile she beamed his way just minutes ago. It was the same something that sparkled in her eyes when she spoke of her preposterous dragon, the something, the very disturbing something, he had caught sight of when her gown slipped back to reveal skin as luscious as cream and breasts made for the tasting.

Yes, Victoria was a lot of things. But she was not mad. Not the kind of madness Westin spoke about, the kind that drove Roger to his death. In the few weeks he'd known her, even Gabriel had come to know that much about her. He was surprised Westin didn't.

As quickly as it had formed, the ice in Gabriel's stomach melted. He ignored the fact that some of the heat undoubtedly came from the memory of Victoria in the library, carefully picking up cards one by one, each careless movement exposing more of her body to him than she would have imagined. No, this was more the flame of righteous indignation, the kind that was bound to assail a man when he heard a woman—any woman—tried and condemned before she ever had a chance to commit a crime.

Gabriel pulled himself up and balled his hands into fists. He stopped himself before he took a step and eyed Westin with sudden interest.

In the few times they'd met, Spencer Westin never seemed more than a mere shadow, not a whole man at all. He fawned over Victoria. He was only as polite as he need be to Gabriel. He took every opportunity, as graciously as he could, to remind them that he was far superior to both of them in every way that counted and probably in a number of ones that didn't as well.

Gabriel had played cards with such men. He had seen them win huge sums of money; affecting civility, feigning indifference, and going in for the kill so swiftly and unexpectedly, that they left their opponents' heads spinning.

Muscle by muscle, Gabriel willed himself to relax, to control the curiosity that burst through him so fiercely he could taste it at the back of his throat. He unclenched his fists and flexed his fingers. He rolled his head. He went back to the table and finished off his glass of brandy, not because he wanted it, but because it gave him something to do, and made him look thoroughly indifferent.

"Yet you want to marry her." He did not say the words as a question, but merely spoke them as true. He poured another glass of brandy and twirled it in his hands. "You do not think Victoria is mad now, but you think she may be some day. And yet you want to marry her."

"You know about that, do you?" Westin's cheeks darkened. He did not meet Gabriel's eyes, but danced a kind of nervous hornpipe over at the window, his feet shuffling back and forth against the wine-colored carpet. "I confess, it's true and it may seem foolish to a man as worldly

as you, Mr. Raddigan. But to me, it is the obligation of a
friend. If Victoria is . . . if she might ever be . . ." He could
not bring himself to say it. He pulled his hands from his
pockets and made a small gesture of surrender.

"I would take care of her if she would let me," Westin
said. "Perhaps take her from this place. From the memories. Perhaps that is the only way to turn her from her sad
destiny."

"Perhaps." For all his posturing, Gabriel could not
drink the brandy. He was sure it would never make its
way past the lump of anger that was quickly replacing the
taste of curiosity in his throat. "You talk as if the girl's
already insane." The words racketed in Gabriel's ears,
harsh reminders of their significance. "You are playing
judge, jury, and executioner. You've passed sentence
before—"

"I know it seems heartless." Westin shook his head
sadly. "I do not mean to seem so cold. It's just that
. . . I saw what happened to Roger. I know what to look
for. If . . .when it happens, I would implore Victoria to
seek help as soon as possible. It may be the only thing that
can save her. Money is no object, not when it comes to
Victoria, and there are specialists in London and Paris
. . . If she begins . . . if she acts odd in any way, you will
tell me, won't you, Mr. Raddigan?" He looked directly at
Gabriel. "You swear you will let me know?"

Gabriel let Westin's question hang in the air, long
enough to make the other man uncomfortable. He wasn't
sure why he derived such pleasure from seeing Westin
discomfited, he only knew he did. It was perverse, Gabriel
supposed, perverse and perhaps a little vicious, but then,
he was only living up to the opinion Westin already had
of him.

Gabriel rocked back on his heels. He kept his eyes on
Westin, hoping to gauge his reaction when he answered

Westin's question with one of his own. "Did you know she saved my life?"

"She?" Westin blinked, quick, convulsive movements like an owl blinded by sudden light. "She? You mean Victoria?" He laughed. "Really! That does not sound at all like the Victoria I know. I cannot imagine it, and while I do not question your integrity, Mr. Raddigan, I wonder at the episode. Amazing! Most amazing."

"Yet it is true." Gabriel allowed a slow smile to brighten his expression. "Does that sound like the act of a madwoman to you?"

"Well, I don't know. I can't say." With his feet apart and his face furrowed into a thousand, thoughtful lines, Westin looked for all the world as if Gabriel had just challenged him to some great debate. He tipped his head to one side, thinking. "I would need more information before I could offer an opinion. What is it, exactly, that Victoria did for you, Mr. Raddigan? Did she call for help when you fell into a river? Find a constable when you were threatened by some ruffian?"

It was Gabriel's turn to laugh. He threw back his head and the sound of his laughter echoed through Westin's cottage. "Better than all that," he said, still smiling. "She kissed me."

Westin's mouth dropped open. His eyes bulged from his head. "K . . . k . . . kissed you? That's outrageous! It's preposterous! It's . . . it's . . ."

"It's the absolute truth." Gabriel was enjoying himself more than he dared admit. He tipped his head back, savoring the delicious realization of what his disclosure was doing to Westin. At least he hoped that was the only reason he felt so good. He dreaded the thought that some of the warmth that filled his insides might come simply from the memory of Victoria's lips on his. Not willing to bring the thought out into the light where he might examine it, he shuttered it behind an insolent smile. "Kissed me," he said. "And put her arms around me. Hoisted up her skirts and—"

Gabriel was cut off by the choking sound coming from Westin. His face was the color of the claret he had served with dinner. While Westin was still spluttering, the dining room door snapped open and Victoria peeked inside.

"Done with your brandy, are you?" They weren't; their two glasses still sat on the table and Gabriel's was full. Torie pretended not to notice. She'd had enough of sitting in the garden by herself. She swept into the room, quickly and effectively cutting off any opportunity they had to object to her presence. "Good, then we can be on our way. It is very late."

She looked from Gabriel to Spencer, waiting for either one of them to respond. For what seemed like a very long time, neither did. Curious, Torie studied the scene, and the longer she studied it, the more curious she became.

Spencer looked as if he'd just swallowed a chicken, complete with the feet, beak, and feathers. Swallowed the poor thing whole. His cheeks were crimson. His mouth hung open. His Adam's apple bobbed up and down as he fought for every breath. Torie could imagine that his heart was thumping like one of the steam engines she'd once seen demonstrated in London. He looked, Torie thought, as if someone had announced with unquestioned accuracy, that the Second Coming was scheduled for tomorrow afternoon at precisely two o'clock. In fact, Spencer was so perturbed, he was hardly aware of her presence, and that in itself told Torie something unusual had taken place.

She did not have to wonder long about where his distress had originated. One look at Gabriel told her all she needed to know. He was standing with his hands clasped loosely behind him, a smile so innocent on his face, she knew without a doubt that he had said something to precipitate Spencer's condition.

A portion of Torie was tempted to ask exactly what they'd been discussing; another, wiser self, cautioned against it.

"It's very late," Torie said again, looking from one of them to the other. "We should start for home."

"Then we're off!" Gabriel was the first to move. Still grinning, he offered Torie his arm.

Before she had a chance to take it, Spencer stepped between them. "Not so quickly, surely," he said. Whatever had troubled him when she came into the room, he hid it now behind one of his amiable, earnest smiles, the kind that had never made Torie uneasy until that day he'd proposed marriage. Now every time he smiled at her, she couldn't help but remember that this was the man who had offered her a lifetime of complete serenity, total harmony, and quite perfect monotony.

It was not a cheery thought, and Torie shook it away. She could not so easily rid herself of the hold Spencer had on her arm. Clutching her elbow a little more firmly than need be to either attract her attention or lead her to the door, he steered her a safe distance from Gabriel. "You will have a cup of tea before you go, won't you, my dear?" he asked.

Spencer's tea was far too strong and always too sweet. But as surely as Torie knew she would not enjoy it, she also knew she could not refuse. If she did, Spencer would be sorely disappointed.

As if she could already taste the cloying sweetness of the honey Spencer spooned into every cup of tea he served, Torie gritted her teeth, and smiled her acceptance.

His fists on his hips, Gabriel paused atop High Brill. It was well past ten o'clock and completely dark, but the sliver of a moon that hung snug against the horizon gave just enough light for Torie to see his face. He turned back in the direction of Spencer's cottage, his chin thrust out, his eyes narrowed.

"He calls you Victoria," Gabriel grunted.

It was the first thing he'd said since they left Spencer's a quarter of an hour ago and, startled, Torie pulled to a stop at Gabriel's side. She eyed him through the darkness, trying to gauge some measure of his mood. He had been devilishly self-satisfied when they left Spencer's, but with each step they took further from the warmth and light of the cottage, he grew more and more quiet.

What it all meant was impossible to say. Gabriel might be angry, though she didn't know about what. He might be worried, though she couldn't imagine why. Whatever it was, it certainly had nothing to do with the fact that Spencer called her by her Christian name.

She raised her eyebrows. "I beg your pardon?"

Again, Gabriel poked his chin in the direction of Spencer's cottage. "Him," he said, and even from that one word she could tell with absolute certainty what he thought of Spencer Westin. "He calls you Victoria."

Baffled, Torie shook her head. In spite of the fact that she could still taste the sweetness of Spencer's tea in her mouth, she felt her mood sour. "Spencer is a good friend," she said. "A man I have known for some time. I see no impropriety in him calling me Victoria. It is my name, after all."

"Yes." Gabriel pulled his gaze from the cottage and turned to her, his eyes shadowed by the night. "But your brother called you Torie."

She had not heard the name spoken aloud since Roger died, and never with such intensity. Torie recoiled from her emotional reaction to it and listened as the last notes of Gabriel's voice echoed through the rolling hills and sailed away into the star-studded sky.

It took her another moment to realize that Gabriel was watching her carefully, as eager to read her thoughts as she was to interpret his. It was not a comfortable feeling, being examined like a specimen in a laboratory, just as it was not comfortable realizing how instinctively she reacted to the warmth in Gabriel's voice. Hoping to dismiss the subject, Torie smiled nervously.

"And how would you know that, Mr. Raddigan? I doubt Roger spoke of me often when you were up at University together. I take it scholars are far too busy discussing matters of import to spend their time in idle chatter of home and family."

She might have known Gabriel could not so easily be steered in another direction, one that was far less personal. He replied as neatly as if they'd been discussing the weather rather than the fact that, as she knew full well, he'd been rummaging through Roger's personal papers all afternoon. "His letters, of course," Gabriel said. "And his journal. Torie. He always called you Torie."

Again he said her name, and again, it wound through Torie, a curl of warmth. "It's nothing but a pet name," she said, fighting to suppress the ungovernable smile that threatened to betray her. "Nothing but a silly pet name."

But even as Torie spoke the words, she knew they were lies. Coming from Gabriel's lips, the name did not sound silly at all. It sounded more of an endearment.

Even though it was dark, Torie turned away, just to be certain Gabriel could not see how her cheeks reddened. She clutched her hands at her waist and stared down at them, all too aware that Gabriel was still watching her.

Gabriel let his gaze drift over Torie, all the way from the top of her head to her waist. If he'd tossed down a few more brandies, he probably would have dared to look even farther, down to where her gown hugged her curves as smoothly as the moonlight caressed the surrounding hills. But he was not foxed, not by any means. And though he could not keep his body from responding impetuously and enthusiastically to even the suggestion of such thoughts, his brain was sober enough to caution him against letting his mind ramble where it had no business.

Right now, it had no business thinking about Torie Broadridge. Not in the way he was tempted to think about her.

It was Westin's fault, damn him. Westin, with his gloomy talk of lights and spirits. Westin with his dire warnings about Torie's supposed frailty and her imagined affliction.

If it weren't for that high-arsed popinjay, Gabriel never would have noticed that Torie was exactly the opposite of what Westin painted her to be. Not frail, but forceful. Not insane, but stubborn, and opinionated, and a damned sight more intelligent than any woman was supposed to be.

If Westin hadn't been an absolute scoundrel, if he hadn't planted notions in Gabriel's brain of Torie as delicate and doomed, Gabriel never would have given her a second thought. He never would have had the feelings he was having right now.

Gabriel had no intention of letting his errant thoughts get in the way of his common sense, but there you have it. Good intentions were one thing, carrying them out another all together.

If there was one thing Gabriel had learned in his life, it was that.

It was sometimes impossible to separate the two, and this was one of those times. Like it or not, Gabriel found his gaze drifting over Torie again, this time past her waist, over her hips, down to that intriguing curve at the back of her gown. He did not even have to try hard to imagine how round and appealing her bottom must be, he need only remember how smooth and silky her skin was, how enticing her breasts.

Torie stood as still as stone. She could feel Gabriel's gaze at her back, as sure as if it were a physical thing. It touched her hair. It moved along her shoulders. It slid down her spine.

In spite of the mildness of the evening, Torie shivered. She wasn't sure why Gabriel was watching her with such interest, she knew only what the look was doing to her composure. She was as warm as if she were hard at work in the hot summer sun. As wobbly as a calf new born. As shaky as if she had joined the gentlemen for brandy after dinner and taken far too much to preserve either her reason or her equilibrium.

She could not have said how long they stood that way. Here on the downs, time seemed an insignificant thing, as immeasurable as the hills themselves. Torie supposed she might mark off the seconds by counting the beats of her heart, but that would be a poor touchstone indeed. Her heart was pounding so fast, counting its beats would serve no purpose.

It did not help her self-possession one whit when she felt Gabriel move nearer.

Torie fanned her face. "My father called me Torie when I was very young," she said, endeavoring to hide her agitation in trivial conversation. To her mortification, she was convinced that the tumult she felt inside was very much evident in every syllable she spoke. "As we grew older, Roger just naturally assumed the habit."

"Torie." Gabriel said the name precisely, as if trying it on for size. "It suits you." Torie imagined him nodding his acceptance. "And did you know, Torie, that Westin still wants to marry you?"

"Don't be absurd!" This time, Torie did not need to pretend a thing. Her laugh was genuine. Grateful that he had changed the subject even though she was quite sure he hadn't meant to, she turned back to Gabriel.

Her confidence melted the moment she saw him.

Though she knew Gabriel had come close, she had no idea he was this close. He was standing not one foot from her, his eyes reflecting the starlight that glimmered all around. His breathing was as erratic as hers. That in itself was enough to make Torie panic, and her panic froze her to the spot. As much as she would have liked to turn and march on toward home, she could not move. Not an inch. She stood paralyzed, watching Gabriel's chest rise and fall beneath his white linen shirt, imagining how his heart beat against it, quick and hard.

If she did not know better, she would have guessed he was as unsettled as she, though she could not for all the world guess why. Gabriel was not the type of man who was affected by the pull of moonglow and starlight. Not one who would let his imagination run rampant simply because he was out on the downs at night with a woman.

Not this woman, at any rate.

Torie brought herself around with the sobering thought.

Surely she was imagining things, and just as surely it all had something to do with the strange buzzing noise that had begun in her head and the sudden twist she felt in her stomach. It had everything to do with the rich and heavy meal Spencer served, she told herself, and nothing to do with the night, or the dark, or Gabriel.

Just to be certain, Torie took a step back, away from Gabriel's disturbing nearness. Convinced that saying something, anything, was better than allowing the possibility of Gabriel reading her thoughts, she pulled together the threads of their conversation as deftly as a fisherman drawing in his nets.

"I explained the reasons for my refusal to Spencer quite clearly the day he made his proposal," she said. "He was most understanding. We are friends now as we were then. That is enough for Spencer, just as it is more than enough for me."

"That's as much as you know about it." A chuckle rumbled through Gabriel. "I tell you, he's not convinced you meant it when you declined his touching proposition." Gabriel gave an exaggerated sigh and brought one hand to his heart. "It seems there is still a glimmer of hope flickering in the nearly spent passion of Mr. Westin's soul."

Torie could not possibly reply. She hadn't any idea what Gabriel was trying to draw her into. He may have been looking to embarrass her. He may have been trying to drag her into a rousing debate. More than likely, he was simply doing all he could to irritate her. It would be far easier to decipher his motives if she could interpret the peculiar look in his eyes. A look that made her feel as if he were searching for something inside her, a clue that would help him solve some mystery he was trying desperately to understand.

"Thank you for supporting my views on Hutton." It was a ridiculous, inappropriate thing to bring up now, but Torie could not for the life of her think of anything else to say. "Spencer can be quite rigid when it comes to scientific principles. And a bit old-fashioned."

Gabriel did not reply, and that in itself was enough to make Torie continue babbling like one of the streams that crossed the downs and led out to sea.

"There is only one form of scientific accuracy as far as Spencer is concerned, and that is the kind that agrees only with his opinions. It is helpful to have someone support your views when you are attempting a discussion with him."

Again she gave Gabriel an opportunity to join in and, again, he declined. He stood scrutinizing her as one might examine a painting in a museum.

"Spencer was never that inflexible when it came to discussing things with Roger, of course," Torie breezed on. "But then Roger did not have very strong ideas about—"

She caught herself before she could say more and

mumbled a word of disgust, surprised by her own care-
lessness. What had come over her, that she would let her
tongue wag like that of an old lady?

Nervously, Torie coughed into her hand. "That is,
Roger was in agreement with most of what Spencer believed and—"

"Roger." Gabriel took a step nearer, closing the space
between them. "We are back again to talking about
Roger."

When he was standing this close, Torie had to look up
to see Gabriel's face. His hair was blacker than the sky
behind him. His eyes were unreadable, but they held her
spellbound. He gave her a lopsided smile. "Do you always
talk of Roger and Westin when you are with other men?"

"I am not often with other men," Torie admitted, her
voice far too breathy for her liking. "Any other men. We
had visitors, of course, over the years. Men of science.
Men Roger knew at school. There is little chance for a
mere sister to talk to men such as those. Sisters are extra-
neous, after all, unless they are skilled at needlework,
yearning to give a man heirs, or smart enough—but only
just—to know when to keep quiet."

It seemed the harder she tried to save herself from the
situation, the deeper she got into trouble. Torie shook her
head. It was all the fault of this dizziness she felt in her
brain, she told herself. Otherwise she would not be making such a muddle of every word she said.

While she had been busy trying, and failing, to steer the
discussion clear of anything that was the least bit personal,
Gabriel was busy letting his gaze roam over her. The
realization did nothing to calm the whirling in Torie's
brain. He searched her face. He inspected her gown. He
let his gaze rest upon her breasts.

As smooth as the shadows, Gabriel moved closer still,
until Torie could feel the warmth of his body only inches

from hers. It was an odd sensation, unfamiliar and quite disturbing. It made her pulse throb and her head ache.

She passed a hand over her eyes.

If only she could concentrate. But she could not, not any more than she could move when Gabriel took her gloved hand in his.

He twined his fingers through hers. "I expected more of a commotion, Torie, I will admit that much to you. As a matter of fact, I will also admit I was rather looking forward to it. Me taking you in my arms. You battling like a Spartan, even though I knew you didn't mean it, not for an instant." He smiled down at her and with his free hand drew her close against him. "Or are you so swept away, your voice has gone as well as your reason?"

"My voice is fine. And my reason is quite intact." That was as much a falsehood as anything she had ever told him. Her voice sounded as muzzy as her brain felt, and Torie was convinced her reason was as far gone as it had ever been. Perhaps that was the reason she felt herself relax beneath the warmth of Gabriel's touch. Perhaps that was why she leaned against him and did not move, not even when his arm went around her waist.

The last time she had been this close to Gabriel, they were in a darkened walkway, with two ruffians and one outraged manservant not five feet from them. Even then she was alarmed by the feel of Gabriel's arms about her, by the way each of his deep, rough breaths pressed his chest against hers, by the sound of her heart drumming in her ears and the beat of his, only a hairsbreadth away.

Out here on the downs, in the darkness and miles from the next living soul, the feeling went beyond alarming. Well beyond.

Panic mixed with some other, indefinable emotion to make Torie's knees feel weak. When Gabriel flattened his hand against her spine, she instinctively pressed against him, and when with thumb and forefinger he stroked the tip of her chin, she tilted her head to receive his kiss.

Gabriel smiled down at her, a slow, irresistible smile that destroyed what little was left of Torie's willpower. But though her rationality was certainly gone, and her self-control not far behind, Torie's pride was left quite intact. Try as she might, she could not meet Gabriel's seductive smile head-on, not without betraying her nervousness. Hoping to remind herself that the rest of the world was still there, that it had not disappeared leaving only the two of them locked in each other's arms surrounded by an endless pool of moonlight, she let her gaze flicker over Gabriel's shoulder.

What she saw there made her blood feel like icy water in her veins. Torie pushed away from Gabriel, her hand automatically going to her throat.

"Torie?" Gabriel leaned nearer, trying to capture her gaze.

Torie did not move. She couldn't. Her gaze was riveted to the horizon and to the tiny, bright lights that hung there just above the ground, flickering at her with silent laughter, mute heralds of madness and death.

The lights danced to the rhythm of some terrible, silent song. They glimmered, blue and yellow specks, bright as fallen stars, elusive as butterflies, there one second, gone when Torie moved her eyes, their glow fading and rising, dimming, then sharpening, calling to her.

Just as they'd called to Roger.

"Torie? What the hell—?" Gabriel's expression was as confused as the look he tossed over his shoulder. "What's wrong with you? What are you staring at? There's nothing there."

Gabriel didn't see the lights. The realization ripped into Torie, and that, more than anything, caused her to panic.

How she made herself move when her legs felt so unsteady and her head so light, Torie could not say. She whirled around and rushed away, heading blindly down the path that led toward home.

"Torie!" Gabriel's voice followed behind her like the echoes of a dream. "What in the bloody hell is wrong with you? Torie! Torie!"

She did not stop, and she did not dare to look behind her. The tension she felt when she realized Gabriel was about to kiss her was nothing compared to the feelings that filled her now, and though some small portion of her brain instructed her to calm down, Torie knew she was well beyond listening. Other, more primitive emotions had already taken control.

Disbelief. Panic. Fear.

Torie lost herself in them, heedless of the small streams she splashed through, unmindful of the gorse branches that scratched at her face and tore her dress.

Once inside the house, she slammed the door closed and leaned her back against it. Her breath came hard and fast, her heart pounded a painful beat inside her. Settling her hands on her knees, she bent and tried to regain her senses.

"It's not possible."

She heard her own voice, as if it came from a million miles away.

"They're not real. They can't be."

Just to prove it to herself, Torie chanced a look around. There was no sign of the lights in here. All was as they'd left it earlier this evening. Everything tidy. Everything quiet.

The awareness should have made Torie feel better, but it didn't. She remembered that Roger had never seen the lights inside, either, not until that final night when they followed him over the threshold and snatched away all that was left of his mind.

"Torie! Torie!"

From outside, Torie heard the echoes of Gabriel's voice. It seemed he was capable of keeping pace with her when he had a mind to. He was close to the house, and getting closer each second.

Pulling herself to her feet, Torie swiped at her tear-stained cheeks with trembling hands.

She would need an explanation ready for Gabriel when he got here and from the sound of his voice, that would not take long. What would she tell him when he asked why she ran like a frightened horse? What would she say when he faced her with the facts and asked what was wrong?

Torie shook her head. She didn't know. She honestly did not know, and with her eyes burning and her head pounding, she did not think she could possibly come up with an explanation that would satisfy him.

All she knew was that she could not tell Gabriel the truth, for right now, she wasn't sure herself what it was.

Was it her own fancies and her memories of Roger's illness that had caused her to see the sparkling lights? Or was it panic, her apprehension about being in Gabriel's arms and her realization that her reaction to his every touch was far more potent and unexpected than was right or wise?

Or was it true?

Had she seen the lights?

The fear and panic drained from Torie, leaving nothing but a cold sense of awareness.

For she knew that if it was true, if she really did see the lights, then surely there was only one explanation.

She was just like Roger.

Mad.

Chapter 9

He'd had far too much to drink already but, damn, what else was there to do?

Gabriel settled back in his chair. He refilled his glass from the bottle of brandy that he had found waiting for him in the library this morning, left anonymously and mysteriously as if by divine intervention. He'd opened the bottle not an hour ago and it was already half empty but, by God, he would not let that stop him.

Not tonight.

Gabriel crossed his right arm over his chest and settled his left elbow on it, the tumbler of brandy dangling loosely in his fingers.

For the last few weeks, he'd been faithful to the promise he'd made that first cursed day he came to Sussex. He'd had little more than an occasional glass. But there were only so many games of Patience a man could play, only so many times he could read and reread Roger's magnificently prosaic correspondence. Boredom bred monotony, and monotony gave rise to ennui. The combination had the remarkable effect of working up a powerful thirst, one that, sooner or later, demanded to be quenched.

Gabriel took another sip of brandy, then spent some minutes watching the amber liquid swirl in his glass. Tiring of that, he looked up at the portrait of Roger Broadridge that hung over the fireplace directly across from where he sat.

Nothing had changed in the five minutes since he'd studied the painting the last time. Or the time before. It still showed the same Roger, looking the same as Gabriel remembered him. Proper as a parson. Dour as a rain cloud. Austere as old Cromwell himself.

"To you, Roger old man." Gabriel raised his glass and glared at the painting, his voice heavy with sarcasm. "And to your charming sister, Torie."

Torie.

The name soured in Gabriel's mouth, scattering the nice, hazy fog of brandy fumes where he'd kept himself isolated most of the evening, and completely destroying his mood.

Not even an entire bottle of brandy was enough to drown the pictures that materialized in his head. He knew that as sure as he knew it was foolish to even try. The more he attempted to rid himself of the disturbing images, the more intense they became, until his whole head seemed filled with them:

Torie, whose straw-colored hair and clear green eyes sparkled in the starlight.

Torie, who felt so good in his arms.

Torie, who had bolted from him like the proverbial ladybird from its fiery house, and hadn't spoken more than ten words to him since that night they dined at Westin's.

Gabriel frowned into his glass.

Though the fact that Torie had fled the moment he came too near was troubling to both his vanity and his masculinity, it was only just another entry in the long list of things that disturbed him about her.

She still disappeared every morning before Gabriel was awake, and she stayed out all day long. She still never said a word about where she'd been, never told Gabriel a thing about the work she wanted him to do, never shared a minute of her day or asked what he'd done with his.

That was bad enough.

But in the four days since her mysterious vanishing act on the downs, other things had happened. Things that made Gabriel uneasy. He didn't notice it the first night. He hardly paid it much mind the second. But by the third night, the pattern was unmistakable.

Where before, Torie disappeared each morning and came back close to dark, now she was certain to be in the house long before nightfall. Where before, she ate heartily and encouraged Gabriel to do the same, now she did not join him for dinner. Where before, she came into the library and wrote furiously in her journal, now she wrote in fits and starts, and ended up the night pacing the room, stopping every now and again to peer out the window as if she expected to see something outside waiting for her.

Gabriel couldn't help but remember Spencer Westin's dire warnings about Torie, about her heritage and her sanity. This time, like every time before, he dismissed Westin's rhetoric with a snort. Westin was the madman, surely. And Torie?

Gabriel turned the thought over in his head while he turned his glass in his hands.

Torie was neither mad nor haunted. He was certain of that. She was just being a woman.

And that, he supposed, was worse than either.

With a heavy sigh, Gabriel finished off his glass and poured another. He did not have a chance to drink it before the library door opened.

Gabriel did not turn around. He knew it was Torie. He heard her footsteps, light against the faded carpet, and recognized the sound of the bundle she seemed always to be carrying as it thumped against the floor.

She did not speak, but walked to the window and looked outside. Satisfied at seeing, or not seeing, whatever it was she was looking for, she went over to the desk that took up most of the far wall of the library. From there, she could see Gabriel quite clearly. He knew that. He also knew he didn't have to look her way to know what kind of expression she wore on her face. If she could see him from the desk, then she could also see the half-empty bottle on the table next to him.

Her lips were puckered, her eyes were frosty. Gabriel didn't have to see that, either. Even from all the way over here, he could feel the sting of her icy glare.

But even the fact that he was swilling brandy here in her library in plain sight of both herself and the portrait of her sainted and dearly-departed brother, was not enough to elicit a reaction from Torie, at least nothing more than a perfectly ladylike snort of disdain. Gabriel waited for more.

There was nothing. Nothing more than the sounds of Torie pulling back her chair, turning her key in the lock, sliding open the top drawer, and drawing out her journal. He heard her open it, smooth out a page, and begin to write.

"I might have known you'd be home soon," Gabriel said, his voice in counterpoint to the scratching of Torie's pen against the paper. As tempted as he was to glance her way, he kept his gaze fastened to Roger's portrait. "It's almost dark."

Torie didn't answer.

Gabriel wasn't surprised. If tonight was anything like last night and the night before, she would scribble in her journal for the next hour or so and then disappear into her room, all the while doing a damned good job of pretending he wasn't here.

There was a stir of anger in the emotions that flooded through Gabriel, but that wasn't the only thing he felt. There was exasperation, too, and frustration, annoyance, and curiosity. There was something else, as well, something that tightened in his gut and made his blood sing as if it were full of the finest brandy. Something Gabriel recognized but refused to name.

Suddenly too uneasy to keep still, though he dared not think why, Gabriel stretched out his long legs toward the fire that Mrs. Denny had laid before she left for the evening. On another night, he might have kept silent, allowing Torie her privacy and himself the all-too-familiar pretense of comfortable drunkenness. That would not work tonight.

Tonight, there was some demon inside him. He could feel it eating away at his self-control, annihilating what was left of his common sense. It was an imp that goaded him on, challenging him to elicit some response—any response—from the woman who sat at the desk, silent and mysterious as the Sphinx.

"Perhaps I could be of some service to you this evening," Gabriel said, forcing a note of laughter into his voice. "You can sit there writing, pretending I don't exist, and I can pace back and forth to the window and peer outside for you. Does that work?"

No answer.

Damn her! Gabriel shifted in his seat. He'd have something out of her tonight, even if it was only a word about the weather.

Gabriel drank down the rest of his brandy and considered pouring another glass. He decided against it, banging his tumbler against the table instead and smiling spitefully when the resultant noise startled Torie enough to cause her a slip of the pen. He heard her mumble a word of disgust, heard the sounds of her nib scratching away her mistake.

"I've noticed you're home early every night." Gabriel kept talking. "Ever since the night we dined at Westin's. I can't help but wonder at it. But then, I'm here all day with nothing much to do but wonder."

This time, Gabriel did not have to introduce a note of derision into his voice. It flowed as effortlessly from him as the brandy from his bottle.

Torie went on writing, her head bent over her book.

Gabriel grumbled a particularly vulgar word, one that seemed to suit the situation to a nicety. Barely controlling his temper, he tried a different tack. "I've been visiting with Roger," he said.

That was enough to get Torie's attention. Her head came up.

Gabriel refused to let her know it mattered. Keeping his gaze fixed on Roger's sullen expression, he waved carelessly at the painting. "We've been reminiscing," he said and chuckled. "Or at least, I have. Roger's not one to say much, is he?"

"You've had too much to drink." Torie snapped her journal shut and he heard the click of her spectacles as she set them on the desk. She pushed back her chair and stood. "It's really most unsuitable."

"Is it?" Gabriel laughed. It was a small enough victory, getting her to talk, but it made him feel remarkably self-satisfied. "I think it's quite excellent. A nice warm, cheerful way to feel." He burrowed further into the chair. "You really ought to try it. Perhaps a dram of warm spirits would dissolve your icy silence and melt your frosty disposition."

"Perhaps," Torie said, rounding the desk and heading for the door, "dinner would help sober you. I'm told food in the stomach counteracts the disgusting effects of alcohol. Mrs. Denny left meat and cheese on the sideboard. Why don't you go in and eat. Then, perhaps, you might consider sleeping it off. Go to bed."

"Alone?"

It was the brandy talking, and Gabriel cursed both himself and it. Still, he had gone too far to control things now, and even if he could, he wasn't sure he wanted to.

As Torie went by, he caught her arm and reeled her in. Before she ever had the chance to struggle and he ever had the chance to stop himself, she was sitting on his lap.

Gabriel dragged in a breath of surprise. He hadn't bothered to look at Torie at all this evening. If he had, he would have realized she was wearing the same dress she wore that day he'd flung the cards all about this very room. The black dress that showed her shoulders to such perfection. The one that was cut even and low over her bosom so that, this close, he could not fail to see the swell of her breasts and the dark, tantalizing shadow that showed between them.

Swallowing hard, Gabriel fought back the swift and conspicuous physical response he feared would betray him.

Women with breasts as appealing as these should be kept covered from head to toe, he decided, at least those who were real ladies and not the kind who advertised themselves and their wares for sale to the highest bidder. It was the only way men like him could be safe from their own treacherous human natures.

But Torie was not covered from head to toe, and Gabriel's human nature was not so easily indulged.

He allowed himself another look, and concluded beyond a doubt that a law was needed. One that required that the stuff women used to clothe themselves be thick and sturdy. He was not familiar enough with fashion to know what that fabric might be, but he was certain it should be so heavy that it necessitated shapeless, formless, completely innocuous gowns. Ones that did not cling to every curve as seductively as Torie's did. Ones that were so circumspect, he would not have the slightest chance of noticing the appealing size of her waist, or the intriguing length of her legs, or the tempting swell of her nipples.

A sudden dryness parched Gabriel's mouth, but he did not chance letting go of Torie long enough to reach for his glass. She had recovered enough from the temporary numbness caused by her surprise for her to struggle, and Gabriel grabbed both her arms above the elbows and held on tight, refusing to let her go.

That should be another requirement of the law, he thought with the clear-cut precision that could only be attributed to the amount of brandy he'd taken. The law should require that women not squirm too much when you were trying to hold on to them. For then nothing, not even that nice, thick, heavy fabric he so fancied, could prevent you from feeling the soft press of their buttocks against your legs, and the supple, provocative movement of their thighs.

Another thought struck Gabriel and he smiled in spite of himself. His imagined law should also require that men who had the audacity to seize women and force them into close, intimate contact, should damned well know what in hell they were about. If not others might find themselves in his predicament, with a bellyful of desire, a throbbing in his loins, an enticing woman on his lap, and not the slightest idea of what to do with her except hold on tight, and see where the madness would take them.

It took just a second for Torie to realize what was happening, but it was one second too long. By the time she gathered her wits enough to struggle, Gabriel's hold on her was too solid to shake off. He grabbed both her arms just above the elbows and held on tight, and no matter how much she squirmed, he wasn't about to let go.

She gave up, glaring at Gabriel with the kind of look that, over the years, she had used so effectively to wither other men.

But Gabriel Raddigan wasn't other men, and he was far too soaked in brandy to wither easily.

Torie sniffed the strong aroma of the liquor and clicked her tongue. Her voice was sharp with disgust. "The results of dissipation are quite unbecoming. You really need to learn to temper your habits, Mr. Raddigan."

"Oh, I've tempered them, right enough." Gabriel's words escaped on the end of a sigh. He slid his gaze over Torie's shoulders. He grazed it across her collarbone. He glided it to her breasts. He kept it there long enough for Torie to feel a hot flush rising in her, and she realized, to her mortification, that must have been his intent. He followed the blush as it flooded her chest and raced up her neck and into her face and when his eyes met hers, he smiled lazily, like a man would if he knew a woman's secrets.

"I'm bloody tired of tempering my habits," Gabriel said. "I've had three weeks of moderation. Three weeks of abstinence. I warned you I would not be happy watching the moss grow on the window ledges." He ran his tongue over his lips. "A man needs more than that, I think. Much more."

It was just the kind of impertinent vulgarity Torie had expected from Gabriel from the first. In the portion of her mind that was not in a panic from the way Gabriel was looking at her, Torie congratulated herself for being such a fine judge of character. What a relief to know that Gabriel was the kind of man she thought him to be. The kind she had gone to Oxford purposely to find.

More than a few times in the last few weeks, she'd had misgivings. She'd been certain she made a terrible misjudgment. She feared she'd gotten a scholar instead of a scoundrel, a gentleman instead of a rogue. It was quite gratifying both to her pride and to her intellect to realize she'd been right all along.

The only problem was, now that she had assessed Gabriel and found him all she feared him to be, what was she to do? And how was she to extricate herself from the precarious position in which she now found herself?

"I really do not understand why you are looking at me

that way, Mr. Raddigan." Torie pulled her dignity around her like a suit of armor, one designed to keep out the most determined of assaults. "It would be a great deal easier to talk to you if you would stop. And a good deal more comfortable if you'd allow me to get up."

"Not for me!" Gabriel's eyes twinkled and she cursed him for it. He settled himself back in the chair, his hands still tight around her arms. His voice had a dreamy quality she suspected came from too much drink and a much too active imagination.

"I was just thinking back to a night in Oxford," he said, his gaze finally leaving her, thankfully, and traveling to the picture of Roger above the fireplace. "I think it must have been Michaelmas term, our first at University, because there was a group of us and we had Roger with us. That could have never happened second term. By then, we'd all come to learn what a . . ." He threw her a glance and dismissed the rest of the curious statement with a laugh.

"No matter!" Gabriel said. "We'd all gone out that night for a few hours of drinking and wenching. Yes, Roger, too," he added quickly when Torie tried to challenge the ridiculous and highly improbable assertion. "At least Roger made a good show of wanting to join in the fun. He drank his share at the first two public houses we called at, but by the time we visited the third and got down to taking a serious look at the bits of muslin available for purchase, your brother got cold feet."

Torie's spine stiffened. "That is not at all surprising," she said. "Roger had principles. He was a responsible student and a man of morality and ethics. Depraved companions may have enticed him to join in drinking a pint or two, but he would never—"

"Wouldn't he?" Gabriel's grin turned into a wide smile. "Then you didn't know Roger as well as you thought you did. Oh, for a while it looked as if he was going to live up to your lofty expectations. I will admit that. He sat by himself in a dark corner, staring into his ale while the rest of us looked over the serving girls who were willing and for hire. I suppose he was gathering his courage. Watching the way the rest of us handled the ladies. Then one particularly pretty young thing caught his eye. Good old Roger!" Gabriel chuckled and threw one last look at the painting.

"Roger was never one to mince words. He didn't say a thing, no doubt because he didn't know what to say. He simply grabbed the girl as she walked by. Grabbed her and pulled her into his lap." Gabriel shifted his gaze to Torie and looked her up and down, as if he wasn't quite sure how she got where she was. He raised his eyebrows, clearly pleased that his own situation so neatly mirrored the one in the story.

"That poor girl was dumbstruck," he said, continuing his tale, a smile on his face. "She didn't say a thing. If she had, it would have saved us all a neat bit of trouble. Well, Roger took her silence for consent. He kissed her."

Even as he told the story, Gabriel's smile faded. By the time he got to the last word, it was gone completely. His dark eyes glimmered with an emotion that was as far from amusement as any Torie had ever seen. He let his gaze flicker over Torie and back up to her eyes.

"May I demonstrate?"

She had not expected him to ask permission. Not ever, not for anything he wanted. Given the opportunity to refuse him, Torie found she could not. She was as speechless as the poor girl in the story and, like Roger, Gabriel took her silence for consent.

"Roger sort of . . ." Gabriel slid his hands up Torie's arms. He settled them on her shoulders, his fingers cool against her skin, but his palms hot as flame. "He held the girl something like this. Rather awkward, I think you'll agree."

Torie was glad Gabriel did not wait for her reply. She could not have looked him in the eye and lied to him. Not about this. She could not have admitted, as much as she would have liked to, that while his touch was a lot of things, it was certainly not awkward.

Gabriel was close now, so close, she could see the copper-colored flecks that flashed in his eyes like heat lightning. She could smell the sweet, heavy scent of brandy on his breath.

"You have to understand, I am not anywhere near as foxed as Roger was," Gabriel explained, his voice faltering as he inched his mouth nearer to Torie's. "Roger couldn't hold his liquor well, you see, and he'd had a great deal to drink. He was inexperienced and nervy as hell. To the delight of the onlookers and the obvious disappointment of the poor girl in his arms, he blundered his way through the kiss." Gabriel spoke the words against her lips and Torie heard him gulp in a great draught of air, as if he were struggling for breath.

"Roger . . . Roger . . ." Gabriel surrendered with a sigh. "Oh, hell!" he moaned. "Who gives a bloody damn what Roger did!"

He brought his mouth to hers so suddenly, Torie barely had time to ready herself. Gabriel braced her with his arms, his one hand sliding over her shoulders and down her back to her waist, his other holding her firmly in place. It was as if he could read her mind and interpret the signals of her body, the ones that made it quite clear that if he did not hold on to her, she would surely swoon.

It was impossible to say how long the kiss lasted, or even if it was one kiss, or two, or even more. Torie supposed, in what was left of the rational portion of her being, that there were those who made a science of such things, just as there were those who would certainly remember every deft move of Gabriel's hands.

She was not one of them. Not one who could ever sort

the emotion from the physical sensations, the kiss from the tingling that surged through her body, the touch from the heat it generated.

All she felt was the fire. The warmth of Gabriel's hands as they moved over her shoulders. The wetness of his mouth as he slid it from her lips and trailed a series of long, slow kisses down her neck. With one finger, he nudged aside the black lace that edged the low-cut neckline of her gown. He grazed his finger across the tops of her breasts and smiled when Torie let go an unintentional murmur of delight, caught by the unexpected pleasure of it.

"What did Roger do then?" It was far too late to redeem herself, but Torie felt she had to try. Her breathing was no more even than Gabriel's. Her heart pounded in her ears. "What happened after that?"

"After that?" Gabriel finished his story, but he did not stop stroking her breasts. "After that, the innkeeper arrived on the scene, no doubt to collect his portion of whatever it was we were willing to pay his doxies. He was a burly man with fists the size of anvils. And the weight." He glanced up at her and smiled. "Roger found out the hard way that the girl he was fondling rather clumsily wasn't a Cyprian at all, but the man's daughter."

Gabriel let out a roar of laughter. He leaned back, pulling Torie with him and settling her into the circle of his arms. "Before we knew what was happening, we were all of us thrown into the street, but not before we'd been witness to an impressive exhibition of the innkeeper's pugilistic prowess and got a fair amount of cut lips, bruised bones and"—he grazed the tip of one finger under Torie's nearly healed eye—"blackened eyes in the bargain."

It was such a preposterous story, Torie had to laugh, too.

Her laughter died when Gabriel skimmed his thumb

beneath her chin and raised her face to his. His eyes were
dark with desire. His voice simmered with temptation.
"Will the story have a happier ending tonight, I wonder?"
he asked.

If only it could.

Suddenly uncomfortable, both with the way Gabriel
was holding her and her own instinctive and highly irrational response to it, Torie bolted off his lap. She retreated
to the fireplace and kept her back to Gabriel, afraid that
if he saw her face, he would surely know what was going
on inside her head.

She wished the story could have a happy ending, both
for him and for her. But how could it?

How could it, when Gabriel was a man who laughed in
the face of all she esteemed? A man with no honor. A man
with no ambition. A man who lived for his luck: with the
cards, with the horses, with the ladies. One who had
abandoned a brilliant future and settled instead for a life
of dissipation and debauchery.

And she?

Though Torie had vowed time and again these past
days that she would not look, her gaze moved automatically to the windows. A chill like death settled in her soul,
banishing the heat of Gabriel's touch.

She was a woman who saw lights flashing out on the
downs. One who, for the last four days, had lived in the
shadow of those lights and all they implied.

Torie closed her eyes, momentarily overcome by the
memory. In the last days, there had been no further sign
of the ghostly lights, no further indication that her eyes or
her mind were playing tricks on her. But she could not
help but think about them. Hour after hour. Day after
day.

She could not help but remember how much they had
surprised and frightened her. She could not help but think
what they might mean, just as she could not help but

dwell on the scraps and shards of her memories of Roger, and the horrible, painful death brought on by his madness.

Was she next?

It was a question that had haunted her every waking moment these last few days. One that kept her from sleeping. One that in and of itself, prevented this night or any other from having a happy ending.

Gathering her courage, Torie swung around to face Gabriel. She did not meet his eyes. She could not, not with the taste of brandy and passion still warm upon her lips. "I should ask you to leave," she said, her voice wavering more than she liked.

"Will you?" Gabriel didn't sound worried. He sounded mildly interested, mildly amused.

It was not a question Torie was prepared to answer, simply because she did not know the answer herself. She turned back to the fire, daring only one quick glance over her shoulder. "That was . . ." She stumbled over the words, not sure herself if what had just happened between them was disgusting or delightful. She decided on a more neutral assessment, gleaning some small amount of satisfaction from the fact that even Gabriel could not dispute it. "It was improper and inappropriate."

"It was indeed!" Gabriel let out a long sigh. He sounded far too pleased with himself. There was an undercurrent of laughter in his voice, and she could picture him smiling, sprawled in the chair where only moments ago the two of them had sat much too close together, doing things that, in recollection, were much too disconcerting to even consider.

His footsteps muffled by the carpeting, Gabriel rose from the chair and stepped closer, until she felt him right behind her, the brush of his linen shirt soft against her back. "Just because something is inappropriate and improper," he said close to her ear, "doesn't mean you can't enjoy it."

"But it was—"

"It was wonderful, and you know it." Gabriel laughed. Before Torie had a chance to move, he took her in his arms and turned her to face him. The light of the fire glittering in the hearth sparkled in his dark eyes. "You expect every encounter you ever have with a man will be like those you've experienced with Westin. I'd wager a year's income—if I had one left to wager—that he's never even kissed you. Has he?" Gabriel didn't wait for an answer. He shook his head, as if baffled by the whole thing.

"The fool's never even tried. Perhaps if he did, you'd realize that there are right ways and wrong ways to go about these things. No doubt Westin would go about it all the wrong way. Like your brother did with that poor girl in the pub." Gabriel pulled himself up to his full height and Torie felt his muscles tense.

"Westin would be stiff and formal," he said with an attempt to replicate what he thought Spencer's demeanor might be. "No doubt he's one of those unfortunate fellows who only knows how to give bad kisses. His lips stiff." The corners of Gabriel's lips tipped into a mischievous smile. "When a man kisses a woman, that is not the portion of his anatomy that is supposed to be rigid."

"Really, Mr. Raddigan! That is too much, even for you." With both her hands on his shoulders, Torie pushed Gabriel away. It should have taken a lot more force to push him back, but she was aided in her quest, no doubt, by the amount of brandy Gabriel had drunk as well as the fact that he was laughing.

Torie thanked whatever vigilant angels looked out for the virtue of young ladies. Had Gabriel kept on in his sweet, flattering tone, she might have been drawn anew into the enchantment cast by his dark eyes and his tender kisses. Now, she was reminded again of the kind of man he was, and the reminder was enough to bring back her anger in full force.

"I am sorry if any of my actions this evening were misleading in some way, Mr. Raddigan," she snapped. "As I said the other day, I am not often in the company of men, and I am not used to their wiles. I will admit, you did quite sweep me off my feet. For a moment. But that's all it was. A momentary sort of . . . insanity, I suppose. I have come to my senses and I would hope that after a good night's sleep and a chance to digest the incredible amount of brandy you've consumed, you will come to yours."

Had it been any other woman, Gabriel was quite sure he would have known exactly what to do right then and there. He would have scooped her into his arms, tossed her down on the floor, and used every persuasive method he could think of to change her mind. And it would have worked. He had no doubt of that.

Had it been any other woman.

But it wasn't. This was Victoria Broadridge, and something deep inside Gabriel's brain where the brandy had not yet penetrated reminded him in no uncertain terms that what would surely work with other women would just as surely not work with Torie.

How could it?

How could such superficial things as kisses and caresses move a heart as steadfast as hers? How could such a shallow thing as the passing pleasure of a man's love satisfy a woman like this, one whose eyes were blazing at him even now with more intensity and more insight and far more intelligence than any other woman he had ever had the ill fortune to know?

"Damn!" Gabriel dropped back down in his chair and glared at Torie. If he had learned nothing else in the last few years, he thought he'd learned the fine and laborious art of avoiding the pricklings of his conscience.

He'd thought wrong.

Gabriel ran one hand through his hair. "That was not an appropriate thing to say in the presence of a lady," he said. "I owe you an apology."

"No." Torie swept by him and went to the door. She was already out in the hallway when he heard her final words, terse and clipped and as cold as the look he felt between his shoulder blades. "You don't owe me a thing, Mr. Raddigan," she said. "Nothing but your summer."

"Nothing but my summer."

Grumbling, Gabriel waited until he heard Torie's bedroom door close before he hauled himself out of his chair and went to his room.

The whole matter was a mystery to him, and not a pleasant one at that. He didn't understand it. Not one bit.

All he knew was that once again, he'd scared Torie away.

And once again, he was left to spend the night, sleepless and alone, with a fire in his gut and a single, persistent question tapping away at his brain.

Why?

Chapter 10

The rain beating against the roof was as insistent and bothersome as the question that clacketed through Gabriel's mind.

Muttering a curse, he flipped over in bed and tugged the blankets under his chin. It was bad enough he'd spent all of the night lost in vivid and quite disturbing dreams about Torie, now even the damned rain was attempting to wake him at some ungodly hour even before the sun was up.

He lay motionless for a few minutes, willing himself back to sleep and failing rather miserably. It was some time before he realized why.

There was another sound, too, other than that of the rain. Another sound that intruded on the edge of his hearing. One that came from inside the house.

Gabriel sat up. Cautiously so as not to make any noise, he swung his legs over the side of the bed and sat listening.

The sound was not loud and perhaps that was what worried him. It was quiet, almost stealthy, like the sound a person might make inadvertently while he was trying his damnedest to go undetected.

Gabriel got out of bed and went to the door. His first inclination was to race out into the hallway and see who was there, but he took one look at himself and thought

better of it. He'd been much too annoyed, both at Torie
and at his own uncontrollable longings, to prepare himself
properly for bed last night. He'd peeled off his clothes and
tossed them on the floor. He was as buff naked as a babe.

Gabriel grinned.

He could imagine the kind of scene it would create if he
went speeding from his room and came face to face with
Torie. He wondered what she'd say when she saw him,
how she'd look when her eyes traveled from his face,
down his chest, down further still. Would she be horrified,
or interested? Would her cheeks flame with embarrassment, or desire?

Gabriel banished his smile as well as the shameless
thoughts that caused it, and reminded himself there were
other, more important matters to consider right now. He
bent his ear to the door to listen.

Surely what he heard was the sound of someone walking about the house, he told himself, listening to the
pattern of the noises. And just as certainly, they were not
Torie's footsteps.

A woman's steps were lighter, even in outdoor shoes.
This was the stride of heavy boots, and it was clearly
headed toward the front door.

His curiosity piqued beyond endurance, Gabriel went
to the window. It was probably close to dawn, yet the sky
and earth were as one, slate-gray and as close as the inside
of a prison cell. The world of the downs was walled in by
mist and carpeted with a heavy fog that swirled near the
ground like eddies in a quick-running stream.

Gabriel squinted through the darkness. Looking to his
left, he could see the front door. He leaned closer to the
window, the ledge cold and damp against his bare chest.
From there, he watched the door open. A second later, a
figure stepped outside.

Gabriel cursed under his breath.

If the light had been stronger, the rain less persistent,

he would be able to see better. As it was, he could only make out bits and pieces of what was going on, but what he did see left him amazed.

He could definitely see that the figure was wearing a long, dark-colored box coat, the kind so many of the young bucks of the ton sported. From memory, Gabriel knew the coat had multiple layers of capes fastened at the shoulder and a long row of buttons down the loose-fitting front. That would account for the odd, shapeless silhouette of the figure moving through the mist, that and the fact that the person was also wearing a large-brimmed hat, the kind Gabriel had seen fishermen wear to keep off rain and sea spray.

The figure turned onto the track that led north toward the Tilgate Forest and Gabriel caught a glance of half Wellington boots and heard them tap against the stone-set path, a noise that might have echoed merrily in different weather, but this morning, only sounded a dull crump. Gabriel watched the fellow until he disappeared into the curtain of rain and fog that surrounded the house.

"Fellow, indeed," Gabriel mumbled.

For while it was impossible to get a glimpse of the person's face, there was no mistaking the clothes, or the clump of his boots, or the fact that no woman in her right mind or mindful of her reputation would be out by herself at this early hour and in this terrible weather. The figure was certainly that of a man.

Gabriel twirled around, his back propped against the window ledge, his arms crossed over his chest.

A man?

"God's eyes!" Gabriel could not help himself. The significance of all he'd seen seeped into his brain where only hours ago, brandy and carnal desire had mingled to muddle his senses. He was suddenly wide awake, and as astonished as he had ever been.

It was no wonder Torie acted like a frightened animal

every time he came too near. No wonder she'd kept him
at arm's length last night. No wonder she refused Spencer
Westin's proposal and paced the floors and peeked out the
windows, her stomach tied in knots so that she could not
eat, her hands trembling so that she could not write properly in her journal.

She was not made nervous by Gabriel's nearness or his
attention, as he had been foolish enough to think. She was
not mad and looking over the downs for ghostly lights, as
Westin would have Gabriel believe.

It all made so much sense now that he thought about
it, Gabriel could not fathom why he had not come upon
the idea sooner.

It was there all along, staring him in the face, and he
needed only to see the mist-shrouded figure of the man
leaving the house to put all the pieces together.

As incredible as it seemed, there was only one explanation.

Torie Broadridge had a lover.

He wondered if it could be the rector.

Balancing a teacup and saucer on his one knee, his top
hat on the other, Gabriel let his gaze travel over the
assembled crowd. He assiduously avoided meeting the
eyes of Miss Katherine Wayne, the young lady seated on
his left, certain that if she was given the slightest encouragement, she would once again launch into a recitation of
her virtues, an inventory of her accomplishments, and a
catalog of her good deeds. She was a plain girl plainly in
search of a husband, and she obviously thought it her
good fortune to be seated next to Gabriel for this afternoon's tea.

Gabriel knew better than that.

He'd heard the young lady's mother cajoling the curate's wife to seat her daughter right here. He'd seen the

way the curate's wife twittered at the thought of being an accomplice to the plot. He knew full well what both ladies had in mind and though he did not agree with their methods, he could not fault their motives.

The annual spring fete here at St. John's Church was one of the first opportunities Gabriel had to meet the people of Cuckfield. From what he could see, he was one of a sparse number of eligible bachelors in the neighborhood, and certainly one of the few who was both below the age of fifty and had the unique attribute of being able bodied and still having all his own hair and teeth.

These significant facts had not gone unnoticed by the matchmaking mamas of the town, nor by the green girls who were parading around in their spring finery like peahens at a strut.

It was far too late in a very long day for that sort of nonsense, Gabriel decided. He'd had enough quaint town merriment, from watching the dancing around the Maypole to being a reluctant bystander at a lethargic boxing demonstration.

He had filled up the long, dull hours his own way, trying to sort through the puzzle that had become something of an obsession since that morning a week ago when he'd seen the mysterious figure leave the house and disappear into the mist.

Who was it?

Pretending he didn't notice the way Miss Wayne's face brightened when it looked as if he might glance her way, Gabriel studied Thomas Blankenship, the rector of St. John's, who was deep in conversation with Spencer Westin. They were seated with Torie, halfway around the wide circle of chairs that had been placed here on the lawn.

The Reverend Mr. Blankenship was a doughy-faced fellow, all cheeks and sparkling blue eyes, fresh-scrubbed and shiny as a new penny. He was a sincere young whelp, a man whose parishioners seemed content with his straightforward though unimaginative ministering. His sermons, if they were anything like the one Gabriel had been obliged to sit through this morning, were painstakingly researched, well written, and dull as dirt.

Could Blankenship be Torie's secret lover?

If Gabriel's conscience suggested that he feel guilty for indicting a man of the cloth without the slightest shred of evidence, he paid it no mind. He had seen worse things in his time, he reminded himself, far worse than a young, unmarried rector who found respite from the spiritual by indulging a little in the physical.

Gabriel took another long look at the man.

Blankenship was short enough to match the figure who'd crept from the house, but he was altogether too chubby. Appropriately enough, he looked like one of those cherubs who lived on the ceilings of ornate churches, all round and rosy.

Not a secret lover, surely, Gabriel decided with a wry smile. Not by a long shot.

Gabriel turned his attention to the people seated on his right. Anthony Darnell was another possibility, he thought, ticking off the list like another man might count the pips in his hand of cards. Darnell was the town chemist, a thin, balding man of indeterminate age whom Gabriel had met directly after church services this morning.

Darnell was not an attractive man. His nose was too long and pointed, his eyes were set far too close together. But if Gabriel had learned one thing about women, it was that they could be charmed by the damnedest things. Beneath the most homely of exteriors might beat the heart of a true romantic and that, Gabriel knew from experience, was oftentimes more attractive to a woman than even a handsome face.

Was Torie such a woman?

That, Gabriel was loath to admit, was as much a mystery to him as the identity of Torie's paramour.

There was one other strong possibility, of course, and as much as Gabriel would have liked to discard it, he knew it would be foolhardy to pretend it didn't exist.

He let his gaze wander over the rest of the tea-sipping crowd to where Spencer Westin still conversed with Reverend Blankenship. The morning he'd seen the man leave the house, Gabriel had automatically dismissed Westin as a prospect. Westin was too tall, too thin. His carriage was all wrong, his stride not as easy, and longer than that of the man Gabriel saw in the mist.

That should have been enough to eliminate Westin from the running, Gabriel told himself again and again. But no matter how often he tried to remove Westin from his list, he could not ignore one very important bit of evidence that pointed right at the man.

For the life of him, Gabriel could not remember hearing a sound from Torie's room the night before he'd seen the man leave the house.

Not a murmur.

Not a groan.

And if there ever was a man who would make love to a woman in absolute silence, it was Spencer Westin.

Gabriel felt his expression sour.

It was damned unfair. That's what it was. Even for all her willfulness, or perhaps because of it, Torie deserved better than that.

Just the thought made Gabriel smile wistfully.

A woman like Torie needed better handling. Soft words murmured close to her ear. Caresses that were softer still, bestowed to the accompaniment of a torrent of melting compliments: How pretty her eyes were, especially when their crisp green was softened by passion. How satiny her skin was, especially the skin of her breasts and thighs. How sweet she tasted.

Gabriel sighed.

Especially how sweet she tasted; her lips, and her breasts, and the warm, secret places only a lover was privileged to know.

A woman like Torie should be made love to with words as well as with actions, the sounds in both their ears as much a part of the seduction as every fevered kiss, every desperate embrace. And if it was done right, a woman like Torie would be asking for more before things had gone far, promising as much pleasure as she was expecting to receive herself. She would not speak in whispers. Her voice would not be muted by either embarrassment or propriety. She would talk out loud and laugh and moan, every inch of her being given to the experience.

What a shame that there were men like Westin, men who assumed that quick and quiet was good enough.

Long and loud. That's the way it was meant to be done, and Gabriel pitied Torie if she had, indeed, settled for less.

Leaning back in his chair, Gabriel set down his teacup. Torie was seated almost directly across from him in the chair next to Westin's. Gabriel stretched his legs out in front of him and watched her, his eyes half closed.

Long and loud.

The words echoed in his brain right alongside the disturbing images they conjured.

Long and loud.

A fascinating thought.

Torie did not have to look up to know that Gabriel was watching her. Though she was turned politely toward Spencer and the Reverend Mr. Blankenship, she could feel the heat of Gabriel's eyes. They touched her with that same, probing gaze he seemed to use every time he looked at her of late. The one that made her feel as if his life depended on him discovering her secrets.

Shifting uncomfortably in her chair, Torie offered Spencer a smile when he looked her way to see what might be wrong.

"Do you need more tea?" Spencer was out of his seat instantly. "I'll just run over and get you a fresh cup, shall I?" He didn't give Torie time to refuse or accept. Before she could say a thing, he whisked the empty cup out of her hands and strode across the lawn, heading for the tent where the ladies of the church were serving refreshments.

Thomas Blankenship watched Spencer scurry away. He did not look Torie in the eye but glanced at her sidelong, a tiny smile threatening to destroy the pious expression he tried so hard to maintain at all times. "He is quite devoted to you, isn't he? He has told me all that is in his heart just, as I believe, he has told you." Blankenship's face flushed like a girl's. "I do not believe I am overstepping my bounds, Miss Broadridge, when I say that I believe Mr. Westin would like to do more for you than just fetch you cups of tea."

"More for her? Or to her?"

How Gabriel crossed the lawn and approached without her knowing it, Torie could not imagine. But he was suddenly there, smiling down at them, devilment sparkling in his eyes along with the last rays of the setting sun.

"I beg your pardon?" Blankenship was neither a fool nor an innocent. Torie knew that. He was simply trying his best to maintain some sense of decorum. He gave Gabriel a vacant look, as if he had not heard, or if he had, as if he had no idea what Gabriel might be getting at. "You'll join us, won't you, Mr. Raddigan?" With the skill of an illusionist, Blankenship changed the subject by waving his hand. He indicated the chair Spencer had just vacated. "We have been discussing Mr. Westin's dinner party. The one planned for later in the week. You'll be joining us there, won't you?"

Gabriel settled himself in the chair. "Of course I'll be there," he told the rector though Torie knew full well that Spencer had not yet invited him. "Mr. Westin includes me in all his dinner invitations." He swiveled in the chair so that he was facing Torie. "Isn't that so, Miss Broadridge?"

She was saved from answering by Spencer's return.

The way Spencer's face fell when he saw Gabriel in his chair made Torie think of how Napoleon might have looked had he ever seen Louis, the Bourbon king, sitting on his throne. Spencer's eager smile faded. His shoulders slumped. He shot a look of distaste Gabriel's way, one that was equaled in intensity only by the similar look Gabriel shot back.

"Mr. Raddigan." Spencer nodded, a curt, abrupt movement that made his dun-colored hair flop into his eyes. Just when it looked as if all was lost, that Gabriel had supplanted him both in his chair and in nearness to Torie, he remembered the tea.

A smile lit Spencer's face. Bending at the waist, he proffered the teacup to her.

It was the third cup of tea Spencer had brought her within the hour, and she was hardly anxious for it, but Torie accepted the tea anyway and took a sip. Though she could not for an instant understand it, the antipathy Gabriel and Spencer felt for each other was palpable. It crackled in the air like electricity.

Torie took another, longer, drink and clinked her cup back on the saucer, eager to make some noise—any noise—that might shatter the awkward silence as well as the conspicuous tension that filled the air.

Reverend Blankenship felt it too, Torie was certain of that. He winced as if the seat of his chair was suddenly too hot. "I've been telling Mr. Raddigan about the dinner party," Blankenship said, scrambling for a safe topic of discussion. "He assures me he will join us there."

"Good. Good." Spencer rubbed his hands together. He sounded pleased, but he didn't look it. He cast a quick glance at Gabriel, and Torie couldn't help but notice that his eyes, usually so benign, were dark with distaste. "You and Mr. Raddigan will have much to talk about there, no doubt," Spencer said, turning to the minister. "You have a great deal in common. Raddigan is an Oxford man, too."

It took no more than a' moment for Blankenship to reply, but in that one moment, Torie felt Gabriel go rigid at her side. His manner changed, as abruptly as if the wind had suddenly shifted and come around at them from the other side. Where before he was glib and relaxed, now he was alert, every fiber of his being flashing his wariness.

Torie could not blame him. The subject of Gabriel's ignominious expulsion from Oxford was not one they had ever discussed. It was not something she ever wanted to discuss, not something she ever wanted to even think about. Her opinion of Gabriel's character had been largely formed by what she knew of his past. It was not an opinion that set well with the current of excitement she felt when he looked at her, not one that coincided in any shape or form to the thrill she felt at his touch or the irrational, mercurial effect of his kisses.

She did not understand it. Not in the least. And that meant, of course, that there was only one way to deal with it. She had decided to keep it completely from her mind.

But while Torie was more than happy to avoid the subject of Gabriel's sullied reputation, Spencer was, apparently, not. His smile widened when Blankenship took the bait.

"Oxford? Really?" His hands flat against his knees, his pudgy cheeks aquiver with excitement, Blankenship turned to Gabriel. "I am a Trinity man myself, and was a fellow there for a year or so before this living came available."

"Were you?" It was something Spencer knew, surely, for it was a story Torie herself had heard the Reverend Blankenship tell time and again. Yet Spencer acted as if it were all fresh to him, and all of it exciting. He shuffled from foot to foot, too eager to keep still. "Then you two must have been in Oxford at the same time! You may have heard of Mr. Raddigan. From what I've been told, he was a student of some renown."

Torie saw Gabriel's fingers fold under themselves into fists. His knuckles were white. He did not look away, but kept his gaze fixed on Spencer, a gaze that, had Spencer been more perceptive, he would not dared to have met without backing down.

Torie knew exactly what Gabriel would have told her had he been able to read her thoughts at that moment. He would have told her he could fight his own battles, that he did not need any woman to come to his aid, especially not her.

Yet she could not resist. Spencer's self-satisfied smile made Torie's blood steam like a kettle at the boil. What he was doing to Gabriel was unfair and spiteful. It was unlike Spencer to be so malicious, but right now, Torie did not have the time to wonder why he was acting the way he was, she knew only that she had to do whatever she could to stop it.

"Mr. Westin?" Being careful to maintain an air of perfect indifference, Torie tugged at Spencer's sleeve.

Spencer ignored her.

Gabriel never moved. Torie saw a muscle at the base of his jaw tense. He didn't look at her. He didn't need to. He knew she was trying to rescue him, and it was quite apparent he didn't appreciate her interference one bit.

Blankenship ignored Torie, too. He was so delighted, he fairly leapt from his chair. "What a joy to find another man of learning in these parts!" he said. "Not that Mr. Westin isn't a fine companion, but he is, after all, a Cambridge man." Blankenship laughed at his own joke. "What college were you at, Mr. Raddigan? And what year did you matriculate?"

"Oh, bother!"

Torie let out a cry as her teacup fell out of her hands and onto her skirt. She vaulted from her chair, brushing at the quickly growing brown stain with one hand. "Dear me! I'm so very sorry. I was so engrossed in your discussion, I did not pay attention to what I was doing. Do forgive me, Reverend Blankenship, for disturbing things so." She turned a wide, innocent smile on Spencer, one she did not dare offer to Gabriel. "I'm so sorry. I've interrupted your conversation."

"I'll get you a cloth." Reverend Blankenship was out of his chair in an instant, heading for the rectory.

"And I'll get you another cup of tea." Spencer followed suit, looking, no doubt, to get back into Torie's good graces.

Gabriel didn't say a thing until they were both out of range. "And I'll thank you to mind your own business." He rose from his chair and pulled himself up to his full height, glaring down at Torie. "I didn't need saving."

She returned the glare. "You didn't need saving, or you didn't need me to save you?"

"Don't you remember? I don't need you for anything. I owe you nothing but my summer. And you?" Gabriel looked her up and down. It wasn't the kind of look he'd used when they were alone together in the library earlier this week. There was no invitation in the sparkle that simmered in his eyes, no suggestion of promised delights, only a bite that chilled Torie to the bone. "You don't owe me anything. Not now. Not ever. And I don't ever need a woman to save me."

Spencer chose that very moment to come back with her

tea. Her gaze still fixed on Gabriel, Torie grabbed the cup and drank it down. When Gabriel spun on his heels and headed out across the lawn, she didn't even take the time to thank Spencer. She banged the cup back on its saucer, handed the whole to Spencer, and without a word of explanation, went after Gabriel.

She caught up with him in the churchyard.

Torie did not realize how quickly she'd covered the space between the rectory and the ancient graveyard that stood at the side of St. John's Church. Her head was spinning by the time she got there, the curious dizziness caused no doubt, by the combination of being in the sun all day and the irritation that flowed through her now like a swift running stream.

She grabbed for the closest headstone to steady herself. It was as old as the church and worn smooth by hundreds of years of wind and rain. Even after a perfect day filled with sunshine, the stone felt icy beneath her fingers.

"Are you sure you didn't need saving?" She called after Gabriel. "What were you planning on doing, sitting there merry as May and telling the Reverend Mr. Blankenship the truth? If you recall correctly, the truth is hardly fit conversation for polite company."

Torie's words sounded no more steady than her head felt, but they were enough to stop Gabriel in his tracks. He swung around. What had been a glare before was now a scowl on his face, but he did manage a laugh. The sound of it was as cold as the shadows that crept between the stones. "The truth? What do you know about the truth?"

What did she know?

Torie massaged her temples with the tips of her fingers. Her head throbbed. Her vision clouded as the light dimmed. It was impossible to look Gabriel in the eye and discuss this. She did not know why. She knew only that just thinking about what Gabriel had done at Oxford caused her heart to sink.

Torie looked away.

"I know all I need to know," she said. "I know far more than I think you would like the Reverend Blankenship and the rest of Cuckfield to know."

"Do you?" His face lost in shadow, Gabriel advanced on her. Closing the space between them in three long, restless strides, he stood opposite her, the gravestone between them like an impassable wall. He snatched Torie's hands into his, forcing her to look into his eyes. "What is the truth?" he asked.

"The truth?" Torie's voice sounded hollow in her ears. It was hard to hear with her heart pounding and her blood rushing inside her head like a cataract. "The truth is that you . . . The truth is that at Oxford you . . ." Torie swallowed hard.

She knew the story as well as she knew her own name. Roger had told it to her a hundred times, and she'd heard it repeated again and again on her most recent visit to Oxford. But now that it came down to it, she found she could not speak the words. They wedged in her throat, but whether from emotion or disgust, she didn't know.

Mumbling his impatience, Gabriel cast her hands aside. "The truth is that I was sent down from University. Is that it, Torie? Is that what you find so hard to say? Go ahead, try it. You'll find it gets easier in time. The words used to stick in my throat, too. They don't anymore. I've found that if I keep my gullet well lubricated, the words practically fly out. Brandy serves the purpose nicely, but then, you know that truth, too, don't you?"

This was not what she had come to hear, though why she had even bothered to follow Gabriel into the churchyard was as much a mystery to Torie now as why her hands were trembling. She clutched at the worn gravestone, her fingers fitted around the remains of an angel with a faded face.

"No." She shook her head. "I don't want to hear it. I don't want to know—"

"Don't want to know the truth?" There was a razor's edge of sarcasm in Gabriel's voice, one that cut though Torie like a knife. He gripped the headstone, his hands on either side of hers, and bent to look her in the eyes. His face was as hard as the stone beneath her fingers. And as cold.

"I thought that's what this summer was all about," he said. "A summer of searching for the truth. Bringing secrets into the light. Isn't that what you want to do? Isn't that why Roger was looking for that damned dragon?"

Before she could even think to answer, he seized her shoulders and drew her up against him, the gravestone pressed into her midsection, his face only inches from hers. Gabriel's eyes blazed at her. His words hit her like blows, wounding where they landed. "Do you want the truth, Torie? Because I'm just the man who will give it to you. I'll be more than happy to tell you the truth about what happened in Oxford. About the fool of a faculty member who was down on his luck. He needed money. And I needed all the help I could get on a particularly difficult examination. Had I gotten the highest score, I would have earned a double first. Top of my class in both the classics and mathematics. That's a very important honor at Oxford and the truth is, I would have done anything to get it. I could feel that double first burning away at my insides with that same, fierce fire I sometimes feel when I look at you."

Gabriel laughed again, and Torie wasn't sure if he was laughing at her or at his own folly. His words echoed against the church and ricocheted among the gravestones. "The truth? The truth came out at the hearing, didn't it? The one presided over by the college chancellor. The one attended by every fellow and faculty member. The one that had people waiting in the streets to hear the decision.

And do you know what they heard? Of course you do! If you didn't, you wouldn't be looking at me that way, as if this poor, dead beggar at our feet had more right to dignity than I do."

"No!" Instinctively Torie fought against his harsh words, even though she was certain Gabriel was not listening. His mind was as far away as the look in his eyes.

His gaze traveled from her face up to the dome of flickering stars above, and he shook his head as if, after all these years, he still could not believe what had happened. "I got the double first, you know. But in the end, they said I didn't earn it. They said I bought it. Because I bribed the one faculty member who had the answers to the examination. They had proof, after all. The faculty member's word against mine. A copy of his examination found in my digs."

He pulled himself away from whatever visions darkened his eyes and looked at Torie. "You want the truth? Well, there it is. The truth is, I was sent down, expelled. My reputation was in shreds. The truth is, I went to my father for help. He was a merchant in London. A man of some renown. He didn't want to hear a thing about it. He refused to see me and forbade my mother from having any communication with me. He disowned me." Gabriel's gaze darted to the church. His expression was as hard as granite, but his eyes simmered with anger and some other emotion that was deeper and as endless as the universe of stars that sparked around them. "I never spoke to either one of my parents again," he said. "They are both dead now."

As if discarding the uncomfortable memories, Gabriel twitched his shoulders. A sarcastic smile lifted the corners of his mouth and he darted a look at Torie. "If it wasn't for a doddering uncle I never met who chose to make me his heir, I would have been penniless, out on the street. As it was, the old man was a good enough sport to die before the news of my disgrace made its way to him. I had his fortune to squander, and I must say, I've done a damned fine job of it. Since all my old friends abandoned me, I found new friends. Ones who were only too happy to help me lead a life of dissipation and lechery."

For just a moment, Torie thought he was about to say something more. A muscle at the base of Gabriel's jaw clenched and his lips parted as if there were still words there, ones that he had to fight to contain. He searched her face, his gaze raking, probing, so candid and blunt, it made Torie shiver.

As suddenly as he'd grabbed her, Gabriel let her go. He brushed his hands together as if ridding himself of the feel of her. "You wanted the truth. There it is. Except for the last of it. But of course, you know that, too, don't you?"

This time, he did not allow her the comfort of answering for her. He stood there waiting, his fists on his hips, his eyes boring into hers.

"Yes." Torie could not bear to look at him. "They took the double first from you. They had no choice. They had to award it to the person who really deserved it."

"Really deserved—?" Gabriel's laughter rang through the churchyard. "Good God, you're right! They had to give it to the one who really deserved it. They had to give it to Roger!"

It wasn't what he said. Torie knew the story of how Roger earned his double first. How could she not? By now, it was a part of family legend. No, it was not what Gabriel said that made a shiver snake up Torie's spine. It was the way he said it.

"Can't you leave it alone?" Torie spun away. Her words were angry. Her voice was sharp. She dropped her head into her hands, fighting for control. "It was a long time ago. Do you have to carry it still like a cross upon your shoulders?" Torie passed her hands over her eyes and turned to him. "Do you have to hate Roger because he was better than you?"

Gabriel did not answer. He stood as still as one of the carved monuments, his face as stark and blank as that of the angel on the gravestone.

Torie turned away again. The sun had long since sunk below the horizon and the churchyard was flooded with shadow and as cold as death. But the blackness that surrounded her was more than the darkness of twilight.

This was a blackness Torie could feel, as real as if it were a tight-woven blanket that had been thrown over her head. All she could see were shadows, the shadows of the gravestones and the darker shadows that moved among them. Shadows that swirled, thickened, and crystallized.

Shadows that exploded suddenly into a glittering display of flickering lights.

Chapter 11

"Ah, there you are!"

The vee of distress that creased Spencer's brow smoothed when he saw Torie. He came around the corner from the other side of the church and hurried over to where they were standing. His mouth pinched tight, he cast one quick look of disapproval at Gabriel, then turned his attention to Torie.

"I was quite worried about you, Victoria," Spencer said, his tone as sour as his expression. "It is hardly fitting for a woman to be gone so long by herself and more inappropriate still for her to be alone with a man such as . . . as . . ." The thought made Spencer blanch. Closing his eyes for a moment, he gathered his self-control and began again.

"I was concerned for your safety," he said precisely. "I've been looking all over for you and—!" Spencer took a close look at Torie and his eyes darkened. He lay one hand on her arm. "Victoria, you look odd. Are you ill?"

Torie did not answer him. How could she? If she ever needed proof that she was the only one who saw the lights, she had it now. Both Spencer and Gabriel were knee-deep in flickering lights, yet neither one saw them. They stood watching her, not the yellow lights that sparked among the gravestones like restless souls, nor the blue lights that gleamed against the side of St. John's Church like the flashing eyes of a nocturnal animal on the prowl.

Spencer wrung his hands, his face suddenly pale with worry. Gabriel stood silent, a scornful half-smile making him look more bitter than ever.

She was the only one who saw the lights.

The realization seeped into every corner of Torie's being, chilling her all the way through to her soul.

She may be the only one who saw them now, but she could not forget that Roger had been the first to see the lights.

And everyone knew Roger was mad.

Without a sound, the lights moved over the gravestones, skirting Gabriel and passing through Spencer as if he wasn't there. They closed in on Torie from all sides, captivating, fascinating, mocking her with their mystery and beauty. She tore her gaze from them, forcing herself to look at Gabriel and Spencer, swearing softly that whatever happened, she would not let them know.

She could not.

Pulling back her shoulders, Torie forced a smile. "I feel fine." She directed her statement at Spencer, certain that Gabriel did not care in the least how she felt, especially not now that he had let down his guard enough to reveal the disgraceful details of his past to her.

"It is very late of course," Torie said, picking at a loose thread on her sleeve, eager to give herself something to do to hide her agitation. "I am rather tired. I—"

Torie recoiled as one of the lights shot up from the ground and filled the air between Spencer and herself. It did not touch her, but she was certain if it had, she would have felt its fire scorching her skin.

"You don't look fine. You look ill." Spencer's nostrils flared. When he swung around on Gabriel, his eyes were wide with irritation and alarm. "I say, Raddigan, you haven't enticed Miss Broadridge into tippling any of that infernal brandy you are always swilling, have you? That may work with your town wenches, but Victoria is a lady. She is not used to—"

"Stop acting like a fool!" Gabriel marched over to where they were standing. He bent to look into Torie's eyes and seeing nothing there, he straightened and snorted. "She's as right as rain and you know it." Gabriel gave Spencer a sour look. "Leave the girl be."

"Leave her be? Leave her be?" Spencer flapped around like a butterfly startled from tall grass. "I might have known that would be your reaction." He turned back to Torie and lowered his voice, speaking to her as one might to a child frightened of the dark. "Your skin is pasty. Your breathing is fast and shallow. Your eyes are wide." With one hand, Spencer felt Torie's brow. Satisfied she was not burning with fever, he took her hands in his, casting a glance over his shoulder at Gabriel. He did not lower his voice further and for the briefest of moments Torie wondered why; she was certain Gabriel could hear everything he said.

"I care for you far too much to be treated so poorly, Victoria," Spencer said, his voice petulant. "Please, let me help you. Tell me what's wrong."

The churchyard and everything in it spun in front of Torie's eyes, every inch of it filled with winking, flashing light. She looked away. She would have liked nothing better than to tell Spencer about the lights, to have him try and explain to her how they had somehow crept over the low wall that separated the churchyard from the downs and invaded even this sacred place.

She would have liked nothing better than to point out to him that they were all around, a pool of fire at their feet that could neither be touched nor felt. She would have liked to take Spencer's face between her hands and tip his head up so that he could see the blazing orange light that hung over their heads like a swollen harvest moon, to direct his attention to the roof of the church where the lights taunted her with a macabre dance.

She would have liked nothing more than to ask for Spencer's help. But she could not. It would surely break his heart.

"You're acting like an old woman!" Torie turned back to Spencer and gave him as much of a smile as she could manage. It was an expression he did not return.

Spencer's brows dropped low over his eyes. "You cannot fool me, Victoria," he said. "You're forgetting what I went through with Roger. I know the signs. You see the lights, don't you?"

Torie ripped her hands from Spencer's grasp. Somewhere in the back of her mind she registered an image of Gabriel. His face was nearly eclipsed by the brilliant blue light that trailed directly before him, but she caught a glimpse of his expression. She was not sure if he looked surprised, or angry, and if her head wasn't whirling like a child's toy top, she was sure she would have been more inclined to wonder why. Before she ever had the chance, Gabriel advanced on her and, grabbing her arm, he steered her as far from Spencer as he could.

"You heard her, Westin," Gabriel grumbled. "She said it's late and she's tired. Why you're trying to scare the girl is beyond me. You're making more of this than—"

"You're both acting like fools!" Torie disentangled herself from Gabriel's grasp. Barely containing a sob, she spun on her heels and headed out of the churchyard, being careful to sidestep the lights that sparked around her feet and praying that her leave-taking looked no more than that, and not like a retreat. "I am going home."

"Not by yourself."

Gabriel and Spencer answered as one, but Gabriel was the first to move. Without waiting to see if Westin would follow, he went off after Torie.

He might have known Westin would not miss the opportunity to play the gallant. He was at Gabriel's side in an instant, stretching out his stride to keep pace.

"I told you there was cause to worry," Westin puffed. "You cannot tell me there is nothing wrong with the girl. She's upset. She's terrified. You saw the way she looked about the churchyard, as if there was something there, something she could see but we could not."

The fact that they were within earshot of the church and whatever celestial beings might reside in its environs did not enter into Gabriel's head. He let go with a foul word spoken with great enthusiasm. Before the echo of the single-syllable oath had even died away, he was off across the lawn where most of the residents of Cuckfield were still blissfully enjoying the evening's last cup of tea.

He paid not the least bit of attention to the Reverend Blankenship who bounced out of his chair at the sight of Gabriel, looking like he wanted to corner him for a long, friendly chat. He pointedly ignored Miss Wayne and her matchmaking mother, both of whom looked like starving beggars at a banquet, watching helplessly as the most delectable dish on the table was snatched from under their very noses. He didn't even give Westin another thought, though the man was right beside him every step of the way.

He kept his gaze fixed firmly on Torie's back, watching her carefully as she scrambled through the crowd, heading for the path that led across the downs and on toward home.

Gabriel mumbled another curse though, at this point, he wasn't even sure who he was damning, Torie or himself. It was more than obvious that Torie wanted to be alone. What wasn't obvious, not even to him, was why he couldn't just let her have her way.

What difference did it make, he asked himself, if she wanted to play the coy female and disappear in the middle of the night's festivities? What business was it of his if she chose to be quiet, mysterious, and incomprehensible?

Damn the woman, why did he mind so much that he had relaxed his defenses and revealed himself to her, and that he might have revealed even more given half the chance? Why did her reaction to the details of his past sting inside him in a place he thought no longer existed, a place he counted on as being empty and immune to such responses, the place that used to hold his heart?

His mood already foul, Gabriel let his mind wander further down the gloomy path he had marked off for it.

What difference did it make to him that Spencer Westin thought Torie was as mad as May-butter, and that he wanted to coddle her because of it? Perhaps that was exactly what a woman like Torie needed, a good bit of coddling to go along with the restrained, silent, and perfectly tedious lovemaking that was evidently Westin's specialty.

At the thought, Gabriel pulled to a stop.

Was that what this was all about?

Gabriel stood rooted to the spot and if Westin stopped to see what might be wrong, it was no more than an instinctive reaction, one he conquered in less than a moment. With a look over his shoulder at Gabriel that was almost a triumphant sneer, Westin hurried to catch Torie up.

"Studying how the land lies, are you?" Reverend Blankenship appeared at Gabriel's side. He did not look at Gabriel, but kept his gaze fixed right where Gabriel's was, on the disappearing figures of Torie and Spencer Westin. For all his youth, Blankenship looked as avuncular a man as any Gabriel had ever known, yet his eyes held a sparkle of cunning that would have done some of Gabriel's more disreputable acquaintances proud.

His hands clasped loosely behind him, his weight resting back upon his heels, the clergyman sniffed, politely advancing further into the subject. "As one Oxford man to another," he said, "I feel obliged to tell you, Westin has asked for her hand."

Gabriel stopped himself just short of telling the Reverend Blankenship exactly what he thought of that bit of information. He decided instead that the facts of the matter would serve his purpose more completely than profanity, at least in this instance. "I know all about that," he said, struggling to keep the emotion that accompanied the admission out of his voice. He poked his chin in the direction Torie had gone. "What I don't understand is her. Fine one minute and off like a shot the next, with Westin at her heels like a groveling pup. Was it part of their plan, do you think?"

Gabriel had not meant to speak the question out loud. It didn't make him feel any better when he realized Blankenship wasn't the least bit surprised by it.

"You mean, do I think they wanted to be alone together?" His lips pursed, Blankenship considered the question. "That all depends," he said, and if Gabriel didn't know he was a man of the cloth and didn't trust that because of it, he was more compassionate than lesser men, he would have said Blankenship was playing devil's advocate, that he was answering Gabriel's question with one of his own to force Gabriel to find all the answers himself. "What happened before she left?"

Gabriel leaned back against the nearest tree, one leg bent, his foot resting against the trunk. "Before she left, Torie was as nervous as could be," he confessed. "She seemed agitated, eager to get away."

"And Westin?"

Gabriel couldn't help himself. He grumbled a word he should not have used in Blankenship's presence. "Westin spent a good portion of the time wringing his hands and mouthing words of distress. The bastard's trying to convince the poor girl that there's something wrong with her, that she's as deranged as her lunatic brother."

"But?" In spite of his benevolent expression, Blankenship did not miss a thing. He could not help but remark on the note of skepticism in Gabriel's voice.

"But he didn't look worried," Gabriel said, his eyes narrowing, his mind traveling back to the scene Torie and Westin had played out before him in the churchyard. "Westin didn't look upset. He looked . . ." He grappled with the memory, struggling to find the right way to explain. "He looked anxious," he finally said, satisfied the word reflected the singular mood of the incident.

"Like a man who was waiting for something?"

"Like a man impatient to be alone with the woman he loved."

This didn't seem to surprise Blankenship, either, and the realization did little to improve Gabriel's disposition. Blankenship nodded. "And who could blame him?" A flush of color rose in his cheeks and he glanced at Gabriel out of the corner of his eye. "I may be a cleric, Mr. Raddigan, but I am also a man. She is far more of a handful than I would like to endeavor to tame, but I can certainly see why Westin is interested in Miss Broadridge. She is outspoken and broad-minded and from what I've heard, stubborn as one of those Oxford fishwives who cry their wares on Cornmarket Street." Blankenship sighed. "But she is an attractive woman. There are some men, I suspect, who would look on conquering her as something of a challenge. Like climbing a mountain."

"Or walking through fire."

Blankenship could not be fooled by the caustic tone of Gabriel's comment. Though his eyes sparkled with a hint of mischief, he somehow managed to retain the note of artlessness in his voice. "You could go after them," he suggested.

"I could," Gabriel agreed. "But what do you imagine I'd find when I got there?"

Blankenship's face turned another two shades darker.

Gabriel couldn't blame him. He supposed that even a man of the cloth was bound to think the same things he was thinking right now.

What would he find if he got home just minutes after Torie and Westin?

Would he find them already locked in an impassioned embrace? Or would he catch sight of them even sooner, in some shadowy bower off the side of the path, making love on a bed of sweet spring grass?

Bracing himself against the images that rose in his brain, Gabriel felt his body tighten in response to the thought. He had to admit, the idea of finding Torie and Westin together held little appeal. But the pictures it conjured!

Torie, on a carpet of wildflowers, each petal soft as her skin and touched with the same pink blush that flamed in her cheeks. Torie, with her gown off and her chemise pushed down around her waist, her bare skin iridescent as pearls in the light of the moon. Torie, with her hair like a gleaming veil around her shoulders, long, silky strands of it lying soft against her breasts.

"Hell!" Gabriel banished the disturbing fantasies with a heartfelt oath.

"Indeed." Blankenship shuffled his feet. He looked so embarrassed, Gabriel wondered if in addition to his talents as a preacher and a saver of souls, he was also a mind reader. Too restless to keep still, or perhaps too afraid that Blankenship really might be able to discern the wayward thoughts that floated through his head, Gabriel pushed away from the tree and took off down the main road that led straight through the heart of Cuckfield.

Blankenship followed behind. "There are two ways you can go, you know," he said, laboring to keep up with the pace Gabriel set. "You could take the path around the west side of the village and follow directly behind Miss Broadridge and Mr. Westin, or you could go south and come at the house along the path that skirts High Brill."

Gabriel tossed him a look. "Are you suggesting—"

"I'm not suggesting a thing." Reverend Blankenship pulled to a stop and out of propriety, Gabriel was obliged to do the same. Blankenship gave him a sympathetic thump on the shoulder. "I'm only saying it's a fine night, and you might want to take your time getting home."

With that, the clergyman turned and headed back to the church fete.

His astonishment complete, Gabriel stood in the center of the lane. Was the Reverend Blankenship recommending he go the long way about because he knew exactly what Gabriel would find when he got home?

Gabriel kicked at a loose stone, sending it skittering into the dark. He should follow the man's advice, he told himself, not because he wanted to, but because he knew it was the right thing, the honorable thing, to do. The least lovers deserved was a bit of privacy, and by taking the long way about, he would allow Torie and Westin some time alone.

Gabriel shook his head, as amazed with the thought as he was with himself.

Although he thought he had settled the matter this afternoon, there was still something about the idea of Westin being Torie's secret lover that didn't set right with him. It made his gut feel queer, as if he'd held on too long to a bellyful of cheap spirits.

The idea that it might be jealousy occurred to him, but only for a moment. He dismissed it in short order and got down to the heart of the matter.

This was getting ridiculous, he told himself again and again. This endless obsession about Miss Broadridge and her mysterious paramour was getting out of hand. It was getting so he couldn't stop thinking about it.

About what they said to each other.

About what they did when they were alone together.

There was only one way to stop it, Gabriel told himself, only one way to settle it, once and for all.

He would find out for certain the identity of Torie's lover and at least satisfy himself on that point.

And he would do it soon.

His mind made up, Gabriel headed toward home.

He was far too irritable to give it a second thought, but somewhere in the back of his mind, he knew that the Reverend Blankenship would be proud of him. His head down, his hands stuffed into his pockets, Gabriel took the long way about.

Gabriel watched the mysterious man leave the house the next morning, and the next, and the morning after that. Each day he hoped to discover some clue to the man's identity, and each day he was disappointed.

The first and third mornings, there was too much fog and rain for him to see any more than the man's retreating figure. The second morning, the sun was directly in Gabriel's eyes and he could see little more than a dark silhouette against the glare.

By the fourth morning, he'd had his fill of intrigue, and he was determined to do something to put an end to it.

When the first sounds of the man creeping about the house came to his ears, Gabriel was ready. He waited until he heard the front door open and shut, then he slipped out of his room and followed.

The man set a brisk pace over the downs and on to the south. The morning, though pleasant, was a bit crisp. In spite of the rate at which they walked, Gabriel was thankful he'd been wise enough to throw on his greatcoat before he hurried out the door.

The fellow was bundled against the morning chill, too.

He was wearing the same shapeless box coat and hat that Gabriel had seen him wear every day. Even from here, one hundred or so paces behind him, Gabriel could tell he was carrying something in his right hand, something that looked like a sack.

Gabriel narrowed his eyes, trying for a better look at the bundle. It wasn't as bulky and cumbersome as the one he'd seen Torie carry, but other than that, it looked the same.

His curiosity piqued, Gabriel found himself watching the way the man swung the sack back and forth to the rhythm of his walk. The fact that Torie's lover took a bundle away from the house each morning, and Torie brought one home with her each evening, only served to heighten the mystery.

After a quarter of an hour's walk, Gabriel watched the man stop at the top of a rise and, one hand up to shield his eyes, look out over the vast emptiness of the downs. Fortunately, he did not turn to look back toward the house, for if he had, he was bound to see Gabriel following. Though the lands around here were dotted with forests and an occasional farm, this area of the downs was particularly desolate.

As far as Gabriel could see, there were nothing but rolling hills, blanketed in green grass and gorse bushes, their flowers bright yellow as the morning sun. Here and there, a sheep stood silent, munching its breakfast, or a low stone wall marked some farmer's meager holding. Far over on his left, a half a mile or so from where he stood, Gabriel could see outcroppings of the chalk that formed the groundwork for these gentle hills, and beyond that, the outline of an ancient stone circle, dark and enigmatic against the brilliant morning sky.

His brief rest over, the man ahead took off again. They were not far from the place where the path split, one portion of it leading into Cuckfield, the other heading east toward Spencer Westin's cottage, and Gabriel found himself oddly nervous. With one finger he flicked a thin sheen of perspiration from his brow, and at the same time he wondered at the fact that his hands felt as clammy as his forehead.

It was ludicrous to feel nervy, he told himself, skirting a small stream that split the downs, sparkling like the blade of a knife in the sunlight. It was foolish to wonder what the man would do when he came to the fork in the path.

Would he continue on south? Or would he confirm Gabriel's suspicions and turn off to the left, toward Westin's cottage where tonight, he, Torie, and from what he'd heard rumored, a vast number of their neighbors would gather for a formal dinner party?

Why did it matter so very much?

Gabriel was no closer to an answer to the question now than he had been the last time he'd asked it of himself. Or the time before.

The fact that the mysterious man might be Westin rankled like salt rubbed in a raw wound, though why it should was beyond Gabriel's comprehension. What difference did it make, if Torie's lover was Westin or some other man? A lover was a lover, and no matter who it was, it meant her heart had already been claimed by another.

The thought hit Gabriel like a whack. Unconsciously, he found his hands curling into fists, as if he could somehow strike back.

It was no use, there was no fighting this, and the realization did little to lighten Gabriel's disposition, already soured from too little sleep and far too much mental exercise.

There was no defense against the desire that raced through him each time Torie walked into the room, no protection against the fantasies about her that chose to flit across his mind at the most inconvenient and inappropriate times.

He had no way to guard himself. Not from this. Perhaps that's why it bothered him so. No matter how painful it was, no matter how frustrating, no matter how hellishly baffling, there was no hiding from the truth.

The ache that erupted in Gabriel at the thought was as inexplicable as the ridiculous but undeniable fact that he was tromping over the barren countryside at this ungodly hour, following God knows who, God knows where.

Inexplicable. All of it, inexplicable.

And, still, he was powerless to resist.

The man ahead came to the fork in the path, and Gabriel pulled to a stop, watching his every move. The man did not pause. He headed straight on toward Cuckfield, and Gabriel let out a breath he did not even realize he'd been holding.

It wasn't Westin, he told himself, feeling strangely vindicated by the discovery. His step was suddenly and unaccountably lighter, his head clearer, but whether from the feel of the fresh morning breeze or from relief, even Gabriel did not know.

Revitalized, he hurried after the fellow, carefully closing the gap between them until he could make out details of the man's appearance that, from a distance, had eluded him.

The man was wearing dark trousers, not the light-colored kind that distinguished a gentleman from those of the lower orders. These were loose-fitting and coarsely woven, like the kind Gabriel had seen many a farmer and laborer in the area wear. If Gabriel's eyes were not playing him false, they were also rolled at the ankle, as if they were not originally intended to be worn by the man who was in them now.

The man's boots looked no more elegant than his trousers. They were half Wellingtons and looked to be of reasonable quality, but they were in a dreadful state. The heels were worn, the backs were scuffed and as dirty as the man's coat which was smudged with soil all along the edge, as if it was dragged frequently through the dirt.

Not a gentleman, Gabriel decided with a little snort of something that was not quite revulsion, not quite surprise.

Before he had the time to consider this new and startling development further, Gabriel saw the outline of the village looming upon the horizon like a fuzzy blur on an artist's canvas, only the spire of the parish church rising above the rest, pointing to the heavens like a slender finger. But when Gabriel expected the man to continue into the village, he turned off to the right where, Gabriel knew from talking to the locals at the King's Head pub, there was a quarry where stone was dug for roadbed repairs.

Gabriel paused at the top of the steep slope that led down into the quarry. From here, he could see the mystery man perfectly without any chance of being seen. The quarry was ringed with trees, its perimeter dotted with boulders, and Gabriel concealed himself behind one of these and watched the man scramble down the embankment. He tossed his bundle to the ground, searched through it, and came up holding something that glinted like metal in the light of the morning sun. Dropping to his knees, he got to work.

"Hell and damnation." His mind just beginning to register the significance of the scene, Gabriel sat back and watched. From this distance, it was impossible to see exactly what was going on, but Gabriel knew enough of the methodology to make an educated guess.

The man was digging, digging in a place that had obviously been painstakingly worked before.

The small patch of dirt where the man worked was marked off with long, straight lines that had been scored into the earth to keep it separate from the rest of the quarry floor. There was a small pile of rocks arranged neatly to one side of him, another, larger heap to the other.

What the man was looking for was as obvious as the fact that he had yet to find it.

He was looking for Torie's dragon bones.

Before Gabriel could stop himself, he was on his feet, moving toward the track that led down to the quarry floor.

He really didn't give a damn about Torie's ridiculous dragon, Gabriel reminded himself, hurrying headlong down the path. He didn't really give a damn about continuing Roger Broadridge's work or furthering his reputation. What he did give a damn about was the fact that he'd spent a good bit of the last month staring at the walls and playing Patience, swearing off—as much as any man could—the delights of good liquor and the distractions he might have found in the arms of the local serving girls.

What he did give a damn about was that something was going on here, something he could not quite understand, something that made his pulse pound like a bass drum inside his head and his blood burn in his veins.

Gabriel stood with his fists on his hips and watched as the man carefully dug through the dirt with a small trowel, so completely engrossed in his work, he did not note Gabriel's presence.

Carefully, he scooped away a tiny square of earth, picked through it with fingers already coated with dirt, and started digging again. It was slow, tedious work.

Work Gabriel had been brought to Sussex to do.

The thought reverberated through his brain like cannon shot. Without another second's hesitation, Gabriel grabbed the man by the arm, hauled him to his feet, and spun him around.

He heard the fellow's startled cry, but even that was not enough to penetrate his anger. It was a full second before he realized that the eyes that stared up into his were green, that the face, though pale and drawn as if by worry, was smooth and pink, that the arm beneath his grip was slim.

Gabriel tore the shapeless hat from the fellow's head, and a cascade of straw-colored hair tumbled over shoulders that were slender and far more delicate than any man's.

The shock was enough to cause Gabriel to catch his breath.

He stared at the person caught in his arms, his voice reverberating back at him from the steep sides of the quarry walls, echoing his disbelief.

"You!"

Chapter 12

"Let me go!"

Torie fought to twist free of the iron grip on her arm. Though she tried to sound stouthearted, she could not help but think it would be easier to be brave if she could see her opponent.

But whoever had grabbed hold of her had effectively taken care of that. When he plucked Roger's hat from her head, her hair came down into her eyes. She was blind, and she was frightened.

"I'll give you one last warning," she cried out. "Let go of me!" When that didn't work, she fought back the only way she could. She rammed her fist, and the butt end of her trowel, into the man's midsection. The tactic was certainly not original, but it was quite effective.

"Bloody damn!"

The man yelped and loosened his hold.

Keeping the tool poised in front of her like a sword, Torie darted away. She tossed her head back, scooping her hair out of her eyes.

"Mr. Raddigan!" Her breathing harsh and unsteady, her heart beating in double time, Torie stared across the space that separated her from Gabriel. Both his hands were curled into fists, but it was obvious he was not about to use them to attack her. He had them pressed into his stomach, and his face looked odd, his skin the color of the pale green leaves that overhung the edge of the quarry.

Her eyes wide, Torie stared at Gabriel's hands, half expecting to see a trickle of blood spread between his fingers and soak the front of his greatcoat. She took one step forward and lowered the trowel as a kind of a peace offering. "I haven't killed you, have I?"

The word Gabriel used in reply was not one Torie had ever heard before. She supposed it was because she led something of a sheltered life and for once, she was glad of it. She did not need to know the word to catch its meaning.

"Well, what did you expect?" she said, instinctively defending herself and deciding that if Gabriel was in fine enough form to be talking like his old self, she had done him no real damage. "You scared me to death. You can't just creep up on a person unawares and—!"

Torie's understanding of the situation dawned as her surprise began to fade. She looked from Gabriel to the place where she had been digging, and from there, to the trowel she still held tight in her fingers. Her mouth suddenly dry, she ran her tongue over her lips. "What are you doing here?" she asked.

"I think, perhaps, that's a question I should be asking you." Gabriel uncurled his fists slowly, as if he, too, was afraid there might be blood. Satisfied there was none, he winced and studied the wide smear of dirt that covered the front of his coat. He rubbed his stomach and eyed Torie as if he wasn't quite sure whether she would attack again. "You're damned lucky I didn't have breakfast this morning," he said.

"Then perhaps it's time we went back and got something to eat." Torie tossed the trowel on the ground, brushed the dirt from her hands, and turned to head toward the path that led out of the quarry. "It's getting on to seven o'clock," she said, making a great show of studying the position of the sun. "You must be famished. Why don't we—"

She might have known he could not be so easily fooled.

Gabriel grabbed Torie's arm. He did not hold her tight this time and whether he knew it or not, that was her undoing. He gently turned her to face him, and Torie found she could not look him in the eye.

"I asked what you're doing here," Gabriel said.

"I might ask you how you found me." Torie supposed she sounded confident enough, she only hoped he did not see that her hands were shaking. She darted him a look. "You haven't been following me, have you?"

"Following you?" Gabriel threw his hands in the air. He stepped away from her and Torie breathed a sigh of relief. But no sooner had he moved away when he came back at her again, his voice infinitely patient, but his eyes sparking with barely suppressed annoyance. "No," he said, "I haven't been following you. How in the name of the Almighty was I supposed to know it was you? I've been following the man I saw leave the house each morning."

"Following the man—!" Torie laughed. "Were you worried for my safety, Mr. Raddigan? Or for my virtue?"

Her laughter did nothing to check the tide of anger that swept over Gabriel's face. "Worried, hell!" he growled. "What difference does it make what I was worried about? I followed you. And I found you. Now tell me, Miss Broadridge, what the hell is going on here?"

There was no retreating this time. No escape. Torie cursed herself once for being careless enough to let Gabriel catch on to her scheme so easily, and then a second time for not listening to her heart when it warned her weeks ago that he was not the kind of man who would sit idly by and let the summer pass quietly.

This was not the way it was supposed to happen.

The words pounded in Torie's head, as harsh as the

sound of her own breathing. She had not meant things to turn out this way. But how could she have anticipated the thrill of excitement that would snake through her every time Gabriel looked her way? How could she have predicted that a man with no family, a man with no reputation, a man with no honor, would cause her to feel things she had never felt before?

Torie dashed the thoughts aside with a feeble gesture toward the place she'd been working. "I am digging," she said, and waited, tense and rigid, for Gabriel's reply.

"Digging." Something in the way he spoke the single word made the hair at the nape of Torie's neck stand on end. He looked her up and down, his gaze traveling from Roger's old, dusty coat to Roger's half Wellingtons caked with mud. "Digging dressed as a man." Gabriel shook his head. "And I must be as dull as Jack's dog. I still don't understand. Are you telling me you leave the house every morning dressed in those old clothes and come back each evening—" His gaze landed on the parcel that sat on the ground at their feet.

Bending down, Gabriel tugged the bag open and lifted Torie's old black gown from inside it. He looked up at her, the gown clutched in his fingers. "And come back each evening dressed again as yourself?"

"Yes. That's correct." It was the absolute truth, and Torie wrapped it around herself like a heavy mantle against a winter chill. Confident of the strength of her argument as well as its righteousness, she gave Gabriel a level look.

"And you donned this strange disguise for what reason?" he asked. "To keep me from knowing it was you stealing about the house each morning? Or was it to keep me from knowing where you were going?"

He was getting far too close to the truth, and the realization did little to help calm Torie's already jangled nerves. She tossed her head and dismissed his questions with a ladylike sniff. "I don't see that how I choose to dress is any concern of yours. It may be unusual for a woman to wear her brother's old clothing, but there is certainly nothing indecent about it. As to how I spend my day . . . I am afraid I don't see how that concerns you, either."

Gabriel dropped the gown back in the bag. "Nor do I," he admitted, his voice even. He crossed his arms over his chest and settled back, yet for all his indifference, Torie could not help but notice that his eyes were aflame, sparks of copper and foxy brown lighting their dark depths. "And I wouldn't give a blue damn if you were doing what I thought you were doing. What a fool I was," he said with a sharp bark that was almost a laugh. He gazed up at the bright blue sky as if looking for the answers to the questions that puzzled him. "You see, when I saw that man leaving the house each morning, I thought you had a lover."

Torie felt her cheeks flame. Blessedly, Gabriel did not leave her time to reply, for if he had, she was not certain what she would have said.

Gabriel's expression clouded, but his voice remained as even and casual as if they'd been discussing nothing more momentous than tonight's dinner party at Spencer's. "I wouldn't care if you spent the entire day and half the night on your back with Westin or some other fellow," he said. "What I do care about is that instead, you spend your day digging. Damn me for an idiot, Miss Broadridge, but I could have sworn that's what you were paying me to do."

His words were painful enough. The way he said them could not be endured. Torie controlled her outrage, but it took all her effort and left her trembling.

"This wasn't the way it was supposed to happen," she said, each word carefully spoken. "You weren't supposed to find out this way. You weren't supposed to be the person you are."

Gabriel's brows dropped low over his eyes. "What wasn't supposed to happen?" he demanded, his voice a mix of anger and incredulity. "What the hell are you talking about?"

Now that the time had come to explain, Torie found that she did not have the words. Frustrated, she turned away. "You weren't supposed to care," she said, her explanation sounding feeble and not nearly thorough enough, even to her.

"Wait a minute." Torie did not have to look at Gabriel to sense his frustration. She could hear it in the ragged breaths he drew in and let go, in the fitful, pacing sound of his boots against the grit and sandstone that carpeted the quarry floor. "Are you telling me——?"

There was no keeping it from him any longer, she told herself, and turning, Torie fixed her gaze on Gabriel and refused to look away.

"No one was more surprised than I when Roger earned that double first at Oxford," she said. In spite of the ball of emotion that wedged in her throat at the thought, she managed a small, cynical laugh. "Well, perhaps you were even more surprised," she added with a tart smile. "But not in the same way."

When it looked as if Gabriel might try and speak, Torie raised her hand to silence him. She would not quarrel with him. She would not listen to his protests or his arguments. Not now. Now it was time to let the truth into the open. And the truth hurt.

"I dared express my astonishment to my parents," Torie confessed, and the pain of the memory still stung her heart. "I was told quite explicitly to keep my opinions to myself. Roger was a man, after all, and as such, was divinely ordained to be not only smarter than I, but more accomplished and more successful than I could ever be."

Torie feared her words sounded bitter, but she was past caring. Steeling her courage, she swallowed hard and continued with her story, determined to have done with it before her own quickly failing nerve and the thunderous look on Gabriel's face convinced her to do otherwise.

"The truth is, Mr. Raddigan, I always thought Roger was a poor student. Once he was graduated from Oxford, my suspicions were confirmed. Roger was an incompetent scientist at best. At worst, I suppose I would be forced to characterize him as lazy and disinterested. He much preferred visiting with Spencer and sharing the stories of his supposed findings to actually working to make the discoveries. He had nothing to do with all this. Roger did not find the tooth." Torie passed one hand over her eyes and smiled a bittersweet smile, one that wavered on the edge of tears.

"Dear God," she sighed, "Roger didn't even care about the tooth. The tooth is mine, Mr. Raddigan." She brought one hand to her heart and held it there and her voice shook with the emotion she found impossible to keep in check. "I found it. Me! I am the one who traveled to London and rooted through the thousands of specimens to identify it. I am the one who decided that if there were teeth, there must be bones, also. And I am the one who comes to this place each day and looks for them. It is my discovery. Not Roger's. My dragon."

Gabriel's astonishment could not have been more complete. He stared at her in wonder, his lips parted. Torie listened to the beat of her own heart, waiting until he found his voice.

Gabriel cocked his head and whether he meant it or not, a small smile of begrudging admiration lightened his expression. "I wondered at it, of course," he said quietly, as if talking to himself. "Roger's reputation . . . His studies on comparative anatomy . . . His writings on Huttonian theory . . . I could not walk through Oxford without hearing Roger Broadridge's brilliance proclaimed from the mouth of some academician or another and it always struck me as absurd. Worse than absurd. It was ludicrous! And you're telling me—?"

"I'm telling you they were mine! They were all mine!" Torie lifted her head and held it high and steady.

For years, she'd been lying to protect Roger's precious reputation. For years, she'd been covering up his mistakes and making excuses for his lapses of memory. Each time she had effectively defended Roger. Each time, she had managed to successfully maintain the pretense of his scientific ability, the value of his work, the importance of the man and his methods and his achievements. She had defended her brother so many times, she had almost come to believe the stories herself.

It was time now to scatter the clouds of dishonesty that shadowed her life. Time to bring the truth into the light.

Torie hauled in a deep breath of sweet morning air. "After he received his double first from Oxford, Roger never did another day's work in his life," she confessed. "I wrote the articles, Mr. Raddigan. I completed the research. Of course it all had to be published under Roger's name." She laughed, a sound completely without humor.

"I would be accepted with open arms if I was out and about doing charitable works. I would be proclaimed as a paragon if I could ply a needle and do delicate embroidery. If I chose to give birth to twelve children, I would be blessed, beatified, and canonized. But I do not do any of those things. Instead, I study the earth and what's in it, and attempt to determine what might have lived millions of years ago, right here in this place where we are standing. And because I am a woman, my findings are invalid. Useless. They would be ignored completely if the truth were known. They would be ridiculed. No, the only way my discoveries will ever be accepted is if they are published under a man's name."

"So Roger gave up his manhood. He allowed himself to take credit for all the things you did." If Torie didn't know better, she would have said Gabriel no longer looked surprised. He nodded, as if confirming some long-held suspicion to himself, but he still looked detached, as if the whole thing were nothing more than an interesting mental exercise.

"And last autumn when Roger died . . ." Gabriel began to work his way through it. Whether he realized it or not, his keen reasoning was leading him inexorably toward the truth, and Torie braced herself for the moment he would come to it.

"Last autumn when Roger died . . . ." He started again.

Torie could not stand idly by and watch him suffer. No matter what she thought of the man, of his character, or his past, she could not bear to hear him struggle with the words it was so obviously her duty to speak.

"Last autumn when Roger died, I had to find someone to take his place," she said before she could stop herself. "Someone who would let me be about my work without any interference. I went to Oxford and searched for the most likely candidate. My requirements were quite modest. I needed a man who had no other options, one who wouldn't question me or what I was about. I found only one desperate enough to suit my purposes. You."

"Desperate enough." Gabriel's words echoed her own, but his voice was as different from hers as night from day. Where hers trembled with emotion, his was icy. Where hers faltered, embarrassment and remorse blocking her throat, his rumbled through the quarry like the sounds of an approaching storm.

In the split second before it broke, Gabriel looked as if the blow to the stomach he'd received earlier really had done him some harm. His face drained of color. His expression was blank. The next instant, all that was changed. He looked at her, his eyes flashing, and before she could even think to move away, he snatched her arm and hauled her to him.

"You didn't want Morrison. You didn't want Granger. You didn't want Cronkite." Gabriel's voice sizzled like lightning. "You didn't want any of them because you knew they'd want some say so in what went on here. You wanted me. You wanted me because I was a worthless drunkard." He tightened his hold, his fingers pressing her flesh until Torie winced.

Even so, she did not dare to move. She watched as the significance of all that had happened in the last month penetrated Gabriel's anger. A muscle at the base of his jaw tightened and the expression on his face darkened from anger to stark awareness.

"That's why you didn't care that I spent my days staring at the four walls and that damned, ugly picture of Roger," he said, a vein at the side of his throat pulsing hard to the cadence of his every word. "Is that why you let me kiss you, too, Torie? Was all that part of the plan to keep me off guard?"

"No." Torie looked away, her cheeks flaming with embarrassment. "Mr. Raddigan, I—"

"Call me Gabriel!" His hand to her chin, Gabriel wrenched her face up to his. "You look at me, and you call me Gabriel."

"Gabriel." Torie backed away a step, the force of his grip easing as she spoke his name. "None of that was supposed to happen, Gabriel," she said, and her heart pounded anew at the memory of his kiss. "You must know that's true."

"As true as the fact that you left brandy bottles all over the house hoping I'd spend the day getting good and drunk and keep well out of your way?"

"Do you think I'm proud of what I did?" Where she found the strength, Torie never knew, but she tore herself from Gabriel's grasp. She did not back away or turn from him, but faced him, trading him angry look for angry look. "Don't you think I would have done it some other way if I had the choice? Don't you believe I would have aligned myself with a real scholar if I could? Don't you suppose I would have shared the prestige of the discovery with some respectable scientist if it meant recognition and publication? But I didn't. I couldn't. You men have made sure of that."

The emotions she had suppressed in the months since Roger's death roiled through Torie like a storm-tossed sea. Somewhere inside her, she knew none of it was Gabriel's fault.

The prejudice. The narrow-mindedness. The mockery. He was not responsible for any of it.

But he was here, and he needed to understand.

"Don't you think I looked for another way?" she asked, her words crashing against the sides of the quarry and washing back over her, every one of them filled with the sting of her humiliation. "No scholar worthy of the title would pass the time of day with me. I know. I tried them all. I had a meeting with your precious Morrison. He had me shown from the room before half of what I had to say was out of my mouth. I talked to the eminent Granger, too. He laughed in my face. I did my best to see Cronkite. They wouldn't let me past the gates at Magdalen. When I ran out of academicians at Oxford, I tried Cambridge. You can imagine the kind of reception I got there. I even went all the way to Paris to see Cuvier. Quite brazen of me, wasn't it, taking it upon myself to visit the most illustrious naturalist in the world? You'll be cheered to know you're in good company. He said all the same things you did when he saw the tooth. He said it is undoubtedly the tooth of a mammal. He said I am certainly mistaken to think it came from Cretaceous rock. He patted me on the shoulder and wished me well and looked at me with large, melancholy eyes, as if I were a simple child who only needed humoring to be shown the error of my ways. I don't need humoring!" Torie screamed the words.

"I didn't come to you because I wanted to," she told Gabriel, and the memory of her desperation rose up in her like a physical thing, making her voice thick. "Dear Lord, who in their right mind would have come willingly to you? From the first day I ever set foot in Oxford to find a collaborator, all I heard were stories about you. The notorious Gabriel Raddigan. The infamous Gabriel Raddigan. I remembered your name, of course. Roger had spoken of you, and never fondly. Can you imagine how it felt for me to come begging to a man who personified everything I disdain?" Torie's shoulders slumped, the immense burden of her own folly like a physical weight upon her.

"I came to you because I had no choice," she said. "You were the only one left."

"The only one left."

For a moment, she thought Gabriel was no longer angry. He repeated her words like a man in a trance, the emotion gone from them, only the bare substance left, the plain, painful syllables. It did not take her long to realize it was because he was angrier than ever. Like a fire left to burn without any attempt to smother it, his anger had gone from red to white-hot. He held his arms tight against his sides, his fingers clenching and unclenching, each of his breaths so rough, she could hear them, one after another, scraping away at all that was left of his self-control.

"You expected me to sit back and do nothing." His voice crackled like flame. "And when you were done looking for your dragon—if, indeed, you found your dragon—you expected to slap my name on your research and present it to the world."

"Yes." It seemed too simple, too feeble, yet for all its inelegance, it was the truth. It was all Torie could say.

"You expected me to be a lazy, drunken sot." Gabriel's words rumbled through the quarry. "You expected me to not care a fig for anything past where the next bottle of brandy would come from or where I'd find the next trollop willing to share my bed."

They were well past the point of lying to each other. Torie knew it. As much as she would have liked to deny it, they were well past being tactful, or even prudent. She raised her chin.

"Yes," she said, and her words were as harsh and plain and ugly as his. "That's exactly what I expected of you. But no matter what else you blame me for, you cannot fault me for that. I only expected the man you, yourself, created."

She watched her words crash over Gabriel like icy waves, each word surrounding him, swallowing him. But instead of dousing his anger, they only heightened it. Too furious to keep still, Gabriel turned and stalked up the path, heading out of the quarry, his parting words overlapping the echo of Torie's.

"You needn't bother wearing the black dress home," he said, each word precise and biting. "It seems the need for masquerades is over. For both of us."

Chapter 13

"Why so vexed? This is what you expected, isn't it?"

Gabriel never turned around. How he knew Torie's nose crinkled and her mouth pinched tight at the smell of brandy that greeted her when she opened the library door, she couldn't imagine. Right now, she didn't care.

"I'm sure I don't know what you're talking about." Keeping her irritation to herself, Torie advanced into the room at the same time she wished with all her might that she hadn't left her good kid gloves in here the last time she wore them. If she'd put them back in her bedroom where they belonged, she could have left for Spencer's dinner party without having to face Gabriel again.

As it was, she crossed the room and gave him only the quickest of glances. Not that she needed to do any more than that. She knew exactly where Gabriel was, just as sure as she knew what he was doing. He was sitting in the chair opposite the fireplace, a tumbler and half-empty bottle on the table next to him.

"Don't act so naive." Gabriel's words were slightly slurred, but the look he gave her was as sober as any she'd ever seen. "You know exactly what I'm talking about. You're pretending to be outraged. You're trying like hell to act shocked. Good heavens!" He gave an exaggerated gasp of horror. "How awful to have a no-account scapegrace in the house, swilling brandy within sight of the sacrosanct picture of the exalted and most fraudulent Saint Roger!" Gabriel laughed and refilled his glass.

"Leave off, my dear Miss Broadridge," he added, and all the humor was gone from his voice as surely as if the brandy had washed it away. "You can't possibly be shocked. You're getting exactly what you expected, a good-for-naught tosspot not worth the powder to blow him to hell."

It was not Gabriel's statement that struck her as much as it was his tone. Torie stood motionless, his words shocking her more than his drinking ever could. Although he did his best to try and sound indifferent, no one but a fool could miss the note of desperation that underpinned the anger in his voice.

For a moment, Torie actually thought to remark on it.

She dismissed that thought with a sigh of resignation. They were beyond discussing anything with objectivity, she reminded herself, whether it be personal matters or fossil teeth. It was unfortunate, but unavoidable. They were beyond everything and anything, anything but the thinnest veneer of courtesy.

Why the thought should cause a dull ache somewhere deep inside her was as peculiar as why her heart was pounding like a drum. Dismissing both thoughts, not because they were inconsequential but because she did not understand them, Torie hurried to her desk.

"All I expect is to locate my gloves and leave for Spencer's," Torie said, her words far too clipped to sound as casual as she would have liked. She moved aside a small collection of fossils and reached for her gloves.

They were not where she'd left them.

She peered beneath a stack of foolscap. They weren't there, either.

Grumbling, Torie unlocked the desk and pulled the top drawer open. The gloves weren't anywhere in sight and she clicked her tongue in annoyance, dropped into her chair, and proceeded to search through the other drawers. "Spencer is sending a gig," she said, desperately trying to fill the uncomfortable silence that sat on the room like a storm cloud. "I would not like to keep the coachman waiting."

"A gig! Westin will carry you there in suitable fashion." Gabriel snickered and his voice dropped to a seductive murmur. "And he'll walk you home in the moonlight."

Shoving aside the contents of the middle desk drawer, Torie felt around the bottom of it for her gloves at the same time she tried her best to ignore Gabriel's words.

It was not the thought of spending time alone with Spencer that made her hands feel sweaty and caused her breath to catch in her throat; it was the thought of being out on the downs at night. The thought that, somewhere along the way, she might again have to face the lights.

Torie slammed the desk drawer shut, wishing she could so easily close her mind to the terrifying thoughts that crept, unbidden, into it.

Would she see the lights again tonight?

She had not seen them since the night of the church fete, she reminded herself, but even that thought brought little comfort. She had to admit she had hardly given herself the opportunity to see the lights or anything else on the downs at night. She assiduously avoided going out after dark. She carefully drew the draperies closed on all the windows at night.

So far, she had been safe.

There was no sign of the lights here near the house.

But she could not help but wonder how long her luck would hold.

Torie's nerves were already pushed to the point of snapping by the frustrating and completely fruitless effort to locate her gloves and the cheerful, thoroughly annoying sound of the brandy bottle clinking against the rim of Gabriel's glass. Thinking about the lights didn't help.

Throwing herself into the effort to find her gloves, struggling for anything that might help her forget that, tonight, she might not be able to avoid the downs, Torie yanked another drawer open and rummaged through its contents.

"I wonder," she heard Gabriel say pensively, "does Westin know what kind of woman you really are?"

Though she tried her best to remain perfectly calm, this last provocation was too presumptuous to ignore. Torie sat bolt upright in her chair and slammed her journal down on the desk top. She scowled at Gabriel. "And what kind of woman is that?" she asked. "The kind who offers gainful employment to those who are clearly unemployable?"

Gabriel did not rise to the challenge in her voice. He burrowed his shoulders further into the high-backed chair and stretched out his legs. "The kind who deceives her associates, including the delightful Mr. Westin," he said, taking a sip of brandy and dangling the glass in his hand. "The kind who lies to him and lets him believe all that codswallop about Roger being a brilliant man of science."

Torie mumbled her displeasure. It was as much of an answer as he deserved, she reminded herself, and she vowed to make it suffice. She finished looking through the last desk drawer and, still without her gloves, sat back and sighed.

She'd been so busy, she hadn't realized Gabriel had risen from his seat. He was standing directly across from her, a slow, indolent sort of smile lighting his face, the kind that made him look more brazen and more maddeningly handsome than ever.

"Is this what you're looking for?" He brought one hand out from behind his back. He was holding her gloves.

Torie hopped to her feet. "You know very well that's

what I'm looking for." She made a grab for the gloves and missed. She tried again and, again Gabriel snatched the gloves away just as her fingers were about to close around them. Barely containing a screech of frustration, Torie marched around to the other side of the desk.

"My gloves," she said, and held out her hand, pointedly refusing to back down, even when Gabriel's gaze boldly raked over her in her newest evening gown.

He studied the short, puffed sleeves of the dress and nodded his approval. He scrutinized the ribbon of contrasting color tied snug around her waist, and mumbled something that sounded like a word of admiration. He let his gaze drop to her prettily embroidered slippers before he slowly brought it up again, taking in the trim of artificial flowers at the hem of her gown and the way the slim, cylindrical skirt fell soft and close over her hips, and he smiled.

Through it all, Torie remained stock-still, her hand extended, her heart suddenly pounding. She did not move at all, not even when he let his gaze stray to the rounded, lace-edged neckline that skimmed the hollow at the base of her throat, and by then, it was too late. She could not have moved an inch if she wanted to. He held her there, as if his eyes cast a kind of spell that fixed her in place, just like the sun held the planets by the sheer force of its burning power.

"A lovely shade of green," Gabriel said, his eyes lighting with pleasure. "What we young bloods of the ton used to call pistache. It's a good color for you. It brings out the green fire in your eyes."

"The only fire in my eyes is the fire that comes from being annoyed." Torie glared at him.

"A bit too austere for my taste," Gabriel said, concentrating on the dress and paying her displeasure not the least bit of attention. "But I suppose that's to be expected from a woman as abstemious and unimaginative as you."

Starting again at the top, he let his gaze roam over her. "The hair is fine," he said. He skimmed his hand over her hair, his fingers grazing the soft mass of curls at the base of her neck. "But I much prefer those old-fashioned dresses on you." He frowned and with one finger, traced the curved neckline of her gown. "You know the kind I mean, like that charming black one you used to mislead me. The kind cut square and low." Absently, he trailed his finger over her shoulders and across her breasts.

"Don't." Torie stiffened and backed away.

"What's this?" Gabriel took a step forward, effectively closing the distance she had been so careful to put between them. His words were light and casual, belying the spark of anger that glinted in his eyes. "Don't tell me you're surprised at how I'm acting," Gabriel said. "How can you be? You went to Oxford purposely to find yourself a worthless rogue. You got that sure enough. But don't pretend you didn't know he was a rakehell, too. A debaucher of young women." Quirking his eyebrows, Gabriel moved closer.

Torie moved another step back.

Gabriel smiled, matching her step for step, one forward to each one she took back. "A randy libertine with no more morals than a—!" His smile widened into a grin when Torie backed into the wall, her body neatly fitted into the small space between the specimen case and the door. "I think, perhaps, you knew all that, too," he said, his smile disappearing as he moved yet another step closer and his chest came up against hers. "I think, perhaps, that's exactly what you wanted."

"Don't be ridiculous!" Torie was thankful she was able to sound as infuriated as she felt. It wasn't easy. There was something about standing this close to Gabriel that made her almost forget how angry he made her. "I knew what I was getting, just as you say. But I was also quite confident that you wouldn't be interested in a woman like me.

What's that you called me? Abstemious and unimaginative? Yes, I suppose I am both those things. I have been too long concerned with my work to worry about cultivating the kinds of talents you value in a woman. I find it completely impossible to call up a blush at will, and no matter how I try, I cannot force myself to giggle and stammer and gasp at every word that falls from your mouth. I'm afraid I am not like the women you are used to being with, but then, I suspect those women would not blush and stammer and bestow their affections on a man as irascible as you, either, not if you didn't have enough of a purse to pay for their services."

Her remark hit home. The corners of Gabriel's mouth tightened ever so slightly, and the fire flared in his eyes.

Torie smiled to herself. She had found the chink in his defenses, and she promised herself she would not forget where it was and how to use it to her best advantage.

Satisfied with at least this little bit of a victory, Torie went on. "I think you'll admit, Gabriel," she said, being careful to emphasize his name, "I am not your sort of woman. Not your sort at all."

"For once we are in complete agreement." Gabriel sounded pleased, but he didn't look it. He let his gaze wander over her again, though standing this close, it was impossible for him to see farther than her breasts where they were crushed against his body. "Not more than a month ago, I would have sworn I'd never give a woman like you a second look. But I'd risk every penny I have that I could still seduce you. Right here and now. In spite of everything that's happened, I swear I could, and have you begging for more."

Torie was as startled by the suggestion as she was by the realization that he was absolutely right. To cover both her shock and her amazement, she made a small noise of disgust. "I don't think you'd enjoy it," she said.

Obviously as staggered by the whole thing as she was

and not as loath to admit it, Gabriel shook his head in wonder. "Damn me," he said, "but I think I would."

Torie knew it was impossible for her heart to stop beating, yet she could have sworn that it did. She stood as if spellbound, watching the blue-black lightning that glimmered in Gabriel's eyes, transfixed by the mellow sound of his voice and the full, deep beat of his heart against hers.

She didn't move, not even when he lifted her hand and turned it over in his.

"You were careful to keep your hands from me, weren't you?" he asked, though it was certain he did not expect an answer. "You knew I'd suspect something if I saw how rough your skin was." He studied the countless scrapes and scratches that covered Torie's hand, unavoidable evidence of those times it was impossible or awkward for her to excavate wearing gloves.

Her skin was as work-hardened and as unladylike as he said, and Torie knew that he could not help but feel it, but that did not seem to bother Gabriel in the least. He pressed a kiss to her fingers.

"I could take you here and now," he said, his voice low and ragged, his words creating a swirl of hot, dangerous desire deep in Torie. Twining his fingers through hers, Gabriel pinned her arm against the wall and slid his lips from her hand to the underside of her wrist. From there, he glided his lips to the sensitive, soft place inside her elbow.

It was not a nuzzle and it was certainly not a kiss, but whatever it was, it lasted far too long and was far too intimate, intimate enough to make Torie's knees feel weak.

Gabriel could not fail to miss the momentary flutter in the firm mettle of her resolve. Almost before she could catch her breath, he was smiling down at her again. "You see what I mean? You can't resist. You don't even want to try. I could kiss you . . ." He let his lips chase the words across her mouth. "And you wouldn't complain."

Torie held her breath. "You're talking nonsense."

"Am I?" Moving too quickly for her to have the chance to escape, Gabriel fitted his hands around her waist and brought his lips to hers. "Is it nonsense for me to kiss you before I say goodbye?"

"Goodbye?" There was something irrevocable about the word and the way it reverberated through the silence that filled the room. Torie pulled away and eyed Gabriel carefully. "What do you mean, goodbye?"

The announcement had obviously elicited the response he desired. Gabriel smiled. "Goodbye," he said, and shrugged as if that small gesture alone could explain everything. "I'm leaving."

Leaving.

Why the single word should settle inside her like a block of ice, Torie did not know. She would have liked to believe it had something to do with her dragon, with her hopes of finding the bones and her plan of using Gabriel to publish her results. She very much feared that was not the case at all, for she was certain that not even the thought of losing Gabriel as a collaborator—albeit an unwilling one—could tie her stomach in knots and cause an ache inside her heart.

"You can't leave," she said. But even she did not know why. Half afraid he might ask, she scrambled for some rational argument to back up the assertion. There was only one she could think of. "We haven't found the bones yet."

Gabriel backed away from her, a look somewhere between incredulity and disgust chasing the slightly drunk and pleasantly aroused smile from his face. "I'm leaving," he said again as if he wasn't sure she'd heard him right the first time. "I'll be gone in the morning."

Now that Gabriel had moved away a step, it gave Torie

the perfect opportunity to retreat. As quickly as she could, she dashed to the other side of the room and turned to face Gabriel. The taste of him was still on her lips, and if Torie didn't know better, she would have sworn it was keeping her thoughts as muddled as her words. "But . . . but . . ." She fought the unaccountable, overwhelming panic that filled her. "I've already promised you two hundred pounds," she said because she couldn't think of anything else to say. "How much more will it take to get you to stay?"

Gabriel's top lip curled. "Do you think the money matters?"

"Your bookmaker thinks so." Torie congratulated herself for her fine and quick reasoning. She was not used to thinking about matters of commerce, yet that's exactly what this was. A matter of business. Perhaps all she need do was make Gabriel realize it.

"I doubt your bookmaker has given up the search for you," she said, sounding as pleased with herself as she felt. "It isn't safe for you to go back to Oxford."

"I'm not going to Oxford."

With a lift of her shoulders, Torie dismissed what she assumed was only a momentary impediment in the smooth road of her unassailable reasoning. She went on. "London, then," she conceded. "I'm sure even ruffians like those who destroyed your home have their sources and their friends. They would locate you soon enough. You would be no safer in London than in Oxford."

"I'm headed for America."

"America." Torie let go the word on the end of a sigh. It sounded foreign and very far away. "America is such a long way off."

"Precisely." Gabriel poured himself another drink. "I should have thought of this long ago," he said, studying the liquor in his glass and talking below his breath, as if he'd been through this argument with himself time and

again. "My creditors will never find me there. Oh, perhaps there might be a chance of them locating me in some
large city like Boston or New York. But there are other
places." He glanced up at Torie. "Farther west. I hear
there are opportunities there for a man. Even one who
has no honor." His gaze still fixed to Torie's, he downed
his drink in one gulp.

"What of the prestige, then?" Torie fought back with
the only other argument she could think of. It was a good
argument, she told herself to bolster her courage. A sound
argument. The one and only argument that would have
worked on her if Torie was in Gabriel's place and she in
his, and she threw herself into it, convinced of its merit.

"It won't take me long to find the bones, surely, and
think of the excitement that will be generated once my
results are published. It will be your name on the research, remember, your name linked with the most incredible scientific find of the century. Imagine what
Morrison and Granger and Cronkite will say then. Imagine the pains they will take to overlook everything that
happened back in Oxford. You'll have your reputation
back, your honor."

"Honor!" His expression dark, his eyes shining with
emotion, Gabriel came over to her. Torie could not help
but notice that it took all his willpower for him to keep his
hands from her, and she knew why. If he dared kiss her
again, he would not be able to stop. "You call that
honor?"

Torie knew he was right. Deep inside her where her
heart beat true, she knew what he said was the undeniable
truth and it staggered her, not because she knew it, but
because Gabriel did.

Clasping her hands at her waist, she fought her way
through the jumble of thoughts that assailed her, turning
her beliefs inside out and her world upside down.

She had lied to everyone, Torie reminded herself. She

had fabricated a career and a reputation for Roger and obscured her own talents and abilities behind it.

She had lied to herself, and hidden her real feelings for Gabriel behind what she thought were the firm walls of reason, only to find the walls crumbling to dust the moment he said goodbye.

And all this time, the man she thought had few scruples and even less integrity had been far more ethical than she. He had never lied to her. He had never pretended to be anything he was not. Whatever else Gabriel had done in his life, he had acted far more honestly in their dealings with each other than she had.

The realization settled inside Torie, filling up the hollow places left by the announcement of Gabriel's leaving with something very close to physical pain.

"Gabriel, I—" It was on the tip of her tongue to apologize. One look at Gabriel changed her mind.

He stood in front of her, his shoulders firm, his chin set with determination, his eyes glinting with something very close to loathing.

"I suppose we should say goodbye, then." Torie contained the sob that threatened to reveal her true feelings. She stuck out her right hand, half hoping he would not take it so that she would not be forced to endure his touch. "I may be gone before you are up and about in the morning. We probably will not see each other again."

"Oh, no!" Suddenly, Gabriel was smiling, his eyes glinting like dark jewels. "You'll see me right enough. Have you forgotten?" He offered her his arm. "We have a dinner party to attend!"

Chapter 14

"I hear he's leaving." Spencer stood close to Torie's side, his expression as dispassionate as ever but his eyes gleaming with something very close to exultation. He fixed his gaze across the parlor. All the furniture had been moved out, and the room was ablaze with candlelight and abuzz with the cheerful voices of his guests.

Against the far wall, Gabriel was entertaining Miss Wayne, her mother, and the Reverend Mr. Blankenship with what must have been an engrossing story. Blankenship laughed aloud at something Gabriel said, and Miss Wayne and her mother hung on his every word, coming up only now and again for a bit of air and to fan the heat of excitement from their faces.

"I hear tell that he'll be in Southampton and on a ship to America before tomorrow's over." Spencer's voice droned like the noise of an insect in Torie's ear.

She controlled the urge to brush it away. "Yes," she said, refusing to meet Spencer's gaze. "He's finally leaving."

Spencer chuckled and rubbed his hands together. "Good," he said. "Maybe now you'll come to your senses."

"What!" Torie rounded on him, so astonished she nearly forgot where they were and how many people were about. She raised her voice, and would have raised it even further had they not been in the midst of half their neighbors, or at least the half whom Spencer considered acceptable. She jiggled her shoulders as if getting rid of some uncomfortable feeling. "I don't know what you're talking about."

Spencer frowned. "Don't you? Then it proves my point. You haven't been thinking rationally lately, not since Mr. Raddigan came into our midst. For some time now, I have suspected that his presence had something to do with the way you've been acting." Spencer wrinkled his nose.

"You've been illogical. Capricious. Not yourself at all. There was that unfortunate incident when you dined here last. Your foolish argument about Huttonian theory. And of course, your conduct at the church fete. Dashing away like that as if Beelzebub himself had risen from one of the graves and come after you. Raddigan was there both times, you'll remember." Spencer's frown turned into a grimace. "Really, Victoria! There is something unwholesome about the man. He has you acting like a madwoman!"

The word was barely out of his mouth when Spencer's face paled. His eyes went round as saucers. "I'm so sorry." He grabbed Torie's hand and held on tight. "You know I didn't mean that," he said as quickly as he could. "I did not mean to compare your actions with Roger's unfortunate illness. I did not mean to imply that you might be . . . that is, that you are ever likely to be . . ."

Spencer's apology was so artless, Torie might have felt sorry for him. She might have, except that his words echoed the same, terrifying awareness that had haunted her since first she'd seen the lights. It was not a reassuring thought and she slapped it away, refusing to give consideration to something so disturbing here and now. She decided that it was safer, and less distressing, to concentrate instead on Spencer's absurd notion that Gabriel had anything at all to do with her behavior.

Torie glared at him. "And what, exactly, are you implying?" she asked.

Spencer darted a glance all around and, convinced no one was paying the least bit of attention to them, went on. "I am not implying a thing, my dear," he said, keeping his voice low and giving her a look that said he wished she would be sensible enough to do the same. "I am merely pointing out that a man as charming and handsome as Mr. Raddigan could quite easily turn the head of a young lady. Any young lady. Look what he's done to our poor Miss Wayne."

Torie followed Spencer's gaze. Katherine Wayne was practically falling over herself in an effort to make Gabriel notice her. She blushed prettily when he finally glanced her way, and she looked as if she might swoon when he took her arm and invited her to join him in the waltz that was just beginning.

"Mindless cretin." If Spencer had asked which of the dancers she was talking about, Torie wasn't sure she'd know the answer. Eager to steer Spencer away from such a question, she added, "Surely Miss Wayne knows he's leaving. Gabriel announced his departure at dinner, and he hasn't been at all reticent about discussing it with anyone who will listen. What does Miss Wayne hope to gain, do you think, by trifling with a man who will be gone by morning?"

Spencer's smile was almost as annoying as his nonchalant shrug. "Perhaps she believes that love can change a man. Perhaps she thinks that if she can make him fall in love with her tonight, he will not leave in the morning."

Torie was very close to repeating a word she'd once heard Gabriel use when he was annoyed. She controlled the urge, but only with the most conscientious of efforts, dismissing both Katherine Wayne and Gabriel. "And what does all this have to do with me?" she asked, lying so effortlessly, she might even have fooled herself. "I don't see how Mr. Raddigan's departure will change much of anything in my life."

"It will leave you without someone to carry on Roger's work." Spencer's eyes lighted, and for all the world, Torie was reminded of a hunting dog, hot on the trail of a fresh and promising scent. "You will need someone to do the work for you, Victoria, and while I admit that Roger's shoes are indisputably large ones and not too easily filled, I would offer myself." He bowed from the waist. "I am at your service, madam."

"At my service?" Torie didn't know whether to laugh or scream. After all the trouble she'd caused by hiring Gabriel for work she had no intention of ever letting him do, the last thing she needed was to get herself involved with another collaborator. "No," she said, a bit too quickly and much too firmly. "I don't think so, Spencer. I—"

"But, Victoria. You know I can do it."

Spencer was so earnest, Torie couldn't help but smile. "I know. I know you can. You are a clever man. An imaginative thinker." The words soured in Torie's mouth. Spencer was imaginative, right enough, but his imagination always seemed to have a way of erring on the side of ideas that were hopelessly old-fashioned and impossibly lackluster. Another night, she might have been tempted to argue the point. Tonight, she did not want to press it, just as she did not want to hurt Spencer's feelings. "This has nothing to do with your competence," Torie said, setting out again onto the straight and narrow path of the strict truth. "It isn't that at all. It's—"

"If you are uncomfortable about my previous proposal of marriage, I would ask you not to be." It was as if Spencer had rehearsed this whole conversation beforehand. He had an answer to her every objection, a parry for her every thrust. "I have given it a great deal of thought, Victoria," he announced. "I realize now that I was very wrong."

Spencer mistook Torie's relief for consternation. "Not about you," he said before she had the chance to speak. "Not about wanting to marry you. I realize though, that a woman, being a frail creature and slave to her emotions, needs more than just the assurance of security, the promise of a comfortable life and a husband who will take such care of her that she will never need to trouble herself with using her mind. I know that is as foreign to women as emotion and caring are to men."

Again, Spencer looked around self-consciously and again satisfied no one was paying them the least attention, he turned back to Torie.

"You need to hear that I love you and . . . and I have decided that I do. I have feelings for you, Victoria, feelings which are perhaps not proper for a man to entertain about a woman who is not joined to him in holy matrimony." A bright red and totally uncharacteristic flush raced up Spencer's neck and stained his cheeks, and if Torie didn't know better, she might have thought he had somehow called it up on purpose to win her sympathy and melt her heart.

But in spite of Spencer's tender words and his attempts at looking lovestruck, Torie could not find it in her to warm to his declaration. She did not even bother to wonder why. Even as she tried her best to listen to Spencer, she heard the low rumble of Gabriel's voice as he sped by with his arms around Miss Wayne. Even as she looked into Spencer's eyes, she could not help but think of the way Gabriel had looked at her in the library this evening, his eyes dark as thunderclouds and hard as flint, his expression speaking his disdain for her so eloquently, she could feel her heart burst and break inside her, just at the thought.

It had been so all night.

For the entire time Torie had talked to the Reverend Mr. Blankenship this evening, she had relived in her mind the scene in the library with Gabriel. For the long and tedious minutes she had chatted with Mrs. Wayne and her dull-witted daughter, she had been distracted by her memories of the past month, lost in the words "America" and "goodbye" and all they implied.

It would never be any other way, she realized, and the awareness did little to lighten her mood. She did not know how it happened. A month ago, she had been sure it never could. She now knew only that Gabriel's departure would leave her somehow less whole than she had been when he was a part of her life, and marrying Spencer would only make it worse.

The awareness that Spencer would insist on being in charge of the excavation of the bones was bad enough. The fact that he would never concede that his wife could have an original thought was worse.

But most dreadful of all was the realization that every time she looked at Spencer, she was bound to think of Gabriel. Every time he took her in his arms, she was certain to remember Gabriel's fevered embrace. Every time he kissed her—if, indeed, a man like Spencer ever saw fit to kiss his wife—she would surely remember the feel of Gabriel's mouth on hers, the taste of his lips, the sweet, slow arousal that built inside her when he traced her mouth with his tongue and nudged her lips apart to probe even deeper.

Every time she looked at Spencer, or any other man, she was sure to think of Gabriel.

The fact was puzzling, but there it was.

Torie clasped her hands at her waist, bracing herself against the astounding impact of the truth.

She could deny it to the world, but she could no longer deny it to herself, she conceded. It was baffling. And annoying. And so exciting, it made her feel as if there were a creature of fire inside the icy exterior of reason and logic where she had for too long kept herself prisoner. She had been a hostage to her own pride and stubbornness, a captive whose only hope of escape would himself be fleeing before too long, leaving for some wild place and taking with him, if not all hope for her happiness, then at least all hope of finding out if he was ever destined to be a part of it.

". . . so I suppose I always have loved you. I just did not know how to express it."

Somehow, the sound of Spencer's voice broke through Torie's thoughts. He had been carrying on the entire time, she supposed, though it seemed as if he had not gotten any farther than when she'd stopped listening.

As if preparing himself for an important announcement, Spencer coughed into his hand. "It is with love and esteem," he said a bit too woodenly, "that I again ask you to be my wife."

Torie fanned her face with one hand. She feared she was acting far too much like Miss Wayne, anxious and all agog, but she could not seem to help herself. Spencer's first proposal was enough of a surprise but that, at least, was rational and clearheaded. His declaration of love was nothing short of astonishing, and coming fast on the heels of the unsettling thoughts that had been filling her head, it was also more than a bit embarrassing.

"I . . . I . . ." Torie stumbled over her words. It did not help her composure when the dance brought Gabriel and his partner to this side of the room. Gabriel's arms were firmly around Miss Wayne, but his gaze was fixed on Torie, his look no friendlier than it had been all evening.

Torie turned her back to the dance floor. "I'm sorry that I am forced to say all the same things I said last time," she told Spencer. She glanced at him out of the corner of her eye, afraid she might see him looking far too much like a wounded animal. To her dismay, he did, but she went on just the same. "I only fear that now that I know your true feelings, my words will hurt you more than ever."

Spencer drew in a long breath and let it out. "That's quite all right," he said. Trying his best not to look cut to the quick, he patted Torie's shoulder as if she were the one who needed comforting. His effort at acting detached was not quite effective. One corner of Spencer's mouth twitched as if with emotion or excitement, and he blinked rapidly, like a man startled by a bright and sudden light.

"I understand," he said, and as abruptly as his agitation came, it left him. His expression was suddenly as composed as if some unseen hand had passed over him, erasing all emotion from his face. It left him perfectly calm and gravely serious, like a man who had long debated some momentous decision and had finally made a choice.

"Let me get you a drink, shall I?" he asked, and before Torie could accept or refuse, he was gone.

The music stopped, and Torie watched as the dancers retired from the floor. They were hot and flushed; the ladies fluttering delicate ivory fans, the gentlemen hurrying to the punch table. She might have known Gabriel would head her way the moment the dance was over, and she cursed herself for not realizing it sooner and retreating to another room.

Gabriel was not at all out of breath from the exertion of the dance. Every ink-black hair in place, every fold of his snowy white cravat as perfect as if he'd just arranged it, he strode over to where Torie was standing. In spite of the way he'd laughed and talked to Miss Wayne all the while they were dancing, he didn't look any happier now than he'd looked at home this evening. He glowered at her. "Having fun?"

Torie dismissed his question with a toss of her head.

"Of course I am having fun," she said. "Spencer is a perfect host."

"He's a perfect ass!"

"Really, Mr. Raddigan!" Torie did her best to look disgusted, though she feared she too was at the point of beginning to agree with Gabriel's frank evaluation of Spencer.

The thought was certainly uncharitable. And tactless. Torie chided herself for it at the same time she cocked one eyebrow and glanced across the room to where Katherine Wayne was talking to her mother. Miss Wayne's words were coming so fast, Torie could nearly see them spilling from her mouth. If there was any doubt as to what they were discussing, it was dispelled when Miss Wayne glanced over at Gabriel and blushed from the tip of her angular chin all the way to the roots of her hair. Hair, Torie noted with a sour smile, that was far too yellow to have come by the grace of Nature alone.

"You are obviously having such a delightful time with Miss Wayne," she said, turning to Gabriel. "I cannot for the life of me understand why you came all the way over here simply to talk to me. I would have thought we said all we had to say to each other before we left the house this evening."

"I dare say, we did that and more." Gabriel gave a sharp bark of laughter. "But I am considerably more sober now than I was then."

Torie rolled her eyes. "Don't tell me you've reconsidered," she said, sarcasm heavy in her voice though in her heart, she was half hoping that was exactly what he was about to say. "Are you telling me you've come to your senses? Decided that my work really is important? Resolved to set aside your masculine pride and let a woman take charge?"

"Masculine pride be damned," Gabriel growled. "Do you think I'd be standing here talking to you if I had the choice? After all the things I found out today?" He snorted in mockery of the very idea. "I've been watching you and Westin," he said, his eyes darkening. "I don't like it. I don't like it at all."

It was Torie's turn to laugh, though her laughter was no more genuine than his. "I thought it was no concern of yours what I did with Mr. Westin or any other man. Remember? You don't care if I spend all night and half the day on my back with—"

"Damn it, Torie, listen to me!" Gabriel was obviously not in the mood to be reminded of what he'd said in the quarry this morning. He moved a step closer and grabbed her arm, his hand stealing beneath the lace-trimmed sleeve of her gown. He lowered his voice at the same time he tossed a look over his shoulder.

The fact that they were talking to each other was causing no undue amount of attention from the other guests. Torie could see that. However, the fact that Gabriel was holding on to her as if she were a slippery eel and he the unfortunate fellow who had been given the task of keeping her in one place, was making a few heads turn.

The Reverend Mr. Blankenship looked over and looked away too quickly to be certain of his expression, but if Torie did not know better, she would have sworn he was smiling. Miss Wayne and her mother looked positively thunderstruck.

Gabriel must have seen exactly what Torie saw. He muttered a curse and pulled his hand away. "I don't trust the man," he said simply, and she knew he was talking about Spencer. "And I don't want to spend my life worrying what he might be up to. I am finally to be rid of you, and I refuse to go through the rest of my days wondering if I could have said or done something to keep you from harm."

Torie made a great show of smoothing her skirts. "I am quite safe, thank you," she said, her voice icy. "And I have no idea what you might be getting at. Spencer is a gentleman, hardly the type who would threaten any woman. I doubt he has ever pinned one to the library wall and . . ." Even at the thought of the kiss Gabriel had slipped from her fingers, to her wrist, to her arm, Torie felt her knees grow weak and her heart pound. She disguised her reaction with a shake of her shoulders. "I am safe, I think. You can rest easy."

"You two always look so at odds with one another when I come upon you alone!" Spencer arrived with a wide smile and a tray of drinks, effectively putting an end to their conversation. "I am not sure who is luckier that you are leaving, Mr. Raddigan. You, because you will no longer be head to head with Victoria all the time. Or me, because now you are going, perhaps she will pay me some attention." He proffered the tray to Torie.

It held three glasses. Two of them were large brandy snifters. The third was a tiny crystal glass filled with golden liquid that sparkled like spring sunshine.

"Something special," Spencer said, his smile widening when Torie reached for the pretty little glass. "A tisane of herbs and liquors. I think you will find it delightful. Let us toast Mr. Raddigan's departure."

Because she could not possibly ignore the toast without being rude, Torie raised her glass when Spencer raised his and took a drink when both Gabriel and Spencer did. She was not used to strong spirits, and whatever was in the splendid little crystal glass burned down her throat and all the way into her stomach.

"Good luck, Mr. Raddigan," she said, wondering what tasted worse, the liquor or the bitter words in her mouth. "Perhaps one day you'll return. I hear those who are daring and able come back from America as rich men."

After no more than one small, obligatory sip, Gabriel set down his glass. "Perhaps," he said, "those who are daring and able are the ones who never leave at all."

The orchestra began another waltz and for a moment, Torie concentrated on the music, thankful that she and Gabriel were far enough estranged from each other that he would never ask her to dance. It was one thing to stand here and trade platitudes with him, one thing to offer a toast and pretend to mean it. It would be another altogether to have to dance with him, his arms around her, his body moving close to hers in time to the music.

Again, Torie found her thoughts wandering to places where they had no business, and again she dismissed them as quickly as she could. She took another sip of her drink. Whatever its faults, she thought, rolling the liquor over her tongue, Spencer's odd-tasting spirits had one virtue. It was especially potent. The peculiar combination of its heady power along with the heat of the close-packed room and the noise of the revelers was nearly enough to drive away her melancholy thoughts and make her forget that after tonight, she would never see Gabriel again.

Nearly.

"You're not enjoying your drink."

Torie looked up to find Spencer making little waving motions, urging her to down the rest of her drink. She obliged and set the glass on the tray.

"Of course I enjoyed it," she said, gritting her teeth as the last of the spirits seared its way down her throat. "But that is quite enough for me." She waved one hand in front of her face. "It is dreadfully hot in here, is it not?"

Neither Spencer nor Gabriel answered. Spencer watched her with a grimly satisfied look akin to that a disgruntled governess might use on a child who, adamantly refusing to eat its dinner, is finally subdued and forced to finish every last bite.

Gabriel looked the way he'd looked all evening, his face a mask of stone, his eyes those of a man who despises what he sees.

It would be bad enough to be the object of either look. Both together were intolerable.

"Yes. Definitely hot." Torie was not at all sure if she was being prudent or simply beating a hasty retreat. Before either of the men could protest, she swept past them and out the doors that led into Spencer's garden.

It was cooler outside, and almost dark. Her head in her hands, Torie dropped onto one of the benches alongside the garden wall, willing her heartbeat to slow, reminding herself that she had little reason to feel so unnerved and wondering all the while that she did.

It was more than just the way Gabriel looked at her, she decided, gulping in a large swallow of air and finding that even that did nothing to relieve the tight, aching feeling that gripped her chest. It was more than just the thought that he would be gone in the morning. More than just the terrible certainty that she had done him an injustice and owed him an apology, one she knew she would never have the chance to say aloud, and even if she did, one she knew that he would never listen to.

It was more than that. Much more.

This was a feeling very like the one she'd had in the graveyard after the church fete. A sense of overwhelming panic. A feeling of paralyzing fear.

Torie tensed. Suddenly, her heartbeat was pulsing in her ears, each beat faster, stronger than the one before, until her heart was thrumming far more rapidly than it was ever meant to. Her palms were moist, and the neat knots and borders of herbs that filled Spencer's garden faded and blurred when she looked at them, their heady, oily scent catching at the back of her throat, making her retch.

Slowly she raised her head. She knew what she would see. As certain as she knew that finally, they had come for her.

The lights.

Hanging from the tree branches. Suspended above Spencer's roof. Blazing a path through his hollyhocks.

This time they did not merely glimmer and slowly wind their way toward her. They tore through the garden at remarkable speed, hurrying at her like frenzied, rabid animals, intent on tearing her sanity to shreds.

One hand against the wall for support, Torie hauled herself to her feet, only one thought making its way through the panic that filled her head.

She could not let the lights near her. Not so close to the house. Not with this many people about.

Torie put one foot in front of the other, moving out of the garden like a sleepwalker, each step as labored as if she were fighting her way through a morass that sucked at her shoes and threatened to draw her down into its airless depths. Finally, her hand touched the latch on the garden gate. She flung it open and staggered out onto the downs.

Once the garden wall was between her and the lights, Torie felt as if she could breathe more easily. She passed one hand over her eyes, glancing back toward Spencer's. Like stars fallen from the sky, the lights still dangled over the house, crackling like fire, burning like the hottest flames of hell.

Torie did not wait to see any more. Moving as quickly as she could, she scrambled toward home.

By the time she got to High Brill, it was completely dark. She paused atop the rise and bent at the waist, struggling to catch her breath. She had run most of the way, the lights nipping at her heels, mirroring her every move. Somehow, she had managed to keep always a step ahead of them.

Torie spun around. They were still there.

The phantom lights were behind her, turning the path to Spencer's into a river of flame.

She looked around her. They were on either side of the hill, spreading like an unstoppable flood of fire.

She stared ahead of her. The lights were there, too. Blocking all route of escape.

Torie's hands were cold as ice and she could not keep herself from trembling. She could see the lights, as clear as day, yet all else around her was indistinct, the downs and all its familiar landmarks obscured as if by a cloud.

Even as she watched, the lights began their final advance, silently slipping up the hill, orbs of fire that hung just above the grass, balls of yellow and blue and intense, glaring white, closing in, inch by inch.

"Gabriel!"

Torie did not have the chance to wonder why she called Gabriel's name. She heard her own voice, small and frightened, even as she reminded herself that he was nowhere near.

"Gabriel!"

She could not seem to help herself. He was the only one who could help. Somehow, she was sure of it, and she screamed his name again, her voice gaining strength as the first of the lights snaked over her, winding around her ankles, twisting around her legs.

"Gabriel!"

The intimate sound of his name rose from her like the cry of a wounded animal. It died there on her lips as the phantoms closed around her and she was swallowed by blinding, impenetrable light.

Chapter 15

"Damned rabbits."

Gabriel barely missed stepping into a rabbit hole that certainly would have turned his ankle. He stuffed his hands into his pockets, hoping with all his heart that wherever he lived in America, it would be someplace without rabbits.

"Damned rabbits and damned Sussex. Damned Spencer Westin." He didn't bother to look back over his shoulder toward Westin's cottage and the dinner party that was still in progress, just as he didn't bother adding one final name to the series of invectives.

He didn't dare.

It wasn't that he was afraid to say it. Even out here on the downs in the pitch-dark with the moon floating over his head like a bloated, grinning skull, he was not a man to believe in ill luck or the power of curses.

He wasn't afraid to say Torie's name.

He was dead set against it.

He couldn't, not without thinking about her. And when he did that, his blood boiled in his veins and his anger roiled up inside him, just as it had back at Westin's when he made the mistake of speaking to her after the dance. Gabriel skirted a small stream and scrambled back onto the path that led to Torie's. It was just as well he'd left without going out to the garden to say goodbye to her, he told himself. He wasn't sure he could face her again and keep what was left of his temper.

It wouldn't matter in the morning.

The thought cheered him as much as anything could right now, and he allowed himself to savor it as he covered the distance back to the house, his strides long and restless, his speed fueled by his anger.

In the morning, none of it would matter.

In the morning, he'd be gone.

"Gabriel!"

Like the whispers of a half-forgotten dream, he heard a voice call to him from over the downs.

Gabriel stopped, his head tilted, listening.

If he didn't know better, he would have sworn the voice was Torie's.

But that was impossible.

Pulling himself back to his senses, Gabriel started off again.

Torie was back at the party, he reminded himself in no uncertain terms. She was not out here in the middle of nowhere.

But if that was true, why did Gabriel hear her call to him again?

Quickening his pace, Gabriel scanned the horizon.

Ahead of him stood High Brill, rising up bulky and dark, blacker even than the sky that lay beyond. There was no sign of Torie or anyone else on the path that led to its summit, but up at the very top, he could just make out a shape. It looked to be a woman, standing stiff and still as a statue. Her dress, colorless in the pale light, reflected the glow of the moon and gleamed like one of the spirits said to haunt the downs.

"Hell!" Gabriel grumbled the single word and started up the slope. "Just when I think I've gotten rid of you . . ."

By the time he got to the top, he was slightly out of breath, but that didn't keep him from mumbling a string of crude words. His colorful tirade was aimed at the darkness, the gradient of the hill, and the baffling woman who simply stood there, not moving a muscle and not giving the least sign that she knew he'd come in answer to her call.

"What is it?" Gabriel would have liked to believe he didn't intend his voice to sound quite so sharp. He couldn't. The anger that had seethed inside him since this morning finally burst its dam. He marched over to Torie, grabbed her shoulders, and twisted her to face him. "I asked you—"

When he saw her face, the words fell dead on his lips.

Torie's eyes were wide, but it was clear she wasn't seeing a thing. Unblinking, she stared not at Gabriel, but through him, with no expression on her face and no indication that she knew he was there. There was no emotion in her wide, green eyes but one, and that one made Gabriel's stomach go cold.

It was fear. Intense, stark, horrible fear. A fear so staggering, it held her fast in its unyielding grip as if she were frozen in time and space.

Gabriel slid his hands from Torie's shoulders to her arms and from there to her fingers. Her skin was as cold as death. Instinctively, he felt her face. Her brow was fiery, her cheeks burned.

Her breathing was rapid and so shallow Gabriel wondered if she hadn't run all the way to High Brill. Her skin glistened in the moonlight, her upper lip and forehead slick with perspiration, her cheeks wet with tears.

"Torie?" His face only inches from hers, Gabriel bent and tried to capture her gaze. It was no use. Whatever strange enchantment held her, it was clearly a powerful one. He shook her and called her name, but he got no response.

Before he even had a chance to mutter it, the curse Gabriel had been ready to direct at no one in particular was smothered by the sound of Torie calling to him again. This time, her voice was high and tight, and as tormented as the cry of a wounded animal.

Something told Gabriel he didn't have a minute to spare.

Scooping Torie into his arms, he lifted her and carried her home.

"You're home, Torie. You're safe. I'm not going to let anything happen to you."

Gabriel lay Torie on her bed and lit the candle on the table beside it. His stomach tied in knots of apprehension, he watched as she scrambled into the corner formed by the wall and the bedstead, her knees drawn up under her chin, her arms wrapped around her legs. Her eyes were still wide with fear and confusion. Her face was the color of ashes, except for her cheeks. They were as red as the hideous stain on Gabriel's shirt, remnants of the mix of Westin's liquor and blood which Torie had coughed up as he carried her home.

"You're home and I'm here." Because he did not know what else to do, Gabriel sat down on the bed and reached for Torie's hand. With a shriek, she snatched it away.

"Damn it, Torie!" The fragile hold Gabriel had on his self-control snapped. His mouth set in a thin, hard line of determination, he moved closer, trapping Torie in the corner. He wrapped his arm around her shoulders, and when she recoiled and cried out, he refused to loosen his hold.

"It's me," he said. One hand beneath her chin, he wrenched Torie's face up to his. Try as he might, he could not disguise the frustration and anger that built in his voice. "It's Gabriel."

"Gabriel?" Somehow, this much of what he said penetrated her daze. Torie's brow cleared and her eyes brightened. But the expression did not last long. The next moment, fresh tears welled in her eyes and cascaded down her cheeks.

"Don't let them touch you." Fitfully, Torie brushed her hands across Gabriel's cheeks and down to his chin. She swept them over his shoulders, as if struggling to scatter some unseen thing. "Don't let them. They'll take you."

Gabriel's anger melted beneath the excruciating look of distress in Torie's eyes. She wasn't worried about herself, she was worried about him, and the realization tore at Gabriel's heart. Suddenly, it didn't seem to matter in the least what she was talking about. She was trapped in a personal hell, shackled by some horrible vision that held her prisoner, body and mind, and he was the one who had to deliver her.

"No." Though she continued to fight against him, Gabriel gathered her into his arms and stroked her hair, the anger in his voice replaced with tenderness. "They won't take me, and they won't take you either, Torie. I won't let them."

"Already . . . have me." The more Gabriel tried to hold her still, the more Torie fought against him, and the more frenzied and peculiar her words became. "All around us. In the house. On you." She slapped at his arms and shoulders. She twisted and turned, fighting to get away from him, and when she realized she could not, she clawed at his face, hissing like a cat.

"Hell!" Gabriel recoiled from her attack, but he refused to let go. With one hand, he tried to grab hold of both her wrists, while with his other, he fought to press her closer still, leaving her no room to move.

It didn't work.

With more strength than he knew she possessed, Torie fought on. Gabriel dodged another assault, only avoiding feeling the sting of her fingernails again by ducking out of the way and pivoting around so that he was kneeling behind her. He grabbed her, one arm around her neck, and was already congratulating himself both for his genius and his dexterity when he felt her teeth pierce his skin.

"Devil take it!" Gabriel cried out in pain and clutched his arm.

It was just enough of a distraction to give Torie the advantage. She leapt off the bed, heading toward the door.

She never got there. Ignoring the pain in his arm as well as the dictates of common sense, Gabriel dove off the bed and caught Torie around the ankles. She tumbled to the floor and he rolled on top of her, pinning her beneath him.

As incredible as it seemed, Gabriel found himself smiling, a smile completely without humor. "Go ahead," he said, a note of challenge in his voice. "Scratch like a cat. Bite and howl. I don't care. It's some response, at least. Some indication you know I'm here."

"No!" With both hands, Torie pushed against him. "Can't keep me here. Can't let them have you, too. Let me go! Let them take me. Leave you here."

The smile fled Gabriel's face. Carefully keeping a tight hold on Torie's hand, he sat up. "Who's going to take you?" he asked. "What are you talking about?"

She did not answer him, but looked to the doorway, her eyes round with fear and worry. Her straw-colored hair, so meticulously arranged at the beginning of the evening, was wild around her shoulders. "Won't let them take you," she said, her words as erratic as her breathing. "Won't let them."

He'd lost her again and Gabriel grumbled a curse, desperate to retain even that small, fragile grip on reality she'd shown only moments ago. Spinning her in his arms, he shook Torie. "What's wrong with you? What are you talking about?"

Torie didn't answer. Panic stricken, she looked around the room. The same, heartrending fear Gabriel had seen in her eyes out on the downs came back, made all the more frightening by the familiarity of the room and the peculiar shadows that stroked her as the bedside candle guttered.

"Lights," she said, and the one, simple word chilled Gabriel like an icy wind. "Yellow. Blue. White lights."

Gabriel closed his eyes, steeling himself against the significance of her statement. "Lights." He repeated the word, his voice suddenly as dry and harsh as hers. "And it isn't the first time you've seen them, is it?"

Torie tipped her head and gave him a look that was so ingenuous, it tangled around his heart. "Spencer's dinner," she said. "And the churchyard. They came for me." A thin trickle of blood dribbled from the corner of her mouth. "Just like Roger," she said. "Mad like Roger."

It was all she could bear. The burden of the realization darkening her expression and flashing through her eyes, Torie fell once again into the strange trance.

"No, damn it!" Gabriel hauled himself to his feet and pulled Torie up beside him. She was weak, her legs shaky, and she staggered and might have fallen if he hadn't gathered her in his arms and carried her back to the bed. He laid her against the pillows and straightened her gown around her. "I'm not going to let you do this, Torie," he said, frowning down at her. "I won't let you slip away again. And I refuse to believe you're mad. Not like Roger. I won't allow it. There must be something else causing all this. There must be another reason."

Gabriel fell to pacing beside the bed. "Why didn't you tell me sooner?" he asked, though he wasn't sure Torie could hear a thing he was saying and he knew she would give him no answer. "Why didn't you say something that

night after Westin's? Or after the church fete? Why didn't
you tell me? No one else would have known. Westin was
so busy getting you cups of tea, he never would have——"

A feeling not unlike that of being punched squarely in
the stomach caused Gabriel to pull to a stop. He steadied
himself against the bedstead, an idea so astounding entering his head, he could scarcely grasp the whole of it. He
wasn't sure what was more excruciating, the sudden tenderness that welled inside him as he looked at Torie's still
form, or the anger that followed close on its heels as the
pieces to the puzzle fell into place inside his head.

"Why didn't you tell me?" Gabriel dropped to the edge
of the bed, looking from Torie to the bloody stain on his
shirtfront. "Why didn't I see the sense of it all before
now?"

He might as well have been talking to the wind, or to
the mute moonlight that streamed through the window,
touching the room with icy fingers.

Torie did not respond. She didn't move. Her eyes
drifted closed and she lay there, motionless as a corpse,
her face so smoothed of the fear that had marked it, her
breathing suddenly so weak that Gabriel bent and placed
his hand at her neck, feeling for her pulse.

It was thin and thready but it was there, and Gabriel
might have breathed a sigh of relief had it not been for the
feel of Torie's skin. Where before she was cold, now she
was hot as blazes. Her brow streamed perspiration. Her
dress clung to her like wet paper. It wouldn't be long
before a chill set in and Gabriel knew he couldn't let that
happen.

Apprehension swept through Gabriel like a cold wind
and he swallowed hard. He knew what he had to do.

His fingers trembling, his breathing more ragged even
than before, he began stripping away her clothes.

Undressing her was more difficult than he imagined,
and he admitted to himself with the smallest of smiles, he

had imagined it enough times to know. It was bad enough
fighting with laces and buttons, stiff fabric, and ribbons
that refused to untie. It was worse still when her gown was
cast aside and she lay there clad only in her petticoat and
corset, the shadows dancing over her, darkening that soft,
secret place between her breasts. It was nearly unbearable
when those garments, too, were tossed aside and Torie's
naked body was outlined by the mix of candle glow and
moonlight.

Gabriel sat back, the urgency of the situation warring
with an aching, primal need that tightened through his
gut and pounded like fire through his blood.

The situation won out.

He knew it would.

Forcing himself to his feet, Gabriel made his way over
to the wardrobe on the other side of the room and rummaged through it until he found a nightgown. He slipped
it over Torie's head and pulled it down around her, tying
the light-colored ribbon at the neck that cinched the gown
closed.

Settling her beneath a soft white blanket, Gabriel left
the room. Outside the door, he drew in a deep breath,
fighting to calm himself. It was not the least bit effective,
but it was the only thing he could think to do, the only
thing that might help dispel the disturbing pictures that
filled his head.

Pictures of Torie's naked body, shimmery in the moonlight.

Gabriel shook the image from his mind but it refused
to stay away. He made a brief stop in the library before
he went in search of a basin, a cloth, and cool water. But
no matter how busy he tried to keep himself, the same,
unsettling pictures pushed aside his thoughts again and
again.

It didn't matter that Torie was perfection, he reminded
himself.

It didn't matter that her breasts were small and round and firm, that her legs were lean and just long enough. It didn't matter that she had slim hips and creamy thighs, the kind that would make any man in his right mind yearn to caress them. It didn't matter that she had a small pink birthmark on her ribs just below her left breast, a mark in the shape of a lacy flower, or that there was a jagged scar on her right knee, the result, no doubt, of some childhood misadventure.

It didn't matter, Gabriel told himself again and again. None of it mattered.

All that mattered was that Torie's body was burning with fever, that her heartbeat was so weak, he wondered how it could possibly keep her alive until morning.

All that mattered was that he was very much afraid that Torie was going to die.

That one thought chased the others from his head, and Gabriel went back into Torie's room, dipped the cloth in water, wrung it, and held it to her brow.

"Damn it, Torie," he said, stroking the cloth over her arms and neck, attempting to cool her off a bit before he placed the basin on her lap and forced her to vomit. "Why did I have to realize all this now, when it may be too late?" He shook his head, amazed at himself. "Now I'm not sure what frightens me more, the thought that you might die, or the thought of what I would do without you."

Her body hot, her breathing barely perceptible, Torie lay with her eyes closed. Her skin was taut across her cheekbones. There were black smudges beneath her eyes. Like a marble sculpture, every vein stood out against the ghostly white of her hands so that she looked no more alive than a stone effigy from an ancient tomb.

Casting aside the unsettling thought, Gabriel stretched,

rolling the stiffness from his shoulders. He closed the book on his lap and set it on the floor before he knuckled his eyes and scraped his hands across the stubble of beard on his chin and jaw.

He hadn't slept a wink all night. He hadn't even tried. More than once during the night, Torie had called out for him. More than once, she'd sat up straight as an arrow, her eyes open, her expression vacant, and muttered something about the lights, something about the madness she was so sure had come to claim her as it had Roger.

More than once, Gabriel had done his best to quiet her fears. He'd taken her in his arms, stroked her, and settled her back in bed. More than once—so many times more than once—he'd waited for her to calm down and then gone over the evidence of all he suspected, and each time he did, he seethed with anger and the desire for revenge.

Even in the glaring light of late morning it seemed an incredible theory, perhaps even more extraordinary than it had last night, with the eerie moonlight glimmering all around and Torie's warnings about lights and phantoms ringing in his ears. Still, there seemed no other explanation, not unless he was ready to believe Torie mad.

With a snort, Gabriel rejected the idea.

Soon enough, he would be proved right or wrong, he reminded himself. Soon, he would know the truth.

A noise like something falling in the library brought Gabriel's head up. His jaw rigid, his mouth set in a firm, hard line, he went to investigate.

And found exactly what he expected.

Spencer Westin was rummaging through the library, scattering books all around, throwing papers to the floor, peering behind tables and under the specimen shelves that lined the walls.

Gabriel paused before entering the room. He was tempted to congratulate himself. He'd been right. He was sure of it. But there was little satisfaction in the truth.

Completely blocking the only means of escape from the room, he settled himself in the middle of the doorway and held up the hard-sided valise that contained Torie's reptile tooth. "Is this what you're looking for?"

At the sound of Gabriel's voice, Westin stopped dead and swung around. His skin went white. His mouth dropped open. "Raddigan." Westin licked his lips. "Whatever are you doing here?"

"I might ask you the same thing." Gabriel advanced a step into the room, the valise still dangling from his hand. He didn't say a thing about the disarray or about the fact that Westin had Torie's journal tucked up under his arm. He didn't need to. He cast a glance at Westin that made it clear he hadn't missed a thing. "It's a deucedly uncommon hour for a social call, wouldn't you say?"

Westin cleared his throat and shifted from foot to foot, fighting to regain his composure. "It's close upon eleven," he said. "Eleven. And you're meant to be well on your way to Southampton by now."

"Yes, I know." Gabriel set the valise on the nearest table and crossed his arms over his chest, his feet planted, his eyes narrowed. "And Torie's meant to be dead. That is how it was to work, isn't it?"

A muscle at the corner of Westin's right eye twitched. "I don't know what you're talking about," he said. "It's nonsense. Pure nonsense." He made a great show of looking beyond Gabriel. "Isn't Victoria here? Isn't she well?"

"She might be well. She might not." Gabriel's voice was so calm, it surprised even him. Fighting to keep his head as well as his temper, he scoured one hand over his chin and down his neck. He looked at the bloody stain on his shirtfront, then up at Westin. "If she were not well, I might be tempted to ask your advice. After all, I believe you are something of an expert when it comes to botanical concoctions."

He gave Westin as much of a detached look as he could manage, and took another few steps into the room, finding some small amount of pleasure in the fact that Westin retreated two steps for each one he advanced.

"I've been reading all night," Gabriel said. "At least that part of the night when I wasn't sticking my finger down Torie's throat or grappling with her fever. But a night's reading isn't enough. Not enough time to learn everything you've taken a lifetime to learn." Gabriel perched on the arm of the nearest chair. "Indulge the pride of a former scholar, will you? Let me see if I've spent my study time wisely. Tell me, which was it, foxglove or lily of the valley? I suspect lily of the valley myself, but I am hardly an expert. Poisoning is not something I know very much about."

"You're not making the least bit of sense." Gabriel had to give Westin credit, he pulled together the shreds of his dignity as quickly as he slipped on his usual appearance of innocent confusion. As casually as if it were the most natural thing in the world, he set down Torie's journal, nudging it with trembling fingers until it sat square in the center of her desk.

"You frighten me, Raddigan," he said, glancing up at Gabriel with that same, condescending look Gabriel had seen him use so many times on Torie. "Talking such nonsense. You act as if it is some matter of life and death."

"Isn't it?" Gabriel clenched and unclenched his fists. "It never occurred to me before last night," he admitted. "It should have. It seems as clear as crystal now. I should have realized it the night we dined with you, but I admit, my head was muzzy from your brandy and the intriguing possibility of finding some excuse—however preposterous—to kiss Torie on the way home. She saw the lights that night. But, you know that, don't you? She saw them again the night of the church fete."

"Girl's as crazy as her brother!" Westin spit out the words, his face screwed into a grimace of distaste.

"Is she?" Gabriel rubbed his thumbs across his knuckles. "Tell me, when did Roger first exhibit signs of his madness?"

It was not a question Westin expected, and for a moment, it was obvious he was not sure how to answer. "Years ago, I've been told," he began. "He—"

"Yet I knew him at Oxford, and while he was irritating and deceitful and utterly intolerable, Roger Broadridge was not mad."

Westin twitched his shoulders. "He certainly was when he lived here. I've told it all to you before. He believed in the lights. He saw them. Obviously, he was already unhealthy, his mind weak."

"And is Torie's mind weak, too?"

Westin snorted. "You know it is. She is a woman who thinks herself equal to a man, and that in itself proves some infirmity. She has ridiculous ideas. Preposterous theories. Her ideas about the dragon, for instance—"

"Are so preposterous, they're worth killing for?"

Westin threw back his head and laughed. "Your years of drink and dissipation have obviously affected your mind, Raddigan. That much is clear. Think of it, man, what possible reason would I have for wanting to kill Victoria?"

"The same reason you had for killing Roger." Gabriel snapped open the valise and lifted out the tooth, weighing it in one hand. "Here's your reason. Torie's dragon. Despite your outmoded beliefs and your limited abilities, you recognized the tooth for the significant find it is. You made Roger think he was mad and then you killed him because you believed the tooth was his discovery. You thought that with Roger out of the way, you'd simply marry Torie and take over Roger's work. Luckily for Torie, things weren't quite that simple."

He had Westin's interest now. Gabriel was sure of it. Westin's mouth puckered as if he'd tasted something nasty. "Thought it was his? What are you talking about? Of course the tooth was Roger's! Who else's would it be?"

Gabriel laughed. For the first time in as long as he could remember, he laughed. It felt damned good. "The tooth," he said quite simply, "belongs to Torie."

He waited to go on, long enough for the significance of his statement to make its way into Westin's hard head.

He knew when it finally did. A rush of color stained Westin's cheeks and his eyes flew open wide.

"Torie's the one who found the tooth," Gabriel continued, enjoying the spectacle Westin was making of himself. "Torie's the one who realized its significance. She's the one who went to London and rooted through all those specimens to determine its relationship to modern animals. She wanted to see her findings published, so she and Roger concocted the story about him discovering the tooth, just as they pretended all her other research was his work."

Gabriel wasn't sure Westin's mouth could fall open any further, but it did.

"So you see, Westin," he said, "you wasted your time and your acting ability. You didn't need to try and make Torie believe you were the ever-attentive friend, concerned about her welfare. You didn't need to bother pretending you were in love with her. Torie's not the kind of woman who can be so easily persuaded. And she's not a woman who will ever give herself to a man unless she loves him."

"She doesn't love you, either."

Westin's statement was true and it stung more than Gabriel would ever admit, but he wasn't about to let Westin know it. He kept his teeth clenched behind a savage smile.

"You started your campaign to steal the tooth in Oxford, didn't you? That ruffian who tried to rob Torie wasn't after her money. He was after the valise. When that didn't work, you tried a proposal of marriage. And when that failed, too, you decided on poison. It was in the tea you brewed for Torie that night, wasn't it?" he asked. "And in all those cups of tea you brought her at the fete. The first few times, you used just enough to bring on the hallucinations. Just enough to scare Torie into believing herself mad. You were hoping she'd run to you for advice and protection. You were planning on convincing her she was unstable. The next step would have been for you to have yourself declared her guardian. Am I right?" Gabriel's top lip curled with loathing.

"She fooled you, Westin. She fooled us both. Torie's so strong, she doesn't need either damned one of us."

"Nonsense. That's what it is." Westin mumbled to himself while he sidestepped Gabriel, heading for the door. "There's not a bit of it you can prove. Let me remind you, on those occasions you say Torie saw the lights, you were also with her. It could just as easily have been you."

Gabriel ignored him. "When you realized you were getting nowhere, you decided to raise the stakes," he said. "Last night, you increased the dosage of the poison and administered it to Torie in that little glass of liquor you presented to her. The spirits made the drug work faster. And that made it more lethal. By this time today, you thought she'd be dead and I'd be gone." He deposited the tooth back in the valise and snapped it shut. "You've come to collect the spoils of your labors."

Westin's tongue flicked in and out of his mouth, like a snake's. "You could have just as easily killed Roger," he said. "You knew him in Oxford. And from what I've heard you say, you were not friends."

"But I didn't kill him," Gabriel snarled. "Damn the son of a bitch, I thought about it. But I didn't. I was miles away when Roger died. But you? You were right here, Westin, and I'd wager Windsor Castle itself that you killed Roger Broadridge."

"Roger?"

A voice from outside the library door brought them both spinning around.

Like a wraith, Torie stood in the gloom of the passage-way, her white nightgown floating above her bare feet, her hair in a tumble around her shoulders. Her eyes were glazed, her lips were cracked. She swayed back and forth, the gaze she turned on both of them feverish.

"Roger?" Shaking her head slowly, she turned to Westin. "You . . . killed . . . Roger?"

"Victoria! Don't believe a word this madman is saying." His hands held out in supplication, Westin took a step in Torie's direction.

"Stop right there." The cold note of danger that threaded its way through Gabriel's words was enough to stop Westin in his tracks. "You go near her and I'll break every bone in your body."

"Killed Roger?" Torie made a feeble gesture in Westin's direction.

"It's all right." Gabriel went to her, pulling her close into the circle of his arm. "It's over now, Torie. All of it. Over. The lights are gone."

Being careful to keep his distance from Torie as well as Gabriel, Westin edged his way out of the library and headed to the front door, his back to the wall, his eyes nervously watching the way Gabriel's hands balled into fists.

"You can't prove a thing." Westin's words were as fitful as the movements he made toward the door. "It's theory. All of it."

"But sound." Gabriel nodded with satisfaction. "And when Torie's better and I have a moment to myself, I intend to speak to the local magistrate about it."

Westin already had the door open and was partway out of it when Gabriel stopped him.

"And, Westin?"

As Gabriel hoped, Westin paused and turned back to him.

"If you ever come near Torie again," Gabriel said, his voice heavy with warning, "you will be sorry for it. And if she dies?" Gabriel narrowed his eyes. "If that happens, it won't matter what the authorities know or don't know. I swear, if Torie dies, I'll kill you myself."

Chapter 16

The dreams had no beginning. They had no end. They tugged her down into some strange, unreachable place where time and space had no measure, where all was chaos, and fear, and horrible, bright white radiance.

Torie had a vague recollection of walking home, a vaguer remembrance still of pausing atop some place high and broad. After that, there was only one thing clear in her mind.

Lights.

Lights that danced around her ankles and snaked around her legs. Lights that enveloped her, blinding her to all else. Lights that taunted her and mocked her, sizzling through her like fire, hissing and crackling their way past the last of her defenses. Lights that pulled her down, finally and inexorably, into inescapable madness.

They blazed behind her eyes. They flashed inside her brain like skyrockets, bursting and exploding, deafening her to all but their unrelenting roar. Like the hottest fire, they burned for what may have been hours. Or days.

Still, the lights tormented her.

The slow slide into insanity which had begun a month ago had turned into an avalanche of madness. Suffocating, sightless, mind-numbing madness. A place of no form and no feeling at all except blistering heat that seared her body, heat that turned the very next moment into deathly cold that chilled her through to her very soul.

There was no way past the lights. There was no respite. Even in her madness, Torie knew that.

There was no escape.

"You'll feel much better after you eat something."

Gabriel knew his smile wasn't the least bit convincing. He didn't much care. Keeping his voice as cheery as was humanly possible, he threw back his shoulders and marched into Torie's bedroom.

"I made it myself, you know," he confided, looking from Torie to the tray he held in his hands. His gaze traveled from Torie's best porcelain teapot—now slightly chipped thanks to his wet hands and the hard kitchen floor—to the pitcher set next to it, its contents sloshing over the edges with each step he took until the entire tray was awash in a creamy sea.

"Brewed the tea without any help," Gabriel continued, uncommonly pleased with himself. "Wait until Hoyle hears about it! He'll be green with envy, poor chap. He'll be certain I no longer need his services. And that, you can be sure, will break the old fellow's heart."

Torie didn't respond to him and she didn't move.

Firmly fixing his smile in place, Gabriel sat down on the edge of the bed and placed the tray on her lap. He'd propped Torie up on a mound of pillows just before he went to fetch her breakfast and she sat there still, her eyes closed, her cheeks the exact color of the single red rose he'd picked to brighten her breakfast tray.

Gabriel gritted his teeth around his smile, acting for all the world as if he and Torie were engaged in the most scintillating of conversations. Acting. That was the right word, he told himself with a grunt. But even he wasn't sure for whose benefit, Torie's or his own.

Setting the disturbing thought firmly aside, Gabriel moved his gaze back to the tray. "It looks delicious, doesn't it?" he asked. He was so used to eliciting no reply at all from her that he went right on without waiting for one. "There's tea and porridge, a coddled egg, and a nice, thick slab of toasted bread."

Even as he recited the litany, Gabriel felt the edges of his smile wilt. There was tea and porridge, right enough, toast and an egg. Yet it was just as well Torie's eyes were closed and she couldn't see them.

Gabriel hadn't eaten porridge in years, not since the days when his nanny cooked it for him in a black iron kettle hung over the massive fireplace that dominated one corner of his nursery. But he suspected porridge was not supposed to look like this.

Gingerly, he poked a spoon into the mixture, his face screwing into an expression of revulsion as the runny, gray cereal dripped back into the bowl.

"Well, perhaps not porridge." Gabriel pushed the bowl to one side of the tray. "I think, perhaps, I did not cook it long enough. The egg's still good and so is the bread." He eyed them hopefully. "I think."

They weren't. They weren't even close to good. He knew it as soon as the words were out of his mouth.

If the porridge was cooked too little, the egg was cooked far too much. And the toasted bread was beyond hope. Gabriel shook his head sadly. He was fairly certain coddled eggs were not meant to have yolks the consistency of stone, nor was toasted bread meant to be as black and hard as coal.

Gabriel sighed, remembering the perfect, mouth-watering breakfasts Hoyle used to prepare with such seeming ease. Even the plain, hearty meals Mrs. Denny had always provided them seemed elegant compared to this.

Setting aside the tray, Gabriel poured a single cup of tea and skimmed a dense and rather disgusting looking layer of floating tea leaves from the top of it with a spoon. He passed it under Torie's nose.

"I'll try Mrs. Denny again tomorrow," he said, encouraged beyond measure when she responded to the scent of the tea. She sucked in a tiny breath, her tongue flicking from between her cracked lips. "She's been feeling a bit indisposed herself and hasn't been here since you took ill." Gabriel kept up the conversation, lying with the ease that came from years of dealing with recalcitrant bill collectors, inflexible merchants, and unreasonable bookmakers. Though he was fairly sure Torie could not hear him, he did not dare put voice to the real reason Mrs. Denny had not been in to do for them these past few days.

Mrs. Denny refused to come anywhere near the house. So did just about everyone else in the village.

Spencer Westin had made sure of that.

Upon leaving the other day, Westin had gone to the village and immediately began spreading the rumor that Torie was completely mad.

As it always did when he stopped to think about it, the thought hit Gabriel somewhere between the heart and stomach, like the good, solid blow of a pugilist's punch. He controlled his anger, but only because he was afraid Torie might notice it in his voice, and he would not for the world cause her further distress.

"I can't blame Mrs. Denny," he said, speaking his thoughts out loud while he used a spoon to force some of the strong, heavily sugared tea between Torie's lips. "She's a simple enough creature and can't be criticized for being afraid, though she might have stopped by to tell me herself that she was leaving us without someone to do the cooking. If it wasn't for the Reverend Mr. Blankenship, I would never have heard what was going on."

He ventured another spoonful of tea and yet another, smiling when Torie's eyelids fluttered open briefly and she swallowed greedily. "Blankenship's a good chap. He doesn't believe a word of that damned nonsense Westin is spreading, and though he hasn't come right out and said it, I think he's mounted something of a campaign of his own, refuting every word out of Westin's mouth. 'We Oxford men, we must stick together.' That's what he told me and, by the Lord Mansfield's teeth, he's been true to his word. Blankenship has been here to see you every day. You'll never imagine what he told me when he stopped by yesterday." Gabriel brightened at the idea of telling Torie something so truly astonishing, it might just be the thing to bring a smile back to her face.

Half the cup of tea was gone, and deciding that was more than enough for Torie's first try, he set it down and sat back. "Blankenship told me that he had something of an epiphany that night at Westin's." Thinking about the dinner party made the familiar anger surge in Gabriel again, but he forced it down and continued, determined to cheer Torie.

"It seems sometime between the soup and the syllabub, Blankenship took a good, long look at Katherine Wayne and decided she was the one and only woman in the world for him. Remarkable, isn't it? They've already read the first banns." Gabriel laughed, a genuine feeling of amusement sweeping through him. "There's a match made in heaven if ever there was one, a lovesick rector and a lady whose one goal in life is to find herself a husband."

The words sobered Gabriel and he reached for Torie's hand, lifting it gently between his own. "And yours is to find bones." He brushed her fingers with his, heartened by the simple fact that there seemed at least some warmth in them, and looked at her, sincerity burning through him so that he was certain she could see it in his eyes, if only she would open hers.

"I've had something of an epiphany myself, Torie," Gabriel admitted. "I've had a great deal of time to think everything through. Since that day I met you, I knew you were the most maddening woman in the world. And the most irresistible. You know, I hate to admit it, but you were also the most accurate. Damn me for a fool! You were right. Back in the quarry that morning. You were absolutely right. You went to Oxford to find a good-for-naught wastrel, and you did. You found me. What you didn't know was that you weren't there just to employ me. You were there to save me."

Gently, he pressed a kiss to her fingers. "It took you shouting at me to make me see the truth of it. And it took nearly losing you for me to realize how much of a difference you've made in my life. Thank you." He breathed the words against her hand. "I've no right to say it, I suppose, and no way to show it that I can think of except one. The Reverend Blankenship is to sit with you these next few afternoons," he said. "Where will I be?" He laughed, answering the question he wished she had asked.

"I've been reading your journal," he explained. "And I think you're right. The quarry does seem the best place to find bones for that's where you found the tooth. I think you're very close, and I won't see all your work go wanting just because you won't be up and about for a while yet. So if you need me, Miss Victoria Broadridge, I will be out excavating."

Her hand still in his, Gabriel leaned forward and kissed Torie's cheek. "You were right," he said, looking down at her and wishing that he had done something—anything —in his life that would merit him the privilege of saying a prayer and having it answered.

"I am exactly the man I made myself," he told her. "More's the pity. I've wasted the last years of my life feeling sorry for myself. I've let Roger's deceit and cunning ruin my life. I've had enough of it. It ends today."

Gabriel sat back. "There's only one thing more I have to do. Will you excuse me for a few minutes?" He stood and moved to the door.

"I'll be back," he promised. "As soon as I've disposed . . ." he said the word carefully after determining it to be just the right one. "As soon as I've disposed of some of the things that are standing in the way of my being a decent man again."

The dream changed abruptly.

Torie sank back against her pillow, anxiety and apprehension giving way to softer, more pleasant emotions.

The lights were gone and in their place, she saw the flash of Gabriel's smile and felt the warmth of his touch. Though she could not think why or how she knew it, she realized somehow that she was safe.

She was safely tucked beneath a fresh-smelling duvet, safely wrapped in a clean, cozy nightgown. There were lights still against her eyelids, but they were not the ones that ate away at her reason, sending her tumbling into dreadful, endless nightmares. This was sunlight, bright and wonderful, and though she was too weak to open her eyes and enjoy it fully, she found herself smiling.

Comfortable and safe at last, Torie fell back into a sleep that was deep and restful, a sleep interrupted by only one more dream.

In it, Gabriel brushed a kiss against her hand before he touched another to her cheek, and a sensation of warmth and affection flooded through Torie, bringing tears to her eyes.

The dream was remarkably real.

It even had its own sounds, sounds so genuine she would have sworn they were real, too.

Torie turned over in bed.

The sounds were discordant and should have vexed her. Instead, they lulled her back to sleep.

The odd and oddly sweet sounds of bottles breaking.

"You didn't leave."

Torie sat near the window, her elbows on her knees, her hands under her chin, her face pulled into the kind of deep, studious expression Gabriel had seen on the faces of hundreds of scholars over the years, the kind that was both earnestly contemplative and honestly puzzled.

There was a deep vee between her eyes and her chin was furrowed. Even though it was evident she was talking to him, she did little more than glance at Gabriel when he came into the room. That, and the fact that he had not thought to see her out of bed, caused him to skid to a halt just inside her bedroom door.

"You're awake!" Gabriel hurried to set down the tray he was carrying. "I didn't think you'd be up and about so soon. You look . . ." He let his gaze sweep over her, from the top of her quite disheveled head to her pale face, from her sunken eyes to her cracked lips, down to where her bare toes peeked from beneath the hem of her gown. "You look wonderful!"

Torie sat up and clasped her hands on her lap. "You needn't lie," she said, leveling a look at him that said as much as she appreciated his attempts at flattery, she would brook no foolishness. "I believe, were you being more honest and less politic, you would say rather that I look like hell. I feel like hell." Torie closed her eyes and swayed slightly in her chair, the exertion of saying so much after spending so long saying nothing at all, robbing her of what little was left of her strength.

Gabriel was at her side in a moment, his hand at her elbow. "You should rest. Let me help you back to bed."

Torie did not answer him, but shook him off, and when

she opened her eyes, they sparkled with some emotion he could not read. "You didn't leave," she said again, as bewildered as ever. "I remember you said you were going. That night of the dinner party. You had booked passage on a ship to America and you were leaving in the morning. But it is long since that morning, isn't it?"

"Long since," Gabriel admitted. Reluctant to meet her eyes and just as reluctant to admit to himself why, he shifted his weight slightly from foot to foot. In the past days, he had wondered how long it would take her to ask the question just as he'd wondered if he would ever have the courage to give her the honest answer to it. Now, he braced himself against what he knew was coming, still not certain how he would respond.

Torie tipped her head to one side. "Why?"

Gabriel shrugged, admonishing himself the moment he did. It was a poor answer, an ambivalent answer, and he owed her more than that.

"Poor, hell." He grumbled to himself. It was inadequate. It was insufficient. It was cowardly.

It branded him a milksop, a man who did not have the mettle to make known the thoughts that had, these past weeks, been trampling through his brain with all the subtlety of one of Torie's thirty-foot reptiles. It was foolish of him. And spineless. And he would not allow it to happen again.

Drawing in a deep breath, Gabriel decided to give voice to the emotions that had taken possession of him, body and soul. It would be easy enough, he told himself, to bolster his courage. He would be glib and suave, urbane and amusing. He would simply sweep Torie away as he had swept so many other women away, with a charm and a sophistication that was so effortless and so spontaneous, it sometimes shocked even him.

Readying himself for the moment, Gabriel pulled himself up to his full height. And shrugged again. "I don't know," he said.

He pulled a face and cursed himself for his ineptitude, wondering why he had never had such a problem with a woman before. Had Torie been any other woman, he would have given her a shrewd wink and a hearty chuckle. Had Torie been any other woman, he would have swaggered just a little, so pleased with himself it would be impossible to contain his conceit. Had Torie been any other woman, any other woman in the entire world, he would simply have told her the truth.

He would have laughed a hearty and carefree sort of laugh and said he did not go to America because he could not endure the thought of being thousands of miles away and wondering what had happened to her. He would have gazed deep into her eyes and confessed that he stayed because he could not look himself in the mirror if he left so brave a woman to fight her demons alone. Like the hero of some melodramatic play, he would have strode to the fireplace, one hand on his hip, and swung to face her, telling her with a voice wavering on the infinitesimal edge between passion and sentiment, that he stayed because he could not bear to leave her; he could not live without her.

But Torie was not any other woman, and suddenly, the words that should have come to him as naturally as breathing, stuck in Gabriel's throat. He tried clearing them with a cough.

"You needed my help," he said, congratulating himself for being able to speak at least a part of the truth. "I couldn't desert you. You were ill and you needed someone to help you get better."

"Ill? Was I?" Torie's eyes changed from clear green to deep, troubled emerald. "I think perhaps you are trying to spare my feelings and I think, perhaps . . ." she fixed him with a look, "we are beyond that, you and I. Tell me the truth, Gabriel. Did I imagine it all? Was that all part of the bad dream? I remember standing in the passage-way outside the library. You were there. With Spencer. You said . . . You told him you knew what was wrong with me and . . ." Just when it looked as if she could not bring herself to finish the thought, she raised her chin, gathering her courage far more effectively than Gabriel had been able to gather his. "Is it true that Spencer killed Roger and wanted me dead, too?"

Whatever self-consciousness Gabriel felt evaporated in-stantly in the face of Torie's question. He crouched down, bringing his face on a level with hers and tucked a way-ward strand of her hair behind her ear. He took both her hands in his.

There was no way to soften the blow though, Lord knew, he had tried his best to think of one. Gabriel cap-tured Torie's gaze with his own, determined to see her through this, the last of the nightmare.

"I'm sorry," he said quite simply. "You didn't dream it. I'm afraid it is true. I think Westin realized the value of the tooth and decided to do whatever it took to obtain it for his own. I can't prove a thing, of course, but I am certain he killed Roger. He stuffed Roger full of stories about eerie lights and restless spirits, then administered a poison to make him hallucinate. Bit by bit, he convinced Roger and everyone else that Roger was mad. I think Westin meant Roger to give up his research when he felt his mind going. I think he meant him to turn it all over to Westin. It was a poor plan, of course, because the work wasn't Roger's, it was yours. When Westin's plan failed, he killed Roger."

"And offered to marry me." A shiver snaked over Torie's shoulders. "When I refused, he determined that there was only one way he'd ever have the tooth." A single tear spilled from her eye and cascaded down her cheek. "I suspect there is a great deal I need to thank you for," she said.

"No." Gabriel smiled and brushed the tear aside with his thumb. "I explained all that. While you were ill. I sat right here and explained that I am the one who should be grateful."

Torie's expression clouded. "I don't understand."

"I do," Gabriel admitted with a laugh. "And I will be more than happy to explain it all to you. But not until after you eat. There's only so long a person can live on sugared tea, you know. I've brought you a proper breakfast."

"Breakfast." Torie repeated the word as if it were foreign and her face took on a distinctly green cast. "I have some memory of one of your breakfasts. Was it yesterday, or longer ago than that?" She didn't wait for him to answer, but shook her head as if to straighten her thoughts. "I think I will pass, thank you."

"Oh, no!" It wasn't often in the last weeks that Gabriel had the chance to gloat. He wasn't about to let the opportunity pass unnoticed. He hopped to his feet and went to retrieve the tray. Offering her a dazzling smile, he swept the tray onto her lap.

In one corner of the tray stood her best silver teapot, its surface gleaming. There were beautifully cooked eggs and perfectly toasted bread on a plate, jam and honey in sparkling crystal pots.

"I . . ." Torie looked up at Gabriel. "I don't know what to say."

"Don't say a thing. Eat." With a wave of one hand, Gabriel urged her to get started. "We'll talk later."

"No!" Torie grabbed for his hand and held on tight. It seemed an instinctive movement and it was so quick and heartfelt, it surprised even her. A bit of pure pink color rose in her cheeks.

"How long has it been?" she asked.

"How long has it been since you've seen a breakfast this splendid?"

His banter wasn't enough to distract her. "How long have I been ill?" she asked. "If the way my stomach is responding to this food is any indication, it's been a very long time."

Convinced that the sooner Torie knew the truth, the easier it would be for her to accept it, Gabriel answered instantly. "Ten days," he said and he could not help but admire the way Torie took the news.

She did not recoil or look horrified, she simply nodded. "Ten days. Then it is no wonder at all that this is the most marvelous-looking breakfast I've ever seen." Her eyes lit with the smallest of smiles.

"Then eat it."

Torie was not about to give in so easily. She shook her head and gave him the kind of penetrating look he remembered so well. "Not until you explain it. I may not recall much of the past days, but I do remember your porridge." She shuddered. "Am I dreaming again?"

"No." Gabriel laughed. He would have liked to take credit for the whole thing, from the gleaming silver pot to the skillfully cooked eggs, but even his scruples would only allow so much.

"Hoyle is here," he admitted. "He has taken over Mrs. Denny's cooking duties and is well on his way to taking over the operation of the entire household." Gabriel grimaced, half because he thought it might make Torie smile and half because he was genuinely staggered by how quickly and efficiently Hoyle could turn chaos into order.

"A month away playing attentive uncle has done little to mellow Hoyle's temperament," he told Torie. "He is as testy as ever. He has ensconced himself in the kitchen like Zeus atop Mount Olympus." Gabriel muttered a mild curse, more to keep up appearances than because he meant it. "I don't know why I bother to keep the man around except that he knows how to cook eggs."

"And you do not."

"No." Gabriel smiled, encouraged that Torie was feeling well enough to offer some show of humor. "I do not. As is Hoyle's wont, he is already running roughshod over me," he added. "But you needn't worry. As I explained back in Oxford, Hoyle has a soft spot in his heart for maidens in dire straits. All you need do is sit back and recover. The rest is in Hoyle's more than competent hands. The place is already running like clockwork. The silver is polished. The clothes are laundered."

Chewing on a mouthful of bread, Torie looked down at her nightgown, then up at Gabriel. "Tell me," she said, washing down the toast with tea. "If Hoyle has taken over Mrs. Denny's duties, then that means Mrs. Denny is not here. And if that is true . . ." Torie glanced away, her cheeks suddenly flushed, her eyes pressed closed. She swallowed with an audible gulp. "Who undressed me and put me in my nightgown?" Her face still screwed up in dismay, she opened her eyes a crack and peeked at him. "It wasn't you, was it?"

Gabriel might be adept at prevarication when it came to merchants, bookmakers, and women who were burning with fever and, therefore, could neither dispute nor question what he was saying, but he was hardly comfortable with lying to Torie when she was looking so innocent and embarrassed.

"Of course it wasn't me!" Determined not to let Torie see his face because he was certain it would reveal his guilt, Gabriel turned his back to her and paced to the other side of the room, wondering at the same time whose feelings he was trying to spare.

It would be bad enough for Torie if she knew he was the one who had stripped off her nightgown each morning and bathed her. It would be even worse for him if she saw his face when the truth came out and realized just how discomfited he was by the whole thing.

Even now in the full light of day with Torie sitting on the other side of the room, waiting for him to tell the truth, he could scarcely keep the memories from overwhelming him.

He could see every contour of her naked body. Without even closing his eyes, without even trying, he could picture every curve, every detail, every inch of ivory skin, every one of the hundreds of freckles that dotted her shoulders and flowed like a flurry of cinnamon-colored snowflakes over her breasts.

If only he tried the slightest bit, he could imagine the silky feel of her skin beneath his fingers, the way sleek strands of her hair skittered over his hands as he tried to hold it out of the way to stroke her neck with a soapy cloth, the brush of her breath, soft and warm, against his cheek.

Gabriel let go a sigh. Torie may have been ill these last, long days, but he was as healthy as ever, and much to his dismay, his body responded to the thoughts as any healthy man's would.

"You were right thinking me a libertine and a scoundrel," he said briskly, hoping to trick both her and his errant self with his bluster. "But even you cannot think me so depraved as to have the temerity to strip an unconscious woman!"

"Then Mrs. Denny was here?"

Gabriel jumped at her suggestion. "That's right," he said. "She has not been well herself and has not been in to cook, but of course, she is the one who has been taking care of your personal needs."

Torie looked as relieved as Gabriel felt. She took another bite of toast, another drink of tea. "I didn't mean to suggest that—"

"No." Gabriel interrupted a little too quickly. "I never

thought you thought . . ." He cleared his throat and with a deep, calming breath, steered himself as clear of the subject as he could. "May I pour you more tea?"

With a smile, Torie accepted his offer. Her smile faded as she watched him and she narrowed her eyes, studying his face.

"Is something wrong?" Gabriel asked.

"There's something wrong with you," she replied. Reaching for him, Torie ran one finger over the row of nearly healed scratches on Gabriel's cheek. Her touch was light and gentle but it held him in place, like the spell of a sorceress. "You look to have had a fight with a very angry cat."

Gabriel opened his mouth, some inadequate explanation ready on his lips though he was not certain what it would be. Before he had a chance to even begin it, Torie grabbed his hand and stared at his arm, and Gabriel cursed himself silently.

The afternoon was warm, and he had rolled his shirt-sleeves above his elbows. In his haste to bring Torie breakfast and his relief at seeing her up, he'd completely forgotten his arms were bare. He followed Torie's gaze down to where his right forearm was bruised, the imprint of Torie's teeth still bright red against the purple.

"Dear Lord!" Some obscure memory made its way into Torie's brain and her face paled. She held one hand to her heart. "I'm sorry. I didn't know. I didn't remember . . ." Tears slipped down her cheeks. "You must think me awful. And after you saved my life!"

In spite of her miserable expression, Gabriel found himself smiling. Kneeling on the floor in front of her, he whisked the tray from her lap and took her into his arms.

Much to Gabriel's delight, and just a bit to his surprise, she did not struggle or try to extricate herself from his embrace. At the same time he told himself it was surely because she was still too weak to fight, he could not help but be inordinately pleased by her reaction. A strange, warm feeling tangled around his heart and he dropped a kiss onto Torie's brow, another on the tip of her nose.

"You're not awful at all," he assured her. "You're strong, and wise and very, very brave. I may have helped you through the last days, Torie, but I am not the one who saved you. You did that yourself. And saved me in the process."

Torie pulled back just far enough to give him a questioning look, the edges of her expression wavering between laughter and tears. "The breaking bottles?" she asked.

Gabriel chuckled. "You heard that, did you? That's right. Brandy bottles. All of them. I suppose it would have been a little more sensible to simply pour the stuff out, but I was feeling rather dramatic that day. And I have you to thank for it." Laughing, he pressed her into a ferocious hug. "You made me see what no one else has made me see these past years," Gabriel told her. "You made me realize I have to believe in myself before anyone else will believe in me."

Women were the most wondrous of creatures.

The incredible premise intruded on Gabriel's thoughts as he watched Torie's smile widen at the same time fresh tears cascaded down her cheeks.

"And you are the most wondrous of all," he said, amazed at himself, and by the feelings she aroused in him, and by the simple fact that the twists and turns of his life had brought him here to this, the most unlikely of places.

Gabriel touched Torie's lips with a light, undemanding kiss, sucking in a sharp breath when she returned the kiss with one of her own.

"Damn me for a fool, Victoria Broadridge," Gabriel said smiling down at her, and wondering why he had spent so many wasted hours practicing fine and fancy words for a declaration that was so simple and so straightforward. "Damn me for a fool," he said, "but I am in love with you."

Chapter 17

"You seem to be feeling better today."

At the sound of Gabriel's voice, Torie stopped her pacing in midstride. She'd spent the entire morning going from one end of her bed chamber to the other, and the sudden suspension of the aimless routine sent her equilibrium into a spin. Holding herself upright, one hand against the wall, she glared across the room at him.

"How much longer do you plan on keeping me prisoner here?" she asked, her words as icy as the look she gave him.

Much to her annoyance, Gabriel laughed. He tossed the bundle he was carrying onto her bed. "I'm right," he said. "You are feeling better. You are practically your old self again. Full of spit and vinegar. I see your daily constitutional has restored your temperament." He gave her a sly smile and let his gaze slide from the top of her head to the tips of her satin house shoes, his eyes lighting as he paused almost imperceptibly at her breasts and hips. "And it has certainly benefitted your body."

How something so simple as a smile could send a prickle of awareness over her was a mystery Torie thought she might never understand. Right now, she did not even try. She accepted it as she had accepted every other one of the extraordinary events that had touched her over the past weeks, each one nudging her in its own singular way to the special and quite surprising intimacy she and Gabriel suddenly seemed to share. It never failed to take her breath away when she stopped to consider it, and today was no exception.

Torie felt her cheeks flush, but whether because of Gabriel's open look of admiration or because she was so easily upended by it, even she didn't know. She shook the thought away. How dare he tempt her with such irresistible looks when she was trying her best to goad him into an argument!

"My temperament is quite as placid as it ever was," she assured him, trying her best to sound petulant so that she could get the argument back on track. "And as for my body . . . a walk in the garden each morning with Hoyle can hardly be considered a constitutional. He is a pleasant enough companion, but he has his duties to attend to and he is always eager to get back to them. And on those occasions when I have ventured to suggest that we go a little farther afield, he has assured me in no uncertain terms that you have strictly forbidden it. That is unconscionable! And it is unfair. This is my home, after all. Last I noticed, I was still mistress here. And I am certainly above the age of consent. You cannot keep me captive."

Her attempt at logic had little impact on Gabriel. He was still smiling at her, simply smiling, and Torie tossed her hands in the air, barely stifling a small screech of frustration. "I'm so very bored!"

Still Gabriel did not reply, and vexed that her confession had elicited no more response than had her reasonable analysis of the situation, she went over to where he stood, not sure of what she might do when she got there, but desperate enough to try anything to make him see her point of view.

It would be a good deal easier to stay angry at him, she

decided, if his eyes did not sparkle so in the light, like dark jewels caught sight of beneath the surface of a brook.

It would be a great bit simpler keeping her mind on track if Gabriel's smile did not wind through her like a tendril of ivy, twisting and twining its way around her heart until it eroded the walls she'd built there to shield herself from the world, leaving in their place something fresh, and wonderful, and growing.

It would be far easier to remain irate if the man who stood before her now was the same man she'd sat across from that first day in Oxford. The one who was fleshy and jaded. The one whose eyes were as flat and lifeless as stones. The one whose real self was so carefully camouflaged beneath a layer of scathing humor, a heavy haze of excess, and a cloud of brandy fumes.

The Gabriel who stood before her now had a burnishing of color across his cheeks, a token of the sun and wind of the downs. There was a new and quite surprising outline of hardened muscle showing beneath his white linen shirt, and a line to his shoulders that made him look far less like he was ready to fight the world and far more like he was willing, finally, to accept those gifts with which it had graced him.

This Gabriel smiled more than he scowled. He laughed far more than he cursed. He sat with Torie quietly by the fire each night, her hand in his, and they talked about a future that, until now, seemed as unattainable as reaching for the moon. A future together.

It was difficult trying to stay angry at him. It meant not paying the least bit of attention to the sensual curve of his mouth, or the tiny thread of desire that grew inside her every second they were together, until she felt as if she might burst from it.

It was difficult. But Torie did her best.

She gave him as peevish a look as she could manage. "I never see you at all," she said, hoping for at least some sign of the guilt she tried to make him feel. "You are already gone somewhere or another when I rise in the morning. You are gone all day. I spend the morning pacing here in the bedroom. In the afternoon, I might move to the library. It's quite intolerable, you know. I'm feeling much better and I think it is time I got out a little."

"I do, too."

It was so unlike Gabriel to agree so readily that for a moment, Torie did not know what to say. She stared at him, her mouth open, hoping some clever rejoinder would suddenly pop into her head and make its way to her lips. It didn't, and she said the only thing she could think to say. "I beg your pardon?"

Laughing, Gabriel flopped down on the sofa near the windows and patted the seat next to him. "I said you're right," he told her after she had accepted his invitation and settled herself beside him. "I can see you are feeling better. And I know you are bored. I think it's time for you to get back to work."

Torie nearly clapped her hands with excitement. She controlled the urge to place a kiss on Gabriel's cheek, but only because she feared it would distract them both from the subject at hand. "When can we get back to the quarry?"

"Oh, no!" Frowning, Gabriel shook his head. "I didn't say anything about excavating. I said working. And in your case, working means catching up on your reading."

Whatever excitement Torie felt melted like a candle left too long in the hot summer sun. Her expression soured. "There isn't a book in the library I haven't read these past two weeks since I've been out of bed," she said. "And there are a few I've read more than once. Don't tell me—"

"But you haven't read this." Gabriel proffered her a letter.

"It's addressed to you," she said, looking from the letter

to him, not quite understanding what this was all about. "Who is it from?"

"Read it."

Torie cast a glance around the room. "I don't have my spectacles. I'm sure I've left them in the library and I can't stand to wait to find out what you've been up to. Tell me. Please."

Gabriel gave in with as much good grace as possible. But he didn't unfold the letter, and he didn't read it. It was obvious he knew every word it contained, and just as obvious that, now that he'd been given the opportunity, he couldn't wait to tell Torie about it.

"It's from Cronkite," he said. "In Oxford."

"Phineas Cronkite?" Torie's head came up and she looked at him in wonder. "The same Phineas Cronkite who turned his back on you when you were sent down? The man who made sure the gates of Magdalen were closed to me when I sought him out to speak to him about the tooth?"

"The same." Gabriel laughed. "And before you castigate him for his past deeds, or me for communicating with him, let me tell you what it says in his letter." With great ceremony, Gabriel unfolded the paper, smoothed it, and ran his finger down the page. He found the passage he was looking for, cleared his throat, and began to read.

" '. . . it is therefore with less than great pleasure, but with a sense of duty and a serious thought to the obligation I owe the scientific community that I—' "

"That pompous, old fool!" Torie could take no more. "He says that? He actually says that in his letter? Let me see." She grabbed for the letter.

Gabriel snatched it away before she had a chance to look at it. "Will you allow me to finish?"

She crossed her arms over her chest. "I am not at all sure I want to hear anymore. The oaf! I cannot think why you wished to correspond with him, just as I cannot think why you are not more annoyed by his rude statements. Less than great pleasure, indeed!" Torie grunted her disapproval. "I am glad now that he left me waiting out on the street like a common tradesman. I do not think I would like Professor Cronkite so very much."

"Nor do I, but if you would let me finish—"

"Sense of duty!" Torie could not be so easily placated. The condescending tone of Cronkite's letter rankled as much as the fact that Gabriel thought it important to write to the man. There was only one reason she could think of for ever having to communicate with Cronkite.

The truth hit Torie like a thunderclap and she sat up straight. Her mouth suddenly dry, she grabbed for Gabriel's sleeve, twisting it in her fingers so that the fine linen bunched and crumpled. "The tooth? You've told him about the tooth and—"

"Please, madam, you are interrupting. Do let me finish, will you?" Gabriel tried his best to sound as pretentious as he could but it was a poor fiction, indeed. A tiny muscle at the corner of his mouth twitched and he could scarce disguise the fire of excitement that burned in his eyes. He began again, hurrying through the first words of the paragraph as if fearing Torie might launch into another outburst.

" '. . . it is therefore with less than great pleasure, but with a sense of duty and a serious thought to the obligation I owe the scientific community that I"—here, Gabriel slowed down and raised his voice—"invite you to appear before the British Association for the Advancement of Science which will be meeting in Oxford on the fifteenth day of July, and present your findings to that august body.' "

Torie knew if she let go of Gabriel's sleeve her hands would be shaking like leaves on a blustery day, so she held on tight. "I can hardly believe it!" she said. "How did you convince him?"

In one smooth move, Gabriel took one of her hands in his. He slipped his arm around her shoulders. "Cronkite may be an old prig, but he is a hardheaded man of science. He couldn't resist something this delicious, even if it did arrive with my name on it. I'll give the old man credit, it took some backbone for him to arrange the thing, especially since I will be the presenter. I think he knew if he did not agree, I would go to Cambridge with it. Cronkite is a lot of things, but he isn't a fool. He can smell a major find when he gets wind of it. Hoyle has heard from one of his friends in Oxford who says the University is already abuzz with the news. There is hardly an hour goes by, the man says, when he doesn't hear more rumblings about Raddigan and this new, incredible discovery. They are not sure what it is, of course, but Cronkite has put the word abroad that it is something important." Gabriel grinned. "It seems you were right, we are about to revolutionize the world of natural science."

Right now Torie could not say what was having more effect on her, Gabriel's news or the smile that shimmered in his dark eyes. It was clear he was enjoying the excitement of the moment as much as she, and the realization tugged at her heartstrings, drawing her even closer to him.

"The fifteenth of July!" Torie considered the incredible news. "That's only two weeks from now." A new thought struck her and she sat back, her voice falling as her spirits plummeted. "You will have to tell him no, of course."

Gabriel looked at her in wonder.

Unable to endure his disappointment just as she was unable to deal with her own, she rose and walked to the other side of the room. "We have the tooth," she said, seeking to explain as clearly as she could. "But that's all we have. It isn't enough. Not for a presentation to the British Association for the Advancement of Science.

They'd eat you alive if you came before them with such meager evidence. The tooth is a curiosity, but in and of itself, it doesn't prove a thing. We need more, Gabriel. We need bones."

"As I said earlier, you have some reading to catch up on." Gabriel produced her journal from beneath the bundle he'd carried into the room. "I know, I know." He waved away her objection before she had a chance to utter it. "You don't have your spectacles. Here." He flipped through the pages. "Allow me to help." Finally finding what he was looking for, he brought the journal over to where Torie was standing and pointed at a line written in some strange hand.

"Yours?" Torie looked up at him.

"Mine," he said. "Where do you think I've been off to every day? I've been at the quarry. Here." He tapped the page. "You can read what I've been up to. You can at least see some of it without your spectacles, can't you?"

It wasn't easy. Gabriel's handwriting was as different from hers as candlelight from sunshine. Torie's script was small and compact but it was eminently readable. Gabriel's was wide and sprawling, his letters spiraling across the page with all the abandon of a sailor on leave, drunk on too much ale. She squinted at the page, trying to bring the unfamiliar hand and her inadequate eyesight into some kind of agreement.

Most of Gabriel's hand was completely indecipherable. She ignored the place he was pointing to, searching for some letters that at least looked as if they had been written in English. Finally finding some she could untangle, she fought her way through the word.

" '. . . meta . . .' " She paused, struggling to make some sense of the rest of the word. "Metal?" She looked at Gabriel. He shook his head. "M-e-t-a- . . . I can read that much of it. 'Metamorphic' perhaps, but that makes little sense in this context. The only thing that would fit would be meta—"

A clutch of excitement gripped Torie's stomach. "Metacarpal. The word is metacarpal." Almost afraid he would dispute her deduction, she darted a look at Gabriel. He was smiling.

"Metacarpal!" Torie laughed, and linking her hands around Gabriel's neck, she smacked a kiss to his lips. "You've found them, haven't you? You've found bones."

"Come see for yourself." Taking her hand, Gabriel tugged her over to the bed. He pointed to the bundle he'd brought into the room with him. "Here," he said. "Your work clothes. Why don't you get dressed and you'll see for yourself what I've found."

Tearing open the bundle, Torie lifted out Roger's trousers, shirt, and jacket. She pressed them to herself, barely able to contain the feel of exhilaration bubbling in her. Too eager to wait any longer for what she'd waited for all this time, she pointed Gabriel toward the door.

"Go!" she said. "Let me get dressed. I'll be ready in a minute."

Gabriel didn't move. He stared at her, his gaze going to where she had the rough work clothes pressed to her breast. His smile sat upon his lips as if it were frozen there. "I could help." He offered the proposal in a light and casual voice, but there was nothing indifferent about the look in his eyes. They darkened to the color of onyx and flickered with an invitation so clear and so very tempting, Torie was certain had she consented, he would have been startled and even a little disconcerted. But he would have accepted.

The thought made her skin tingle and her head feel giddy. It was the first time since her illness that he had broached the subject of physical intimacy that he had always, until now, treated so cavalierly. There was something about this new thoughtfulness of his that was far more seductive than the confident, maddeningly poised looks he used to give her, something that curled through her like fire, threatening to decimate all sense of reason, all traces of logic in its path.

"I do not believe that would be either wise or prudent," she said, her breathy words dissolving into a laugh when she saw how relieved Gabriel actually looked.

"I thought as much." Still smiling, he went to the door. He was already outside in the passageway when he stuck his head back in, quirking his eyebrows at her and offering a smile that made her heart turn over. "It wouldn't be wise or prudent," he said. "I fully agree. Perhaps that is why the idea is so very appealing."

Torie threw back her head and laughed, enjoying the feel of the sun on her face, the sting of the fresh breeze that blew in off the Channel, and the singular freedom that came from wearing Roger's old, comfortable clothes and roaming again, at last, over the downs. At the rim of the quarry, she paused only long enough to catch her breath, then started down the path that led to the quarry floor.

"Oh, no! Don't go running off." Planting his feet and grabbing her hand, Gabriel held on tight, keeping her firmly in place. "You've already overtaxed yourself. We should have taken our time getting here. But you wouldn't listen. You had to go racing off like—"

"Stop worrying." Gabriel's attempt at nurturing was so uncharacteristic and at the same time so endearing, Torie couldn't help but smile. "I feel wonderful," she assured him. "Nothing could exhaust me. Not today. It's so good to be out of the house! And the thought that you have actually found bones—"

"I said I found something. I didn't say they were bones.

Not for certain. That was all in the section of the journal you didn't bother to read."

In spite of Gabriel's attempts at curbing her enthusiasm, Torie went right on smiling, her gaze already ranging over the quarry, registering and recording the places where Gabriel had been working these last few weeks while she had been recuperating.

The floor of the quarry was beginning to resemble the patchwork covering on one of the eiderdowns she'd seen Mrs. Denny work at. Neat, exact lines were scored into the soil to divide the area into squares, every one of them containing an outcropping of sandstone boulders. Each larger square was divided again into smaller sections, and in three of these, each a good bit distant from the others, Gabriel had set posts topped with fluttering bits of white cloth.

Torie turned to him, a question in her eyes, the tingle of excitement so strong inside her, she could barely keep still. "You have three spots marked. Three? Have you found three deposits of bones?"

"I promised I would explain fully when we got there," Gabriel said, looking as pleased with himself as a cat that had just cornered an especially juicy mouse. "We are not quite there. Not yet." He stepped in front of her when she made a move toward the path, "And we won't get there at all if you don't take a moment to rest."

Half in annoyance, half in resignation, Torie sighed. Deciding to look relaxed and at ease so that Gabriel would allow them to proceed as soon as possible, she lowered herself onto the nearest boulder. "You are quite as fussy as Hoyle. He is just as determined to make me feel like an invalid."

"And I am determined not to have to carry you home." Even before Gabriel was settled beside her, his face lit with a mischievous grin. "Though it is not altogether an unpleasant thought."

Torie had to admit, it was not. But pleasant or unpleasant, now was not the time for it. She was too near her goal, too close to an ambition too long held to let herself be distracted by thoughts as unsettling as those Gabriel suggested. Tucking the image away so that she might bring it out later and savor its delicious implications, Torie concentrated instead on the scene before her.

The last place she remembered excavating was in the center of the quarry, an area no more than ten feet by ten feet. It was bordered by two especially large blocks of sandstone which at some forgotten time in the past, someone had begun to cut and shape. The blocks were never finished and never removed. Their straight sides and rounded corners rose up from the pebble-strewn quarry floor, but their bases were still anchored firmly in the ground, sloping down into the soil as if they were sprouting from it.

The site had seemed the most promising to Torie; the rock formations were Cretaceous, just like the one in which she'd found the tooth, and there were indications of other fossils in the rock, shells and even some fish. But no little white flag fluttered in the center of her plot, and Torie sighed, her shoulders rounding with a sudden feeling of discouragement.

She had not been close, she noted, letting her gaze wander to the flags Gabriel had set up to mark his finds. All her years of study, all her days of hard work here at the site, all her reading and analysis and investigation—and she had not even been close.

"I told you you were close!" As if reading her thoughts and purposely contradicting them, Gabriel leaned nearer and gave her hand a squeeze.

"Close?" Setting aside her discouragement before it could spoil the thrill of the moment, Torie concentrated on the orderly sections into which Gabriel had divided the area. "It looks as if I would have spent a good deal of the next few years digging about in the wrong part of the quarry. What made you decide to look there?" she asked, pointing to the post that was farthest from them. "I saw no other signs in that area of sediment that contained fossils."

"Precisely." Gabriel smiled an enigmatic smile and offered her his arm. "Shall we go have a look?"

Torie did not wait to answer him. Jumping to her feet, she hurried with him down the path that led to the quarry floor, her steps so quick and eager that for once, he needed to scramble to catch her up.

Needles of excitement prickling over her arms and legs, Torie headed to where the closest flag flapped in the breeze.

"Not there." Gabriel tugged her further along the path, stopping only long enough to retrieve a brush, trowel, chisel, and gloves from a bag he'd left next to the two sandstone blocks.

"Here." He pointed to an area not two feet from where Torie had last worked, handing her the tools as he did. "Ready to get to work?"

"But . . . ?" Torie looked from the bare plot over to the others dotted with flags. "But this one isn't marked. Doesn't that mean—?"

"It means Westin would never think to look here." Gabriel chuckled when Torie's mouth fell open. "You don't think he'll surrender so easily, do you? He hadn't the vaguest notion about following you when you were working here. He didn't realize you were the one to follow. But I've been here these past few weeks and word must have gotten around to him. All he would have to do if he wanted to locate the bones is follow me, and as a matter of fact, I'm fairly sure he has a time or two. But there's no use making it easy for him, letting him know the exact spot. Here."

Smiling both at his own cleverness and Torie's reaction

to it, he thrust the tools in her direction again. His voice dropped, his words wrapping around her like warm wool. "The honor is yours, my darling Torie. You are the one who had the wisdom to believe."

Her hands trembling, Torie accepted the tools. She fell to her knees and tugged at his trouser leg, waiting for him to kneel beside her.

Fortifying herself with a great draught of air, she looked to Gabriel for reassurance. "Where?" she asked.

Gabriel moved aside a mound of rocks and a small cache of pebbles that were piled against one of the large sandstone blocks. Using his hands, he scooped away some of the loose soil at the base of the block, revealing a large section of previously buried sandstone. In one corner of it, something dark and shiny and still partially buried caught the light and winked at Torie.

"Right here," he said, pointing to where Torie was looking. "I covered it back up after I found it. Didn't want Westin to see."

The soil was loose and it moved aside easily. Still Torie took her time, carefully scooping out the dirt and brushing it aside. Bit by bit, more of the fossil was revealed.

"I told you you were close." Gabriel peered over her shoulder at the small patch of exposed rock, and whether he knew it or not, his voice vibrated with all the excitement she felt. He gave her shoulder a pat of congratulations and encouragement. "That's as much as I've seen of it," he said. "I wanted you to be the one to take it from the ground."

The work was painstaking and took the better part of the afternoon.

Torie and Gabriel took turns working at the rock, one of them carefully notching the sandstone all around the fossil with a chisel while the other brushed aside the soil. Hoyle had been considerate enough to pack a light luncheon and a bottle filled with lemonade, and they took turns at that, too, alternately working and eating as the sun topped the rim of the quarry and dissolved the long, cool shadows.

By the time they were done determining the contours of the fossil and scoring it, Torie found that even her enthusiasm was not enough to sustain her. It had been far too long since she'd indulged herself in any exercise and the forced inactivity had taken its toll. At Gabriel's urging—and the threat that if she didn't rest they would leave for home immediately—Torie sat back and watched while he chipped the rock containing the fossil away from the sandstone block.

Even once the rock was freed, their work did not end.

Invigorated, more by the emotion of the situation than by her brief rest, Torie sat up and, grabbing for the trowel before Gabriel could convince her to sit back down, she worked it into the space between the edge of the rock and the sandstone block and pried upward. The trowel was serviceable, but only to a certain point. When it looked as if it might damage the rock and its precious contents, Torie tossed the trowel aside and went to work with her fingers. Gingerly, she dug around the rock, smiling to herself when Gabriel joined in. He followed her example, scooping the soil aside with one finger, brushing it out of the hole.

"There you have it." Gabriel sat back on his heels, swiping his sleeve across his forehead. "It's loose enough to remove. Go ahead. Lift it out."

Torie shook her head. "Not by myself." Leaning forward, she took Gabriel's hands in hers and carried them to the fossil. "You take that end," she suggested. "I'll take this."

Gabriel placed his hands beneath one end of the rock and waited while Torie did the same thing at the other end. He looked up long enough to glance at her. "Ready?"

"Ready."

Together, they lifted the rock, and the bones it contained, out of the ground.

They set it down between them and for what seemed like a very long time, neither one of them spoke a word. Torie could not tear her gaze away from the rock and its precious contents, a perfectly preserved clutch of bones that were almost certainly metacarpal, the bones of an animal's forefeet, or hands.

They were larger than any bones she had ever seen, far bigger than the bones of an elephant or hippopotamus, and the strata that contained them was almost certainly Cretaceous.

"It seems your dragon was just as you imagined it." Gabriel's voice was hushed and as solemn as if he were saying a prayer. Reverently, he glided one finger along the fossilized bones. "Look at the size of these bones! The thing must have been enormous."

Torie barely heard him. Casting aside her gloves, she followed the path Gabriel's finger had taken over the surface of the time-smoothed bones with her hand. She was scarcely able to believe that she was finally seeing and touching what had been to the academic community nothing more than a fool's illusion and what had always been to her, a dream.

"Sixty-five million years. That's as long as these bones have been hidden in the earth." Torie's voice was a whisper that even she could barely hear above the pounding of her heart. "It's like touching the past."

"Or the future." Gabriel pulled off his own gloves and twined his fingers through Torie's. "It is as if we've linked ourselves with a time millions of years ago."

"A time when there could not have been reptiles?" Torie knew it was wicked of her to tease him, but she could not seem to help herself. "You believe me now, don't you?"

"Believe you?" Gabriel pulled her closer. "I believe you," he said, his voice suddenly as husky as it had been somber only moments ago. "I believe you have led us into the future. You." With his thumb and forefinger, he traced the line of her jaw, from her left ear, to her chin, and back up again to her right ear, stopping only long enough to brush a smudge of dirt from her cheek. "You are as amazing a creature as your—" He gave the bones a dubious look. "It needs a name, I imagine. What will you call your dragon?"

Torie had given the matter careful consideration in the past and she was not at a loss for words. "Iguanodon," she said. "That's what I should like to call it. The name means iguana tooth."

"Then iguanodon it is." Smiling, Gabriel pulled her to her feet and scooped her into the circle of his arms. "If we were in Oxford, I know just how we'd celebrate this brave new age of science," he said, grinning down at her. "Someone would send for the oldest bottle of brandy in the cellar and we would toast all around."

"But we are not in Oxford." Torie returned his smile with one of her own. "We are here in Sussex. Just the two of us. And, thank the Lord, there isn't a brandy bottle anywhere to be had."

Gabriel chuckled, a warm, wonderful sound that vibrated through his chest and shivered against Torie's fingertips. "Then we shall have to find our own way to celebrate," he said, still smiling. He held Torie far enough away to look her up and down. "You are a sight, Miss Victoria Broadridge. That is for certain. Your hair is tousled, your face is streaked with grime, and your clothes are a mess." He shook his head in dismay, but Torie could not help but notice that he was a poor actor, indeed. He did not look as disillusioned as he tried.

He looked delighted. And exhilarated. And though he wore a smile that traveled all the way from his lips to his eyes, she knew beyond a shadow of a doubt that there was nothing in the least bit frivolous in what he said or what he did.

Gabriel let his gaze flicker over her, from her hair to her clothes, his scrutiny leaving a curious aching in her breasts and a trail of fire that followed the path of his eyes.

"You look a sight, right enough," Gabriel said, his voice as wonderfully shimmery as his look. "The most beautiful sight in the world. Lemonade is not suitable enough for this celebration. And not at all what I need to slake my thirst. I think perhaps there is a better way to celebrate, don't you?" He bent his head, his lips only a fraction of an inch from hers. "I think we should celebrate with a kiss."

Chapter 18

Gabriel did not wait for Torie to agree or disagree. Something told him she would not object. Something as old as the fossil that lay at their feet. Something as certain and irrefutable as the track of the sun through the sky, or the sigh of the wind that ruffled the hair at the nape of his neck and pushed Torie's borrowed shirt close against her, molding itself to her breasts.

Gabriel lowered his mouth to Torie's, abandoning his past and himself to the taste of her lips and the beguiling promise that came when he deepened the kiss and she responded, opening her mouth for him to taste the sweetness of her tongue.

"Even the finest brandy could not be that good." He smiled down at Torie long enough to catch the dreamy, heavy-eyed look on her face.

A less experienced man might think she was simply weary, exhausted from her long confinement and the exertions of the day. But Gabriel knew better. He knew desire when he saw it, and he had never seen it so untainted by greed or lust, so honest and unfeigned.

The thought wound through him like flame. It brightened those places deep inside him that had been too long lost in shadow. It burned away the last of those excuses which had kept his head from responding where all this time, his heart and body had tried to lead him.

With his thumb, Gabriel traced the outline of Torie's lips. "A mouth made for kissing, not arguing," he said, quirking his eyebrows and looking at her hopefully.

Torie tried her best not to smile. "There's a right time and place for both," she countered. "I may allow you a kiss now, but you can be certain I will be just as adamant about debating with you should you ever say anything so ridiculous as to deserve my scorn."

Gabriel laughed. He cupped her chin in his hand, and there was no regret in his voice, just as there was none in his heart. "Stubborn as ever," he said. "I can feel it. Right here." He stroked his thumb along her chin. "In the muscles that bunch up into a frown when you're displeased."

"And always will." She scowled at him for good measure, the grimace tempered by the tiny smile that tickled the corners of her lips and the spark of laughter in her eyes. "Just as yours do when you are angry." Torie brushed his mouth with a touch as light as the whisk of a butterfly's wings. "This is where your frowns commence, like thunderclouds coming over the downs." She laughed, the sound of it echoing through the quarry like the delicate music of fairy bells, and Gabriel wondered if she had any idea how beguiling she looked with the sun glinting off her flaxen hair and a streak of dirt across her nose.

Probably not, he decided, just as she had no idea how the touch of her fingertips seared through him like a brand, no concept of how her breasts pressed against his chest each time she moved even the slightest bit, and how each small movement shot him through with longing.

"I warn you, you may have more cause than ever to glower and groan," Torie said, still smiling. "I fear I will not be so even tempered as you have known me to be in the past."

"Even tempered! God's teeth!" Gabriel shook his head in wonder.

"Exactly. Now that I have seen there is more to you than bluster and scathing repartee, I may not be as likely to back away from an argument."

She had meant the comment as nothing more than sly raillery, Gabriel was certain of it. Yet, in spite of the sweet aftertaste of Torie's kiss, her words left a sudden, sour bite in his mouth. He searched her face, his pleasant mood dissolving. "More to me than bluster and scathing repartee. Is there more, do you think? It will come as a shock to Granger, Morrison, and Cronkite, that is for certain. They and the rest of the damned Oxford academic community are convinced—"

"Stop!" Though Torie silenced him gently with one finger against his lips, all the dreaminess was gone from her face and from her voice. Her golden eyebrows dipped low. Her eyes glinted with green fire that wavered somewhere between aggravation and disappointment. She clutched his sleeve with one hand and moved the other to his cheek, obliging him to look her in the eye.

"What Granger and Morrison and Cronkite think doesn't matter any longer," she said. "Our iguanodon has taken care of that. It will astound them! It will astound scholars all over the world and have them vying for your regard. But never have a doubt, Gabriel. Granger and Morrison and Cronkite and all the others will never forgive you for your mistake. Not until you forgive yourself."

"A mistake, was it?" Gabriel took a step back, instinctively putting distance between Torie and himself just as for the last years, he had sought to put some distance between himself and the truth. "Two months ago, you did not consider it a mistake. You thought it but another of my character flaws, another bit of evidence that piled up with all the rest to prove me worthless. You despised me because I was sent down. You hated me because I was the one who tried to steal Roger's precious double first. You thought me a man with no honor."

His words were like blows, each of them beating against Torie, each one causing her to retreat a step until there was a full arm's length between them, a space that might just as well have been a million miles. But for all the bitter truth of his words, she did not look as if she was about to back down from them.

Torie threw back her shoulders and met Gabriel's gaze with one that was as unyielding and merciless as his own, her voice not as bitter as his, but her words as resolute, her manner every bit as tenacious. "That was before I learned that honor is more than some prize that a university bestows on a man, like a BA or a double first," she said. "That is a mistake I admit that I have made. One I need to forgive myself for and one for which I need to ask your forgiveness. I judged you before I knew you, and worse than that, I judged you by the standards of the close-minded, narrow-hearted, mean-spirited, inflexible academicians who set themselves up as judge and jury of a man before they know his true worth."

"Granger and Morrison and Cronkite didn't see you in Oxford when you chased away that lout intent on stealing my purse even though you thought me the most bothersome termagant of the town. They don't know that you worked hard to find the dragon, even though I treated you so poorly, never telling you the truth of why I wanted you here. They can't possibly know that you stayed here with me when you could have left. When you had every right to leave. That you sat by my side day and night and nursed me back to health when you could have left the country and been rid of your memories, and your debts, and me.

"Oh, Gabriel!" Torie's voice was thick with emotion, her eyes were bright with unshed tears. "Don't you see? Honor isn't what other people think of you. It's what you think of yourself. It is what you do and what you are. You don't need Granger's or Morrison's or even Cronkite's approval to make yourself into the man you are capable of being. You need only your own pride. You need only—"

Torie's words dissolved in the face of what she was about to say, but her determination did not. Even though she looked suddenly as shy as a schoolgirl, her cheeks bright with color, she held her ground, firmly refusing to look away.

"You told me you loved me," she said. "And you have never asked for my love in return. But I offer it to you, Gabriel. And I promise you that my love and your own self-dignity will be enough. It will have to be."

"Damn!" Gabriel ran one hand through his hair, dislodging a shower of soil and rock chips that sprinkled over his shoulders like a hard rain. "You can't love me." It was the wrong thing to say, but he couldn't seem to help himself. He desperately wanted Torie to love him. He knew it in his heart and in his soul. He felt it in every fiber of his body, in the ache and the need and the maddening, exhilarating rush that bolted through him when their hands met or their bodies touched.

But how could she love him? How could she when she did not know the truth?

"Damn!" Unable to face either the incredible tenderness in Torie's eyes or the annoying but indisputable questions that pounded through his head, Gabriel turned away.

"You won't put me off that easily." Behind him, he heard the sound of Torie's boots against the stone. She gripped his sleeve and somehow found strength enough to whirl him around to face her. Whatever reticence had marked her features and colored her cheeks was gone. In its place was the fury, not so much of a woman scorned, as it was of a woman who refused to be ignored.

And that, Gabriel knew, was far more dangerous.

"Don't you dare to presume you can love me and I cannot reciprocate," she said, her eyes sparking like they had so many times before, her chin set with a resolution that was truly remarkable to witness. "I don't care what happened in your past. Damn the double first! And damn Granger and Morrison. And Cronkite, too! If I cannot love you because you are gallant and determined and just as obstinate as I am, then at least let me love you because every time you look my way, I feel as if my heart is tumbling through me, and my skin is too tight to hold me, and my knees are weak. It may not be much, but it is a beginning, I think, and right now, it appears that a beginning is exactly what we need."

Gabriel could not help himself. He started to laugh. He laughed at the expression of wonderment that came to Torie's face. He laughed at his own foolhardiness. He laughed because every word that came out of her made his blood sing in his veins and his spirit feel as light as air. His laughter stopped only when he thought that the time had come to tell her the whole of the truth. He prayed that once he did, she would still look at him with the same trust and love.

"Just when I thought I'd gotten rid of my damned conscience once and for all." Gabriel seized Torie's hands and held them to his heart. "Thanks to you, here are my scruples, knocking me over the head so that, no matter how hard I try, no matter what the consequences, I cannot ignore them."

She was still looking at him in bewilderment, but he did not give her a chance to ask what he was talking about. He pulled her into his arms.

"It's getting late," he said. "Hoyle will be searching high and low for us. We need to get home. And I," he drew in a breath and let it out again, "I have something I must tell you."

Again, it looked as if Torie would have liked to ask what he was talking about, and again, Gabriel did not give her the opportunity. He couldn't. Now that the time had come to tell her all that was in his heart, he couldn't risk any distraction.

In an uncomfortable silence, they stowed their tools and set the fossil in a satchel to take it with them. It wasn't until they were out of the quarry and at the top of the path that led toward home that Gabriel dared to speak.

"It's the double first," he said, launching into the story without any of the slow and reassuring preamble he had always meant to give it. "It was mine, you see."

Torie didn't see. Matching him stride for stride, she gave Gabriel a sidelong look, hoping to gauge his mood as well as his meaning, and frowning when in spite of her scrutiny, both remained incomprehensible.

Gabriel was no help at all. For the next few minutes, he walked on mumbling to himself. It wasn't until they were halfway home that he let out a highly ingenious and rather colorful curse and pulled to a stop. He set down the bag containing the fossil in the soft grass along the side of the path and grabbed for Torie's hand, holding her in place.

"I didn't want to have to tell you this," he said, his eyes shimmering blue-black in the late afternoon light. "I never thought it would matter. But it does matter now. Because of you. Because of us. You have to know. We cannot begin any sort of a life together when there is so much of the past still between us." He searched her face as if willing her to read his thoughts. "The double first was mine."

He desperately wanted her to understand. Torie knew that. But no matter how much he wanted it, no matter how much she would have liked to oblige, he could not expect the impossible. She shrugged and gave him a questioning look.

"You said that. You said the double first was yours. But that doesn't make the least bit of sense. The double first was awarded to Roger because . . . It went to him when it was discovered that you . . ."

In spite of the fact that Gabriel was holding on to her and that she was quite sure she was standing on firm and solid ground, the world seemed to shift before Torie's eyes. She swallowed down the sudden nausea that accompanied the movement and held on tight to Gabriel to steady herself.

She did not entirely understand her fierce resistance to the simple sentence she had been in the midst of speaking. It was an instinctive reaction to something she knew in her heart but could not put into words for her head to comprehend. She tried again, reasoning through it all, forcing herself to go slowly so that she might follow where it was leading.

"The double first was taken from you." Even as she spoke, she felt the terrific burden the words carried with them, the implication of all they had meant to the incredible promise that had once been Gabriel's life. "Somehow, the University discovered that you'd paid for the answers to a very important examination. I know all about it. I have for years, and what I did not know, you told me that night of the church fete. You said you obtained the answers by bribing the don who had prepared the examination."

"Oh, Miss Broadridge! Where are your powers of deduction?" Had they been discussing anything else, Torie was certain Gabriel would have enjoyed the singular delight of challenging her. But they were not discussing Huttonian theory, or extinct reptiles, or diluvial deposits and what fossils they might or might not contain. They were discussing a man's life—Gabriel's life—and in her heart, Torie knew what he had to tell her would affect both of them forever.

Gabriel's gaze bored into hers, forcing her to see the truth. "I did not say I bribed the don, I said that was what the University tribunal determined. They are two very different things, Torie, what a tribunal decides happened and what really happened."

Again, the involuntary reaction, the quick, violent tug, as if the fabric of the world were being pulled out from beneath her feet; the sudden, stifling feeling, as if she were being smothered.

Torie fought back automatically. "A copy of the examination was found in your digs."

"Yes," Gabriel said, "it was."

"And the double first went to Roger because he was . . . he was second to you." There was only one place her analysis could lead her, and Torie found herself there, poised as if at the brink of a precipice, pausing only long enough to wonder what would happen when she took the final step over the edge.

She clutched Gabriel's arms. She looked into his eyes.

She took the step, and found it not a walk into the void but more a plunge into icy water. The truth seeped through her, chilling her to the bone.

"You earned that double first honestly, didn't you? And Roger was second to you . . ." Torie drew in a great gulp of air. "Roger was second to you even though he had the answers to the examination. He bought them. And he arranged it so that you looked to be the guilty one."

Gabriel did not respond. He watched her as if his very life depended on her answer to his question. "Do you believe it?" he asked.

Did she believe?

The question burned through Torie's brain, but she did not have to look far for the answer. She need only remember how Roger had spent the last years of his life, sitting idly by while she studied and worked to earn him a reputation he did not merit and barely valued.

She need only shift her hands in Gabriel's and feel how his skin was work roughened, his fingers scraped and scratched from the hours he'd spent searching for the bones. She need only glance at him to see that his body was hardened and bronzed from long days working in the sun.

And if that was not enough?

Torie raised her gaze to Gabriel's, a sensation like sunlight flowing through her when their eyes met.

If that was not enough, she assured herself, she need only look into Gabriel's eyes. The answer was there.

And here.

Torie placed her palm against Gabriel's chest, measuring each strong, even pulse of his heart.

"I can't believe I was so blind!" She wrapped her arms around him and buried her face against his chest. "I believed Roger because I wanted to believe him. I wanted to think there was more to my brother than just a man who desired nothing more of life than to take credit for the honors earned by someone else. I never suspected . . . I never would have thought . . . I should have, of course. I should have realized Roger was never anything but an imposter." Pulling herself upright, she sniffed back the tears of anger and disappointment that clogged her voice. "Why didn't you tell me sooner? Why didn't you try to do something about it?"

He ignored her first question and Torie knew why. They both already knew the answer to it. Gabriel had not told her of Roger's perfidy because he had hoped to never tell her. He had been terribly wronged by Roger, and yet, he let Torie keep the foolish fantasies she entertained about her brother's abilities.

The realization filled Torie with warmth. But it did little to chase away the cold left by her second question, one he had still not answered. "Why didn't you try to save yourself and your reputation?"

"Do you think I didn't try?" Gabriel's one-sided smile was filled not so much with self-regret as it was with the anguish of bitter memories, an anger that spilled over into his voice. "Roger had always been jealous of my academic achievements. That is why we shared digs for only one year. He was vindictive and lazy. I suspected from the first that he was behind the thing. I think he communicated with the don in writing, using my name. But neither of them was foolish enough to have kept the proof, of course. I think he took my greatcoat and hat and met to buy the examination in a dark place where he would not be recognized. But I could find no one who saw the incident. I was certain that Roger was the one who left the examination in my digs where it was sure to be found. But I was out a great deal, and many people came and went throughout the college. How could I ever prove any of it?"

Beneath her hands, Torie felt Gabriel's muscles tense. She could not help but sense the fury and desperation that must have possessed him then, a brilliant scholar at the start of an even more brilliant career. His future was ripped from him, and there was nothing he could do to protect it.

As if confirming her opinion, he went on, "I pleaded with the dean. I petitioned Granger, and Morrison, and yes, even Cronkite. I reminded them of my reputation, my potential. And they?" Gabriel snorted with derision. "They didn't see any farther than the ends of their noses. All they wanted was to keep the whole thing as quiet as they could and that meant getting it taken care of quickly. They found the damned copy of that damned examination, and they saw it as a convenient solution to their problem. It was much like the situation we find ourselves in with Spencer Westin. We suspect. But we cannot prove a thing. And, as the magistrate told me when I went to see him about Westin, without proof . . ." Gabriel shrugged as if not deeming the thought worthy of further consideration, but Torie could not help but notice the remnant of the hurt and anger that still lingered in his eyes.

"I owe you more than an apology," Torie said and this time, she did not even try to control the tears that cascaded down her cheeks. "My brother destroyed your career. He ruined your life. It is no wonder you disliked him so, just as it is no wonder you resented me because of him."

Was it anger she saw glimmering in his eyes? Or something deeper and more splendid? Torie was not sure. Not until Gabriel spoke again.

"Roger suffered for his sins, I think," he said, his voice dropping. "I suppose that was his punishment for what he did. I am only sorry that you ever had to learn of it."

"Sorry?" Torie could not believe her ears. "I am the one who should be sorry."

"Not for me, I hope." Unaccountably, Gabriel was smiling. He looked neither relieved nor pleased, only glad to be free of the burden of his secret and sorry that Torie had to share it. Even through her tears, Torie could see that. His eyes were gleaming and his face was smoothed of the lines of worry that had marked it.

"I think, perhaps, that it was all meant to be," he said, mirroring her action, his arms around her waist. "I think, perhaps, life is very much like your iguanodon. A great deal remains hidden until we work at seeing what is beneath the surface. If not for Roger and all he did, you would not have come to Oxford looking for me. And I would know neither the singular pleasure of your company nor your exceptional beauty."

Gabriel sighed, not with remorse, but as if he were expelling the past. His muscles relaxed, the tension gone from them. With one hand, he traced an invisible design over Torie's back, his touch as soothing as the slow, even tempo of his breathing, as comforting as the warmth of his body against hers.

They may have stood there for minutes, or hours. Torie wasn't sure. She knew only that there was peace within the circle of Gabriel's arms, peace and a happiness she had never known existed.

But sometime while they were lost in the embrace, the sun settled against the far horizon, sending its last, fiery rays against the downs. Long fingers of purple shadow stretched over them and in spite of the close comfort of Gabriel's nearness, Torie shivered.

She glanced around. Ahead of them, a stone fairy ring stood out against the orange evening sky as if it had been cut from black paper and pasted there. On either side of her, the soft, green downs disappeared into a haze of amethyst and gray muted to the color of a mole's fur.

"I have not been out at night since the dinner at Spencer's," she said, determined to disguise her uneasiness. "It seems so . . . so different. So foreign."

Gabriel could not be so easily deceived. He interpreted her thoughts and put into words what she felt too foolish to say, his voice dipping low in deference to the evening quiet that settled around them. "There are no lights." After he retrieved the fossil, he linked his arm through hers, steering her toward home. "They're gone. You won't see them again."

"I know." Torie believed every word he said, but it was troublesome getting her body to acquiesce. Despite herself, she could not help but dart a glance around.

There was no sign of the lights.

"No more." Gabriel leaned over and dropped a kiss on her brow, understanding somehow what was going through her head. They were nearing the house and when they got as far as the garden gate, he set the fossil down and took Torie into his arms, his voice rich and full of laughter.

"No more," he said again, whirling her around. "There is nothing out here but the night and the stars and the two of us. There is nothing for either of us to be afraid of anymore."

He kissed her again, and Torie gave herself to each of the incredible sensations that wound through her. There was that first scintillating moment when his mouth covered hers, that instant when her blood effervesced through her and made her head spin. The moment dissolved into two, then three, and the effervescence stilled to a hum that whirled through her, body, mind, and soul, dissolving the last of what was left of those obstacles that had kept them so long apart.

The moments merged, every one with the next, each affirming in its own way something Torie had for so long suspected, but never admitted, not even to herself.

This was something she wanted.

She wanted Gabriel's arms around her, his body close to hers. She wanted his mouth on hers, his kiss deeper and more insistent with each passing second. She wanted him to caress her, to somehow relieve the throb of desire that was growing inside her, causing her a startling but not unpleasant awareness of her own body. She wanted him to commit every inch of her to the memory of his touch, to scoop her hair atop her head and learn the contours of her neck and shoulders, to stroke her breasts and glide his hands along her legs.

She wanted him to taste the flavor of her skin, just as she wanted to taste his. To draw his scent into her lungs and hold it inside her. To feel the length of him pressed against her just as it was now, his one leg tucked between hers, his hands trailing over her back, up to her shoulders, and over her breasts.

She wanted it. Just as she wanted him. More than she had ever wanted anything else in her life. "More than anything."

"What was that?" Gabriel raised his head long enough to glance at her, his eyes dancing with laughter and the reflected light of the moon just topping the horizon.

"More than anything." Torie purred like a contented cat. "I said I want this more than anything."

"Then for once, we are in full agreement." Gabriel's smile widened into a grin that melted Torie's heart. "No argument. No contention. For what I hope will be the first of many, many times, we both want the same thing. That is something as singular as our iguanodon, I think, and something to be celebrated. Here," he tugged her off the garden path, over to where the grass was soft and long.

"Not here!" Torie's reaction was involuntary. She glanced at the house. "But Hoyle—"

"Hoyle goes to bed early and he sleeps like a stone!" Still smiling, Gabriel dropped to his knees and pulled Torie down beside him. "And the room he occupies is at the other side of the house. And—" He pressed one finger to her lips when she tried to speak. "And we are sheltered enough here. Your roses to one side." He glanced over his shoulder. "The garden wall to the other. It is as private as can be." He kissed her once, twice, and yet another time, and in that portion of her brain that was still able to function, Torie was certain he did it most deliberately, addling her head and astonishing her senses so as to leave her too dazed and flustered to renew her opposition.

He smiled down at her one last time before he brought his lips to hers again. "Do you wish to debate my analysis of the situation?"

Torie shook her head. She did not wish to debate him because she knew he was right, and even if she did, she was certain she could never make her head and mouth work in concert. Right now, her head couldn't think beyond the delicious possibility of what Gabriel might do next, and her mouth was fully occupied.

Debate was the farthest thing from her mind, especially

when Gabriel tugged her shirt from where it was tucked into her trousers and slipped his hand inside.

He had touched her before. Torie could not help but remember it. Once when he'd had far too much to drink, he'd nudged aside the lace edging of her dress and run his fingers over her breasts, tempting her, though he could not have possibly known it, and vexing her, for that was surely his plan. Once when he'd been far too angry to think clearly, he'd used the exquisite potency of his touch to mock her for her spinsterhood and punish her for her lies.

Now, his touch was neither mocking nor impudent, but gentle and almost reverent, each movement filled with the promise that he would not only take his pleasure of her, but give it back as well.

He stroked her breasts where they rose above the top of her corset, and dipped his fingers inside. Torie caught her lower lip between her teeth, marveling that so simple an action could feel so exquisite and make her feel at once so content and so dissatisfied. She wanted more of him, much more, and she leaned forward, instinctively closing the space between them at the same time she glided her hands across Gabriel's shoulders and along his chest, savoring the feel of hardened muscle and the crush of his fine linen shirt beneath her fingers.

Gabriel slipped his hand from beneath her shirt and brought it to the collar, undoing the two buttons there and moving the fabric aside. His chest rising and falling with each uneven breath he took, he sat back and stared at what little of her skin was exposed, fitting his hand at the back of her neck and stroking his thumb along the front.

"I could not want you more than I want you right now, Torie." Gabriel's voice was rough, his breath catching in his throat. "I'm only afraid I might wake and find that this is nothing but another one of the distressing dreams that has troubled me this whole summer."

"Dreams? About me?" Something about the idea sent a current of pleasure through Torie. She looked at him from beneath her lashes. "What do you dream about me?"

Torie thought Gabriel might not answer. He continued to stare at her, his gaze fixed to where his thumb was tracing small, slow circles against her skin. "I dream of holding you," he finally confessed, raising his eyes to hers. "I dream of touching you just as I am now. I dream of seeing you naked in the moonlight, your skin the color of pearls, your eyes sparkling with desire and pleasure and need. I've spent a good bit of the last months dreaming about bedding you in the soft, warm grass."

"Really?" Torie smiled and gave him a sly look. "And here I thought you were simply watching the moss grow on the window ledges. Do you mean, all this time—?"

"All this time, I have wondered what it would be like to hold you and touch you, yes." By this time, Gabriel was smiling, too. A deep chuckle rumbled through his chest. "I've spent hours dreaming about touching you here." He caressed her throat, then slipped his hand again to her breasts, and even through the layers of her shirt and corset, Torie could feel his longing. He flattened his hand and rubbed his palm over her nipples, his eyes sparkling with satisfaction when Torie arched her back so that he could more easily stroke her.

"I've spent even more hours dreaming about stripping away your clothes." Gabriel fitted both his hands around Torie's waist and slid them upward, taking Roger's old linen shirt with them. He tossed it aside and sat back to admire her, his gaze sparking fire everywhere it touched.

"In my dreams, I think I counted every one of your freckles." Laughing, Gabriel tapped his fingertips along her shoulders and down to her breasts as if it really were possible to count the thousands of freckles that dotted her skin. Each feathery, playful pat coursed through her like honey, as warm and delicious as the sound of Gabriel's voice. "I dreamed they would taste like bits of sugar."

His lips followed the trail his fingers established, the warm, wet touch of his mouth moving with delectable, agonizing slowness along her neck and down to her breasts. He dropped a kiss between her breasts at the same time his fingers found the ribbon tie that held her corset closed. He tugged the end of the ivory ribbon and sighed contentedly.

"I've certainly dreamed of doing this," he said, slowly pulling out the bow. "And this." His fingers splayed, he spread the corset aside. He cupped her breasts, one in each hand. "And this." He brought his mouth down, first to one breast, then to the other, his tongue tracing their shape, learning their size. He drew her into his mouth, holding her there until she groaned.

"And this." Gabriel sat up only long enough to toss Torie's corset over his shoulder before he bent to run his tongue over her breasts again, smiling as he felt her nipples harden like small, fine gems, and smiling even more when a shudder of pleasure ran through Torie's body.

"I dream of tasting every inch of you," he admitted, sliding his tongue between her breasts. "I dream of everything I will do. Everything I will say. And now that the time is here, I curse myself for not having said and done it all sooner."

Gabriel did not need to look at Torie again to gauge the measure of her desire. He could feel it tingle through her skin, like the heat lightning that sometimes flickered in the summer sky, and he wondered why he had been so stubborn, and why he had been so foolish, and why he had waited so long when this much pleasure had been right before him all summer, and he had been too blind to see it.

It had never been the time or place, he told himself, carefully swinging Torie around and laying her down. He sat back to relish the sight she made, her hair loose around her shoulders—though he could not for the life of him remember releasing it from its pins—her eyes heavy with desire, her skin pale as ivory and soft as satin against the summer grass.

It had never been the time, he reminded himself, sliding his hands over her stomach. Not when they first met, and Torie convinced him to come to Sussex. Not when they quarrelled their way through the spring and on into the summer, each one of them determined to hang on to the rigid beliefs and uncompromising convictions that kept them apart.

It had not been the place, he remembered, trailing a line of kisses over Torie's rib cage. Not when they walked together across the downs after that first dinner at Westin's, or when Gabriel sat at the church fete surrounded by the good people of Cuckfield, wondering, always wondering, what it would be like to make love to her.

But now time and place had come together, like the past and future that lay forever entwined in the iguanodon fossil.

Gabriel's heart squeezed with joy at the same time a certain other, far more sensitive part of him reminded him quite explicitly that he had waited for this moment for a very long time.

Silencing his runaway imagination along with his capricious impulses, he reminded himself that they had all the time in the world and that he had decided long ago their lovemaking would be long and loud.

He nearly forgot that promise when Torie stroked her hands over his shoulders, undoing the buttons at his throat just as he'd undone hers. "Do you still think me unimaginative and abstemious?" she asked, tugging at his shirt until he discarded it.

"You remember that, do you?" Gabriel shook his head and chuckled, but Torie did not give him either the time or the allowance to express his regret. Raising herself on her elbows, she trailed her tongue over his bare chest.

"Did I ever say unimaginative?" Gabriel wondered if he sounded as out of breath to her as he did to himself. "It was, apparently, a transitory bit of madness. I should have known a scholar of your intelligence would have incredible imagination."

Torie murmured something that sounded like a blend of contentment and agreement. "And abstemious? Do you still think me abstemious?"

"Abstemious." Gabriel tipped back his head and smiled, considering the word while Torie dropped a string of kisses over his neck and shoulders. "It's a harsh word, abstemious. I am usually much more charitable. You must have pushed me to the limits of my patience in order for me to have spoken with such insensitivity. I'm sure all I meant was—"

A new thought hit Gabriel and he pulled himself up straight. He stared down into Torie's upturned face, his mouth suddenly dry.

"Abstemious." His voice sounded the way paper does when it tears. "I meant to hurt you with the word then, but it is true, isn't it?" He licked his lips, thinking out loud. "It's a damned awkward problem."

Torie could not have looked more surprised. She leaned back on her elbows, the moonlight shimmering against her breasts. "Problem?"

Gabriel swallowed hard. "Yes. You see, I don't believe I've ever had a . . ." That was far too blunt, and he tried again. "That is, you are inexperienced and I . . ." That was not much better. He gave up trying, discarding his mortification without a thought for where it landed, just like he'd tossed away Torie's shirt and corset. "I don't believe I have ever done this with a virgin," he admitted. "It suddenly occurred to me. I don't want to—"

His feeble protest was cut short by the sounds of Torie's laughter. She sat up and trailed her fingers through the fine mat of dark hair on his chest, her voice low and inviting, her words curling through him as her fingers swirled over his skin. "You said it yourself, I am a woman of intelligence and imagination. I am quick to learn and even quicker to put what I learn into practice. What I lack in experience, perhaps I could make up for in enthusiasm." She traced his lips with the tip of one finger. "If only you will teach me the right thing to do."

It was an offer he couldn't resist.

Gabriel's momentary doubts vanished. "I can show you right enough, if you will promise to tell me if I am going too fast. I have no wish to frighten you or hurt you. I—"

Torie kissed away the last of his words. "I am not a porcelain doll," she said. "But flesh and blood." Taking her hand in his, she laid it on her breast. "You have felt it, I think."

Indeed.

Gabriel abandoned the last of his misgivings to the feel of her body moving against his in a soft, slow rhythm.

"Do you think me unteachable?" She whispered the words in his ear.

As an answer, Gabriel pressed her back against the grass and trailed his hand between her legs. "Not at all," he said, stretching out beside her. "I think you will make a fine student. And if I am not wrong—and I seldom am—I believe there are some things the pupil may teach the master. Besides, it is all so much simpler with you in those clothes! If you only do as I do—"

He hadn't even finished before Torie was following his lead. She ran her fingers over his thigh and brushed them across the front of his trousers. "There are advantages to being a virgin," she said, cupping her hand around him and stroking him slowly. "There are wonderful surprises."

"And more where that came from." Moving his hand to her waist, Gabriel unbuttoned her trousers.

She did the same to his.

"I have dreamed of this, too, Torie," Gabriel whispered, his voice rough with longing. "Of holding you close against me." He drew a line with his tongue from her stomach up to her breasts. "I've even dreamed of that birthmark you have on your side. The one that looks like a pretty little flower."

"Birthmark?" Torie stiffened. The slow, sweet swirl of her fingers stopped. Cocking one elbow, she rested her head in her hand and gave him a look that wasn't in the least playful. "What do you know of that birthmark? And don't tell me you've just seen it. Your lips have been far too busy to give your eyes time to explore."

"I—" Gabriel groaned. It was clear this would have been far easier if only he'd confessed it when he had the chance. He brushed his hand over her breasts and, giving her a teasing smile, he ran his gaze the length of her body. "I saw it when you were ill. I saw a great deal of you when you were ill. Mrs. Denny never came to care for you, you see, and I—"

"What?" Torie sat up as if she'd been shot through with a current of electricity, the glimmer in her eyes suddenly a spark. "You were the one?"

Gabriel sat up, too, though he knew the second he did, that it was a mistake. If he'd stayed in place, reclining in the grass, he would have been far less likely to destroy the mood. Now they were nose to nose, and damn him, Torie's nose had that look about it, that little twitch. The one that told him she was as angry as a cat with its tail caught on a hot fender.

He fought back instinctively, forcing himself to stay

calm, and wincing, but only just a little, when his words came out far more patronizing than he intended. "It was an innocent enough thing. Someone had to care for you."

"Yes, I agree." The corners of Torie's mouth pinched with disapproval. "But you could have admitted doing it when you had the chance. Were you ashamed of what you did, or only of what you were thinking while you were doing it?"

There was something in the sharpness of Torie's words that warned Gabriel to back away. But he didn't. No matter how sensible the voice that told him to swallow her protests with his lips and smooth the furrow of anger from between her eyes with a shower of kisses, he could not ignore the other voice, the one that reminded him that she was being illogical and stubborn and that her bullheadedness was the one thing that had always irritated him the most. She was being irrational, as only Torie could, and her unreasonableness nearly made him forget that they had been exceedingly close to completing the long and torturous seduction that, he realized, had begun in Oxford all those weeks ago.

Nearly.

The thought of having her good graces and her lovemaking snatched away when they were finally both to be his was enough to make Gabriel act just as irrational as Torie.

He crossed his arms over his chest. "I didn't see anything then that I'm not about to see now."

"You think so, do you?" Torie fished behind herself with one hand. She came up holding Roger's shirt and slipped it over her head, successfully ignoring the look on Gabriel's face which, he was sure, was an absurd combination of anger, disbelief, and absolute despair.

"You can't mean it!" Gabriel's heart rose in his throat at the same time another portion of his anatomy fell. "Just because I—"

"You lied," Torie said. Before Gabriel had either the presence of mind or the sense to stop her, she hopped to her feet. "How can I trust you with my body when I cannot even trust you to tell the truth?" She kicked through the tall grass until she found her corset and once she did, she held it close against her like a shield. "It hardly matters if you did or you didn't undress me while I was ill," she said. "Not anymore. Tonight, you have seen nearly all there is to see and I have no doubt there were other nights when you saw a great deal more. But it does matter that you lied about it. That is unforgivable."

"Lied? I—"

Before Gabriel could defend himself further, Torie spun away from him and stomped off in the direction of the house. She disappeared inside.

"Damn!" Gabriel breathed the word in absolute amazement. He sat in the grass, stunned.

His shock did not last long. In a burst as quick and hot as a flash fire, his astonishment was incinerated by a good, healthy dose of anger. "Damn!" Propelling himself to his feet, Gabriel grabbed the satchel and tromped into the house. He slammed the door as hard as he could.

"Damn!" He yelled again when he passed Torie's closed bedroom door. "You are the most mulish, obstinate, recalcitrant hellcat ever born!"

There was no answer from inside her bedroom, though Gabriel was certain he heard the sound of footsteps treading the floorboards, as if Torie was pacing.

"Good!" He snorted the word, uncommonly pleased with the realization that Torie was no more composed than he. Spinning on his heels, Gabriel marched to his own room. Once he got there, he banged the door closed and paced back and forth in front of it, his anger warring with what was left of his desire.

The anger won.

"Termagant!" He grunted the word and poked his chin

in the direction of Torie's room, as if she could see him. "Termagant!" He said it louder so that at least she would know he had not surrendered without a fight.

"Heartless cad!" Her voice flew to him, as sharp-edged as his. "Callous rake!"

"Hellcat!"

"Uncaring scoundrel!"

"Mulish woman!" Too angry to keep still, too frustrated to pace and go nowhere, Gabriel dropped down on his bed. He propped himself against the bedstead, his ankles crossed, his arms over his chest, and smiled a spiteful smile when he realized Torie was still pacing.

"That's a lesson to be learned, isn't it?" Gabriel yelled the question so that she would be certain to hear it. "A woman of learning! A woman of intelligence! Better to take a woman to bed who doesn't have a brain in her head. Then she wouldn't question what you say or do. Instead, I have to fall in love with a bluestocking, one who thinks herself equal to a man in all she says and does."

He tossed a scathing look at the door at the same time he grabbed his pillow and pitched it across the room. There wasn't much comfort in that, he decided. Not even when the pillow hit something and the sound of breaking glass filled the air.

In fact, there was only one bit of comfort he could find in the whole, pitiful affair, and Gabriel consoled himself with it.

"Damn!" he said, not feeling any better in spite of the revelation, but tossing out the scathing words as his Parthian shot.

"No doubt you would want to be on top!"

Chapter 19

Gabriel supposed he'd had hangovers that were more dreadful than this, but right now he couldn't remember one.

And the most terrible part of it all was that he hadn't even had anything to drink.

Still, his head throbbed like a steam engine. His eyes burned. His muscles ached. He hadn't gotten one moment of sleep last night and his reflection in the mirror that hung outside the library door confirmed his worst suspicions. The misery of each one of the endless, restless hours was etched upon his face, and even a morning bath and one of Hoyle's diligent and perfectly executed toilettes had done little to help.

Neither had Hoyle's coffee.

Gabriel scowled at the half empty cup in his hand, finding no comfort in the fact that even Hoyle's strong and justifiably famous coffee, which had served him both as crutch and restorative on many such a painful morning in the past, did little to help today.

"Fool!" He frowned at his reflection. "To let a woman affect you so. And yet . . ."

And yet, try as he might—and he had spent a great many hours trying—he could not forget last night. How could he when he'd spent every minute of every hour of the night with thoughts of it pounding through his brain? How could he when every shadow in his room reminded him of the night-soft place between Torie's breasts? When every sigh of the wind put him in mind of the soft groans that had escaped her when he'd explored her body with his hands and mouth?

"Damn!" Gabriel turned from the mirror, too disturbed by the memories to face himself.

He glanced up and down the passageway, half expecting to see Torie emerge from one of the rooms further down the hallway. When she didn't, he breathed a sigh of relief.

He hadn't seen her all morning, and he intended to keep it that way. He'd purposely stayed in his room far later than usual, until he could be sure that Torie had already left for the quarry.

"You're afraid to face her, aren't you?" Over his shoulder, Gabriel glowered at his reflection, thankful that no matter how wretched he looked on the outside, at least no one could see the craving and desire that was eating away at his insides like an acid. He grumbled a word he'd learned from one of the more notorious of Oxford's bookmakers, a word that though it had served him well in the past, never seemed more appropriate than today.

"You don't know what you'll say to her when you do see her, do you?" he asked himself. "You don't know what you'll do. And the hell of it is, you have no idea what she might do, either."

Gabriel shook his head in disgust and gulped down another mouthful of coffee, grimacing when the cold, bitter liquid hit the back of his throat.

It wasn't that he didn't know what he'd like to do, he told himself.

All night long, the same scene had played and replayed itself inside his head. He knew exactly what he should have done last night, and he should have done it as soon as Torie started raising a howl about the simple fact that he'd lied to her.

He should have marched right into her room and thrown her down on the bed. He should have ripped away her clothes and tossed them to the floor. He should have taken her, right then and there, and the consequences be damned.

He should have.

Gabriel's shoulders slumped.

But he hadn't.

Always, there was some voice in his head that made him hesitate. Always, there was some small prick from his conscience, one that told him this was not the casual roll in the hay that it had been with so many other women. Always, he reminded himself that he wanted more than that from Torie.

He wanted Torie's love unconditionally. He wanted it given freely, not taken or inveigled. He wanted her to melt into his arms as their lips met, to fuse with him as their bodies joined.

He wanted all of her. Not just her body, but her incredible mind as well. Her indomitable spirit. And yes—Gabriel admitted with a rueful smile—even her extraordinary willfulness.

Now, he wasn't sure there was ever a way they would come again to that special understanding they had shared last night. New walls had replaced the old ones that had been built between them. And new walls were always stronger than the old.

Setting his mouth in a thin line of disgust, Gabriel punched open the library door.

At least he had all day to consider what he was going to do about it. He was certain he wouldn't see Torie again until evening. And if nothing else, that meant he had all day to himself to worry.

* * *

Torie pushed her spectacles back up to the bridge of her nose and tried to make herself concentrate on the journal page open in front of her.

It was no use.

The more she tried to make herself focus on her writing, the more her thoughts wandered. And the more her thoughts wandered, the more they ended up right back to Gabriel.

Torie groaned.

She was still angry at him, she realized, still upset that he'd deceived her. "And yet . . ." Torie's words dissolved in an avalanche of memory.

And yet, she could not forget the feel of his arms around her, just as she could not forget the taste of his lips, or the exquisite touch of his hands as he laid a path of desire across her body. She could not forget that in spite of the fact that he'd lied to her, he was still the most incredible man she had ever met and that she had been ready to give herself to him. She could not forget—she would never forget—that all night long, she had regretted the fact that she had not.

It was quite the most frustrating thing she had ever encountered, so frustrating that it had kept her awake long past the time when she and Gabriel had stopped trading barbs. She had spent the night staring at the blackness outside her window, wishing with all her heart that she had the self-possession and the mettle and at least humility enough to go to Gabriel and beg him to take her again into his arms.

But she didn't. She couldn't.

And now she sat with her head pounding to the rhythm of her blasted expectations, and her body aching as if her skin were too tight.

At least she would not have to face Gabriel this morning. That was one consolation.

Absently, Torie flipped through the pages of her journal, purposely avoiding those that Gabriel had written. She congratulated herself for being canny enough not to emerge from her room until she was sure he'd left for the quarry.

At least he would not see her this way, her hair around her shoulders, straight as a pound of candles, her eyes ringed with weary smudges, her face, no doubt, still as pinched and drawn as it had been when she looked into her mirror earlier.

At least she could spend the day planning what she would say to Gabriel when he came back this evening.

At least she could spend the day alone in the peace and quiet of the library, worrying.

When the library door flew open, Torie's head came up. She watched Gabriel stride into the room and stop dead at the sight of her, his expression a perfect likeness to the mixture of surprise and utter trepidation that, no doubt, marked her own features.

"Oh, it's you."

Spoken in unison, their voices washed over each other at the same time their gazes locked.

Torie was the first to look away. Clutching the desktop and praying that Gabriel would not notice that her knuckles were white, she gave him as much of a smile as she could manage, one that she feared looked very like a snarl. Forcing herself to relax, she kept her voice as level as possible. "Good morning."

"Good morning." Gabriel's words were no more congenial than the look she knew he was giving her. She could feel his eyes as they moved from the top of her head down to what he could see of her behind the desk, and she wondered that at the same time his gaze could scour her, it could send her heart racing and make her pulse beat fast and hard.

Torie knew it was also making her blush. She could feel the heat in her chest and neck and she knew Gabriel would be certain to notice it, too. Adjusting the lace edging along the neckline of her black gown with trembling fingers, she forced herself to raise her gaze to his.

Instantly, Gabriel looked away. He offered her a brusque bow, and trying to make it look as if he wasn't retreating and failing rather deplorably, he scurried over to the window. He stood with his back to Torie, his hands clutched behind him. "I trust you slept well last night."

"Like a log!" Grateful he was not facing her to see it, Torie stifled a yawn. Taking off her spectacles, she rose from the desk and closed her journal with a defiant snap. "I hope you are as well rested."

"Absolutely!" Gabriel whirled around. He didn't look well rested, but Torie was prudent enough not to mention it. At least not yet. For now, she decided to ignore the fact that his eyes were a maze of red lines and his skin was unusually pale. She would save that bit of powder and shot for later, in the event their argument heated up and she was in need of fresh ammunition.

"Ah!" Gabriel drew in a chestful of air, trying mightily to look like a man eager to meet the challenges of the day. "There is nothing like a long, untroubled night's sleep to invigorate a man."

"Indeed." Torie came around from behind the desk and stopped. With Gabriel standing where he was now, she would have to pass perilously close to him to get to the door, and something told her that would be far from wise.

Keeping her head high at the same time she staunchly held her place, Torie clutched her hands at her waist and traded Gabriel look for look. Perhaps if she was thinking more clearly, if her head wasn't muddled with memories of last night and her body wasn't humming with the peculiar vibrations caused by Gabriel's nearness, she might have seen some humor in the situation. It was like a scene from an amusing farce, she supposed, two people who were, only yesterday, so close to being lovers, today acting as if they'd never set eyes on each other before.

The thought did little to improve Torie's mood and even less to relieve the tension that stretched through her body, taut as harp strings.

"You're going to the quarry today?" Gabriel's question snapped her from her thoughts.

"I think not," Torie replied. "I thought rather to spend the day . . ." She hastened to find some explanation that would have the effect of both providing her with an excuse and excusing her from the room. "Studying," she said, wincing just a little at how lame the rationale sounded. "I am so invigorated from my long night's rest that I think my mind will be in top form today. And you?"

Gabriel didn't look any more sure of himself than she felt. It was impossible to miss the fact that he nearly let down his guard long enough to shrug, and just as impossible to notice that, at the last moment, he realized that would be an admission of the fact that he was just as disconcerted as she. He concealed the movement by coughing politely behind his hand and darted a look at the door as if it were the gates of heaven and he the wretched soul who desperately sought entrance. "I think I shall go see what Hoyle is about," he said. "There is much we need to discuss before we leave for Oxford and—"

"Hoyle isn't here." Torie had never been one to believe in the supernatural, but as soon as the words were out of her mouth, she felt as if she were suddenly one of the ha'penny-a-reading fortune tellers who worked the country markets and hiring fairs. She knew something was going to happen. As surely as she knew her own name.

She braced herself for it, her body tingling with anticipation, her head buzzing with excitement.

"Hoyle isn't here?" Gabriel moved a step closer, his expression brightening just enough to tell her that her instincts were unerring. "And where is it that Hoyle's gone?"

"Cuckfield." As if her feet moved of their own volition, Torie took a step, too, one in Gabriel's direction. "For the day."

"The day." Another step brought Gabriel a little closer. "He'll be gone—"

"For hours." The words were not even out of her mouth before Gabriel swallowed them up, his lips covering hers in a ravenous kiss.

"I didn't sleep a wink last night thinking about you." Excitement vibrating through his body and making his voice breathless, Gabriel ran his hands and his mouth over Torie's neck, down to where her low-cut dress skimmed her shoulders. He pushed the black gown over her arms and down to her waist and tore away the ribbon that held her corset in place. His fingers were quick and impatient, his touch not delicate as it had been last night, but reckless and wanton, his kisses like flame against her bare skin.

He looked down at her long enough to give her the kind of imperious, exasperating smile that never failed to send her heart banging against her rib cage. "I didn't sleep, and neither did you. So you see, we're even. We've both lied to each other. And, damn me, right now I don't care which of us is on top."

He took her breast in his mouth and Torie gasped with pleasure, her own fingers somehow finding Gabriel's cravat, loosening it, and tossing it to the floor. His shirt followed though she was not quite sure how or which one of them took it off, just as she was not exactly sure how the rest of her clothing ended up in a pile on the floor, with Gabriel's on top of it.

In that one, rational part of her brain that still seemed to be functioning, Torie told herself that they should have taken the time, at least, to look at each other. She knew that last night they would have. Last night, they would have spent long, lush minutes examining each other, exploring, enjoying the feel of bare flesh against bare flesh, savoring the taste of each others' skin.

Today, it didn't matter. Not in the least. There would be other times for such leisurely lovemaking, other times when they could relax and take their unhurried pleasure.

But this was not one of them.

Without a word, Gabriel scooped Torie into his arms and laid her on the carpet in front of the hearth. Without a word, he moved over her, nudging her legs apart and settling himself between them. Without a word, he thrust himself into her, waiting only a fraction of a second to determine that she was not in any discomfort before he began to move against her in a fierce, primitive tempo.

Torie wound her arms around Gabriel's neck as the rhythm spiraled out of control, until it was the only thing in the world, the only thing that mattered. There was nothing outside the invisible circle of trust and love that surrounded them, nothing save this wondrous here and now, this feel of their bodies moving against each other in exquisite symmetry, this knowledge that somehow, at last, they had come to a place where they had always been meant to be.

Torie felt her heart squeeze with love at the same time the curious tension that had been building in her all summer exploded in a shower of sensation that left her breathless and trembling.

At the same time Gabriel called her name she heard a high-pitched, delirious sort of sound that bounced merrily against the walls of the library. It took her a moment or two before she realized it was the sound of her own voice.

Gabriel collapsed against her, and making a noise halfway between a groan of absolute contentment and a chuckle of delight, he nuzzled his lips against her neck. "There you have it," he said, dropping a kiss on the tip of her nose, another on the peaks of each of her breasts. "And next time, I promise, we'll take our time." He smiled down at her before he brought his mouth to hers again. "And you can be on top."

Gabriel looked down at the peculiar object cradled in Torie's hands. It was still covered with dirt, still partially encased in quarry sandstone, but there was no doubt, it was something fabulous, something the likes of which neither of them had ever dreamed of finding.

He tapped the peculiar fossil with the tip of one finger. "What do you think it might be?"

Torie gave him an exasperated look. It was the kind of look he had not seen in all the days since they had become lovers and he found an odd sense of comfort in it, like coming upon a familiar though not sorely missed friend after a long absence.

"It's a logical enough question," he said, defending himself instinctively as he always did against that look, but this time with a smile on his face. "I thought you might not know—"

"Of course I know." Torie's lips pinched with annoyance. She straightened her shoulders and glared at him. Her expression was a perfect imitation of an Oxford don, one who had been pushed too far by clottish young lads whose last thought in the world was to actually learn anything up at University.

But Gabriel had hardly ever seen a don thrust out his bottom lip, not the way Torie did. And he had never, ever seen one do it as defiantly. Or as seductively. "I should think I've learned that much, haven't I?" she said, disdain dripping from her voice. "It's a . . . It's a . . ." Her pretense was convincing, at least for as long as it lasted. Torie dissolved into laughter. "I haven't the slightest idea what it is!" Shaking her head, she sat back on her heels and stared at the fossil.

Gabriel studied it, too.

They had discovered this new and highly unusual specimen while digging only a short distance from where they'd found the metacarpal bones. Those were easy enough to identify, for except for their incredible size and obvious age, they were not so very different from the bones of modern-day reptiles.

But this?

This was something else all together, and Gabriel could not help but share both Torie's puzzlement and her exhilaration. This was something new, something unexpected, and the implications of the startling find were only just beginning to make their way into Gabriel's head, muzzy as it was from a day spent too long in the sun and a week's worth of nights in which he'd gotten very little sleep indeed.

Not that he was complaining.

Gabriel glanced over to where Torie knelt in the dirt. The fossil in her lap, she carefully brushed bits of rock chip away from it, looking for all the world like the able, experienced, and highly competent scientist she was.

Only he knew there was another side to Torie.

At the same time the thought brought a smile to his face, Gabriel amended it.

There was not only one other side to her, he reminded himself, but many. Each time they had made love in the past days, Torie had revealed a new, and sometimes startling, facet of her character to him.

There was the playful side of her, the woman who tantalized him with her kisses and teased him with her

touch. There was the sensuous side of her, the woman
who only last night, had artfully arranged herself in front
of the window so that the moon painted her naked body
with frosted light. There was a wicked side to Torie as well
and the thought made Gabriel's body tighten. That was
the woman who had quickly learned that there were
many pleasures she could bestow upon him, and who,
much to Gabriel's delight and to both their satisfaction,
had not been bashful about employing her new skills.

The memories were as delectable as they were fierce
and, had they been anywhere else, Gabriel might have
acted on the capricious notion that sped through his
bloodstream. They had already made love in his bedroom
(twice last night), her bedroom (only once the night before
but that had been an especially lusty adventure and had
robbed them both of all their energy), the library (three
times, he thought, though he couldn't be quite sure), the
garden (in the moonlight), and—Hoyle would be shocked
to know it—the kitchen. They could add the quarry to the
list, he supposed, if it were not quite so rocky and so
accessible that anyone who happened by might see them.

Still, it was a tantalizing thought, and Gabriel did his
best to pretend he was studying the fossil while he turned
it over in his head. He watched Torie chip away at another bit of rock and blow away the flakes from around
the fossil. Her fingers were long and thin and, as he had
good cause to know, as deft and agile as could be. Her
cheeks were red from the sun, as flushed as they were
wont to be after they made love. Her lips were pursed,
ready to blow at the bits of rock and dirt again, and
Gabriel could not help but remember the feel of them
against his. Even bedecked in Roger's old clothes, she was
every inch a woman, and every inch of her was now
familiar to Gabriel, to the touch of his hands and the
brush of his mouth.

This last thought was almost enough to upend him,

almost enough to make him forget where they were, and how public a place it was, and that they had already made love once this morning before they ever left for the quarry.

If Torie noticed that Gabriel's blood was crashing through his veins, if she noticed that his body was aching with need, or even that he was suddenly breathing far too irregularly for a man who was doing nothing more strenuous than sitting amid a pile of boulders and rock chips, she paid it no mind. She glanced over her shoulder at him and smiled, her face aglow with that special fervor she reserved for only two things: Gabriel and fossils.

"It is Cretaceous strata, don't you think?" She poked at the rock and asked her question even though it was apparent from the incandescence of her expression that she was certain it was. "And near enough to our other finds to make me think it belonged to the same animal. But where?" She lifted the fossil as if fitting it against some giant, unseen animal's body.

It wasn't easy putting aside the tantalizing ideas that still lingered in his head and made his body sting with longing, but, somehow, Gabriel managed. He watched the sunlight glint off the surface of the fossil, seized by a sudden desire to know all there was to know about it.

It was nothing like the physical desire that burned through him when he was with Torie. Nothing like the intangible, but just as powerful, need that made him yearn for their spirits to merge as their bodies joined, to melt one into the other, two halves of the same wonderful whole.

This was intellectual desire, the hunger for learning, the passion for knowledge, and Gabriel felt it jolt through him like the kick of a horse. It put him in mind of those days, long past, when he woke every morning with the fever of scholarly excitement burning through him, and

reminded him that, thanks to Torie, his future held the
promise of such wonders again.

From what he could see of it still partially encased in
the rock that had held it for the past sixty-five million
years, Gabriel judged that the fossil was about thirty centi-
meters long. It was thick and rounded at one end, and it
tapered off into a point, much like a—

"Dermal horn?" Gabriel offered the suggestion, making it into a question because it seemed at once so far-
fetched and so fabulous. "You know," he said, taking the
fossil from Torie and holding it up to his brow. "Like a
rhinoceros."

"Yes!" Torie's eyes lit. "It's the right shape to be a
tubercle, isn't it? Imagine what our iguanodon must have
looked like with that thing on its nose!"

"Imagine what they will say in Oxford when we add it
to the list of fossils we will be presenting to the British
Association for the Advancement of Science."

"You mean the ones you will be presenting." As surely
as if someone had blown out a candle, the light of excitement went out of Torie's eyes. She ran one finger over the
fossil absently, but Gabriel could not help but notice that
there was anything but indifference in her expression.
"You will be the one giving the presentation," she reminded him, though she had no need. "I will not even be
allowed into the assembly."

"I know." His attempt at consolation was undoubtedly
hackneyed and probably worthless, but Gabriel could
think of little else to say. "It's insufferable and offensive.
You know I agree with you. But it can't be helped. It is
tradition, and the University is ruled by tradition." He
ran one hand up and down her arm in a small gesture of
comfort. "First let us turn those old cocks at Oxford on
their ears with your iguanodon, shall we? Then we will
work on seeing that women can attend scientific lectures."

"And be students of the University," Torie added for good measure.

Gabriel smiled. "And be students of the University." He echoed her wish though as much as he would have liked to see it come true, it was difficult for him to envision a day when such an unimaginable event might ever happen.

"And be fellows there," Torie added, unequivocally.

"And be fellows there," he agreed.

"And vice-chancellors as well."

"And vice-chancellors as well." Gabriel couldn't help himself, by this time he was laughing. He was not ridiculing Torie's radical ideas, but rather reveling in them, like one did in a fresh spring breeze that blew away the last of winter's stale air.

"I would have thought it all impossible before I met you," he said, leaning forward to brush away the smudge of dirt on her cheek before he kissed her. "But nothing is impossible in the face of such determination. You've convinced me of that." The closeness of Torie's body and the heat that radiated from it made all the disturbing thoughts Gabriel had been so eager to put aside come crashing back over him, like a wild surge of seawater.

"Or we could forget Oxford all together," he suggested, bringing his mouth to her ear and lowering his voice, each word a caress. "We could forget the unimaginative and tedious scientific community. We could even forget our iguanodon with its odd teeth and its big feet and its peculiar horn. We could stay here in Sussex forever, watching the moss grow on the window ledges from the vantage point of our bed."

Torie could not possibly have thought he was serious, but she smiled anyway and made a satisfied sound from deep in her throat. The idea was surely as appealing to her as it was to him.

"We could," she said, "but we would not want to miss

the opportunity to turn the world of science on its ear."
She ran one finger along Gabriel's jaw, from his ear all the
way down to his chin, and if he thought he was aroused
before simply thinking about her touch, he'd been wrong.
Nothing could compare to the exquisite thrill caused by
the real thing. "However," she said, her voice as low as
his, "we do not have to leave for Oxford for a week yet,
and we could go home now and watch the moss grow on
the window ledges from the vantage point of our bed."

It was not something to which Gabriel needed to give
a second thought. Offering Torie a hand, he pulled her to
her feet. They deposited the new fossil in a bag and
headed out of the quarry.

Once or twice, Gabriel had to remind himself to slow
down. Torie's legs were not as long as his and he did not
want to tire the poor girl out even before they arrived
home. Once they were there . . .

Gabriel smiled, savoring the thought.

Once they were there, he had every intention of tiring
her out, and himself along with her.

"We'll have Hoyle leave dinner outside the door," Gabriel said, thinking out loud and liking the thought very
much indeed. "We can have him bring us a bowl of plums
and some of those plump gooseberries that—"

They rounded the corner of the house and Gabriel's
pleasant thoughts dissolved. Hoyle was standing near the
garden gate and one look at him made both Gabriel and
Torie stop in place and exchange worried looks.

Hoyle's hair was standing on end. His face was as pale
as death. His eyes brimming with what looked to Gabriel
very much like panic, Hoyle darted a frantic glance
around the garden. But even when his gaze finally
alighted on Gabriel and Torie, he looked no more relieved than before. In fact, it seemed as though he did not
see them at all. He looked right through them, his face a
mask of shock.

The dazed look on Hoyle's face was highly peculiar, but even more distressing was the fact that Hoyle's cravat was askew. And that, Gabriel knew for certain, meant something was very wrong.

Gabriel gave Torie's hand a squeeze and glanced at her briefly, signaling her to stay back until he could ascertain what had happened.

"Hoyle?" Gabriel marched over to the garden gate and stood square in front of his valet. "Hoyle, what is it? What's wrong?"

His stratagem with Hoyle had no more effect than the one he'd used on Torie. Gabriel might have known she wouldn't listen. No sooner was he with Hoyle than he heard her right behind him.

"I don't think just speaking to him will help much." Torie stepped between Gabriel and Hoyle and, taking one of Hoyle's hands, rubbed it between both her own. "He's as cold as yesterday's fire." Dropping Hoyle's left hand and moving on to chafe his right, she opened the gate and stepped into the garden. "Come on," she said to Gabriel. "We've got a bottle of sherry somewhere about. Let's get him inside and—"

Something in what Torie said snapped Hoyle back to life. He held back and there was a glimmer of recognition in his eyes. He gave Gabriel a look that was a mixture half of pleading, half of warning.

"Not the front way, sir," Hoyle said, his voice quavering in spite of the fact that he was trying his damnedest to keep his composure. He held his shoulders so stiff, it made Gabriel's muscles ache to watch him. "The kitchen door, sir, might be better, sir." Hoyle cast a glance at Torie. "For Miss Victoria, sir."

Gabriel didn't ask for further explanation. Not here. Not now. He led the way into the house through the kitchen door and they sat around the scrubbed wooden table where, most days, Hoyle would be busy at this hour preparing the evening meal. In silence, they watched Hoyle drink not one, but two large tumblers of sherry and when he was done, Gabriel leaned forward in his chair and pinned his valet with a look.

"All right. Out with it, Hoyle. What's happened that has you so distressed, man?"

Very deliberately, Hoyle set down his empty glass in the center of the table. As the spirits made their way into his system, a rush of color invaded his cheeks, making the rest of his face look more waxen than ever. He drew in a deep breath and for just a moment, allowed his eyes to flicker in the direction of the door that separated the kitchen from the rest of the house.

Hoyle shook his head. "Gorblimey, sir, it's the most horridous thing what I ever saw."

Torie looked at Hoyle in wonder, but Gabriel paid her little mind. He knew exactly what was happening. It was obvious the sherry had done more than just help to soothe Hoyle's jangled nerves.

That and Hoyle's distress had also loosened his valet's tongue, bringing to fore Hoyle's humble London origins, a fact which Gabriel had known for years and had always held in the strictest confidence. It wasn't that Hoyle feared what the public in general might think if they learned that in spite of a bearing fit for a royal duke and a dignity second to none, he was born within the sound of Bow Bells, the son of an East End butcher. It was his fellow valets Hoyle was worried about. Gabriel made a mental note to swear Torie to secrecy with regard not to whatever Hoyle might be about to say, but the manner in which he was about to say it. As soon, that is, as they could get him to say something.

Gabriel drummed his fingers on the tabletop.

"I know. I know." Hoyle's gaze traveled briefly to Gabriel before he brought it again to the empty tumbler and kept it there, as if the sight might help banish other, uglier, images that rose in his head.

"It's that 'orrible Mr. Westin, I'm afraid, sir," Hoyle finally said. " 'E's in the library, sir. And, Goramity, sir. 'e's deader than Julius Caesar!"

Chapter 20

Of course, Gabriel insisted Torie should not accompany them. Of course, Hoyle concurred, mumbling something that sounded suspiciously like, "somethin' awful what a young lady shouldn't in no way see, sir."

Of course, Torie listened to neither one of them.

Allowing Hoyle and Gabriel to lead the way, but only because she knew it would satisfy their need to feel as if they were safeguarding her, Torie followed them to the library.

But in spite of Hoyle's warnings, in spite of Gabriel's hand which clamped on her shoulder the second they walked into the room, Torie felt the scene spin in front of her eyes.

She did not know what she expected when Hoyle said Spencer was dead.

But she did not expect this.

The library was a shambles. Books were spilled from the shelves. The specimen cases along the walls were overturned, their glass fronts smashed, shards littering the floor like fallen stars.

The room was in such a state that it took Torie a full moment before she realized that beneath a mound of books and a table that had been toppled in the center of the room, lay the body of Spencer Westin.

Neither she nor Gabriel had seen Spencer since that day after the dinner party when, thinking she was dead and Gabriel gone, he had come to the house in search of the tooth. Still, Torie had known Spencer long enough to recognize him anywhere. But she would not have recognized him now, not if Hoyle had not warned them who it was.

Spencer lay in the middle of the library floor, his body twisted into an awkward position, his legs bent at impossible angles. His mouth was agape in a silent, unending scream. His eyes were wide with horror.

Torie clutched Gabriel's sleeve with both hands. She told herself to look away, yet she could not. Her gaze was drawn from Spencer's staring eyes to the wound on the left side of his head, a wide, flat hollow that looked to have been made by something heavy, a wound so broad, it laid open Spencer's skull.

There was blood everywhere. Clotted blood coated Spencer's brow and darkened the fabric of his dark jacket. It pooled on the carpet beneath his head. Even the walls were spattered with it, the pattern of bright red hideously stark against the white paint.

For fear she might scream, Torie covered her mouth with her hands. Instinctively, she took a step back at the same time that, in the split second it took for him to assess the situation, Gabriel stepped in front of her to block the view. His arms went about Torie and he cast a glance over his shoulder in Hoyle's direction, one that said quite clearly that he was not at all pleased.

"Lordy, sir, I tried to warn you." Hoyle began a brisk defense, a display so uncharacteristic as to show how distressed he was by the whole situation. "I told you as how I didn't think Miss Victoria should—"

"Yes, yes. You're right." Torie knew it was as much of an apology as Hoyle was likely to get from Gabriel. Wrapping one arm around her shoulders, he piloted her out into the passageway and from there, directly back into the kitchen.

This time, he poured two glasses of sherry. He handed one across to Hoyle. "And you," he said, sitting next to Torie, his arm around her. "Drink this. Then we'll talk."

The spirits burned down Torie's throat and into her stomach, but she didn't much care. The heat felt good. And something about it made the scene in the library seem less real. When she had drained her glass, she leaned against Gabriel's shoulder.

"I know what Spencer tried to do to me." Torie's words sounded suspiciously hysterical, even to her, but she could not seem to control them. They bubbled out of her before she could stop them. "He killed Roger and he might have done the same to me if not for you." She burrowed further into the safety of the circle of Gabriel's arm. "But to have this happen to him . . . Here in my own home . . ." Torie gulped down a painful breath of air. "I don't understand."

"I'm afraid I do, miss. And if I'm any sort of judge of a man—and I believe it is not misplaced vanity to say, I am—I think Mr. Gabriel here, he does, too." The third glass of sherry seemed to have worked a charm on Hoyle. He was nearly himself again, his celebrated composure back in full measure, his eyes bright. Only a few lingering cockney inflections betrayed him, and somewhere past the shock that filled her, Torie remarked to herself on how odd it was. She would ask Gabriel about it, she promised herself, some time when all their energies and emotions were not caught up in the horror of all that had happened.

"I went up to Cuckfield this morning," Hoyle said, turning to Gabriel and beginning a brisk, lucid explanation of the events. "After you and Miss Victoria 'ere left for the quarry. Today is market day, you see, and I went to get fruit and fowl for this evening's supper." He looked over to where his purchases sat on the sideboard along the wall, untouched and, until this moment, forgotten. "When I returned—"

Hoyle looked from Gabriel to Torie, his face, which had only a short time ago been so pale, suddenly red all the way from his chin to his ears.

"When I returned, I 'eard noises coming from the library. Excuse me for sayin' it, sir . . . miss . . ." Although Hoyle addressed them directly, his gaze was fixed firmly to the ceiling. "But I thought as how the two of you might 'ave come back from your diggin' early. Beggin' your pardon," he coughed politely behind his hand, "but you 'ave been known of late to cause a bit of a din when the two of you are alone together."

Forcing his way past his embarrassment, Hoyle brought his gaze back to Gabriel's and his eyes darkened with disturbing memories. "But it weren't you, sir. It were that hawful Mr. Westin. Mr. Westin and another man."

"Another man?" Gabriel sat up straight, sudden interest and concern humming in him until Torie swore she could feel it vibrating through his body. "What sort of other man?"

"I suspect you already know the answer to that." Hoyle swallowed audibly. "It was that misbegotten beggar, sir. You remember. The big, ugly brute with the silver-headed walking stick. The one what smashed his way through Paradise Square."

"Damn!" Gabriel vaulted off his chair and stalked to the other side of the kitchen. He slapped his palms against the window ledge. "Did he say how he found me?"

"Odd that you should ask that, isn't it? Isn't that just the point where I walked in. As I said—didn't I?—I 'eard sounds, and it didn't take me long to realize that it weren't the two of you. These was voices. Mens' voices. And they was angry as bulls in heat." This time, even the tip of Hoyle's nose turned red. He gave Torie a quick look of apology. "Beggin' your pardon, miss," he said. "It's a way butchers 'ave of talkin' if you know what I mean, miss. Anyways . . ." Hoyle cocked his head to one side, considering the last bit of the story he'd related.

"They weren't both the voices angry," he decided after some thought. "Just one of them. The other man sounded timid. Apprehensive like."

Rising from his chair, Hoyle went over to the sideboard and reenacted the scene. He pretended to be putting down his purchases, then looked up, his attention caught by the voices.

"I went into the library straightaway," he said, going as far as the kitchen door before stopping and turning back to Torie and Gabriel. "Just as I got to the door, I heard that bastard—" Realizing his blunder, Hoyle gulped audibly as if he could swallow down the word. "That ruffian," he amended with a quick glance at Torie, "say something to Mr. Westin about The Article. That's exactly what he called it, you see, 'The Article,' as if he wasn't quite sure himself what he was talking about. I made to open the door and just as I did, he ordered Mr. Westin to turn The Article over to him or there would be hell to pay. Only you see, sir, if you're gettin' what it is I'm sayin', he didn't know it was Mr. Westin."

Torie was completely confused, but one look at Gabriel told her he knew exactly what Hoyle was talking about. His hands curled into fists.

"That blackguard thought—"

"He thought Mr. Westin was you, sir." Hoyle completed the thought for him, looking no more pleased with the turn of events than Gabriel did. "Remember," he continued, whether for Torie's benefit or Gabriel's, Torie was not sure, " 'e never saw you that night at Paradise Square. He came lookin' for you, found me to be the only one at home, and proceeded to destroy the place while his nasty-looking accomplice stood by and watched. It was the other man what knowed you by sight, am I right, sir?

So, naturally, today, when he came into the 'ouse and found Mr. Westin in the library, he assumed—"

"Assumed it was me." Gabriel nodded thoughtfully.

It did not take long for Torie to logic through the rest of it. "And Spencer was here," she said, "because he knew we were all gone. He'd come to find the tooth! That's why the library's in such a state. He was looking for the tooth. He planned to steal it!"

"No doubt." Gabriel came to stand behind her. He placed one hand on her shoulder. "And it's a good thing we anticipated it, isn't it? Westin had no way of knowing that we'd left the tooth and the metacarpal bones with Reverend Blankenship for safe keeping. He came here looking for the fossils and got himself coshed for his efforts. I can't say I'm sorry. After what he did to you . . ." He caressed Torie's shoulder. "The bastard deserved to die as painful a death as the one he tried to make you suffer through."

"It's a poor end for a man." Whatever anger Torie had felt for Spencer was gone now, vanished in the face of the horrifying look of fear on the dead man's face, one she could still see so clearly in her mind's eye. "It is a dreadful way to die, I think," she said, her voice sinking very low. "A dreadful thing to happen to any man, good or evil."

Gabriel grunted something, but Torie could not tell if it was agreement or derision. He pulled away from her and faced Hoyle, his mind obviously still caught up in the mystery of what the ruffian from Oxford had been doing in Sussex. "You didn't tell that bullyboy that he had the wrong man?"

Hoyle looked at his boots. "I suppose I might have. I suppose I should have. But I hardly had the chance. The brute grew more insistent, his threats, uglier. Mr. Westin, of course, begged him to listen. He told 'im who he was. But you know how it is, sir. Once a man like that is enraged, there is little can be done to stop him. I burst into the room just as 'e was bringing the heavy top of that walkin' stick of his down on Mr. Westin's head. There was a tremendous crackin' sound as you can imagine and then . . ." Hoyle shivered and all the high color drained from his face.

"Then Mr. Westin just crumpled, sir, like a discarded bit of rag. I went to him immediately, of course, even though one look at him told me it wouldn't do no good. Beggin' your pardon, sir, for you have been a splendid employer for all your faults, but that's when I made my big mistake. I was upset, you see, and I wasn't thinkin' clearly. I . . . I'm afraid I went over to Mr. Westin and I called his name. That's when that bugger realized 'e'd killed the wrong man."

What had happened this afternoon was all too clear now, and even the lingering heat of the sherry was not strong enough to chase away the chill that invaded Torie. Spencer had come for the tooth, yes. That was quite clear and awful enough in its own way.

But even more frightening was the certain knowledge that the ruffian from Oxford had come for Gabriel.

Torie closed her eyes, the horrible implications of the situation making their way through her like ice water. "And what will happen now?" she asked.

For a few heartbeats, no one dared to put into words the frightening thoughts that were, no doubt, reeling through all their minds.

Much to Torie's surprise, Hoyle was the first to move. He cleared his throat and when Torie opened her eyes, it was to find him looking very much like his old self. His shoulders were thrown back. His head was high. Only his eyes betrayed his agitation.

"There's more, I'm afraid, sir." Hoyle's voice was no more than a rough whisper. "That murderin' beggar, he told me to give you a message." Hoyle never turned his head, but his eyes darted to Torie. "If you'd rather I saved the rest of it for some time when we might converse in private, sir . . ." he began.

Gabriel dismissed the suggestion with a brisk wave of one hand. He dropped back into the chair next to Torie's and took her hand in his. "Go right ahead," he instructed Hoyle. "It's as much Miss Victoria's fight as it is mine. They are her articles." He emphasized the word. "What concerns me and the bones certainly concerns her."

"Very well, sir." Hoyle agreed, but he didn't look pleased. Darting an uneasy look between Gabriel and Torie, he continued. "That ruffian, he says that word of your find has made its way over the length and breadth of Oxford. Everyone's talking about it. Word has gone 'round town that you will be giving a scientific presentation and that you'll be bringing something to it the likes of which no one has ever seen before. Something rare, sir. Something valuable. He says as how the man he works for—you know the one well enough, sir—he says as how he is particularly interested in that thing, sir, and he reminds you that if it is as valuable as everyone says, then you could sell it and pay off the money what you owe him. He says if you don't . . ." Hoyle's composure broke. He blinked rapidly and the muscles around his mouth twitched.

"He swears quite convincingly, sir, that if you don't, the same thing will happen to you as what happened to Mr. Westin."

It was exactly what Torie expected Hoyle to say, yet hearing her worst worries put into words had more of an effect on her than she could have imagined. Fear tore at her insides like the claws of some hunting animal. She clutched Gabriel's hand and forced herself to work through it, but even then the fear did not vanish completely. It settled like fog sometimes did out on the downs, sinking into crevices where you would never expect to find it and rising up when you just happened by, the unexpected, damp of it chilling even the warmest morning.

Her worry colored the edges of her words. "This isn't your friend Kresgee?" she asked, but as soon as the question was out of her mouth, she knew the answer to it. "It couldn't be, could it? For before we ever left Oxford, I agreed to pay the money you owed to Kresgee myself. This is . . . someone else? The man who ordered Paradise Square destroyed?"

"That's sure enough." Gabriel slammed his palms against the table. Rising from his seat, he paced the length of the kitchen. "And for the same reason. Bloody hell!" He stopped in the center of the room, his eyes dark with anger and with no more than a look at Hoyle, made it clear that he wished for he and Torie to be alone.

Hoyle reached for his hat. "I shall go into Cuckfield, why don't I, sir, and let the authorities know what's happened to Mr. Westin."

Gabriel kept up his pacing long after Hoyle left. Finally, he pulled himself to a stop opposite Torie. "There are other people I owe money to, you see," he began, looking rather sheepish, "and I——"

"Of course you do!" Torie rose from her chair and brushed off her trousers. "My nerves may be jangled. And I certainly admit that I am disturbed by all that happened here today. But I am not simpleminded. I realized you had enemies that night we encountered those two bullyboys in Oxford. But I did not realize they were this dangerous. There's only one thing to do, of course. You agree?"

For his part, Gabriel looked nothing if not relieved. He had been expecting a confrontation of some sort, though why, Torie did not know, and obviously finding her much more reasonable and accommodating than he expected, he smiled. "Of course I agree. If you start readying yourself now, you can be on the morning coach and——"

"Morning coach?" Torie looked at him in wonder. "I'm not going anywhere," she said decisively. "What I meant, of course, is that we must pay off the money you owe this horrible man and—"

"Oh, no!" Whatever trepidation Gabriel felt came back in a rush. His lids dropped over his eyes until they were hooded and as menacing as a hawk's. His fists went to his hips. "That is out of the question!"

It was not the time for an argument.

Torie knew it. And she reminded herself of it again and again.

They had troubles enough, that was for certain, and more to come from the looks of things.

This was not the time for a row. Not the time to quibble about words. They were both upset. Both worried. Both disturbed by all that had happened. Neither one of them was thinking clearly.

No.

With a click of her tongue, Torie discarded the thought.

Her head was quite clear, thank you. It was Gabriel who needed help to order his thoughts.

"Out of the question." She repeated his last words, giving them an inflection that, she was convinced, was certain to make him see how ridiculous they were. "Is it out of the question? Why? I am a woman of some means, after all. I have my parents' fortune at my disposal as well as that money which Roger left to me. We can easily settle whatever debts you owe."

"Can we?" Gabriel crossed his arms over his chest. His eyes glinting with the slightest hint of challenge, he named the sum he owed the bookmaker in Oxford.

It was a staggering amount, even to a lady of Torie's means, yet she refused to let it intimidate her. "That is more than I imagined," she admitted. At the same time she congratulated herself. Not only had she somehow managed to modulate her voice so that it did not betray her astonishment, but, as usual, she kept her eminent rationality, reasoning her way through the problem with lightning speed before she ever dared to discuss it. "But it is not such a sum that it cannot be handled," she added. "So you see, it is not out of the question that I assist you. Why should it be?"

Just as typically, Gabriel could not seem to see the logic of her argument. He pulled himself up to his full height and pinned her with a look. "Because I don't take money from women, that's why."

"Women!" In spite of her warnings to herself, a spark of anger ignited in Torie. This time, it was impossible to keep it out of her voice. "Is that what I am, then? Just another woman?"

"You know I didn't mean it that way." His hands out in appeal, Gabriel took one step toward her. Whatever he might have been about to say, he reconsidered it, taking a step of equal measure back into place. His palms flat, he made a sharp, unequivocal gesture with both hands. "I won't have people talking. That's what I meant. I won't have your reputation ruined by rumors."

"Rumors? What sort of rumors?"

Gabriel drew in a deep breath, refusing to meet her eyes. "I won't have it be said that I bedded you for your money."

Torie dismissed his argument with a toss of her head. "And who would say such a thing? Certainly not me. And Hoyle would never breathe a word about it. He is thrilled at our relationship. I sometimes see him smiling like a benevolent uncle when he thinks neither of us is aware of it. And, if it has slipped your mind, may I remind you that you did not have to persuade me overly much to share your bed. And"—she raised her voice when it looked as if Gabriel might try to interrupt her—"and, let me remind you that you bedded me long before today, long before we realized there was a problem with these people who seem so intent on wrenching their money from you."

"Long before you knew there was a problem."

Gabriel countered her argument so quickly, it took Torie a full minute to sort through what he was trying to get at. "Long before I knew." She revised her last statement despite the painful knob that seemed to have wedged itself, suddenly and unexpectedly, somewhere between her throat and her heart. "You knew, of course. You have known all along. But you wouldn't—"

"Of course I wouldn't." In three strides, Gabriel closed the gap between them. He took her in his arms. "Damn the rumormongers." The curse reverberated through his chest. "Yes, I've known about the money all along. When you are indebted to a man the likes of Simon Stone, it is not something you can easily forget. Yes, I've known there was money he'd be expecting and that he was the one who sent those two ruffians to Paradise Square. But I wasn't worried. I knew I'd work it out some way. But that has nothing to do with the two of us. You know that, don't you? It has nothing to do with why I bedded you and why—God help me because it is surely not the time—why I would bed you again right now if I could." Gabriel brought his mouth to hers for one fierce kiss.

"You're in my blood, Torie," he said, running one hand through her hair. "In every breath I draw. I know you make your offer in friendship and love. But you have to understand, I decline it for the same reasons. It's not a way for us to begin a life together, not with rumors swirling around us." Holding her close against him, Gabriel propped his chin on Torie's head.

As much as Torie was loath to admit it, she knew Gabriel was right. Yet there seemed no other solution to the problem. No other way but one.

Even with the warmth of Gabriel's body close to hers and the feel of his arms around her, Torie shivered. Her hands wrapped tight around his arms, she braced herself against the question she felt obliged to ask. "You are not suggesting—" The words caught in her throat and she cleared them away and started anew. "You are not suggesting we sell the fossils, are you?"

For what seemed like a very long time, Gabriel did not answer, and Torie swore softly to herself. If only she could see his face!

Pushing back out of Gabriel's arms, Torie carefully reworded the question. "Do you agree with what these people suggest? There are undoubtedly private collectors and desperate scientists like Spencer who might do anything to own our fossils and usurp our work. Do you think we should sell the iguanodon?"

Gabriel did not answer. Before she could ever hope to analyze whatever emotion might show on his face, he turned from her and went to stand at the windows. When he spoke, his voice was flat. "You know I would never ask you to do that."

He had not answered the question. Torie couldn't help but notice it. "You would never ask, no. I know you well enough to realize that. But would you have me do it, Gabriel? They are as much yours as they are mine, after all. You worked as hard as I did to find them. Would you have us sell the fossils and use the money to pay your debt to this Stone fellow?"

Even when Gabriel turned to her, it was impossible to read his expression. The sun was behind him, its light spreading a fiery halo around his head, his face lost in shadow. "There are better ways to best a man than joining him at his own game," he said and seemingly changed the subject by asking, "Can you be ready to leave for Oxford in the morning?"

"I—"

"Can you?"

As much as Gabriel tried to hide it, there was a certain

note of urgency in his voice that made Torie's skin prickle with apprehension. She hugged her arms tight around herself. "You think he'll come back?"

"I think it's a possibility." Gabriel pushed away from the windows. Taking her arm, he steered her toward the passageway that led to her bedchamber. "You start getting your things together. With a little effort, you and Hoyle can be on that coach, I think."

Torie skidded to a stop. "Me? And Hoyle? What about—"

"I'm not going. Not yet." With another tug on her arm, Gabriel urged her along, his words as confident as each of his quick, sure steps. "You will go on ahead. And you'll have the fossils with you. I'll meet you in Oxford in time for the presentation. That way—"

"That way, those ruffians will come after you, not us." Even Gabriel's persistent nudging was not enough to move Torie this time. The worry she had felt earlier was back in full measure, and she planted her feet and refused to move, instinctively fighting the fear as she had, so many nights, fought the terror of the lights out on the downs.

Still, like a cold fog, the fear slithered up her arms and along the back of her neck. It washed over her and settled in her soul, more terrifying even than the illusion of the lights.

For this time, she was not afraid for her safety or even for her sanity. This time, she was afraid for Gabriel. For his well-being. For his life.

There were logical arguments against his foolhardy plan and, surely, Torie told herself, had she the time and the presence of mind, she would have been able to think of them.

But she did not have the time. She could tell as much from the flame of determination in Gabriel's eyes as from the grim set of his mouth. And she did not have the presence of mind, for all she could think, regardless of

Gabriel's assurance and the flood of affection and admiration she felt at his reckless courage, was that she might lose him.

The awareness tore through Torie, and when she spoke, her voice was sharp with disapproval and tears sprang to her eyes. "You cannot offer yourself up as a decoy—"

"Why not?" His dark eyes flashing, Gabriel dropped his hand from her arm and faced her. He might have challenged her. He might have lectured her on the suitability of ladies who, like children, were seemingly meant to be seen and not heard. He might have done either, or both. Instead he took one look at the tears that cascaded down her cheeks and his exasperation dissolved. Taking Torie in his arms, he pressed her close, his voice rich and warm. "I am the one who got myself into this mull," he said, stroking his cheek against her hair. "At least allow me to get myself out of it."

He was right.

Torie sniffed back her tears. She wasn't pleased about it, but she knew he was right.

She would leave for Oxford with Hoyle in the morning and let Gabriel keep his pride and work out whatever plan he had devised to vindicate himself. She would take Gabriel's advice this one time, because she knew he was right and because she had to do all she could to support him.

She would let him take her to her room. She would pack her trunks and go to Oxford with Hoyle, taking the fossils with her.

But in spite of her resolve and Gabriel's best intentions, by the time they got to Torie's bedchamber, Oxford was the farthest thing from both their minds.

Torie did not begin packing her trunks for a very long time.

* * *

It was only for one week.

Hoisting the hard-sided valise that contained the tooth onto the table in her room at the Golden Cross Inn, Torie tried her best to push aside the aura of melancholy that hung over her like the heavy gray rain clouds outside the window.

It was only one week until she would see Gabriel again, she reminded herself. Only one week until he would arrive here in Oxford. One week until he was scheduled to speak to the assembled scientific community.

The thought sizzled through Torie's bloodstream, making her miss Gabriel all the more. Only a few hours had gone by since they said goodbye in Cuckfield, yet it felt a lifetime ago.

With half the town already up and about their chores this morning and many of them watching the leave-taking curiously, they could not possibly kiss each other goodbye. Gabriel had done nothing more than kiss Torie's hand. It was a polite gesture, gallant and fashionable, yet she could swear that the heat of his kiss still burned on her skin, just as the heat of yesterday's lovemaking still blazed through her body.

Torie set the thought aside. There was no use torturing herself with such memories, she reminded herself, no use tormenting herself by reliving every kiss, every touch.

Gabriel would be here in one week and then there would be enough time for all they had promised each other yesterday. Enough time for every lingering kiss. Enough time for each heated caress.

In one week, Gabriel would astound the world with the revelation of their iguanodon. In one week, just as they'd planned before she left Sussex, he would present the fossils as a gift to the Ashmolean Museum.

It would seem odd not having the bits and pieces of her iguanodon about the house, she thought, like missing a child who was away at school. Yet both she and Gabriel knew it was for the best. Once the fossils were ensconced at the museum, they could be studied, not only by her and Gabriel, but by any number of other scientists who might offer insight into the form and habits of the mysterious animal. There were other benefits to the plan as well, Torie knew, and although she and Gabriel had not discussed it, they both knew that once the fossils were in the Ashmolean, they would be out of harm's way, safe from unscrupulous scientists like Spencer or dangerous men like the bookmaker, Simon Stone, and his sinister bullyboys.

Still, Gabriel's plan made her uneasy.

All of yesterday evening, Gabriel had tried to make her believe the whole thing was nothing more than a lark. He'd spent a good deal of time—when they were not making love—extolling the virtues of his scheme, reminding her of what fun it would be to outwit Simon Stone, telling her that it would do her good to spend a week in Oxford by herself, just as their forced separation would give him time to put the finishing strokes on the presentation he was scheduled to give at the Sheldonian Theatre, a presentation they had labored over together.

Torie rubbed her hands over her arms. It was a chilly day, and damp, and she chided herself for letting the foul weather affect her mood.

It was only a week, she reminded herself. And yet she could not seem to forget that every kiss Gabriel had given her yesterday was as intense and fevered as if it were his last.

A knock at the door roused Torie from her gloomy thoughts and she opened it to find Hoyle with the case that contained the iguanodon metacarpal bones and dermal horn.

He crossed the room, deposited the trunk on the floor and turned to her, swiping one hand across his forehead.

"That's the last of it," he said. "And a heavy one it is, too. Is there anything else I can do for you, miss?"

"No." Torie dismissed him with a quick smile. "I am sure you have friends here in town with whom you are anxious to reacquaint yourself," she said. "I won't be needing you for the rest of the evening."

When Hoyle was gone, Torie went over to the trunk that contained the fossils. Kneeling on the floor, she stroked her hand over the lid.

"Like a child going away to school," she said, her voice hushed, a bittersweet smile on her face. "I shall miss having you about, my iguanodon." She popped open the lid and reached inside for the fossils.

It was no wonder Hoyle had such a time carrying the trunk up to her room. Gabriel had filled it with rocks. She sifted through the pile, certain that he had added the extra rocks to disguise the fact that the fossils were in it.

But they weren't.

Puzzled, Torie sat back on her heels and a tremor of alarm skimmed over her shoulders, like a cold hand on her back.

She scolded herself for it the moment it happened.

Of course the fossils were here. She had seen Gabriel carry the trunk out of the Reverend Mr. Blankenship's house herself.

Carefully, Torie unloaded the case. One by one, she placed the rocks on the floor beside her until the trunk was empty.

The bones and horn were nowhere to be seen.

Torie bolted to her feet.

It was ridiculous, of course. It was impossible. The notion that sprang to her mind was utterly preposterous.

Yet she could not put it out of her head.

Gabriel had never answered her yesterday when she questioned him about selling the fossils.

Gabriel had brought the trunk to the coach, and the fossils were missing from it.

Gabriel had brought her the hard-sided valise, too.

Torie went over to the valise, cursing herself when her hands trembled so much that she could not open it.

She hauled in a deep breath and bracing her hands against the worn leather, she popped the catch and flipped the top aside.

Her dragon tooth was gone.

Chapter 21

"Gorblimey, Miss, I just can't believe it." Hoyle shook his head sadly. "I can't believe it of him."

It was not the first time since she'd told Hoyle that the fossils were missing that he'd said the same thing. It was not the second or the third time, either. Hoyle had been repeating the same thing over and over for the last hour, and Torie was at the end of her patience. Slapping her hands against the tabletop, she spun away from where Hoyle was kneeling, staring into the empty trunk.

"I can't believe it, either. Gabriel wouldn't have——" The words that had been clamoring through Torie's brain all of last night and all of this morning refused to make their way out of her mouth. Pacing across the room, she cursed beneath her breath and started again. "Gabriel wouldn't have done it. He wouldn't have taken the fossils. I know him well enough to know——"

"As do I, miss." Hoyle rose to his feet. Like a mourner at a funeral, he stood with his hands clasped in front of him, his gaze cast down at the trunk. "Yet the evidence is here before us. Or rather, isn't, if you know what I mean. Mr. Gabriel was the last one to handle these trunks, and he told me specifically that he had checked the contents of them before he carried them from the vicarage out to the coach. They have not been out of our sight since then, miss, except for the time when they were on the same coach as we were on. There's nobody could have touched those fossils. Nobody but Mr. Gabriel, that is."

Hoyle was right, and Torie knew it. Still, she refused to believe it.

"No!" She swatted at the draperies when she went by the windows. "I won't believe it. I don't believe it. Gabriel said he had something planned. A way to pay this Simon Stone fellow so that he'd never bother us again. He wouldn't have . . . He couldn't have . . . Would he?"

Torie's last words rose up on the end of a sob. Poor Hoyle looked at her in desolation. She knew he wanted to help. He wanted to console her. He simply didn't know what to say.

"He couldn't have gotten to Oxford before us, could he?" Desperate to try and reason through the thing, Torie asked the question, praying Hoyle would give her the answers that would make the whole, horrible thing impossible. "I mean, there's no way he could have removed the fossils and—"

"Certainly he could have, miss."

Hoyle had not intended his comment as a condemnation, yet that is certainly how it sounded. It was her own fault, Torie told herself, fighting against a wave of despair that threatened to reopen the flood of tears that had overwhelmed her last night, the one she had been able to suppress until now, but only barely. It was her own fault, she reminded herself again in no uncertain terms. She had asked a question. Hoyle had merely provided the answer.

"What I mean, miss, is . . ." Hoyle's ears got red. "I mean, I didn't mean to imply anything, but what I mean is—"

"Oh, Hoyle! Let's both of us let off acting like two fools, shall we?" Torie dropped into one of the chairs pulled up to the table in front of the window. She pulled out the chair beside her and motioned Hoyle to sit. "There's only so far our shock and surprise can get us. I should know." She shook her head in disgust, her voice filled with the dregs of the disquiet that had kept her from sleep last night. "I spent all of last night being shocked and surprised."

"And you should have called me, miss. You should have let me know." As much as Hoyle might have liked to disguise it, he could not conceal the expression of sympathy that crossed his face. He masked it as soon as he possibly could. His bushy eyebrows dipped low over his eyes and he frowned, as if envisioning a scene and not liking it at all. "Heaven help me if Mr. Gabriel were to find out that I left you by yourself all night, fretting and worrying. What I mean to say, miss, is if there ever was a man who worshiped the ground you walked upon, it's Mr. Gabriel and—"

Again, Hoyle's mouth outpaced his brain and, again, he scrambled, trying to get the one caught up with the other. "That is, I didn't mean to remind you, miss—"

"That's all right, Hoyle. We won't speak of that, either." Torie clutched her hands together on her lap, her brisk determination fading just a little beneath the implications of all Hoyle said. "For now," she suggested, both for Hoyle's sake and for her own, "let's not speak of our surprise or our disappointment. Let's reason through this thing, the both of us. I think perhaps we'll find that we've underestimated Mr. Raddigan."

The promise of a rational discussion as well as her defense of Gabriel had just the effect Torie desired.

Hoyle sat in the chair beside her and resumed his usual, brisk demeanor. "All right then, miss," he said, twining his fingers together and planting his hands on the table in front of him. "You asked if Mr. Gabriel could have gotten to Oxford before us, and I will answer as truthfully as I can, even if it isn't the truth either one of us wants to hear.

"Yes, miss, I think Mr. Gabriel could have gotten to town long before us. After all, the coach is not the fastest way to travel. With a good horse and dry roads—which we had until we were almost here, you will remember—Mr. Gabriel could very well have arrived here in Oxford before we did. He is an excellent horseman."

"Very well." Torie clutched her hands a bit tighter. "If he got here yesterday before we arrived, what would he have done?"

"The way he's been acting lately, miss . . ." Hoyle gave her a sidelong glance. "Begging your pardon for being so presumptuous and all . . . but the way he's been lately, I should think he would have been here waiting for you."

"As do I." Torie's voice sank under the weight of her worry. She tried to slough it off with a shake of her shoulders. "But that is obviously not what happened. We're here and he is not."

"As far as we know, miss."

"As far as we know," Torie concurred. "If he was here in town, where would he be, do you think?"

Hoyle scratched one hand through his hair. "There's any number of places he might lie doggo, if you catch my drift, miss. There's been times aplenty in these past years when someone's been on his trail and he's needed to disappear for a day or two. Mostly it's been one of the bookmakers after him, like this Stone fellow. But there's been the odd tradesman, eager for some payment or another, and once or twice a young lady who—"

Hoyle's face went as white as the walls. "Beggin' your pardon, miss." The words escaped him in a breathless whisper. "But—"

"Never mind that." Too frustrated to keep still, Torie shot out of her chair. "Where would he have gone, do you think? And why?"

With an audible gulp, Hoyle recovered his aplomb.

"Well, the way I see it, he could be any one of a number of places." He glanced over his shoulder at Torie as if uncertain what her reaction to his next suggestion might be. "He might have stayed in Sussex, miss, just like he said he was going to do."

"And kept the fossils with him?" Torie dismissed the notion instantly. "It doesn't make sense, does it? He said he wanted us to take the fossils in case Stone's bullyboy came back. If Gabriel was still in Cuckfield, why would he have kept the bones with him? That would have left both him and the bones in danger."

"Good enough, miss." Hoyle conceded. "But then, if he were here and he . . ." Again, Hoyle swallowed hard enough for the sound to be heard. "If he were here and he brought the fossils with him, he'd be at even greater risk. Stone's sure to hear if Mr. Gabriel's back in town and Mr. Gabriel, he's sure to be in trouble when Stone finds out. He wouldn't have brought the fossils here, miss. Not unless . . ."

The rest of Hoyle's statement hung, unspoken, in the air between them.

They were the same words Torie had been hiding from all of yesterday night and all of this morning.

The same words she found it so hard to speak now.

Holding her fists tight at her sides, Torie drew in a sharp breath. "Unless Gabriel brought the fossils here so he could sell them."

Hoyle didn't reply, but his shoulders slumped and he bowed his head.

Torie needed no more of a reply than that. "We've got this muddled somehow, I know we do," she said, almost to herself. "Gabriel would never sell the fossils to pay off Stone. They mean too much to him, just as they do to me. Unless—"

A new idea hit her and Torie stopped, a thread of hope winding through her at the same time a cord of fear tangled around her throat, cutting off her air. "This whole thing might be a ruse to protect me, don't you think, Hoyle?" she asked, her voice suddenly high and excited. "He is just foolish enough to think that if he hides both himself and the fossils this week, we will not be in danger. But he will be, won't he?"

Striding to the door, Torie threw it open. She was already out in the passageway before she heard Hoyle's chair scrape back.

"Miss? Miss?" He stood in the doorway and if Torie had either the time or the inclination to turn around, she was certain he would be staring at her, stunned. "Miss, where is it you're off to?"

Torie started down the stairs. "Don't you see?" she asked. "Gabriel's in danger. We've got to find this Stone fellow and pay off the debt before Stone finds Gabriel."

Behind her, Torie heard the sounds of Hoyle's scrambling footsteps. He was beside her in an instant, his chin high, his head steady. "Right you are, miss," he said. "And I'm with you every step of the way. But there's no way you're going to see that crafty bugger alone."

"A most generous offer, Miss Broadridge. Most generous, indeed."

Behind his mahogany desk, Simon Stone folded his large, square-fingered hands on the brocade waistcoat that strained over his stomach. He raked Torie with a look, one that might have made her chastise him had she not been so worried about Gabriel and so relieved at finally finding Stone that she refused to give him any reason at all for sending her away.

After six days of searching for Stone, she had learned one thing sure enough: A man who did not want his whereabouts generally known could not be easily found, and once he was found, there was no sense risking the chance of losing him again.

Six days.

Torie scanned the room where she stood before Stone's desk, her thoughts as scattered as the pattern of whorls and flowers that graced the Persian carpet at her feet.

It had been six days of frustrations, six days of blind roads and disappointment. Six days of worry.

Between Hoyle and herself, they had talked to every one of Gabriel's friends who could have even the faintest indication of where they might find Simon Stone. One place led to another, that place to another still. It was obvious from the first that Stone was not an easy man to call on. The morning of Gabriel's scheduled presentation, they had finally run Stone to ground in Wolvercote, a village outside of Oxford, in a house as unobtrusive outside as it was sumptuous within.

And now that they finally had him, Torie told herself, there was nothing he could say, nothing he could do, that would make her turn tail and run.

"You must pardon me for being quite so impertinent, of course," Stone continued in a voice as smooth as treacle, "but it isn't often a lady comes here looking to help out one of the hapless fellows who happens to have the misfortune to be in my debt. Not a real lady, if you get my meaning." Stone slid a look from Torie to Hoyle who stood near the door, a look that clearly said he was not used to being called on by the type of young lady who brought a servant with her, and that he was not quite sure how to deal with either one of them.

"You don't look Gabe's type," Stone said frankly, his gaze sliding back to Torie. Rising from his leather chair, he came around to the front of the desk, his small, ice-blue eyes skimming over her, his pudgy cheeks quivering with approval. "I have known Gabe since the days he was sent down, and I must say, you don't look his type at all."

"What type I am is hardly the question." Torie traded Stone look for look. In spite of her resolve to remain as polite and detached as possible, she refused to be pulled into whatever game it was he was playing. Instead, she steered the conversation back to where it had started when they were first ushered into his private chamber a few minutes ago. "The question, as I am sure you remember it, is if you will accept my money in payment of Mr. Raddigan's debts."

Stone rested his short, stout frame against the desk. "Of course." He chuckled. "A woman of business, are you? Straight and to the point. I can see how that might appeal to Gabe. As you will then, Miss Broadridge. We shall be businesslike, you and I. Straight and to the point. You say you are willing to pay off the debt, but you do not state exactly how." Stone looked her up and down again and this time, even Hoyle did not fail to notice the lewd gleam in his eye. Hoyle took a step forward and might have come at Stone if Torie had not raised one hand to stop him.

"A delightful offer," she said, with all the charm and as much of a smile as she could force to her lips. "But I thought rather to simply pay you the money. It is so much less involved and so very much less disgusting to contemplate. I know the sum, of course, and I am willing to add one hundred pounds to it."

For all his insouciance, Stone made a noise that was as close to an astonished and blatantly rapacious gasp as any Torie had ever heard. "A hundred pounds besides!" His beady eyes twinkled in the light of the crystal chandelier that hung above their heads. "You are as generous as you are beautiful, Miss Broadridge," he said, inclining his head in a gesture of esteem. "I would be a rich man, indeed, if I could learn what magic Gabe has worked on you. He has captured your heart, I see."

"My heart is my business, Mr. Stone. What concerns you is my purse."

Stone laughed, his head back, the light gleaming off teeth that were pointed, like a cat's. "I cannot help but think you are wasting your time on a wastrel such as Gabe."

"Who I choose to waste my time on is my business and mine alone," Torie said, firmly refusing to have her thoughts drawn to Gabriel for fear that her self-control simply could not stand the strain. "In exchange, however, I need your assurance that you will no longer trouble us, that Mr. Raddigan will no longer be in danger from you or from anyone you employ."

Like a confused innocent, Stone raised his shoulders and held out his hands. He looked from Torie to Hoyle. "Danger? I assure you I don't know what you're talking about. I'm a businessman. Nothing more. I would never—"

"No. I'm sure you never would." Torie was not in the mood for either his prevarication or his excuses. She pinned him with a look. "But nonetheless, in exchange for the money, I would have your assurance of it."

For the first time since their interview with Stone had begun, he looked perplexed. Turning from them, he went back around to the other side of the desk. He did not sit down, but drummed his fingers against the desktop.

"Well, that's the devil of it, isn't it, Miss Broadridge?" Stone shook his head and Torie had the impression that, whatever the reason, they were seeing a glimpse of the real man behind the flamboyant exterior. There was genuine regret in his expression, though why, she could not imagine.

"I will admit, there is nothing I would like better than to take you up on your generous offer," Stone said. "All Gabe owes me plus another one hundred pounds besides." He rubbed his palms together, letting go a long, low whistle beneath his breath. "It is a munificent offer, no doubt of that, and one I am most sorry to have to decline."

It was the last thing Torie expected him to say. "Decline!" For one second, she allowed her astonishment to show. It was a strategic error. She knew it the moment Stone's face lit with a triumphant smile.

Even this small victory was enough to make a man like Stone radiate contentment. "Decline, yes," he said, skillfully raising the shields that had, for that brief moment, given her a look behind his mask. "You see, you are too late. A few hours too late. Just this morning, Mr. Raddigan paid his debt to me in full."

Hoyle did not approve.

Neither, Torie suspected, would any of the other two thousand or so scholars who were assembled beneath the fresco of the TRIUMPH OF RELIGION, ART AND SCIENCE OVER ENVY, HATE AND MALICE that decorated the ceiling of the Sheldonian Theatre.

None of them would appreciate that there was a female in their presence—if only they knew it—just as none of them would approve of the fact that the particular lady in question was dressed in her brother's clothes and had her brother's hat pulled firmly down around her ears, all a ruse to disguise her appearance and delude them as to her presence.

Not that she cared.

Two hours after visiting Simon Stone and finding out that Gabriel's debt had somehow been paid, Torie was not sure she cared much about anything.

It had been a hellish day. One fraught with doubt and despair. One charged with emotion that vacillated wildly between worry over Gabriel's safety and anger every time Torie faced the inescapable fact that Gabriel's debt had been paid and that the fossils—and Gabriel—were still missing.

It seemed impossible to do further damage to a heart that had been broken the moment Stone's statement left his lips, yet the very thought made a pain erupt inside Torie. She quelled it as she had silenced every other doubt that had assailed her this past week, telling herself over and over that Gabriel would not and could not have betrayed her so.

But if he would not, if he could not, where was he?

Torie's gaze traveled instinctively to the double doors on the main floor of the theater. Even though she and Hoyle were seated in the last row of the balcony—a tactic Torie found unnecessary but which Hoyle had insisted upon to protect their identities—Torie could clearly see the area where, only a few minutes from now, Gabriel was scheduled to begin his presentation.

Except that so far, there was no sign of Gabriel.

Scraping her sweating palms against the legs of her trousers, Torie shifted in her seat and glanced around the auditorium. Her gaze landed on Hoyle, who was seated to her right, and she was reminded that she was not the only one on whom the last week had taken its toll.

Hoyle was sitting as straight as an arrow with his hat atop his knees, glancing surreptitiously and unbelievingly around the room like a two-penny thief who had somehow found himself face-to-face with the Crown Jewels. He clearly thought himself out of place and just as unquestionably, he could not wait to escape.

Even for all that he was as tense as Torie, Hoyle did not fail to catch the look she cast his way. He swiveled slightly in his seat, and Torie had the distinct impression that he might have patted her hand if he had not remembered her disguise and known without a doubt that such a gesture might be perceived as even more scandalous than the fact that there was a woman present.

He leaned nearer, keeping his voice down, as if he were afraid that in spite of an accent that was every bit as proper as any scholar's, his manner of speaking might somehow betray him as an interloper. "He'll be here, won't he?" Hoyle asked.

"Of course he'll be here."

Her back ramrod straight, Torie peered down into the lecture area. Following Hoyle's example as well as the nervous glance he cast to either side, she kept her voice to a whisper. "See, things will be starting in just a few minutes. There is Professor Cronkite waiting to commence. Gabriel will be here soon." She held her hands on her lap with her fingers wound tight around themselves. "He has to come."

But he didn't.

The lecture was scheduled to begin at two o'clock.

By half past two, there was a general rumbling in the audience, like the sound of some distant storm. By fifteen minutes to three, the crowd was more than restless, it was disgusted.

"It's a shame, that's what it is." The man seated next to Torie lifted himself out of his chair, shaking out his flowing black robes.

A friend seated directly in front of him followed his example. "Pity," he said, though the tone in his voice sounded far more bored than pitying. "Promised to be interesting. Of course, one never could count on Raddigan for much of anything."

"Anything but debauchery," the first fellow added with a laugh.

Torie curbed the stinging retort ready on her lips, but only because Hoyle darted her a glance of warning. Biting her tongue, she watched as the man and his friend left the theater.

They were not the only ones to go. All around them, Torie watched as the crowd, which had been so eager such a short time ago, grew restless and decided, for the most part, to leave. By the time three o'clock came and went, there were fewer than two hundred people left in the auditorium and those who stayed did so only because they'd stopped to chat with colleagues.

Still, Torie sat in the last row of the balcony, her gaze fixed to the double doors. Now and again, she saw Cronkite, Morrison, and Granger with their heads together, mumbling to each other and nodding seriously as if to say "I knew this would happen." Now and again, she noticed that another group of scholars would leave, their noses out of joint, no doubt, because their precious time had been wasted. Now and again, she heard Hoyle clear his throat nervously or stir in his chair. He didn't dare speak a word until fifteen minutes after three.

"Come on, miss." Hoyle didn't worry about lowering his voice this time. They were the only ones left in this section of the balcony and he stood and went so far as to place a gentle hand on her shoulder. "We'll go out looking for him again tomorrow."

"Tomorrow." Though she was quite certain there would be no tomorrow, Torie repeated the word. She looked up at Hoyle and shook her head.

"I'll wait here," she said.

Even now she questioned what fueled her stubbornness, her faith in Gabriel or her anger. It didn't take her long to realize that it was neither.

It was not blind faith for, Lord knew, if she was ever one who depended on hope rather than logic to get her by, she had little of that left inside her now. It was not anger, either, though if she sat very still and cleared her mind of the thoughts that caromed through it, she could feel the fury that stormed through her, the outrage that came when she remembered, whether she wanted to or not, that the fossils were gone and that with them went her life's work.

No, it was not faith or anger that kept her rooted to the spot. It was love. The kind of love that burned through her even now when it seemed all her hope in the world had been lost. The kind that would continue to hold true to Gabriel. The kind that would never give up.

The sound of the double doors being punched open startled Torie out of her thoughts. From this angle, all she could see of the person coming in the door was a dark head and an uncommonly large portmanteau, but it was enough.

Her blood suddenly racing through her veins, her head buzzing, Torie leaned forward.

It was Gabriel sure enough and Torie smiled over at Hoyle and watched as he dropped back into his seat, a wide grin lighting his face.

Gabriel stopped for only a moment to whisper something to Cronkite before he proceeded to the lecture area. What was left of the crowd quieted, but only for a moment.

One look at Gabriel, and the crowd was chattering again.

The remains of what had once been a white handkerchief were tied around Gabriel's right hand. Even from here, Torie could tell the cloth was bloodstained. It perfectly matched the smear of blood on Gabriel's forehead. His hair was disheveled, and if the light and the distance weren't playing tricks on her, his left eye was blackened.

Her initial instinct was to hurry down to him, but in addition to being a superior valet, an excellent cook, and an inestimable companion, Hoyle must also have been a mind reader. He clamped one hand down on Torie's arm to hold her in place.

"Gentlemen, you must forgive me." Gabriel raised his voice and swept the auditorium with a glance. If he noticed that most of the crowd was gone, if he cared, he didn't show it. He held his head up and his shoulders back and spoke to those few who remained as if he were addressing the largest and most important assemblage in all of Oxford.

"I beg your forgiveness for being so late," he continued. "I met an old . . . friend." He gave the word a curious intonation at the same time he looked down at his crudely bandaged hand. "And we were some time sorting out our differences. If Professor Cronkite will be so kind as to allow me . . . ?" He raised his eyebrows and looked toward Cronkite who, because he obviously was not sure if he should be relieved or appalled by Gabriel's condition, had no choice. He nodded his agreement.

Gabriel started into the presentation he and Torie had worked so hard to prepare, and Torie sat back, letting the sound of his voice wind around and through her, drinking in the warm comfort of his presence. She tipped her head back, listening to Gabriel explain about Cretaceous strata, diluvial deposits, and Weald sediments.

He would have made a marvelous professor, Torie noted, a tiny thread of hope winding through her that, after today, he might yet get that chance. Though Torie knew the presentation by rote, she hung on every word. Gabriel's voice was rich and full. His sense of timing, superb. By the time he opened the portmanteau he'd carried into the theater with him, she was convinced no one in the audience could possibly have looked away until they saw what it contained.

But no one could have cared more than she.

Torie sat forward in her seat, watching as Gabriel pulled first the tooth, then the metacarpal bones, then the dermal horn from the bag and showed them around the room.

"Lordy, miss!" She heard Hoyle let out an exclamation of wonder. " 'e's had 'em all along!"

The rest of his presentation was a blur to Torie. She was sure Gabriel said something about the strong, hooflike middle fingers of the creature. She was certain he mentioned that its wrist bones were fused. She was positive he explained the dermal horn and the worn tooth and the relationship between the fossils he held in his hands and the iguanodon remains Torie had studied in London.

She was certain he covered it all, but for the life of her, she didn't hear a word of it. How could she listen to Gabriel when all she could hear was the sound of her own heart pumping wildly in her ears? How could she concentrate on what he was saying when all she could think was that the wound on his hand was still bleeding, and the cut on his brow looked tender, and that she would burst at the seams if she soon didn't find out what had happened to him, and where he'd been this past week, and why he'd taken the fossils out of her trunks and kept them to himself?

Torie listened as Gabriel went through the final portion of the presentation. By the time he explained that the fossil was, undoubtedly, from some extinct and heretofore unknown animal, the audience had lost any skepticism it might have had. Every scholar in the place was on the edge of his seat. Cronkite was smiling like a father at the birth of his first child. Even Morrison and Granger looked pleased.

Torie smiled through the tears that had somehow sprung to her eyes. She listened to the last words of Gabriel's presentation and waited for him to add the last bit of it, the presentation of the fossils to the Ashmolean, so that she might rush outside and be waiting for him when he emerged from the theater.

But he didn't say a thing about presenting the fossils to the museum. He placed them on the table that had been provided for him and turned to his audience, his dark eyes scanning the crowd, his face, in spite of the dried blood and the bruised eye and the smear of dirt across one whole side of it, sparkling with something so close to mischief that Torie and Hoyle exchanged dumbfounded looks.

"Gentlemen, at this point in the presentation, I would be remiss if I did not include another important piece of information, one equally as remarkable as the iguanodon itself." He motioned to the fossils. "You know my theories regarding the nature of the creature. You have seen with your own eyes the proof of its existence and have heard the overwhelming evidence that attests to the fact that we have before us the remains of a fantastic animal that, until now, was unknown. It is an animal of incredible age, one of inconceivable size. But what you do not know is that I am not the one who discovered the creature."

Torie felt her heart stop at the same time a startled murmur made its way through the audience.

Gabriel brought the crowd under control with a lift of his hands. "The animal in question was originally discovered by a colleague of mine, a person who, because of the narrow criteria we place on our assemblage, could not be here today. The iguanodon was originally discovered by a scientist who is intrepid, and intelligent, and far more clever, I would venture to say, than any one of us here in this room. Yet this same scientist would not be allowed through the doors of this distinguished place. It is a sad commentary on our bigotry, gentlemen, that the woman—"

The word was no sooner out of Gabriel's mouth when a roar of protest echoed through the auditorium.

Gabriel ignored it.

He ignored the man in the very first row who leapt to his feet and stomped out of the hall muttering something about "the devil's own work."

He ignored the catcalls, and the jeers, and the open laughter.

He ignored everything.

He stood with his feet planted firmly in the center of the

lecture area, his chin raised so that the light of the afternoon sun streaming in through the windows that circled
around the auditorium gleamed in his face and brought
out the multishaded blues that surrounded his cheek and
eye.

He looked a sight, sure enough.

He looked grimy. He looked disheveled. He looked so
handsome and grand that a lump of emotion formed in
Torie's throat.

Gabriel raised his voice, continuing on as if the distur-
bance had never occurred. ". . . that the woman who
made these discoveries, the one who put together the
pieces of a puzzle that have remained hidden for sixty-five
million years, could not be with us today because we are
too narrow-minded to let her past the front doors."

"Damn me if you aren't wrong there, sir!" Hoyle
bolted out of his seat and nearly danced a jig of delight
right there in the aisleway.

Torie watched as Gabriel put one hand to his forehead,
shading his eyes so that he might better see up into the
balcony. When he caught sight of Hoyle, his eyes lit.
When his gaze moved to the person seated beside Hoyle,
his face broke into a grin.

"That's right. She's here," Hoyle said, grabbing
Torie's elbow and hauling her to her feet. "You know."
He looked around at the audience all of whom, by now,
were staring at the proceedings with their mouths open.
"This is the lady Mr. Gabriel is talking about. She's the
one what found that there dragon thing."

By this time, Gabriel was laughing. "Gentlemen," he
said, bowing in Torie's direction and giving her a smile
that made her heart leap. "May I present the most preem-
inent paleontologist of our time, Miss Victoria Broadridge."

After that, all was chaos. Cronkite looked as if he'd seen
a ghost and, Torie thought, if he was remembering the

way he treated her when she came to him with the tooth, it was no wonder.

Granger would have none of it. His mouth opening and closing, his words unintelligible from this distance, he left the theater with a great number of the audience following in his wake.

Morrison sat in place like Lot's wife, turned into a pillar of salt.

Of those who were left—and it was a pitiful few, Torie noted with a sad shake of her head—most gathered around Gabriel, thumping his back and peppering him with questions, pumping his hand and peering at the fossils, beckoning Torie to join them on the lecture floor.

Gabriel didn't pay any of them the least mind. His gaze fixed on the balcony, he watched as Torie made her way downstairs.

The crowd parted in front of her, most of them, she supposed, as horrified that she was here as they were that she was clothed in such unsuitable attire. But she would give them credit, she heard not one word of criticism.

"The enlightened few." Torie couldn't help but smile, admiring their spirit for staying in the face of such scandal and thinking that, perhaps, there might be hope for a woman vice-chancellor in Oxford after all.

In honor of the courage of these few scholars, or perhaps to spite Morrison and Cronkite who were still quite speechless, Torie plucked Roger's hat from her head. Her hair came down as the hat came off and she shook her head, scattering it around her shoulders. She stopped three feet in front of Gabriel, and the crowd grew silent.

"Miss Broadridge." Gabriel inclined his head politely. "Delightful to have you here."

"Mr. Raddigan." Tipping her head, Torie returned his greeting. "I must say it is delightful to be here. We—" She looked around to make certain Hoyle was beside her. "We wondered what kept you."

Gabriel pulled a face and gingerly touched one finger to his eye. "One of Stone's bullyboys," he said. He held up his bloody hand like a trophy. "The small man with the ratlike face who called at Paradise Square last spring. He wasn't after me—I'll explain all about that later—but still . . ." Gabriel let out an exaggerated sigh. "When I came upon the man who helped tear apart my home and in the process endangered two people who are quite dear to me . . ." He let his gaze slide from Hoyle to Torie. "Well, you can imagine I was more than a little indignant. One word led to another. One thing led to another." He lifted his shoulders in a casual gesture. "You may not be aware, Miss Broadridge, but I have something of a temper."

"As do I." Torie inched forward. "Which brings us to a question I am loath to mention in such a public forum as this, but one I feel obliged to ask nevertheless. Your debt to Stone is paid. Hoyle and I know it. We were in Wolvercote this morning. The question of course is, how?"

Gabriel laughed and took a step in Torie's direction. His voice was as formal as ever, but there was something in his eyes that made Torie wonder how long he could maintain the pretense. "Not the fossils," he said, glancing at them over his shoulder.

"Not the fossils," she returned. "Though why they—and you—have been missing all this time is every bit as much a mystery as our iguanodon."

Cronkite was standing to one side of Gabriel, shifting from foot to foot as if Torie's very presence made him feel as if the building might come crashing in around their ears. Ever so politely, Gabriel pushed his way past him. "It's simple," he said, his eyes never leaving Torie. "I arrived in Oxford the day after you did. I had the fossils with me because I knew you and the fossils would be in danger if you had them. I couldn't make my presence known. Stone was having you watched. I didn't dare contact you for fear that he'd find me. I couldn't come out of hiding until I'd taken care of my debt, and that didn't happen until this morning."

Torie nodded. "A most ingenious plan," she said, and she wondered if any of the score or so of men who were gathered around them had any idea that just being this close to Gabriel made her skin tingle and her body ache for his touch. She dared another step closer, barely containing a smile. "But how did you accomplish it?"

Gabriel, too, seemed drawn by the invisible tie that held them. He took another step so that he was no more than an arm's length from her. From this distance, Torie could see that the cut on his forehead was not as grave as she feared, though she was certain that his left eye and cheek would, by nightfall, change from brilliant blue to lurid purple.

Without a look at the crowd, Gabriel reached for her. He caught her arm and drew her near. "Paradise Square," he said. "I've sold the lot of it. The house. The furniture. Even what was left of the stock of brandy in the cellar."

"Sold it." Torie cocked her head to one side, considering the news, but this time, it was impossible to keep the smile from her face. "And you are planning on doing what, Mr. Raddigan?"

With his free hand, Gabriel took Torie's other arm. He drew her closer, ignoring the fact that the curious looks on the faces of the bystanders had, by this time, turned into horrified stares.

"I thought I might retire," he said, slipping his hands beneath Roger's coat and resting them at the small of Torie's back.

"Sir?"

Behind her, Torie heard Hoyle clear his throat. Both she and Gabriel looked his way.

Hoyle glanced from one of them to the other, his expression perfectly impassive. "If you'll excuse me, sir, I think it only my duty to point out that if you are considering what I think you are considering, you might want to make the young lady an . . ." He searched for the right word and finally finding it, set his chin and looked straight ahead. "An offer, sir."

"Offer, indeed." Gabriel's smile was poorly concealed. "It is no wonder I pay the man so much," he said to Torie, as if it were some secret. "He's invaluable, don't you think? And, as always, he's also right."

Gabriel took a step back and drew in a long breath. "I suppose I should be down on one knee," he said, half to Torie, half to the crowd that was now staring, silent and amazed. He discarded the idea with a quick lift of his shoulders. "But no." He shook his head. "Eye to eye, I think. Face to face. No one on top."

"And just what is your offer?" Torie couldn't help herself. It was terribly cruel of her to tease him so, but the moment was too delicious to let slip by. She stood back, waiting for his response.

Gabriel couldn't keep his distance for another second. Closing the gap between them, he took Torie's hands in his. "Will you be my wife?" he asked.

She did not hesitate. "You know how much I would like that. But——" She interrupted when it looked as if Gabriel might try and say something more. "It is impossible for a true scientist to make any decision without all the facts. Where was it you said you'd be retiring to, Mr. Raddigan?"

Gabriel grinned. "I hear Sussex is a lovely place."

Linking her arms around his neck, Torie smiled up at him. "Lovely, yes. But frightfully dull."

Gabriel glanced around him. "Gentlemen, if you'll excuse us," he said, but he didn't wait for any of them to turn their backs. He scooped Torie into his arms and kissed her the way, she would venture to guess, no woman had ever been kissed inside the Sheldonian Theatre.

"Dull?" He smiled down at her, the late afternoon sun sparkling against the promise of forever that shone in his eyes. "Somehow, I don't think so. If things become too tedious for us, we can always watch the moss grow on the window ledges!"

Author's Note

Although *Earthly Delights* is a work of fiction, it is based in part on the first discoveries of dinosaur fossils in the early nineteenth century.

In 1822, Mary Ann Mantell spotted a giant tooth in a pile of rocks being used for road repairs near Lewes, England. She showed the tooth to her husband, Dr. Gideon Mantell, an avid fossil collector.

Dr. Mantell determined that the tooth (and the bones he subsequently found) were from a giant, extinct reptile the likes of which no one had ever imagined. He named the animal iguanodon.